Mother's Day Out

KAREN MacINERNEY

Mother's Day Out

A MARGIE PETERSON MYSTERY

THOMAS & MERCER

Published by Thomas & Mercer, Seattle

www.apub.com

Amazon, the Amazon logo, and Thomas & Mercer are trademarks of Amazon.com, Inc., or its affiliates.

ISBN-13: 9781477820025
ISBN-10: 1477820027

Cover design by Cyanotype Book Architects

Library of Congress Control Number: 2013920537

Printed in the United States of America

CHAPTER ONE

After eight years of chiseling away at the petrified contents of Tupperware containers, wiping a variety of organic substances off of two small children, and cleaning up after an incontinent Siamese cat, I thought I could stomach anything.

I was wrong.

It was eleven thirty on a rainy Tuesday morning in Austin, Texas, and I had been tailing Irwin Pence, purveyor of toilets and bathtubs to the not-so-rich-and-famous, every morning for a week now. Much of that time involved sitting in a parking lot and waiting, punctuated by me narrowing my eyes into the rearview mirror every so often and mouthing, "Margie Peterson, private investigator." I was trying for a look that was firm and knowledgeable, yet slightly intimidating. So far, all I'd come up with was a puckery expression that made me look like I'd been sucking on limes.

As I sat outside ABC Plumbing and Fixtures, trying to improve on the sucking-limes look, I had the satisfying yet slightly unsettling thought that I was the only mom on the Green Meadows Day School PTA who spent her mornings on stakeouts. Until recently, the main excitement in my life was trying to get my three-year-old and five-year-old from swim lessons to soccer without sideswiping another minivan. Now, though, while the other moms jogged loops around the lake, had their eyebrows waxed, or went grocery shopping, I was a covert operative, stalking an overweight plumbing salesman like a lioness hunting a zebra.

This was my first case with Peachtree Investigations, the PI firm that had reluctantly hired me last week. For the first few days, the thrill of me—me!—shadowing a suspected wrongdoer had made the time fly. But after five mornings of sitting outside ABC Plumbing and Fixtures in my Dodge Caravan, puckering into the mirror, knitting a rainbow scarf for my niece, and trying not to think about my bladder (which is hard when you're sitting outside a toilet store), I had to admit I was starting to have the first inklings of doubt. I mean, it *sounds* glamorous, but the truth is, sitting around in a dumpy parking lot waiting for a fat guy to sneak out and hook up with someone wasn't exactly a thrill. To be honest, I was starting to wonder if it was worth the trouble my husband was giving me for taking a part-time job as a PI.

And then I hit pay dirt.

This afternoon, instead of turning east for lunch at Taco Bell (the supersize combo with three extra burritos, double cheese, and sour cream), Pence broke with tradition and turned south. I made a quick U-turn and gripped the steering wheel hard. Ten minutes later, his blue Ford pickup slowed next to a gaggle of scantily clad women huddled under umbrellas. As I peered through the squeaking windshield wipers, three of them approached the car. A moment later, one of them clambered up into the passenger seat.

I clenched the steering wheel and gave myself a reassuring lime-sucking look as we traveled down Oltorf. I was ready for this, right? If five years of living with small kids hadn't prepared me for excitement, adventure, and frequent brushes with the unexpected (think toilet bowls, Matchbox cars, and Niagara Falls), what would?

Now the pickup and I were in the parking lot of the Como Motel. The rain drummed on the cracked pavement as Pence did a fast waddle to the office. He returned to the truck for a moment to retrieve a grocery bag, then dashed through the rain and wedged himself through the door of room 126. An improbably blond woman in a minimalist leather dress followed him.

I reached for the door handle, but hesitated. I knew I needed to follow them, and I had spent the week preparing for just this eventuality. But now that it came down to it, it felt a bit awkward. I mean, I spent half my life telling my kids to respect others' privacy and be honest, yet here I was, following someone incognito and preparing to take a picture of him engaged in an intimate act.

I gripped the handle again. Why did it matter if he knew I was following him? After all, Mr. Pence was married. And it was his wife who had hired me—well, Peachtree Investigations, anyway—to find out if he was cheating on her. And he'd just gone into a motel room with a hooker, hadn't he? So, if anyone was playing fast and loose with the morals here, it was him. Right?

Besides, I was due at my kids' school in twenty-five minutes.

I had half opened the door when I realized I wasn't the only one in the parking lot. A few doors down from room 126, a scraggly young man and a green-haired woman were loading their worldly possessions into a hatchback. I pulled the door shut and growled.

Not good.

While the young couple rearranged the items for the fifteenth time and struggled to slam the trunk lid, my stomach gurgled. I foraged through the debris on the floor between the front seats until I came up with half a granola bar, munching on it while the couple retrieved a CD that had rolled halfway across the parking lot. The bar wasn't Nature Valley's finest—it was a bit soggy—but I eat when I'm stressed, and it was better than rooting around for stray Cheerios.

Finally, the little car pulled out onto the highway. I popped the last stale fragment of granola into my mouth, grabbed my daughter's umbrella, and scurried across the parking lot. If it were *my* husband,

I reasoned as my tennis shoe sank into a murky puddle, I'd want to know, wouldn't I?

A moment later, I crouched down outside the window of room 126, huddling under my Hello Kitty umbrella and glancing around to make sure I was alone. Then I pulled out my ancient Nikon camera, peered through the gap in the yellowed vinyl curtains, and just about shot the granola bar back up.

There, in the middle of the bed, stood Irwin Pence, all three hundred fifty pounds of him.

The surprising thing was not that he was naked.

It was that he was wearing nothing but Saran Wrap.

I swallowed back a lump of granola. Irwin Pence's back was to the window. His plastic-encased buttocks looked like two misshapen balls of dough that had been left to rise for far too long, except for the coarse black hairs peppering the dimpled surface. I stared, mesmerized, but all I could think was, *Poor Mrs. Pence.*

I swallowed again. Chances were that a wide-angle shot of Mr. Pence's buttocks would be enough for Mrs. Pence to make an identification—how many three-hundred-fifty-pound men with a penchant for Saran Wrap could there possibly be in Austin?—but it would be better to hold out for a shot of his face. And, if I could get it, at least a fragment of the woman who had popped through the motel room door behind him. I assumed she was in there somewhere. I just couldn't see past those massive wads of dough, wrapped up like something in the "We make it—you bake it" case at Central Market.

My stomach churned, but I jammed the camera up to the glass anyway. As I waited for the mountain of flesh to turn toward me, the thought crossed my mind that throwing Tupperware parties might not be such a bad idea after all.

Behind me, an eighteen-wheeler roared past on IH-35. I bounced up and down a few times to keep the circulation going in my calves, focusing my attention on Mr. Pence's vast white body and hoping he would shift around enough to give me a clear shot. I tried a little visualization thing I'd read about, sending him an invisible laser beam with the message *Turn around*, but so far it wasn't working.

A moist breeze from the vicinity of the Dumpster brought a mixed bouquet of rotting vegetables, barnyard, and sewer, which doesn't go well with stale granola. I took a break from thinking about Mr. Pence, focusing instead on keeping the contents of my stomach in place, and glanced down at my watch. It was time to get the show on the road. I was due at my kids' school in twenty minutes, and I was already in the doghouse with the director, Attila the Bunn, for "sauntering in" forty-five minutes late that morning. I sighed. It was just my luck that the day Pence chose to indulge his Saran Wrap fetish would be the one day my kids had early dismissal.

Unfortunately, the mountain of flesh on the saggy king-size bed with its circa-1970 bedspread of burnt orange and avocado green remained buttocks-out. I wrinkled my nose as I considered the variety of activities that bedspread had witnessed—and the number of times it had probably seen the inside of a washing machine.

As I crouched, camera at the ready, my nose started to run. I set the camera down for a moment and dug in my backpack for a tissue. Two fuzzy pacifiers, a half-eaten lollipop, a McDonald's fry phone, and an overdue *Bob the Builder* DVD later, I located a frayed tissue decorated with purse lint. I stuffed the debris back into my bag and was about to blow my nose when a wave of White Linen perfume engulfed me.

"What you doin'?"

I jumped, then craned my neck upward. A tall man in a short skirt stood over me.

My eyes roved over him as my brain churned through possible explanations for crouching outside a motel-room window with a pink ruffled umbrella and a camera. Except for the dusky shadow of a beard, his face could have come out of a fashion magazine—blue-gray eyes fringed with silky lashes, high cheekbones, and plump raspberry lips the exact shade of his umbrella. His legs were encased in sheer silk stockings. His face wasn't quite as smooth as a baby's bottom, but he could have given master classes on leg-shaving technique.

I heaved myself to my feet and shoved the camera into my bag, stammering, "I was just looking for my room key." What I was going to do when I couldn't find it, I didn't know.

"The door's over there."

"Door? Oh, right." I shuffled over a few steps and started digging in my purse again.

"That your husband in there?"

"I'm sorry?"

"Your husband."

I squared my shoulders and set my jaw in what I hoped was a look of matronly indignation. "What makes you think it's my husband in there?"

"Either that or you a Peepin' Tom."

Since all the digging in the world wasn't going to produce a key to room 126, I was more than happy to go along with Mr. Legs's explanation. I attempted a dramatic sniffle, but it came out as a wet snort. "You caught me," I said. "That's him. I was just looking for a tissue." I sniffled again and tried to coax a tear by thinking of something awful. Tragic car accident? Starving children in Africa? A week with my in-laws in a remote cabin in the Adirondacks? I squeezed my eyes shut, hoping for a drop of moisture.

"Cheatin'?"

I nodded and stepped back as he squatted and peered through the crack in the curtains. His brief rubber skirt rose perilously high. I averted my eyes.

"Whoa. You need to get your man on a diet. I sure hope he doesn't like to be on top."

"On top?"

"You know. In bed."

"Oh. Oh no, he doesn't," I stammered as I stole a glance at my watch. Here I was, within five minutes of being late to pick up my two children, expounding on the sexual habits of a man I'd never met to an oversized transvestite.

"What you want to do is get him on that Atkins diet. A friend of mine, Tallulah, she dropped about sixty pounds on that high-protein thing. Got to eat pork rinds and everything." He peered in again for a moment. "Of course, your man's got more to go, but still." He stared through the window again. "He do that at home?"

"Do what?"

"You know. The wrap-and-slap thing."

"Wrap-and-slap? It has a name?"

"Yeah, there are a few of them who have a thing for gettin' trussed up like a Butterball turkey. And then they like the paddle."

"There's a paddle?"

I scooted over and crouched down again. Mr. Pence was now bent across the bed, with the blonde standing over him. She had traded in her dress for a half roll of Saran Wrap, and was giving it her all with a short wooden paddle. Poor Mrs. Pence.

The blonde delivered a particularly energetic whack, and Pence turned his mottled face toward the window. I fumbled in my purse for the camera, but by the time I got it into position, he had turned away.

Mr. Legs spoke from somewhere behind me. "You gettin' a divorce?"

"What? Oh, right. A divorce. I just need a good shot for the attorneys."

"You the kind of woman who don't take no shit. I like that."

A few whacks later, Mr. Pence turned toward the window again. I aimed the Nikon and pushed the button, flooding the motel room with light. Two heads shot up.

I had forgotten to turn off the flash.

"Crap!" I jammed the camera into my purse and dashed down the sidewalk, the worn treads of my sneakers sliding on the wet concrete. As I turned the corner of the building, the door squeaked open behind me.

I pressed myself to the damp cinder-block wall for a moment and peeked around the corner. Mr. Legs was nowhere to be seen, but Pence stood where I had a moment before, wrapped in a grungy white bath towel that frankly wasn't up to the task. He looked around for a moment, a deep crease in his thick brow, and stooped down to pick up something red from the walkway. He turned it over in his hands and disappeared into the room.

I leaned against the wall and cursed. I had dropped Elsie's fry phone, and there was no way to get it back.

I waited a few minutes, then slunk across the parking lot to the minivan, closing up the Hello Kitty umbrella and slamming the door behind me. Then I pressed my forehead to the steering wheel and swore. Why the fry phone? How was I going to explain it to Elsie?

Other kids had blankets, favorite dolls, stuffed kangaroos. Not mine. Since age one, my daughter had gone to sleep every night cuddling up to a McDonald's fry phone.

The fry phone was a plastic toy phone that looked like a packet of French fries. It had been available a few Februaries ago for about three hours. If I'd known its future position as the sun around which all other things in our household revolved, I would have bought out all the Happy Meals in town, creating a cache of duplicate fry phones behind the piles of unused yarn in the back of my closet. But by the time she got attached to it, it was too late. Fry phones had long been replaced by collectible Pokémon figures and Barbie Peek-a-boo dolls.

And now it was gone, snatched by an obese plastic-clad adulterer who sold plumbing fixtures for a living.

I looked back at Pence's motel room longingly. Then I bit my lip and turned the key in the ignition, wishing—just for a moment—that I'd never even heard of Peachtree Investigations.

It seemed like more than a week ago that I'd dropped the kids off at school, squeezed myself into a suit, and headed south on Congress Avenue, looking for an address I'd scrawled on a piece of paper. Until six weeks ago, I hadn't planned on working at all, but the tuition bill that turned up in our mailbox after Nick joined Elsie in preschool was big enough to cause heart palpitations.

Because Texas doesn't have public preschools, Blake and I had enrolled both kids in Green Meadows Day School. It had a good reputation—and a price tag that made University of Texas tuition look like a bargain-basement closeout deal. Blake suggested we take out a home equity loan and pay it back when he got his promotion, but I pooh-poohed the idea. "I've got some time off during the week now," I said breezily. "I'll just get a job." I figured I'd pick up some part-time work at the advertising agency I'd left when Elsie was born.

Easy, right?

Wrong. It didn't take me long to figure out that once you step off the career track, it's not that easy to hop back on. After nearly six years out of the business, and with a schedule that limited my round-the-clock hand-holding capacity, my childless former boss shook her head at me. "I'm afraid we don't have a part-time position. And you've been out of the industry so long . . ."

So I started looking at the want ads and quickly learned that if you're an exotic dancer or a dishwasher, the world of part-time work is your oyster. Otherwise, you're out of luck.

I was about to resign myself to a life of Tupperware parties—unless there was a market for chunky women over thirty, the dancing was out, and as far as I was concerned, I did enough dishwashing at home—when I spotted an ad that looked a little different: *Exciting part-time work, flexible hours. Apply in person.* It looked better than busing tables for the Taco Shack, so I did.

The address was in a seedy part of town, wedged between Ecstasy Lingerie Modeling and Austin Propane Service. I parked the van in the empty lot and inched my way up to the grungy storefront in my too-tight blue pumps, feeling like I'd just come back from a trip to the foot binder. The peeling paint on the smudgy glass door read "Peachtree Investigations." Below it, stuck to the cloudy glass, was a brown-edged peach decal that resembled someone's rear end more than a piece of fruit.

I considered turning around and getting back into the mini-van. Then the list of Help Wanted ads I had seen played through my head: professional dancer, dishwasher, dog trainer . . . At least this job promised to be exciting. Supposedly.

I pushed the door open and stepped into a dingy room reeking of cigarette smoke and mold. As the door clanked shut behind me, a woman with a helmet of orange hair and a large curvy body stubbed her cigarette out in an overflowing ashtray. She narrowed her brown eyes at me over her desk. "I'm Peaches Barlowe. What can I do for you? Husband trouble?"

"No," I said, trying not to wrinkle my nose at the smell. The place screamed for Lysol. "I'm here to apply for the job."

She cast an eye over my navy-blue suit, which was secretly safety-pinned in the back, and snorted. "You're kidding me, right?"

"No." I swallowed and straightened my spine, glancing at the yellowed stacks of paper strewn around the office. A few dead doodlebugs littered the dirty gray carpet. Whatever Peaches was, she wasn't a tidy housekeeper. If she was hiring for a filing position, the pay had better be impressive. "What exactly is the job?"

"Sweetheart, this isn't the type of work you're looking for." She leaned forward over the scarred desk, giving me a view of her breasts, which nestled together like cantaloupes in her stretchy red top. Peaches looked to be on the far side of forty, but she hadn't stopped shopping in the juniors department.

"You don't know that."

"I'm looking for an investigator. This isn't an office gig."

An investigator? It was better than a maid, but I'd never pictured myself as an investigator. I couldn't even find my car keys, much less track things down for other people. I was about to say, "No thank you" when something stopped me. What the heck? At least it didn't require washing dishes. I could at least try it out. "Sounds interesting," I said, pulling my résumé from the leather portfolio I had dug out of the back of my closet and putting on my best professional look. "I don't have any direct experience, but I'm a fast learner."

She ran an eye over the cream-colored paper and raised a penciled eyebrow. "Marigold Peterson. You're named after a flower?"

At least I wasn't named after a fruit. "My friends call me Margie."

She cocked a penciled eyebrow in disbelief. "Contributor to the Green Meadows Day School newsletter?"

"It could be considered investigative reporting."

"Yeah, right. Big in-depth articles on potty training." She scanned it again. "Account executive for BDS&M?" She pushed my résumé toward me. "Honey, the kind of research we do isn't like writing a fancy-schmancy press release, or tracking down the best chocolate cake recipe. We do some pretty ugly work here. I need someone with grit."

Ugly work? I'd seen diapers that would make a biker gang blanch. Grit? I'd survived staying home with my children for five years, hadn't I?

The look of disdain on Peaches's face sparked something in me. What was with people these days? They thought that just because a woman had kids and stayed home, the only excitement in her life should come from attending driveway-stenciling classes at the local library. Even Blake had changed since I had Elsie. We used to have conversations about politics, ethics, the state of the world. Now we talked about the state of his sock drawer.

I took a deep breath. Just because I'd spent the last five years of my life dealing with diapers and dirty dishes didn't mean my brain had turned into Gerber Oatmeal & Banana Cereal.

The safety pin on the back of my skirt strained as I leaned forward. "I know I can do it," I said. "Please let me give it a shot."

Peaches leaned back and adjusted her cleavage. "Honey, why do you want to? This is nasty stuff. These people aren't exactly nursery school teachers, you know. Some of them are downright dangerous." The look of disdain faded, replaced by something like pity. "You look like a nice lady, you're not hurting for money. Why don't you stick to something safe, like the PTA?"

This lady clearly hadn't met the parents at Green Meadows Day School. Give me a gang of delinquents over a group of frustrated MBA mothers with their hearts set on Harvard for their offspring any day.

Margie Peterson, private investigator.

It had a ring to it.

I pushed the résumé back toward Peaches and looked her in the eye. "Give me one case. If I get it right, you pay me. If I don't, my time is free."

She held my stare for a minute, then sighed and reached behind her for a battered manila folder. She shoved it across the desk. "All right. Since no one else has turned up, I'll give you one chance. Infidelity case. Plumbing salesman. If you don't get the proof, you don't get the money. And I still think you're in over your head." My fingers tingled with anticipation as I grabbed the folder. Peaches pulled a packet of Ultra Slims from her top drawer. "Christ," she said. "I don't know why I'm doing this."

I straightened my shoulders. "What do I need to do?"

She flicked her lighter, and an orange flame leaped up. "Follow him and get a picture of him doing something he shouldn't be doing."

"Is there any training?"

"Can you drive?"

"Yes."

"Do you have a camera?"

"Yes."

She took a deep drag from her Ultra Slim and whirled around in her chair. "Consider yourself trained."

CHAPTER TWO

That had been just over a week ago. Today, as I rolled into Green Meadows Day School twenty minutes late, I was feeling a little less excited about the whole PI thing. Sure, I'd gotten the shot. At least I thought I had. But now I was short one fry phone and had probably made myself a prime target for Attila the Bunn.

My suspicions were confirmed the moment I opened the office door and met the disapproving gaze of the director. Except for the absence of green skin, she was a dead ringer for the Wicked Witch of the West in her later, plumper years.

The kids rushed toward me, and I knelt to hug them, burying my nose in Nick's hair and breathing in his puppy-dog-apple-juice-Watermelon-Blast-Shampoo smell. Elsie was wearing the yellow skirt and purple sparkly top she had chosen that morning, but Nick's fire-truck shorts had been replaced by a pink skirt decorated with overblown cabbage roses. I gave the kids a squeeze and stood up, my hand resting on Elsie's black curly head. Mrs. Bunn tapped a pointy-shoed toe and narrowed her eyes at me.

"You're late."

I put on my best concerned-parent look. "I'm so sorry. It won't happen again."

She handed me the missive of the day—there were always missives of the day at Green Meadows Day School—with all the pomp and circumstance of the pope delivering the latest bull. Then her steely eyes focused on Nick, whose chubby toddler body was wrapped around my leg. "Nick had another accident. There were no spare clothes in his cubby, so we had to put him in Elsie's." That explained the skirt.

"Well, I've always tried to have a gender-neutral household."

She harrumphed, sending a jiggle through her jowls. "I'd like to have a meeting with you, Mrs. Peterson, to discuss some issues regarding parental involvement at the school and proper nutrition for the children. There's also a behavior issue I'd like to address . . ." She cocked a bushy eyebrow at Elsie.

I'd been through the nutrition lecture before and was more than familiar with the litany of my sins: using Jif peanut butter instead of the natural and unsweetened variety, white bread instead of whole wheat . . .

But a behavior issue? I looked down at Elsie's black curls and decided it was probably something minor. After all, Mrs. Bunn considered failing to put a napkin on your lap at snack time to be a major lapse of decorum.

"We need to talk, Mrs. Peterson."

My mind cast about for a redeeming topic, something that would reinforce my commitment to Green Meadows Day School and get me out of the office. Should I offer to trim the hedges? Scrub the floors with a toothbrush later in the week? Then I remembered the newsletter. "I'd love to talk about it—I'll call you; maybe we can set something up for next Monday—but I'm on my way to upload the pictures from the class picnic. I need to have them ready for the school newsletter tomorrow."

Her gaze slackened a bit, and I took the opportunity to whisk the kids through the door. "Thanks so much, Mrs. Bunn. See you tomorrow!"

. . .

I pulled into our cracked driveway ten minutes later and made a mental note to ask Blake to cut the grass. Our neighbors' lawns looked like golf course greens; ours resembled something you'd see on a *National Geographic* special on the wilds of the Serengeti.

I kicked over a dandelion that was almost as tall as I was and opened the van doors for the kids. The state of the yard was a little surprising, actually. Faucets might drip for months before Blake got around to fixing them, but he generally worked to keep the outside of the house, a stone cottage built in the late 1920s, looking good. My husband had inherited his mother's Martha Stewart-ish obsession. I, on the other hand, was a little more laissez-faire in the domestic department. Needless to say, our first years together had been an adjustment. With time, though, I managed to come to terms with my husband's quirks, figuring that if color-coded towel-organization strategies were all I had to complain about, I was a lucky woman.

As the kids tumbled from the Caravan and tripped up the front walk to the house, my eyes swept the flower beds—my one domestic pet project—with satisfaction. The Mexican bush sage had exploded into bloom at the end of the driveway, and a drift of pink and purple impatiens bloomed beside the wood ferns. If the grass were shorter, the flowers would even be visible from the street.

The house itself was one of those properties listed as "having great potential." In fact, that was how the agent had sold it to us seven years ago. We'd spent the first six months drawing up plans for major renovations and expansion. Then I'd gotten pregnant with Elsie and quit my job at the advertising agency to stay home, and the grand plans had been downsized to a fresh paint job on the trim. A paint job that needed to be done again, I thought as I unlocked the door; the door's original lime green was threatening to overtake the brick red we had covered it with. I shook my head. I was sure we'd hear about it from Blake's mother soon.

Still, I thought as I closed the door behind me and dumped my keys next to a stack of unopened mail, it could be worse. I was happy here. More importantly, so were the kids. My own childhood had taken place in a series of run-down apartments, and although having a swimming pool on the grounds had been fun for the first few years, the novelty had worn off. My mother had done the best she could; after my father left us for another woman just after my third birthday, she supported us by taking a series of jobs as an apartment manager. Still, I had spent my school years burning with jealousy over my friends' houses, which all seemed to be in real neighborhoods and featured both a mom *and* a dad. Cheery maternal comments, such as "You are *so* lucky. Most kids have their own backyards, not a community play area!" just didn't cut it.

I looked at our tiny kitchen with its ancient white stove and slightly rust-stained sink with affection. Rufus, our Siamese rescue kitty, rubbed himself against my legs, and I reached down to scratch his ears. So what if our house would never be picked as the cover feature of *Town & Country*? So what if Nick occasionally wet his pants waiting for Elsie to vacate the house's one bathroom? At least it was ours.

I checked my voice mail, cringing when I recognized my mother's number. A moment later, her voice burbled into my ear. "Hi, Marigold. I was just calling to see if you'd tried that St. John's wort tea I sent you." I rolled my eyes. Most people had outgrown the hippie movement in the sixties, but my mother had never gotten over it. Last month it was yoga. Now she was dating an herbalist named Karma, and I had started receiving packets of strange-looking green stuff in the mail. "Give me a call when you get a chance, and give my sweethearts a hug!"

I hit "Delete." I'd call her back after I'd gotten the kids to bed and had a glass of wine. Maybe two. Then Elsie came up behind me and hugged my leg. "I'm hungry, Mommy."

"You guys ready for a snack?" I asked.

"Cupcakes!" Nick declared.

"How about Oreos?" Elsie suggested.

"How about cheese sticks and apple slices?" After my run-in with Attila, I felt the need to be virtuous.

They groaned, but two minutes later they were at the kitchen table, squabbling over whose apple slices were bigger.

As the kids bickered, I pulled a package of chicken breasts out of the refrigerator and thought about this morning's job. All in all, I decided, it had gone okay. Sure, I'd lost the fry phone, but I had something to show to Peaches. I put aside thoughts of my daughter's screams when she discovered the fry phone was gone and allowed myself a moment of satisfaction. It was nice to take on a task other than the laundry and get it done.

The kids finished their apple slices and wandered into the living room, leaving the table littered with bits of red peel. Two seconds later, the sound of four thousand Legos hitting the hardwood floor echoed through the house. "You need to clean that up!" I called.

"We will, Mommy."

Yeah, right. "Cleaning up" consisted of each child contributing one Lego to the box, then dropping to the floor in exhaustion. The other 3,998 were mine to deal with.

I chose to ignore the sounds of chaos for now and focus on the yogurt marinade I was mixing up for the chicken breasts. Blake's doctor had recently announced that my husband's cholesterol was dangerously high, and I'd started cooking low-fat dinners and dragging him out of the house for walks. I didn't like the idea of losing him to an early cardiac arrest, but with the hours he'd been putting in lately and the attendant stress, it wouldn't be a shock if he keeled over into his Corn Flakes one morning. Besides, it was good for me, too. I made sure the kids ate a relatively balanced diet, but either the clothing manufacturers were making things smaller or my chocolate habit was edging me into muumuu territory.

As I stirred lemon juice into the yogurt, I thought about Mrs. Pence. Did she cook low-fat meals for her husband? From what I'd seen this morning, I was guessing not. How would she feel when she saw the photo of her shrink-wrapped husband? She must have known something was up—otherwise she wouldn't have hired a private investigator—but seeing the proof would still be a shock. Particularly a photo like the one in my camera.

I covered the chicken with Saran Wrap and winced at the spices dotting the pale slabs of flesh. They looked kind of like Pence's buttocks. Just a whole lot smaller. Why Saran Wrap? I wondered. Had his first erotic experience involved bake-sale brownies? It would certainly explain a lot. I briefly considered sending Mrs. Pence a sympathy card but decided against it. Odds were good that Hallmark didn't have a "Sorry Your Husband Was Sharing His Saran Wrap Fetish with a Hooker" card anyway.

I had just slid the chicken into the refrigerator when the phone rang. I rinsed my hands and picked it up before it went to voice mail.

"Hello?"

"Margie."

I recognized my husband's voice. "Blake! How are you? You're not going to believe what happened this morning . . ."

"I'm sorry, honey, I don't have time to talk. I just wanted to tell you that I've got a meeting with a client tonight, so I won't be home for dinner."

So much for the chicken. "Again? You've been working way too hard lately."

"I know, I know. It's just this case I'm putting together."

I sighed. Maybe we'd do hot dogs and macaroni and cheese, and save the chicken for tomorrow. "Well, we'll miss you. Want me to save you some dinner?"

"Oh, don't worry about that. I'll pick something up. Gotta run . . . Give the kids a kiss."

And then he was gone.

I hung up the phone and scowled, wishing I could expense all of the uneaten dinners I'd prepared lately to Jones McEwan, the law firm that was holding my husband in indentured servitude. "It's just till I make partner," he always said. "Then I can relax a little, and we can work on the house a bit." Yeah, right. It had been four years now, and even though he worked seventy-hour weeks on a regular basis, he was still an associate.

I had just pulled a package of hot dogs out of the freezer when Elsie appeared in the doorway, blue eyes wide. "Can I have my fry phone?"

I swallowed. How was I going to tell her an obese plastic-clad adulterer had swiped her love object? I adopted a casual tone. "You know, honey, I don't know where it is right now. I'm sure it will turn up, though." I guided her through the Lego-strewn living room to the TV. "Why don't I put *Lady and the Tramp* on?"

Tears welled in her eyes. "But I want my fry phone!"

"Honey, I don't know where it is right now."

"You mean it's gone? Forever?"

"No, sweetie, not forever. I'm sure it'll turn up." I stroked her curls and sat through fifteen minutes of Lady and her perfect household until the snuffling had receded to an occasional sniff. Then I retreated to the computer desk, where I pulled up eBay and typed in *Fry phone*. Nothing. Ditto for *McDonald's fry phone*, *French fry phone*, *Happy Meal phone*, and *Freedom fry phone*. Damn.

Why had I taken this job?

I shut off the computer and picked up the phone. Peaches answered on the third ring.

"It's Margie," I said. "I got a photo of Pence."

"You're shitting me." I could hear the surprise in her pack-a-day voice. "When can you bring it in?"

"I'll e-mail it to you," I said. I paused to clear my throat. "I accidentally left something outside the motel room, though, and I was wondering if you could ask Mrs. Pence to see if she can find it for me. Her husband picked it up."

"You left something outside of the room?"

"Yeah." I lowered my voice. "A McDonald's fry phone."

"Jesus H. Christ. A McDonald's fry phone? Like one of those Happy Meal toys? You want me to tell Mrs. Pence that her husband is cheating on her, and then ask her if she can find a McDonald's fry phone my investigator accidentally left behind?"

"I know, I know . . . It was an accident. But it's my daughter's favorite toy."

"A fry phone. Whatever happened to teddy bears? Jesus. How the hell did you lose . . . No, I won't ask. I don't want to know." I could hear the intake of breath as she took a drag from a cigarette. "You need to write a report. Should be a breeze for you, what with all your big reporting jobs for the nursery school newsletter."

I opened my mouth to issue a snappy retort. Unfortunately, all that came out was, "How soon do you need it?"

"Can you get it done today?"

Today? I listened for sounds of trouble from the living room. Except for the soothing voice of Lady's mistress, the house was peaceful. "I think so."

"Good," she said, "and since you pulled off the first one, I got another job for you."

"Wait a minute. I've got the kids this afternoon . . ."

"It's a rush, so we're going to have to be proactive on it. You know what a honeypot is?"

"A honeypot?"

"Yeah."

"Is it some kind of special equipment?"

She snorted. "Special equipment? No, sweetheart. *You're* the honeypot."

"*I'm* the honeypot?" That didn't sound good. "How do I do that?"

She sucked on the cigarette again before answering. "A trip to Dillard's foundations department would be a start. Maybe even Frederick's of Hollywood."

"You mean . . ."

"Infidelity case. I need someone to be the bait. Once you've got him hooked, we call in the photographer, and he gets a shot we can show wifey. I usually use a professional, but Rosita is out of circulation for a few months, and Angie's busy. But if you don't think you can hack it . . ." She trailed off.

"You mean you want me to go to a bar and hit on someone?"

"Yup."

"But I'm married."

"I didn't say you had to sleep with him. Just make him want to sleep with you."

I digested this for a moment. Make someone want to sleep with me? Lately, the only people interested in sharing my bed were two small children with less-than-discriminating taste.

"That's all well and good," I said, "but what am I going to do with my kids?"

"Look," Peaches said. "If you don't think you can do it, I'll just find someone else."

"No, no. Why don't I do it tomorrow? Blake can cover for me. It's been a long time since I've been on the bar circuit, though. I don't know if I have anything to wear."

"Control-top hose, for starters. You got any push-up bras?"

I groaned. "How soon does this need to happen?"

"Like I said, it's a rush job. Lady's anxious. She said he usually goes out on Tuesday nights, so I figure if you follow him from work, you can get it taken care of tonight."

"Tonight? But my husband's not home till late."

She sighed. "I guess I might be able to get Angie . . ."

I thought about the kids in the other room. My friend Becky had already offered to have them over some night this week, and it would probably take their minds off the fact that their daddy wasn't home. Assuming the offer still stood, what did I have to lose? "All right. I'll do it."

"Good. He works at the Bank One building, downtown." I jotted down the details and hung up the phone, wondering how I was going to transform my pudgy thirty-five-year-old self into a vixen by six this evening, and whether Becky would be able to watch the kids. And most of all, I wondered where on God's green earth I was going to find another fry phone.

CHAPTER THREE

An hour later, I was sitting on Becky Hale's bed, watching her rummage through her closet. Becky and I had been best friends and roommates at the University of Texas, but after graduation, she and I had drifted into different careers and separate lives. Then, a few years ago, we ran into each other at a coffee shop on a rainy weekday morning, both of us lugging baby carriers and trying to keep our hyperactive toddlers from upending a coffee-cup display. We exchanged one tired look and our friendship had rekindled.

When I called to tell Becky about my new assignment—and to ask her to watch my kids—she'd squealed.

"How exciting! Can I do you up?"

"Do me up?"

"I've wanted to get my hands on you for the longest time," she said. "You used to look so nice in college, before the kids . . . With those green eyes, you could look like a million dollars." She paused. "Not that you don't already look great, of course."

Yeah, right. "I'd be happy with just a hundred," I said.

Now, as the kids raced around the Hale house screaming, Becky emerged from her cavernous walk-in closet and fixed me with an appraising look.

"Thanks for keeping the kids tonight. Usually I could just have Blake watch them, but he seems to have taken up residence at Jones McEwan lately. I was considering installing a cot in his office, but I don't want to encourage him."

"I know. Rick's been at the office a lot lately, too. But it's no problem. You know the kids love each other. It almost makes it easier."

"Right up to cleanup time, anyway."

"I'll just bribe them with Oreos." Becky pursed her Cupid's bow lips and ran a hand through her curly blond hair. "Now, what are we going to do with you? I think green's a good color for you, don't you? Something short, to show off your legs."

I closed my eyes and relinquished the reins to Becky, who, despite her children, always managed to look like she had stepped out of a Talbot's ad. As Elsie and Nick joined Zoe and Josh in disassembling the house beyond the bedroom door, Becky plugged in a curling iron and squeezed me into a dress two sizes too small. Then she assembled a cadre of brushes and unguents and went to work.

"How did you get this job, anyway?" she asked, clamping a curling iron onto a hank of my hair. I jerked away as the hot metal grazed my ear.

"It was the only thing in the paper that looked interesting." I winced as the hot iron brushed my ear again. As Becky sprayed and crimped, I told her about my first encounter with Peaches Barlowe and Peachtree Investigations. Becky had been at Disneyland with her kids for the last week and a half, so I hadn't had a chance to fill her in.

When I finished, she fluffed my bangs and fixed me with a doubtful eye. "It doesn't sound like a really reputable agency."

"Well, they've got enough work to hire me. And she's right; it *is* interesting." I told her about Mr. Pence in the motel room, and she snorted.

"What does Blake think?" She sucked in her breath. "And what about Prudence?"

Prudence was my mother-in-law, the queen of twin sets and dinners with hand-lettered place cards. I'm not exactly the daughter-in-law she had in mind. In fact, I think she's still reeling from the shock of our marriage, even though it happened eight years ago. So far, I'd skirted the whole issue of my new part-time job, but it couldn't last forever.

"Prue doesn't know," I said. "And I haven't told Blake the gory details."

Becky shot me a wicked smile. "I'll bet not. I'd love to be a fly on the wall for that conversation . . ."

"I'm hoping it will never happen, but I know that's being foolishly optimistic."

"You know, for the sake of marital harmony, you could always sell Mary Kay."

"The last time I bought mascara was before Nick was born," I reminded her.

"You have a point. Maybe not Mary Kay. But you could always do Tupperware. Ellen Bentsen makes loads selling jewelry."

I glanced up at her, but her heart-shaped face was lost behind a cloud of Finesse Extra Hold. "You know, you'd kill me if I suggested you take up selling Tupperware."

"Okay," she said, pumping the sprayer a few more times, "maybe not Tupperware. But why the PI gig?"

"I don't know. We needed the money. To be honest, I didn't know that's what I was applying for at first. And then when I found out, I figured I'd give it a shot."

"At least it's more exciting than being room mother." She sighed. "I'm actually a bit jealous. I could use a little spice in my life." That didn't surprise me. Becky might look a little like one of the Stepford wives, but beneath her polished exterior, she had a yen for adventure that chasing toddlers didn't satisfy.

An image of Irwin Pence and his paddle pal flashed through my mind. "I forgot to tell you, I lost Elsie's fry phone. We talked about it earlier, but if she asks for it tonight, tell her it'll turn up."

Becky drew in her breath as the iron clacked down again, singeing my other ear. "Oh my God. I can't imagine what it would be like if Zoe lost Kermit. She'd just die. How did it happen?"

"I dropped it outside the room, and Pence picked it up."

Becky's eyebrows shot up. "Mr. Saran Wrap? The one with the hooker?"

I started to nod, then stopped when my forehead hit hot metal. "I know. I'm just hoping I can find a new one."

"Ouch." She snorted back a laugh. "I guess you couldn't just knock on the door and ask for it back, could you?"

I shot her a stern look from beneath the curling iron.

"All right, all right. I know it's not funny. But what are you going to do now? I mean, didn't those go out of circulation like five years ago?"

"Yeah. I can't even find one on eBay."

"Not good, Margie," she said, spraying another cloud of liquid plastic. "Not good."

After another half hour of prodding, singeing, and smearing, Becky applied a last dab of mascara and stepped back to inspect her handiwork. "I think you're done. Go take a look."

I blinked at the unfamiliar person staring out of the full-length mirror. My usually droopy reddish-brown hair had been teased to a wavy halo around my face, my thin lips had been plumped and slicked with fire-engine-red lipstick, and my tired green eyes were ablaze in a rainbow of shimmery eye shadow. The rest of me had been stuffed into an emerald sheath dress, which was fine while I was upright. But I felt all circulation shut off to the bottom half of my body the moment I sat down.

"Dear Lord. I look like the Happy Hooker."

A furrow appeared in Becky's smooth brow. "Too much?"

"Oh no," I said. "That was exactly the look I was going for."

• • •

At five forty-five, I pulled the Caravan into a "Deliveries Only" parking spot across from the Bank One parking garage, slid a Hot Chocolate CD into the player, and cranked up "You Sexy Thing." The mascara Becky had applied kept making the lashes of my right eye stick together, and the control-top hose felt like two boa constrictors were getting cozy with my upper thighs. In short, I felt about as sexy as Mrs. Potato Head. As the music throbbed in the minivan's crumb-encrusted interior, I pried my eyelashes apart for the sixth time and focused on the "I believe in miracles" part.

By six o'clock, I was having serious reservations about the life of a private investigator—and about Becky's wardrobe selection. The dress cinched into my waist, pushing my diaphragm up to right under my chin, and my breathing was so fast and shallow, it sounded like I was practicing for Lamaze class. I reclined the seat a few inches to relieve the pressure, convinced that whatever brain cells had survived two pregnancies were now expiring from oxygen deprivation.

I had just inched back to an almost prone position when someone rapped at the window. I hit the window button and rolled it down.

"Hey!" It was a short, skinny redheaded guy in a blue uniform with a Lone Star Delivery patch affixed to the chest. I found myself staring at his nose, which was huge, erupting from the middle of his narrow face like Mount Fuji. "You can't park here. I've got a truck."

I tore my eyes from his nose and saw that he was right. He'd double-parked his truck right next to me, blocking my exit.

At that moment, a red Miata swung out of the Bank One parking garage. I scrabbled for my notes and checked the plate number. It was a match.

"Lady! You gotta move!"

"You're in my way!" I barked, lurching to a sitting position. I threw the van into reverse and slammed into a parking meter. Then I put it in drive and swerved out into the street, smacking the front of the truck with the back half of the Caravan. As I gunned the engine, a shudder ran through the minivan's frame, and something clattered to the pavement.

"Are you fucking insane?" he screeched from somewhere behind me.

I glanced in the rearview mirror. Fuji-nose stood in the middle of the street, shaking his scrawny arms at me. A few feet in front of him, like an orphaned child, lay my back bumper.

I returned my seat to an upright position and tried to concentrate on breathing and following the Miata, but as we wove through the streets of downtown Austin, my thoughts kept returning to my mangled minivan. Was it possible that the damage was just cosmetic? Had I remembered to pay the insurance premium? And how was I going to explain this to Blake?

My mind was still straining to recall the details of my insurance when Jack Emerson cruised into a parking spot on Fourth Street and climbed out of the little red car. He was an attractive man in his late thirties, with clean-cut salt-and-pepper hair and a tall, trim frame clad in charcoal slacks and a white shirt. When I saw his lean body striding down the sidewalk, my already compressed chest deflated further. It was going to take more than a miracle to get Emerson to want to go to bed with me. I was thinking mind-altering drugs and duct tape.

I pulled the minivan into the only vacant space—another "Deliveries Only" spot—and unfolded myself from the driver's seat, enjoying the first full breath I'd had in an hour. Then I took a peek at the back of the minivan and almost choked. The rear-left panel had imploded, and it looked as if someone had tried to pry the rest of the back end off with a crowbar. Could they reattach bumpers? Maybe I could swing by and pick it up later.

A car door slammed somewhere, reminding me that the reason my minivan looked like a can of Friskies after a run-in with a pack of starving cats was that I had been sent out to seduce George Clooney.

I wrenched my eyes away from the carnage. Then I breathed in as deeply as I could, smoothed down my dress, and trotted after Emerson as fast as was possible in a pair of black Ferragamo slingbacks two sizes too big.

After a half-block walk, he stopped in front of a bar and slipped through the dark entrance. Good. Dim lights and liquor. It wasn't duct tape, but it was a start.

I loitered near the entrance for a moment and slipped in behind him, flashing a grimace at the bouncer as I tottered over the threshold.

Entering the chilly darkness of the Rainbow Room was a little like stepping into an oversized meat locker. My eyes strained to adjust to the dim light. At first, the only things visible were streaks of neon and the glow of e-cigarettes. After a moment, I could make out several groups of fashionably dressed men and women clumped around a cavernous room, sending up plumes of nicotine-laced vapor like smoke signals. The building had probably been a warehouse in its previous life. Now, it was dominated by a long runway in the center, cool tubes of blue and pink neon everywhere else, and above it all the heavy beat of dance music. The place reeked of spilled beer, stale perfume, and the musky smell of bodies. This was definitely not the Green Meadows PTA meeting.

When I could see enough to move, I shuffled forward a few steps and scanned the room for Emerson. He was sitting at one end of the curved bar. I adjusted the hem of my skirt, sucked in another shallow breath, and wobbled in his direction.

I hoisted myself onto the vacant stool two down from Emerson, sucking in my tummy and trying to look sultry yet nonchalant. As I directed an airy wave toward the bartender, the gold band on my left hand glinted in the blue light. *Crap.*

I yanked my hand back and buried it in my lap as the bartender, a tall Adonis-like creature whose half-buttoned silk shirt revealed a chest like sealskin, glided over.

"Can I help you?"

"Gin and tonic," I said, tugging at my wedding ring under the bar. It was stuck just beneath my knuckle. "Extra large."

He cocked a sculpted eyebrow at me. "They only come in one size."

"Oh. Well, whatever size they come in, then." He slicked back his blond hair and reached back for a glass. I slid my eyes over to Emerson, who had half turned in my direction, and gave the ring a sharp, desperate tug.

As Emerson's eyes met mine, the gold band slipped past my knuckle and zinged across the smoky room. It made brief contact with the substantial derriere of a short redhead before clinking to the black tile floor and disappearing into a tangle of chrome chair legs.

His eyes followed its trajectory. "Lose something?"

The blood rushed to my face. "I'll be right back." I got off the bar stool and lurched across the room, the slingbacks slipping on the waxed floor as I plowed through the jungle of tables and chairs. Emerson watched with interest as I held my breath and lowered myself to my knees, groping under the chairs for my wedding band. It had landed in a pool of pink gooey stuff.

I pried it up and tottered back to my seat, clutching the sticky ring behind my back. Unfortunately, by the time I returned, a sleek woman with glossy brown hair had sidled over to the bar stool between us and was leaning into Emerson as if he were the only thing holding her up.

On the plus side, Adonis had returned with my gin and tonic. After wrapping my ring in a napkin and burying it in my miniscule purse, I grabbed the drink and downed half of it. Then I shot a glance at the slender brunette, whose handkerchief-size dress exposed several acres of tanned, unblemished back, and drank the rest.

As I perched on my stool, watching the ice cubes in my glass quiver in time to the music, I began to wonder what I was doing here. My dress was cutting off the blood supply to my lower body, my eyelashes were stuck together, and the minivan looked like it had recently starred as a speed bump in a Monster Truck special. And for what? The man I had spent the last two hours preparing to seduce was wrapped around a brunette ten years my junior.

I stirred the quivering ice cubes with a moody finger. Maybe Becky was right, and I should hand in my badge. Or whatever it was that PIs carried to say they were PIs. Which I probably needed to take up with Peaches, come to think of it.

The brunette snuggled in closer to Emerson, and I decided it was time for another gin and tonic. I was trying to flag down Adonis when a woman's manicured hand closed on my right arm.

"You're new here, aren't you?"

I whirled around and blinked. At first I thought she had woolly bear caterpillars on her face. Then I realized they were false eyelashes. My gaze drifted south to her substantial figure, which had been stuffed into a bright orange cocktail dress. The plunging neckline ended just shy of her navel.

"Here for the Tuesday Night Showdown?"

I jerked my eyes back up to her face. Her skin was spackled with foundation the same shade as her dress, accented with two vivid spots of red rouge. "What showdown?" I asked.

She fluttered her furry eyelashes again. "It's a kind of beauty contest, darling."

I waved her away. "Oh no. I'm just here for a drink."

"But you look so gorgeous!" She tugged at my arm. "Come on. It'll be fun."

Maybe it was the gin and tonic. Maybe it was the prospect of getting Jack Emerson to notice me. Maybe it was just someone, even a woman with caterpillars for eyelashes, telling me I was gorgeous when I felt like a water buffalo in Italian shoes. Whatever it was, I soon found myself trailing the woman in the orange dress through the smoky room. She stopped at a clutch of tall, heavily made-up women in dresses that looked more like confections than clothing.

"By the way," she said, "I'm Cassandra Starr. The mistress of ceremonies." She herded me in with the other women, most of whom looked like they were on their way to the prom, and the onslaught of mixed perfumes made my nose itch. "What's your name?"

"Margie."

"Margie?" She squinted at me. "That's a lovely name, dear, but I think for tonight you should be Emerald. Emerald Divine. And I'd recommend another pass with the lipstick, darling. Don't be afraid of color." I blinked as she pulled out a tube of iridescent purple and ran it over her lips.

A moment later she whisked off, leaving me to study the dresses of the women towering over me. The outfits looked like escapees from Elsie's dress-up box: ruffles, silks, satins, sequins. Even fur. Despite the three-inch heels, I felt like an underdressed dwarf.

"First time?" A smoky-voiced woman in a long fuchsia gown bent down, peering at me from above a wrap festooned with bright pink feathers.

"For a beauty contest? Definitely."

"Beauty contest?" She snorted, then focused on the low cut of my dress. "I love your cleavage, though. So natural. I was filling mine out with birdseed in panty hose for a while, but then Samantha turned me onto mastectomy products. What is that, a Wonderbra?"

Before I had a chance to answer, the low lights dimmed further. Cassandra stepped up to the runway, her orange dress glowing in the spotlight. "Good evening, ladies and gentlemen, and welcome to the Rainbow Room. I think you're going to love the lineup of ladies we have for you tonight. So sit back, order another drink, and enjoy."

My stomach did a little flip-flop as I stole a glance at Emerson. He had stopped chatting with the brunette and turned toward the runway. Good. At least I'd have his attention for a moment.

Cassandra smiled at the crowd. "Our first contestant is a new girl on the block, but I'm sure you'll agree she's a class act." She turned and winked a caterpillar at me. I swallowed hard. "Ladies and gentlemen, allow me to introduce the first contestant in the Rainbow Room's Tuesday Night Drag Queen Showdown . . . Miss Emerald Divine!"

CHAPTER FOUR

rag Queen Showdown?

D The blazing light swung over to where I stood, blinking like the subject of an alien abduction. Cassandra swept down the runway and shoved me toward the stairway. I clawed at her satin-clad arm. "No, no. You don't understand. I'm a real woman."

"So are we all, sweetheart," she muttered into my ear. Her eyelashes brushed my cheek. "Now get up there and strut your stuff." She gave me a sharp push. I stumbled onto the runway and stood there with my mouth hanging open.

"Go!" Cassandra stage-whispered at me.

At least a hundred pairs of gleaming, expectant eyes were fixed on me, waiting. Every nerve in my body was telling me to turn and run. Instead, my feet moved in wooden steps down the glossy runway, which looked to be about two miles long, as the room vibrated to the tune of "I'm Too Sexy."

Time slowed to a crawl as I teetered toward the crowd, feeling like one of the dancing hippos in *Fantasia*, my lips pulled back into a rictus of a smile. *Dear Lord*, I thought, *please let nobody recognize me.* I could explain many things to my husband and in-laws. This wasn't one of them.

A few weak whistles trickled from the crowd as I wobbled to the end of the runway. I risked dropping my eyes to the people below for a moment, shuffling backward when I realized an octogenarian in leather pants was peering up my dress. I glanced toward the bar. Emerson had turned back to the brunette, who looked like she shared a trainer with Jennifer Lopez. Was she a man, too?

Finally, I swung around to face the gaggle of women awaiting their turn in the spotlight. Tall, heavy makeup, fancy dresses, husky voices . . . How had I missed it?

Despite the too-big slingbacks, I jogged to the end of the runway, flailing as my right shoe tried to slide off the floor into somebody's drink. Three or four steps from the end, the spotlight still hot on my back, I took a deep breath. As the air whooshed out of my lungs, something slithered down my spine.

The zipper of my dress had given out.

Wolf whistles erupted behind me as I dived into the sea of ruffles and sequins. I clutched at the back of my dress and stumbled toward the safety of a dark corner.

As I leaned against the wall, panting and trying to keep my dress from puddling on the floor at my feet, the woman in fuchsia glided over in a cloud of Obsession. "Not bad for your first time out. Shame about the dress, though." She unwound the pink-feathered wrap from her beefy shoulders and dangled it like a dead tropical bird. "I don't have a safety pin, but this will keep you covered for now."

"Thanks," I said, pulling the prickly wrap tight around my shoulders. It wasn't exactly opaque, but it was a lot better than walking around with my dress gaping open.

"I'm Carmen. What's your name, sugar?"

"Margie."

"Margie? Good name. Much better than Emerald." Carmen rolled her heavily lined eyes. "Cassandra's always coming up with stage names that sound like gay bars."

A smattering of applause came as the second contestant, a tall blonde in a midnight-blue satin dress, sashayed down the runway. Then Cassandra took the stage again, wiggling her orange-clad hips and beaming into the microphone. "Let's have a hand for Selena Sass. And now let's hear it for our next contestant . . . Carmen Bianca!"

My companion's extravagantly styled head shot up. "That's me," she said. "Gotta go. You can hang on to the wrap for now . . . Hope to see you around."

"Sure. Thanks again."

She winked at me and undulated toward the runway. As the spotlight lit her in a blaze of fuchsia, the crowd let out a chorus of enthusiastic whistles. Carmen was obviously a favorite, and after a moment of watching her slinky walk, I could see why. I peered past her swinging hips to Emerson, whose arm had snaked around the brunette's naked shoulders. By the time Carmen blew a last kiss to the crowd and swayed off the runway, they had locked lips. George Clooney and Jennifer Lopez. *Us* magazine would have loved it.

I watched them grope each other for a few minutes. Then I tugged up my dress and dug in my purse for the scrap of paper with the photographer's number on it. Emerson might not end up in a compromising position with me, but it looked like things with Jennifer were getting hot enough for a Kodak moment. I was about to dial when my phone lit up with an incoming call.

I glanced around, looking for a quiet place to talk, and scurried down the corridor leading to the restrooms. I ran into a dark-haired woman—or man, it was hard to tell—in a long, silvery dress. "Sorry," I said. The woman—or man—looked at me, startled, and for a moment, she looked familiar. Probably because her eyes were ringed with the same amount of eyeliner as the rest of the "women" here, I decided. She drifted past me in a cloud of Anaïs Anaïs, and I plunged toward the restrooms, where the throbbing music was slightly less bone-shaking.

"Hello?"

"Margie?"

"Blake. What are you doing home?"

"Nick's throwing up all over the place. Becky couldn't reach you, so she called me. I had to cancel the client meeting to get the kids."

"Sorry about that. Is he okay?"

"He threw up all over the backseat of the Audi. What is going on with you? Where have you been? Becky's been calling you all night."

"I must not have heard the phone. Is Nick okay?"

"Yeah, but the car's in bad shape. It reeks. I'll need to take the minivan tomorrow." I sucked in my breath. The minivan wasn't in great shape, either. "And that stupid cat crapped on my pillow again."

"Just throw the pillow in the laundry room, and I'll see if I can clean up the car when I get home."

"No, that's all right. I'll take the van. You had it cleaned this week, didn't you?"

I cleared my throat. "I, uh, had a little fender bender with the minivan."

"A fender bender?"

I swallowed. Blake considered a door ding a felony offense. "Nothing major," I said. "Don't worry about it."

"How bad? Did you get the guy's insurance?"

"I'll take care of it, sweetheart. Just relax." The phone beeped. I pulled it from my ear; the battery icon was flashing. "Honey, my battery's dying. I've got to go. There are hot dogs in the fridge if you're hungry."

"Hungry? I'm covered in vomit. What's that music?"

"I'm on a job. I'll be home as soon as I can."

"Are you in a bar?" The phone beeped again.

"Yes. Look, I have to make another call."

"When are you coming home?"

"Gotta go. Be home soon. Talk later." I hit "End" and closed my eyes for a moment, trying not to picture my husband's face when I returned home from a bar with a smashed minivan, a zipperless dress, and a hot-pink feathered wrap. I sighed and dialed the photographer's number.

He answered on the fourth ring.

"Is this Gary Mathers?"

"Yeah. What do you want?"

"I'm Margie Peterson. Peaches Barlowe gave me your number. I've got a job for you. Can you meet me at the Rainbow Room on Fourth Street?"

"Now?"

"Yes, now."

"Can it wait a couple hours? I'm in the middle of a football game here."

I glanced toward the bar. Emerson and his friend were still there, but I didn't know for how long. "No, it can't." The phone beeped frantically. "Look, my phone's dying. Will you be here or not?"

He swore under his breath. "How will I know you?"

"Green dress, pink wrap." Silence. "Hello? Hello?"

Nothing. I jammed the dead phone into my purse, hoping he had at least gotten my description, and slipped into the restroom marked "Princesses."

It was lined with urinals.

I wrinkled my nose at the line of pink pee cakes and edged toward the mirror. The shimmery eye shadow had started to ooze down my cheeks, giving me a kind of glow-in-the-dark raccoon look, and the red lipstick was reduced to a crimson line on the outskirts of my lips. When I pulled off the feathered wrap, the green dress sagged from my shoulders and flapped open in the back, exposing rippled flesh and my bra clasp. Great. Now I looked like the Happy Hooker after a rough night. I spent a few futile minutes trying to fix the zipper and then gave up.

After swiping at the green streaks beneath my eyes, I wobbled over to the bathroom's single stall and peered under the door. The stall was occupied by a pair of stocking-clad ankles and sequined pumps. The pressure in my bladder increased as I walked back to the mirror to wait, fluffing my stiff hair with inexpert fingers and rubbing my lips together in a vain attempt to redistribute what was left of the lipstick. I hoped whoever was in there would hurry up. I wasn't desperate enough to try the urinals yet, but that could change soon.

After a few minutes, when no sound came from the stall, I walked back over. "Hello? Are you okay?"

Silence.

I pushed the door, and it swung open.

Positioned on the toilet like a department store mannequin was the contestant in the long blue dress. My stomach heaved. When she had sailed down the runway, her face had been as white as porcelain.

Now it was covered in blood.

I staggered backward, almost tumbling into the line of urinals. I didn't need to check her pulse to know that the woman in the stall was dead. Half her face had been blown away.

My stomach turned over. Was the shooter still here? Was I next?

No, I realized. I was alone; there was only one stall here, and nowhere else to hide. Whoever had done this was gone.

Police.

Call the police.

I ripped my cell phone out, stabbing at the display with shaking fingers. Nothing. Dead battery.

My eyes slid back to the woman—man, I corrected myself—on the toilet. His head lolled sideways, the blond hair dangling as if ripped from his scalp. Beside him on the floor a blue sequined purse gaped open. An iPhone poked out of the top. I crept into the stall and hooked the strap with my finger, pulling the purse across the tiles.

I yanked the phone out of the purse, sending a tube of lipstick skittering across the floor. My fingers fumbled with the touch screen as I attempted to dial 911. Finally, the display said *Connecting*, and I jammed the phone against my ear.

After two rings somebody picked up.

"Hello?"

I froze.

"Hello? Who is this?"

I lowered the phone and stared at the number on the display.

The phone hadn't connected me to 911.

It had speed-dialed my home phone number.

CHAPTER FIVE

I stared at the phone in my hand. Why had the phone of a dead transvestite called my house?

My eyes jerked to the man in the dark blue dress again, and a shudder ran through me. To date, my face-to-face experience with death had been limited to plucking limp tropical fish out of the tank in the living room. The most violence we saw in Austin Heights was during homeowners' association meetings to determine whether spruce green or sage green should make the list of acceptable paint colors. And even then, the worst outcome was usually limited to refusing to invite a neighbor to the Christmas open house.

I dialed 911 again with shaking fingers. I didn't think there was much the paramedics could do for her, or him. But I still had to try.

This time a dispatcher answered. My body felt numb as I reeled out the details.

"Just stay there, and don't let anyone in," the dispatcher said in a warm-cocoa voice that chased away some of the chill that had seeped into me. "Do you need me to stay on the line?"

"No, no," I said, turning my eyes from the woman in the stall. The air conditioner clicked on, creating a breeze that smelled of stale urine. "I'll be okay."

"Hang in there. They'll be there as fast as they can."

"Thanks."

She hung up.

Except for the low thump of music from the bar and the steady drip-drip of a water faucet, the room was eerily still. The man on the toilet was dead, but his presence filled the small room in a most unpleasant way. A single earring twinkled on the floor a few feet from the body—an unusual chandelier, with blue and green crystals that sparkled under the fluorescent lights. It seemed utterly out of place.

I wrapped my arms around myself and shivered, wishing I'd listened to Becky and gone into Tupperware sales. If I'd just turned around and walked back to the minivan instead of going into Peachtree Investigations, I could be home eating Kit Kats right now, instead of sharing a bathroom with the remains of a mutilated drag queen. I moved away from the stall and positioned myself by the door to the corridor, turning to face the urinals.

As I shifted from foot to foot, the patter of dripping water was like a Morse code message to my overfilled bladder. *Emergency!* it tapped out. *Evacuate now!*

I squeezed my knees together, wishing the dead man had ended up anywhere other than straddling the only available toilet. My eyes roved over the row of yellowed porcelain receptacles. If I got desperate enough, I could always try squatting. With my luck, though, Austin's finest would burst through the door the moment the control-top hose dropped to my ankles.

I ignored my bladder and shifted my eyes to the phone in my hand—the phone that had dialed my home number. If I'd been at home when he called, could I have saved his life somehow?

And why *had* he called my home?

I glanced at the man on the toilet again. Could he be one of Blake's clients? It didn't seem likely. Blake dealt mainly with corporations, and the clients' attire tended more toward pinstripes than pinafores.

Everything I'd ever seen on *CSI* told me that I should keep my fingers to myself and wait for the police to investigate. But I'd already touched the phone. Would it hurt to look through the call history? After all, I was supposed to be a private investigator now.

I squeezed my thighs together and pulled up the call history. My phone number popped up on the screen twice. One was the phone call I'd inadvertently made, at seven fifteen. The other call had been made at six that evening, while I was waiting for Jack Emerson outside the Bank One building.

Next I checked the speed-dial list. Four numbers were listed. None of them was mine.

I was about to scroll through call history again when footsteps approached from down the hall. I tossed the phone into the purse and adjusted the neckline of my dress, preparing to greet the police or turn away a person in need (chances were they'd be just as comfortable in the Princes' room anyway). But whoever it was kept going, and the door to the Princesses' room stayed closed.

I looked at the phone again. I must have accidentally hit "Redial" while I was fumbling to dial 911. But why had the woman/man in the stall called my house?

Next to the phone, a brown wallet peeked out from under a tube of lipstick and a Gillette razor. It would be easy to find out the dead man's identity. The answer was right in front of me.

I stooped down, then hesitated. Picking up a phone to call the police was one thing, but my limited knowledge of crime scenes told me that the police wouldn't look too kindly on my rifling through a murder victim's wallet. I listened for footsteps.

Nothing.

I took a deep breath and went for it.

My bladder threatened to explode as I squatted down on the floor and withdrew the wallet, using the feathered wrap as an impromptu glove. Fingerprints on the phone I could explain. Fingerprints on the wallet? Probably not.

I cradled the wallet in a hammock of pink feathers and lifted the edge with a fingernail. It flopped open to reveal a Texas driver's license. The man pictured looked to be in his late twenties, with close-cropped black hair, a bright white shirt, and a red tie.

My eyes darted to the man in the stall. The hair exposed where the blond wig had been torn off was short and black. The hair was a match, but I couldn't tell about the face.

Evan Maxted, read the name under the picture. He was five foot eleven and twenty-nine years old. I gazed from the picture to the person sprawled over the toilet. Somebody's son. My heart twinged. Did his parents know about his double life? How would they deal with the crushing news that their son's life had been snuffed out? My eyes flicked toward the gruesome scene in the toilet stall again, prickling with hot tears.

Get yourself together, Margie. I swiped at my eyes with the back of my hand and forced myself to look away, focusing instead on the wallet cradled in the pink wrap. Evan's picture smiled at me from his driver's license, a dimple in his right cheek. I took a deep shuddery breath and closed my eyes for a moment, trying to regain control of my emotions. *The police are going to be here soon. You'd better get moving.*

Using the wrap to shield my fingers, I pulled out the credit cards tucked behind the license. Platinum Visa, American Express Gold card. Whoever Evan Maxted was, he didn't seem to be hurting for money. Or else he ran up impressive balances.

A short stack of white cards lined one of the inner pockets. I pinched the corner of the top one between my fingernails and drew it out. It was a business card. *Evan Maxted. Vice President, International Shipping Company.* That explained the platinum Visa.

I was about to slip the card back in, when footsteps thundered down the hall outside.

I whirled toward the door, causing the wallet to tumble from its fluffy hammock onto the tile floor. I thrust my hand into the feathers

45

and grabbed at it, tossing it back into the purse next to the phone. The door burst open as the wallet thunked on top of the phone, flapping open like a clamshell. I curled Evan Maxted's business card into the palm of my hand and turned to face the police.

Suddenly, people in uniform—the emergency medical technicians—flooded the room like a swarm of angry but efficient bees, transforming the echoey room into a hive of activity.

"She's over there," I said, pointing at the stall, but they had already located her. As they approached the dead man, I turned away, feeling small and unimportant.

A short man with a head of bristle-brush hair and a torso with the dimensions of a pickle barrel pushed into the room. I hugged my wrap closer and smiled at him weakly.

"I'm Detective Bunsen. Are you the one who called?" he asked in a gruff, no-nonsense voice.

I nodded and inclined my head toward her purse. "I'm sorry. I had to use his phone to call 911. Mine was dead."

His hazel eyes flicked to the purse, taking in the wallet splayed over the phone. Then he shifted his piercing gaze to me. I was just the woman who found her. So why did I suddenly feel like the subject of an interrogation?

"Why didn't you just call from the bar?" he asked.

I shrugged, causing my dress to gape open. I tugged it closed. "I don't know. I panicked, I guess. I saw her phone, so I just grabbed it."

He gave the wallet a meaningful look. "And did you limit yourself to using the phone?"

My cheeks felt hot. My eyes followed his to the wallet draped over the phone. "I just used the phone. I'm afraid things got a little jumbled in her . . . I mean, his purse. I was nervous. I've never seen a dead body before."

As Bunsen crossed his burly arms across his chest, two more men in blue entered the ladies' room. With the EMTs still circling the stall, things were getting a little crowded.

The two cops glanced at the woman draped over the toilet. The younger of the two turned pale.

The older one turned to Bunsen. "Do you need me to call forensics?"

"Yeah. Call the coroner, and get the crime scene van out here."

"Will do. Want me to close off the bar?"

Bunsen gave a sharp nod. "Edwards is already working on it. Give him a hand, and call for more backup. Lotta people out there." The two men disappeared through the door again, and Bunsen turned back to me.

"Did you know the victim?"

I shook my head. "Never met her."

He raised a bushy eyebrow. "Her?"

"Her, him, whatever." I squeezed my legs together, feeling like I was about to burst. "I hate to interrupt, but do you mind if I slip over to the men's room for a moment?"

His eyebrows rose in surprise. "You're a man?"

"No. It's just that I came in here to go to the bathroom, and there's only one stall."

He nodded. "Meet me in the hall when you're done."

I pushed through the door to the Princesses' room with relief—relief to be away from the body in the bathroom, and to be away from Bunsen. The thumping music was gone, and the dark corridor was flooded with light. Apparently a corpse in the ladies' room meant party time at the Rainbow Room was over.

Fortunately, the stall in the Princes' room was vacant, and a few minutes later I emerged from the men's room feeling much better. And with Evan Maxted's business card stashed in my purse. Bunsen hadn't emerged from the ladies' room yet, and the corridor was empty. As I leaned against the wall to wait, Cassandra tripped down the hall toward me, her makeup even more garish in full fluorescent light.

She grabbed at my arm just as Detective Bunsen stepped out of the ladies' room.

"Emerald!" she said. "There you are!" She paused to flick an appreciative eye over Detective Bunsen's stocky frame. Then she fluttered her caterpillars and reached to squeeze his upper arm. "Oooh, muscles." Bunsen stepped back. Although his facial expression didn't change, his olive skin reddened. "Is this your boyfriend, Emerald?"

"Margie. And no. This is Detective Bunsen."

"I'll bet you look wonderful in uniform," she purred to him. Then she turned to me. "Anyway, darling, I know there's all this fuss going on—I heard somebody had a tiff in the Princesses' room—but I was just coming to tell you that you won third place."

Bunsen's eyebrows rose. "Third place?"

Cassandra smiled coquettishly. "We have a little beauty contest here on Tuesday nights. Emerald here was a smash hit."

Now it was my turn to blush.

"The trick with the dress was *so* sexy." She draped an arm around me and turned to Bunsen. Her purple lipstick was smeared, and her breath was one hundred fifty proof. "Would you believe it, Officer? It's her first time out, and she takes a bronze!" She leaned toward Bunsen. "And what are all of you handsome men doing here? Did somebody get a little naughty in one of the stalls?"

"Cassandra," I said. "There's been a murder."

Her eyes got big, and she drew in a dramatic breath. "A murder? Who?"

"The contestant in the blue dress."

"Selena?" Color leached from beneath the orange foundation. "Oh no . . . that's awful!" She clutched at Bunsen's arm again. "How did it happen?"

Bunsen pried her fingers from his arm. "You knew the victim?"

"Oh, of course I did. I just can't *believe* it . . . We met at Miss Veronica's tranny school. What a gorgeous girl." She pressed two sausage-like fingers together. "We were like *this*!" Cassandra's eyes were wet behind the caterpillars.

For a moment, I forgot Bunsen was standing next to me. "Tranny school?"

Cassandra perked up a little bit. "Oh, that's where we learn all the tricks for looking glamorous, darling. How else do you think I learned to look this fabulous?"

Bunsen whipped out a notebook. "The victim's name was Selena?"

"That was her stage name. Selena Sass."

Bunsen jotted that down. "And her . . . his . . . real name?"

"Something that started with an *E*, I think. Edward? Edwin?"

Evan, I started to say, but stopped myself just in time.

"Evan," she said. "Evan something."

"Would you mind going and having a seat at the bar?" Bunsen asked. "I'll need to ask you a few questions as soon as I'm done here."

"Oh, of course, Officer!"

"I'll be with you as soon as I've finished with Miss . . ." He turned to me.

"Peterson."

"With Miss Peterson."

"It's a terrible tragedy. Just terrible. Of course I'll do whatever I can to help, Officer." Cassandra squeezed his arm again and sashayed down the corridor. Despite the death of her friend, I noticed an extra waggle in her hips. The show must go on, I suppose.

Bunsen turned to me. "So, you were a contestant in a drag queen contest? But you're a woman, you say." His eyes slid down to my dress, which was gaping open again.

I pulled my dress up and cleared my throat. "It was an accident."

"An accident?"

"I'm kind of on a job."

"What kind of job?"

"I'm a private investigator."

"A private investigator. May I see your license?"

I shifted. "Actually, I don't have a license."

"No license? But you're here on a job. What company are you working for?"

"Peachtree Investigations."

He jotted that down. "And you were in this drag queen contest with the victim?"

"That's right."

"I thought you said you'd never met her."

"I didn't meet her. I just saw her go up after me."

His dark brown eyes bored into me. "Exactly what were you investigating, Miss Peterson?"

"It was an infidelity case," I said. "I was trailing a woman's husband."

He stared at my dress. "Do you always dress like this when you're on a job?"

"No. Only when . . ." I trailed off. I didn't want to tell this man I was supposed to be a honeypot.

"Only when what?"

I sighed. If he talked to Peaches, he'd find out anyway. "Okay. I was here because I was supposed to seduce someone, then call the photographer."

He blinked at me. "You came to a gay bar to seduce someone's husband?"

"I didn't know it was a gay bar."

"The urinals in the ladies' room didn't tip you off?"

"The ladies' room wasn't my first stop."

"You hadn't met the victim, but you and this Cassandra woman seemed pretty cozy. Want to explain that?"

"It was just a fluke. She introduced herself and invited me to join a beauty contest. I didn't realize the rest of them were all drag queens."

He cleared his throat. "So I'm guessing things didn't work out with the guy you were tailing."

I flushed. "No. Not really."

"Well." His mouth twitched upward. "On the plus side, at least you walked away with a bronze."

Anger flared in me. "Look," I said. "A woman—a man, I mean—was just murdered. Don't you have anything relevant to ask me?"

He flipped over a page in his notebook. "Miss Peterson, I'm going to need the number of the agency you work for."

"I don't remember the number offhand, but I can get it for you."

"You don't remember it?"

I shook my head slowly.

He sighed. "Okay, Miss Peterson. Before you found the body, did you see anyone else in the corridor, or in the bathroom? Anyone entering or leaving?"

"No, there was no one. Someone went down the hall while I was waiting for you guys to come, but that was it."

"Did you see who it was?"

I shook my head again.

"Was the door to the stall open or closed?"

"Closed, but not locked. I waited for a while, but it was so quiet, and she didn't answer when I asked if she was okay, so I pushed it open, and then . . ." An image of Evan Maxted's face flashed into my brain again. I swallowed hard.

"And you called from the victim's phone because your phone was dead. Where was the victim's purse before you went through it?"

"I didn't go through it, exactly." Well, not the purse, anyway. Just the wallet. "All I did was get the phone out. Anyway, it was on the floor, open, next to the toilet. That's how I saw the phone."

"If you just got the phone out, then how come the victim's wallet was open on top of the phone?"

I shrugged. "I don't know. It must have happened when I put the phone back into the purse."

He fixed me with a hard stare. "Miss Peterson, this is important. Was the wallet open when you first got there?"

Sweat broke out on my brow. "I'm sorry, Officer. I was in such a panic, I don't remember." I straightened my dress. "And by the way, it's Mrs., not Miss."

"You're married?"

I nodded. "In fact, I have to get home. My son is sick. Do you need anything else from me?"

Bunsen shook his head slowly. "Married. Unbelievable." He flipped to a new page. "I'll need to know where to reach you. I don't suppose you have a card?"

"No, not yet." I reeled off my home address. "I don't have the number for Peachtree Investigations on me, but I can get it to you."

He pulled a card out of the breast pocket of his jacket. "Give me a call when you have it. Show this to Edwards when you leave. He'll let you go. I'll be in touch."

I tucked it into my purse and turned to leave, relieved to be away from Bunsen. As I walked down the corridor toward the dance floor, he called after me.

"Oh, and Mrs. Peterson?"

"Yes?" I turned, cringing. What now?

He smirked at me. "Good luck with your career."

I pulled my wrap tighter around me and stumbled toward the door.

A gangly man with a large paunch stopped me. "You Margie Peterson?"

"Yeah." How did he know my name?

His eyes raked over me. "Nice outfit. I'm the photographer. Where's the happy couple?"

The photographer? I'd forgotten I'd called him. I did a quick survey of the bar. Emerson was gone. "You're too late."

He ran a hand through his thinning hair. "Fuck. The Cowboys were winning, too. And now they won't let me leave. What are all these cops here for?"

"There was a murder. Look, I've got to go. Sorry you came out for nothing."

"It's still gonna cost you, you know. And the longer they make me stay here, the higher my bill."

I tossed the end of my wrap over my shoulder and stalked toward the front door. "Take it up with Peaches."

I flashed Bunsen's card at the cop stationed next to the door and stepped out into the evening's lingering heat. The warm, soft air was welcome after the chilly bar, and I stopped a few yards away from the entry, closing my eyes and letting the events of the evening roll over me.

I'd ended up in a drag queen contest, found a dead body, and been interrogated by the police. Now I had to go home and face my husband and sick child with a crunched minivan and a dress that looked as if someone had torn it off me.

I fished for my car keys as I trudged past the crime scene van, my feet aching with every step. It would be nice to get home and change into something normal. My hand closed on my keys as I got to the parking spot where I had left the minivan.

It was empty.

I whirled around just in time to see my battered Dodge Caravan disappear around the corner, attached to the back of a tow truck.

CHAPTER SIX

The house was dark by the time I climbed out of a taxi and teetered up the front walk, clutching the rear bumper of my minivan. I dragged it up the front walk and leaned it next to the front door, grateful to have made it home.

When the front door closed behind me, I kicked off the slingbacks and crept up the stairs to Nick's bedroom. The sour smell of vomit assaulted my nostrils as I cracked open the door. Except for a pile of soiled sheets, Nick's bed was empty.

I found him in our bedroom, curled up in the crook of Blake's arm. I studied the two men in my life in the half-light leaking from the hall. Nick's broad cheekbones and sandy hair mirrored his father's, and behind the closed lashes, I knew his eyes were the same piercing blue.

When he was asleep, mouth ajar, the years reeled away from Blake. His face, so tense recently, softened, looking more like the face of the man I had married eight years ago—full of hope, quick to smile.

For a moment, the horror of the evening faded. I reached out to touch their faces—first Nick's downy cheek, like the skin of a peach, then the soft bristle of my husband's. As my fingers brushed across Blake's jaw, his eyes jerked open.

"Sorry to wake you," I whispered. "I was just checking on the two of you."

He sat up and ran a hand through his hair. "Where have you been?" His eyes dropped to my gaping dress. "Good God. What happened to you? Did you change your mind and go for the exotic dancing after all?"

I pulled Carmen's wrap tight around me. "I was on a job. Go back to sleep. I'll tell you about it tomorrow." I touched my son's damp forehead. "How's Nick?"

"I hope nobody saw you like this."

I decided this wasn't the moment to mention the drag queen contest. "Is Nick okay?" I repeated.

"You mean aside from throwing up all over the place?"

"He seems to be doing better."

"Well, he is, but my car's not. I hope you cleaned the van out this week, because I've got clients to meet tomorrow morning. First Nick throws up everywhere; then you come home looking like something out of *Moulin Rouge* . . ." He glanced over at the glowing digital clock. "I don't have time to deal with this right now. I need to get to sleep. The alarm's set for five." He jerked the covers up and rolled away from me.

I blinked at him for a moment, startled by his curtness. His breathing slowed as he drifted back to sleep. I knew he was getting ready for a big case, and granted, it wasn't every day I came home in a dress that was half torn off, but what happened to civil conversation? As I watched his chest rise and fall, my mind turned to the cell phone in the restroom of the Rainbow Room. Had the dead transvestite been calling my husband? And if so, why?

My stomach fluttered slightly as I stood up and tiptoed to the bathroom.

• • •

Someone was shaking me.

I swam up through a dream involving Cassandra Starr and Esther Williams, who were performing *Swan Lake* under a disco ball.

"Where is the minivan?" My husband hovered over me, smelling like aftershave and shampoo.

"You smell nice," I said groggily. "What about the minivan?"

"Where exactly *is* it? You brought home the bumper. What happened to the rest of it?"

The events of the previous evening came reeling back to me. "It got towed," I said.

"You smashed it up so much it wouldn't run?"

"No, it got towed later. After the accident."

"*After* the accident?"

I sat up and rubbed the sleep from my eyes. "Why do you need it?"

"Because I have clients to meet with, and my car smells like the inside of a Dumpster."

My eyes shot to Nick, who lay spread-eagled on the bed. I'd forgotten about that.

I bit my lip. "Can you drive it with the windows down?"

His blue eyes were uneasy. "Margie, I don't know what's happening to you. It's like you're turning into your mother or something."

My mother? I'd taken a job as a private investigator, not a tarot reader. I pushed my hair behind my ears and tried to come up with a response, but the first thing that popped into my mind was the call history on the dead woman's phone. Now was probably not the time to bring that up. "Look," I said. "Call a taxi. I'll take care of the car today, and I'll get the minivan back."

He stared at me for a long moment. Then he stalked out of the room, leaving the smell of aftershave in his wake. I glanced at the clock. Five forty-five. As I burrowed back into the covers and tried to banish thoughts of Blake, the Rainbow Room, and the dead woman's cell phone, it occurred to me that I had no way to get my children to school that day. The car seats were still in the minivan.

• • •

"Your home number was on a dead transvestite's cell phone?" Becky asked as we tooled down MoPac toward Green Meadows Day School. When I'd called her at seven thirty and told her about the minivan, she'd offered to help immediately.

I adjusted my seat belt and glanced over my shoulder at the kids. I'd told Becky a few of the details but hadn't had a chance to tell her the whole story. "I don't want to talk about it in front of Elsie and Nick."

"Fine," she said, checking her pink lipstick in the rearview mirror. Then she flipped it up and honked at the station wagon in front of us, which was lumbering along at ten miles an hour below the speed limit. "But as soon as we drop them off, I want every detail."

"What about Nick?"

"He can sit in the car for a few minutes while you fill me in outside."

We arrived at Green Meadows Day School just after eight thirty. Becky stayed with Nick while I hustled the kids to their classrooms and ducked into the office to deliver the photos for the school newsletter.

"Ah, Mrs. Peterson." Mrs. Bunn stared at me from behind her massive desk, a look of anticipation on her bloated features. "On time this morning, I see. I was hoping you would stop by. We need to chat about your daughter."

"Can we set up a time to do that? I'd talk about it now, but somebody's waiting for me in the parking lot." I flashed her a toothy smile and pulled the CD out of my bag. "Here are the pictures for the newsletter, by the way."

As I slid the CD onto the desk, Mrs. Bunn sidled out from behind it like a giant crab. I found myself mesmerized by a black hair bobbing on the end of her chin as she launched into her topic. "I think this is something that needs to be dealt with immediately." She crossed her hamlike arms over her ample chest, and my hand drooped as it reached for the door. "You may not be aware of this, Mrs. Peterson, but your daughter seems to believe that she is a dog."

"A dog?"

"Yes. A dog."

I laughed with relief. From Attila's tone, I was expecting to hear she thought Elsie was a budding ax murderer. "I guess it's from watching *Lady and the Tramp*. At least she's not howling at the moon." Attila blinked, unmoved. I tried a different tack. "I'm sure this is fairly common. Don't all kids go through phases like this? Where they pretend to be something they're not?"

"Mrs. Peterson, I don't think you comprehend the serious nature of this problem. Your daughter refuses to drink from a glass. Miss Pitken caught her pouring her milk into a bowl and lapping it up the other day. She continually moves her lunch box to the floor, where she rips her food apart with her teeth rather than using utensils. Furthermore, she has taken to licking—and even biting—her schoolmates on the playground. I'm sorry to report that she's spent a good bit of time in the office recently."

Mrs. Bunn didn't look sorry at all. In fact, her brown eyes looked almost gleeful. "Mrs. Peterson, is there a problem in the home?" she asked.

Licking? Biting? Barking from time to time was one thing, but even I had to admit that crawling around and licking milk from a bowl was a bit much. I smiled my brightest smile anyway.

"No, no," I said. "Everything's fine." No need to tell her that I'd recently participated in a drag queen contest, my minivan was smashed, and a transvestite had called my home phone number before being murdered and discovered by me in the ladies' room. Mrs. Bunn's brown eyes bored into me. "I'm sorry about Elsie's behavior," I stammered. "She's always had an active imagination, and we've been watching a lot of *Lady and the Tramp* . . . I knew she liked to pretend to be Lady, but I didn't realize it was such an issue . . ."

"And there's another thing."

"Another thing?" I arranged my face into as pleasant an expression as possible. "What is it?"

Mrs. Bunn's beady eyes were like laser beams. "The other day, something occurred that made me wonder . . . Is it possible that there is an alcohol problem in the home?"

"An alcohol problem?" I blinked. Unless you considered an overdose of amaretto cookies an alcohol problem, the answer would have to be no. Although a few more tête-à-têtes with Attila might send me running for the peach schnapps. "Not at all. Why?"

Mrs. Bunn looked unconvinced. Her voice was frosty. "When Miss Pitken asked Elsie to stop barking at one of her classmates on Monday, your daughter asked if Miss Pitken had been . . . *imbibing*."

Before I could stop myself, I snorted. "Elsie asked if Miss Pitken was drunk?"

Mrs. Bunn drew herself up. If she had been taller than five foot three, she would have looked down her hooked nose at me. "I assure you, Mrs. Peterson, that Green Meadows Day School does not consider this behavior a laughing matter."

"Oh no," I said, recovering. "I don't, either. I was just surprised. Blake says that sometimes . . . I'll ask him to stop. I didn't realize Elsie had picked that up."

"Well, that may be the case, Mrs. Peterson, but I still feel obligated to recommend you take the child to a professional counselor." She handed me a card.

"A professional counselor? Are you sure that's necessary? Surely all kids go through phases like this . . ."

"One of her classmates had to visit a doctor after Elsie sank her teeth into his arm on Monday. We tried to call you earlier, but you didn't answer your phone."

"I must have turned off the ringer," I said, feeling guilty.

Mrs. Bunn made a little huffing noise. "I would have to say that the level of delusion and aggression your daughter is expressing is indicative of some deeper issues."

I took a deep breath. "A counselor, though. Don't you think it seems a bit much to send a five-year-old to a therapist?"

"Mrs. Peterson, I must inform you that if you do not choose to avail yourself of a psychologist's services, we will have to ask Elsie to leave the school."

Leave the school? Attila was playing hardball today. I tucked my hair behind my ears and straightened my shoulders. "I'm sorry she's been a problem for you. If you think she needs to see a counselor, we'll take her."

Mrs. Bunn nodded. "Good. And if you continue to have trouble with Nick's toilet training, I highly recommend her for him as well. As I'm sure you know, late toilet training can sometimes be a red flag."

Nick, too? "I appreciate your taking the time to talk to me," I lied. If I didn't get out of here soon, she'd be launching into Freudian theories about my son's reluctance to stop playing with trains long enough to visit the potty. "I'll call the counselor this afternoon."

Mrs. Bunn nodded in approval, the task of ruining my day accomplished. Another thing to check off her list. "And before you leave . . . when will you have that article to accompany the photographs of the picnic?" She inclined her head toward the photo pack on her desk.

With everything that had happened during the last twenty-four hours, the article on the class picnic was pretty low on the priority list right now, right behind cleaning toilets and organizing my sock drawer. "I'll get to it as soon as possible," I said.

Mrs. Bunn nodded sharply. Audience dismissed. I grabbed for the doorknob and bolted into the cool morning air.

Nick was asleep in the backseat when I slid back into the Suburban. As we left the parking lot, I related my conversation with Attila.

Becky's eyes grew round as she turned onto the entrance ramp to MoPac. "She wants you to take Elsie to a therapist?"

"If I don't, she's going to expel Elsie."

"Expel her?" She swerved onto the freeway, narrowly missing a blue Mini. "That witch! There's nothing wrong with Elsie! Kids go through phases. So she thinks she's Lady. Just because she doesn't want to be Cinderella doesn't mean she needs to have her head examined."

"Well, unless I want to find another preschool, I have to take her. Who knows? Maybe it will be good for her."

"Good for her? She shouldn't have to go at all! That woman has gone too far."

I sighed. "I agree. But what am I going to do? She's the director."

"We should pull our kids from the school. Send them somewhere else."

"But where?" Waiting lists for Austin preschools were longer than *War and Peace*.

"I guess you're right. Still, it's criminal, what that woman gets away with." She cut a station wagon off and pulled into the left lane, reaching over to pat my leg at the same time. "Don't worry about Elsie. She's just got a lot of spirit."

I hoped she was right.

Becky glanced in the rearview mirror. "Nick's still asleep. Forget about that Bunn woman. I want to hear more about last night."

My worry about Elsie faded into the background as I filled Becky in on what had happened at the Rainbow Room. When I related my trip up and down the runway, Becky laughed so hard I had to reach out and grab the steering wheel to keep the Suburban from veering into the median.

"You took third place in a drag queen contest?" she wheezed.

"Yes. But don't you tell a *soul* about it. Bunn already thinks we're a family of raging alcoholics. I don't need her thinking we're sexual deviants, too."

She wiped her eyes. "I was wrong about you selling Mary Kay. This is *much* more exciting."

"What gets me is, where are all these transvestites coming from? I mean, I've gone for years without running into one, and now I've met at least a dozen in one day."

"Well you *were* at a gay bar. On drag queen night . . ." She started giggling again.

I gave her a light whack on the arm. "But what about the one at the Como Motel?"

Becky rolled her eyes. "Margie, come on. This is Austin. Ever seen the personal ads in the back of the *Chronicle*? And a transvestite ran for mayor a few years ago, remember?"

"I guess that's what happens when you start having kids," I said. "Your exposure gets limited to old Disney movies and other people with kids."

"I'll bet you meet *lots* of interesting people in your new career," Becky said with a wicked smile. "I can't wait to hear about your *next* case . . ."

"I'll only tell you if you promise not to tell anyone else," I said sternly. "I'm in enough trouble with Attila as it is."

"My lips are sealed. But I can't believe the zipper popped . . . Can I tell Roger about it? Pleeaasse?"

"No. He'll tell Blake, and I don't think our marriage would ever recover."

She sighed. "You're probably right. So tell me how you ended up finding the dead woman. Or man. Whatever."

I described what I'd found in the bathroom, then related what had happened when I tried to dial 911. "I still can't believe a dead transvestite's phone auto-dialed my house. What do you think I should do about it?"

"Did you ask Blake if he knew her?"

"Not yet, but I just can't imagine him being buddy-buddy with a drag queen named Selena. He's so worried about appearances; he doesn't even like it when Nick tries on Elsie's dress-up clothes."

Becky grinned. "Good thing I changed Nick out of that pink skirt, then."

"I forgot to take him out of Elsie's skirt?"

"You had a lot on your mind yesterday." Becky swerved into the right lane. "You know, maybe Blake didn't know her as a transvestite. Maybe they met at conference, or something."

"I don't know. I peeked into his wallet and found one of his business cards. It looked like he had a pretty good day job."

Becky turned to stare at me. "You peeked into his wallet? Isn't that illegal?"

"Watch out!"

Becky's head swiveled toward the windshield again. Her foot slammed down on the brake just in time to avoid crunching the back end of a VW Beetle.

I relaxed my grip on the door handle. "I didn't leave any fingerprints. It turns out Selena Sass was actually a company VP named Evan Maxted during office hours."

"Talk about a double life. Executive by day, enchantress by night . . ." She swerved off the freeway and onto the exit ramp.

I sighed. "This is all so *weird*."

"Why don't you just ask him?"

"I should," I said. "I'm kind of afraid to, though. He hasn't been himself lately. He's distracted all the time, irritable. And this morning, he was pissed about the minivan. I couldn't bring myself to tell him about everything else that happened."

"That man needs to go to sensitivity training."

Normally I wouldn't agree with her. Blake might be anal, but he was also thoughtful. The way he'd been acting lately, though, I had to admit she had a point. I sighed. "Right after I find a school that teaches men to recognize dirty socks."

• • •

Ten minutes later, as Becky waited in the parking lot out front, I trundled through the impound center in the wake of a man with so much snuff jammed under his lip that it looked like he had a tumor. As we moved through a sea of cars, he shot a brown stream of tobacco onto the cracked pavement. I was concentrating on staying out of range when he came to a stop.

"Here she is."

I looked up at the crumpled hulk of metal that was my minivan and swallowed. "Are you sure this is it?"

He glanced down at the form in his hand. "That's what the papers say." He walked around the Caravan, running his hand across the buckled metal. "What did you do to it?"

"I had a little run-in with a truck."

"Looks like you smacked the hell out of it."

"I didn't realize it was this bad. How much do you think it would take to fix it?"

He sucked air through his teeth, somehow managing not to choke on a chunk of Skoal. "All I can say is, I sure hope you got it paid off." He handed me the keys. "Good luck."

"Thanks." As he ambled back toward the office, I slid into the driver's seat and shoved the key into the ignition, praying that at least the engine was functional. I breathed a thank-you to the man upstairs when it roared to life on the first try.

When I rolled through the chain-link gate into the front parking lot, Becky's eyes widened. She rolled down her window. "Oh my God. Blake is going to *die*."

"Yeah. Tell me about it. Is Nick still sleeping?"

She glanced behind her. "Yeah, he is." Then her eyes focused on the Caravan. "What are you going to do?"

I leaned back and closed my eyes. "When I think of something, I'll let you know."

CHAPTER SEVEN

I stepped out of the elevator onto the twentieth floor of the Bartleby Bank building at ten thirty, suddenly conscious of my loose denim shorts and bleach-spotted polo shirt. Perhaps I should have changed into something that looked less like something on the Goodwill bargain table. I had been short on time, though; Becky had offered to keep Nick for a few hours while I figured out what to do next, and I didn't want to waste it trying on khakis that I'd outgrown.

After stopping in a Starbucks for a pumpkin spice latte with extra whipped cream and a big slice of lemon pound cake, I had decided to deal with Blake first. Now, as I pushed through the glass doors into the plush lobby of Jones McEwan, I wasn't sure it was such a good idea.

The building was decorated in Late Twentieth-Century Donald Trump, or, as Becky put it, No Dime Left Unspent. The marble entry gave way to velvet carpet, and the massive mahogany front desk looked like something Louis XVI would have had commissioned. As always, the lobby smelled of furniture polish and money, overlaid with a hint of expensive cologne, unlike the fug I usually inhabited, which was flavored with eau de children.

Minnie, the receptionist, looked dwarfed behind her desk, which was quite a feat. Despite a number of forays into the Atkins diet, she was still a woman of substance. She adjusted her glasses and smiled at me. "Hi there, Margie. Looking for Blake?"

I smiled at her. I had always liked Minnie; she was kind and down-to-earth, and instead of wearing Donna Karan, she dressed her pillowy body in the kind of dresses you expect to see on first-grade teachers. Today's denim ensemble, complete with red gingham patches, seemed out of place behind the chunk of highly polished mahogany.

"Great dress," I said.

"Thanks. I found it at Dress Barn the other day; I got it for half off."

I fingered my ragged shirt. "I may need to head down there myself."

Her blue eyes twinkled. "Oh, don't you worry about that. You look fine. You're a mom. You're not supposed to look fancy."

I laughed. "Tell my husband that."

She rolled her eyes. "Oh, don't be silly. Want me to buzz him for you?"

"Yeah. I need to talk to him for a few minutes. I know he had client meetings this morning, but I was hoping I could catch him."

"I think he's back there. Let me just check." She picked up the phone and pressed a few buttons. "Margie's here. Can I send her back?" She listened for a moment, and then hung up. "He says he's got about fifteen minutes."

"Thanks, Minnie." As I started down the hall to his office, she called after me.

"Can you remind him to sign off on the Christmas party list for me?"

"Christmas party? Already?"

"I know. We start planning it in August, would you believe?"

"It gets earlier every year," I said. "I'll tell him."

As I walked down the hall, I almost ran into Herb McEwan, one of the firm's senior partners. As usual, he was head-to-toe Brooks Brothers. I crossed my arms reflexively over my spotty shirt.

"Margie!" His eyes flicked up and down me. "Doing a little housework today? You really should visit Bitsy's store sometime. She's branching out into casual wear, did you know?"

"I'm glad to hear it's going well," I said. As if I could afford any of the clothes Bitsy sold in her little boutique. All profits to charity, of course. Unlike us, the McEwans didn't need the extra money. "Maybe I'll stop in sometime!" I lied.

"Good, good. I'll tell her to look for you!" He disappeared down the hallway, leaving a whiff of expensive cologne in his wake, and I made a beeline for my husband's office.

Blake was sitting in his leather chair, staring out the window at the view of the Capitol when I slipped through his door.

"Hi, honey."

He swiveled around as I closed the door behind me. His eyes flicked up and down my ensemble, and his mouth pursed in a moue of distaste. "Nice outfit."

"Sorry about that. I was in a hurry this morning."

"Still, it's better than the getup you had on last night. What were you doing, trolling for clients or something? And did you get the minivan back?"

"Yes, I did." I sucked in my breath, then let it out slowly. "I'll probably need to borrow one of your parents' cars for a couple of days while I get it fixed, though."

Now I had my husband's attention. "What do you mean, a couple of days? How bad is the damage?"

I shrugged. "It runs. Look, I wanted to talk to you about—"

Blake's chiseled face reddened. "It runs? What do you mean, it *runs*? Is the other guy going to cover the expense?" He narrowed his eyes at me. "It *was* the other guy's fault, wasn't it?"

Well, not exactly. I banished thoughts of Fuji-nose and the Lone Star Delivery truck. "I'll get it taken care of," I said. "But enough about me. Did your client meeting go okay?"

"You wrecked the minivan." He cradled his head in his hands. "I can't believe you wrecked the minivan."

I took a few tentative steps forward and sat down in a chair across from him.

He looked up at me and then glanced at his watch. "We'll talk about this more later. That, and this 'job' of yours. I've got a client coming in ten minutes."

"There's just one more thing." I folded my arms over my chest. "I'm sorry to bother you at work, but I need to talk to you without the kids around."

His brow furrowed. "About what?"

"Well, first of all, I had a conversation with Mrs. Bunn at Green Meadows this morning. She seems to think that Elsie needs to talk with a therapist."

"A therapist? Why?"

"Apparently Elsie's been acting like a dog at school lately. Licking other kids, even biting them . . ."

Blake shrugged. "So? She's five. Isn't that normal?"

I took a deep breath. "So Mrs. Bunn thinks we've got family problems, and she told me that if we don't send Elsie to a psychologist, she's going to expel her."

He leaned back and blinked at me. "Expel her? You've got to be kidding me."

"I wish I were."

He let out a sigh of exasperation. "Fine. Whatever. Let's just keep it quiet, though. The last thing I need is rumors running around that there's something wrong with one of the kids. Maybe I'll see if I can fit in a phone call to Bunn, find a way to work this out." He glanced at his watch. "Look, Margie, I hate to cut this short, but . . ."

I pushed my worry about Elsie aside for a moment. "There's one more thing."

"What is it?"

Since Blake was in a hurry and there was no way to break it to him gently anyway, I decided to get it over with. "I found a dead body last night. A dead transvestite."

He sat up straight in his leather chair. I noticed a fleck of muffin stuck to his starched white shirt and resisted the urge to reach over and brush it off. "A dead transvestite?" His handsome face flushed a dangerous red. "Where the heck were you?"

"A gay bar. It's called the Rainbow Room."

"A gay bar? What were you doing in a gay bar?"

"Like I said, I was on a job. Anyway, I wanted to ask you if you knew a man named Evan Maxted."

Blake ran his hand through his hair. "Evan Maxted?"

"Yeah."

"What does that have to do with the fact that you were in a gay bar last night?"

"Because that was the dead transvestite's name, and our home phone number was on her cell phone."

A shadow of something flitted across his face as he sank back into his chair. "A dead transvestite called our house?"

"Well, I'm pretty sure she was alive when she made the call. Anyway, do you know an Evan Maxted?"

Blake stood up. "No, I don't." He sighed. "Margie, this job of yours has got to go. What's it going to be next? Hookers? Drug runners? The Mafia?" He walked around the desk and stood behind me, his hands on my shoulders. "Look, sweetheart. I appreciate your wanting to help pay for tuition, and I know how you feel about taking a loan out on the house. But I don't think this is the right thing. For you, for our family . . . for my reputation."

I pulled away. "Your reputation?"

"I know, I know, that's the least of our worries. I just don't want you getting mixed up with all of this. It could be dangerous, and if it got out that you were hanging around in gay bars . . . Look, why don't you join the Junior League? I'll call Herb McEwan. His wife, Bitsy, is president this year. I'm sure she'll sponsor you."

Although I appreciated his concern for my welfare, I was annoyed to be fobbed off on the Junior League. "Blake, I don't want to join the Junior League."

He put his hands up. "Fine, fine. I was just trying to help. How about volunteering at the Wildflower Center? You're a good gardener. They could probably use the help." He glanced at his watch again. "Look, I really have to run. We'll talk more about this later. Did you get the cake for Mom?"

"What cake?"

"It's her birthday tonight, remember?"

I groaned. "I forgot."

"We're supposed to meet them for dinner at seven." He glanced down at my shorts. "And you might want to dress a little. We're meeting at Sullivan's."

"Let's just hope Nick's over his vomiting bug."

"I'll see you tonight," he said, turning back to his desk.

"I love you," I said.

"Love you, too. Let me know what you find out about the minivan," he called after me as I trudged back down the hall toward the front desk.

When I got there, Minnie's seat was empty, but the Christmas party list lay on her desk. I picked it up to see if I knew anyone on the invite list. I hated the annual party. Blake spent most of it schmoozing. But it helped if I had someone to talk to.

After scanning the first page and coming up empty, I flipped through to my husband's client list, a few pages in. I sucked in my breath, feeling like someone had hit me in the stomach with a bowling ball.

The seventh name on the list was Evan Maxted of International Shipping Company.

. . .

My stomach was still heaving when I sank into the driver's seat of the minivan and pulled the door shut behind me. My husband of eight years had just lied to me. *Lied.* Eyes closed, I leaned my head against the steering wheel, fighting back the tears that seared my eyes.

It wasn't just that my husband had lied to me. The thing that had caused a lump the size of a grapefruit to swell in my throat was that I had had no idea he was lying. Despite the late-summer heat, a chill swept through me. I sat up and gripped the steering wheel with trembling hands, sick with the feeling that the foundation of my marriage—the most solid thing in my life—was crumbling beneath me. If my husband had lied about knowing Evan Maxted, what else had he lied about?

As I put the car into reverse and backed out of the parking space, the sun glanced off the tower of glass that housed my husband. I shielded my eyes from the glare. Blake had known Evan Maxted but didn't want me to know it. Why?

An image of Maxted's wig, half-torn from his shorn head, flashed through my mind as I pulled onto Congress Avenue. I drew a shaky breath. What should I do now? I had planned to get a quote on repairing the car, but now all I wanted to do was find out why my husband had lied to me about knowing Evan Maxted. The problem was, I had no idea where to start.

. . .

Fifteen minutes later, I rolled into the pitted parking lot of Peachtree Investigations. I grabbed the folder with the report and the photo of

Pence and pushed through the smeared glass door, my stomach still doing somersaults.

Peaches leaned back in her chair, the phone clamped to the side of her head, a cigarette dangling from her left hand. As I crossed the dirty carpet, she brushed an ash from her green spandex top and winked at me.

I threw myself into the rickety wooden chair across from her. "Gotta go," she said into the receiver. "Call you later." She hung up the phone and swiveled around to face me. "So, how did it go last night?"

"Not so hot." I struggled to keep my voice steady. My life might be falling apart, but I didn't feel like sharing that with Peaches. "It turns out Jack Emerson is gay."

Peaches sucked on her cigarette and exhaled a ribbon of smoke. She studied me through the gray haze. "You don't look so good. Everything okay?"

I swallowed hard. "Yeah."

"Good." She took another puff. "I figured he was gay. Gary called this morning, said he showed up at the Rainbow Room, but you told him the guy was gone." She crossed her legs and leaned back in her chair. "You think he likes the straight-looking ones, or the trannies?"

"He was with someone who looked like a woman."

"Well," she said, "guess I'll call Angelique, then. Haven't had a tranny lover turn her down yet." She patted her stiff red hair. "Sounds like it was an exciting night, though. Gary told me somebody got killed down there."

"Yeah," I said, my voice cracking despite my best efforts. "I was the one who found the body."

"You found him?" She crushed her cigarette butt in an overflowing plastic ashtray. "Jesus. Bad night. Well, don't worry about Emerson. At least you got the Pence case wrapped up." I handed her the folder. She opened it eagerly and studied the four-by-six picture, holding it up to the light. "Wow, you really did get him wrapped up." She pulled a face. "Kinda wish they'd used aluminum foil. You can't see as much that way. Anyway, this is great. Mrs. Pence's lawyer's gonna love you. Maybe we'll get a bonus out of it."

Despite what seemed like a ragged hole in my chest, I felt a faint stirring of pride. My husband might be lying to me, my kid might be acting like a dog, and Attila the Bunn might be calling the Betty Ford Center on my behalf, but at least I'd solved my first case. My shock at my husband's lie was smoldering, turning into something else. Anger? Rage?

I sucked in a deep breath. *Put it aside*, I told myself. *Just figure out what to do next*. My thoughts turned to Evan Maxted again. If I could track down somebody else's errant husband, could I find out more about Maxted's connection to Blake?

I glanced at the yellowed files stacked in untidy piles around the desk. Old case files, probably. Peachtree Investigations might not be the classiest private investigation agency out there, but it had stayed in business long enough to acquire a substantial amount of paperwork. Not to mention an impressive collection of dead doodlebugs.

I might not know how to dig up dirt on Evan Maxted, but Peaches probably did. I watched her as she scanned the report I had typed. I didn't feel like sharing my marital problems with a woman whose favorite textile was spandex and who worked in an office that smelled like a tobacco factory with mold problems. But if my husband was involved with something that could put my kids at risk, what were my options?

I took a deep breath and plunged. "I need your help, Peaches." To my surprise, the quaver in my voice had disappeared.

She looked up from the report, her brown eyes shrewd. "What kind of help?"

"I need to know how you find out about somebody."

"Like a background check?"

I nodded.

"Well, it depends on who the person is. Also depends on what kind of info you're starting with. You got an address, or a social security number?"

I shook my head.

"Who is this person?"

I shrugged. "Just someone I ran into yesterday."

"You got a name?"

"Yes."

She put the report down and tugged at a bra strap. "You just ran into this person yesterday, and suddenly you want to know all about them."

"Actually . . . it's the person who died at the Rainbow Room. I saw something that made me think she . . . he . . . might be connected with someone I know."

Peaches chuckled. "Well, since the guy's dead, I guess trailing him isn't gonna help. Are the police involved?"

My mind flicked to surly Detective Bunsen. "I think so. Yes."

She reached under her desk for a dog-eared phone book. "Well, there are a few things we can do. First, give me the guy's name."

A phone book. Why hadn't I thought of that? "Evan Maxted."

"Well, that's a start. At least it's not John Smith." She flipped through the pages with tangerine-colored nails. "Got a pen?"

I scrabbled through my purse and came up with a leaky Bic.

"Okay, here it is: 501 Fourth Street, Unit 902. I think that's those new downtown lofts. Pretty swanky address. You might want to start with neighbors . . . Say you're a relative or an old friend, and you're trying to track him down." She looked up at me and cocked an eyebrow. "You look pretty respectable. If you play your cards right, maybe one of them will let you in the place."

"Won't the cops have trouble with that?"

"Not if they don't know. And not if you don't leave fingerprints. Too bad he lives in an apartment building, or I'd say you could go through his trash." I wrinkled my nose. As much as I wanted to know about Evan Maxted, I wasn't sure I was ready to try Dumpster diving. "You know where he works?" she said.

"I've got his business card."

"You got a business card?" Her eyes glinted. "I won't ask how you got that, but it looks like you're getting the hang of things already. Anyway, go to his office, talk with his coworkers . . . Sometimes you can pretend you want to do business with the company. While you're there, see if you can get a few minutes in his office alone."

"Isn't that illegal? Like breaking and entering?"

She winked. "Not if you don't get caught. Besides, you're not breaking, just entering. Now, I've got some free time today, it turns out. If you give me what you've got on this guy, I'll see what I can find out."

"Really?"

"You bet."

I handed her the business card I had found in Maxted's purse. She ran a copy on a wheezy photocopier and returned it to me.

"How much access do you have to your friend's stuff?"

My friend? I was puzzled for a moment until I realized she meant my husband. "Oh. A good bit," I said.

"You might want to see what you can find out there, too."

My stomach plummeted. Investigating my husband. She was right, but that didn't make it something I wanted to do.

CHAPTER EIGHT

Peaches was right about Evan Maxted's address being swanky. It was one of those fifteen-story loft buildings that attempt to be both modern and "vintage" simultaneously. This particular building attempted to meld the old and the new by stacking fourteen stories of mirrored glass atop a squat brownstone base festooned with arches and curlicues. According to the big promotional sign out front, the units featured "the chic downtown lifestyle and unparalleled views of the Capitol." The starting price was in the mid–five hundreds.

My heart hammered in my chest as I parked my smushed minivan across the street from Maxted's building. I was still numb from the encounter with Blake that morning, but the shock was wearing off. Replacing it was my fear of getting caught in a dead person's apartment under false pretenses. If I even made it that far. I'd been racking my brain for twenty minutes, and I still couldn't come up with a convincing story to tell the neighbors.

I stared at the building for a moment. Then I pulled out my cell phone, grabbed the phone book I kept under the front seat, and dialed Randall's Bakery. I had to order the cake for my mother-in-law's birthday anyway, so at least it was a valid excuse.

As I waited for someone to pick up, I wondered yet again how to go about gaining the confidence of Evan Maxted's neighbors. Since it was safe to assume that his relatives had been notified of his death, I wasn't comfortable introducing myself as a member of the family. And wouldn't a friend call, rather than show up unannounced on a Wednesday morning, when Maxted would probably be at work?

I was entertaining a scenario involving a confession of secret love children from a prior marriage when someone with an extremely heavy accent picked up the phone. As I described the cake I wanted for my mother-in-law's birthday, I found myself wishing once again that I had taken Spanish instead of six years of French.

Fifteen minutes later, I hung up, reasonably confident that the woman on the other end of the line understood that the cake was for a birthday, not for a retirement party or a First Communion, and that I needed it today.

I cradled the phone for a few minutes, trying to think of someone else to call, but came up blank. Instead, I dug through my purse for quarters to feed the meter, crossed the street, dodging two BMWs, and headed toward the building's glass double doors.

As I tripped up the granite stairs to the entrance, the nasty thought occurred to me that a building selling five-hundred-thousand-dollar apartments might include a doorman. I froze in midstep. How was I going to get past a doorman? I was having a hard enough time coming up with a story that would fool a neighbor, much less a snooty bouncer in a uniform.

I half turned toward the minivan. *Leave the investigating to the police*, I told myself. *You're out of your league.*

But the police didn't know about Maxted's connection to my husband.

I straightened my wrinkled polo shirt, climbed the last few steps, and pushed through the building's front door.

Although a massive wooden desk sat to the left of the door, the red velvet chair behind it was empty. *Whew.* Either the developer hadn't sold enough units to pay a doorman's salary, or the desk was reserved for nighttime security.

The developer might have skimped on the doorman, but everything else in the lobby was top dollar. I looked at the dark paneled walls, the soaring ceiling, and the huge chandelier that looked as if it came from the set of *Phantom of the Opera*. And I wondered what it would be like to live in a building where the finishes didn't include spilled apple juice and congealed chocolate milk, and where the neighbors talked about the latest Versace collection at Saks Fifth Avenue rather than the sale on kids' sweatpants at Target.

As my sneakers squeaked across the marble floor, the elevator disgorged a fashionably anorexic blonde and an equally fashionable Pomeranian on a rhinestone-studded leash. The designer duo clicked toward me on high-heeled shoes (the blonde) and pink-painted toenails (the Pomeranian). The blonde tugged at the leash with a manicured hand as the dog yipped and scrabbled toward me on the slick floor, looking like a powder puff that had escaped from an expensive toiletry set. Although the temperature was in the nineties, the Pomeranian wore a pink cashmere sweater, and a satin bow nestled atop its fluffy styled head.

Even the dogs in this building wore designer clothes.

I smiled at the blonde, maneuvered around the yapping dog, which had now bared its polished teeth and started to growl, and stepped into the elevator. My stomach lurched as I pressed the button for the ninth floor. What was I doing here? I still had no idea how to approach the neighbors. Then, as the Pomeranian's blow-dried tail disappeared behind walnut-paneled elevator doors, I had a flash of inspiration. All I needed was for one of the neighbors to have a key to Maxted's apartment.

A moment later, the doors slid open to a long hallway that looked just like a hotel's, the only difference being that there were only four doors.

It wasn't hard to figure out which one belonged to Evan Maxted, since a piece of yellow crime scene tape dangled from the doorjamb. I loitered at the end of the hall for a moment, waiting for somebody to emerge from Maxted's apartment. When nobody did, I crept up and put my ear to the door, half expecting to hear Bunsen's deep voice on the other side. There was nothing but the hum of an air-conditioning system.

It was time to put my plan into action. I took a few deep, cleansing breaths, just like they'd taught me at Lamaze class, and turned to face the door across the hall. It hadn't helped then; it didn't help much now, either. I straightened my shirt, squared my shoulders, and knocked.

Nobody answered.

There were only two doors left, and one of them had a pile of newspapers out front. I waited a minute before padding past the pile of papers toward the door at the end of the hallway. If no one answered, I told myself, I had done the best I could. I could go home.

I knocked, half hoping that no one would answer.

Someone did.

A frail seventy-five-year-old woman in a green and gold turban peered out of the cracked doorway. I was taken aback; she was about as different from the chic waif in the lobby as was possible. "Are you a solicitor?" she asked in a gravelly voice. "Because soliciting isn't allowed in this building."

"Oh, no, no, no," I said. I was trying to get into someone's apartment under false pretenses, which was much worse, but decided not to share that. "I'm a friend of Evan's. Evan Maxted, your neighbor down the hall?"

"Yes."

I took a deep breath and went forward. "He was keeping my cat for a while, and I was supposed to swing by this morning and pick her up, but Evan's not here, and I can't reach him. And now there's this crime-scene tape; I'm worried. Do you have any idea what happened?"

"I know; I'm worried, too. I saw the tape, and there have been officers in and out of his apartment, but they won't tell me a word."

She cocked her head. "What's this about a cat? I didn't know he was keeping a cat."

"Oh, yes. Snookums. He's wonderful."

"I thought you said it was a she."

"I did?" I tossed off a brittle laugh. "Well, ever since we got him neutered, I get confused. Anyway, I'd really like to pick him up. Do you have any idea when Evan will be back?"

"I didn't know he was keeping a cat."

"It was just while I was out of town."

"Well, I don't know what's going on," she said, "but like I said, when I came out to get my paper this morning, there were police officers all over the place."

I swallowed. "Really? I hope he's okay." I knew otherwise, of course, but lying was like learning to ride a bike, I was discovering. Once you got rolling, it got a lot easier.

"I asked them about it, but they wouldn't tell me what was going on. What did you say your name was again?"

My name? "Prudence," I blurted, then cringed. It was my mother-in-law's first name. Since I had just spelled it out six times for the woman at the bakery, it was the first thing that popped into my head.

"Prudence . . ." She looked at me questioningly, and I realized she was waiting for my last name.

I opened and closed my mouth a few times, unable to think of a single surname. The woman's eyes narrowed slightly. "Schultz," I choked out, cringing again. My brain had just coughed up my maiden name. Not exactly the cloak of anonymity I was going for. "And you are?"

"Me? I'm Willhelmina Bergdorfer, but everybody calls me Willie." She adjusted her turban. "My, what a nice, old-fashioned name Prudence is. Not like all of those Brittanys and Tiffanys running around these days. And how do you know Evan?"

"Oh, we were in school together."

"In school? Pardon my saying so, but you look quite a bit older than Evan."

"Too much time in the sun, I guess."

"Well, I probably shouldn't, since it's a crime scene, but if your cat's in there . . ." She sighed. "Why don't you come in while I see if I can find the key."

The key! "Thank goodness you've got one. If something's happened to Evan, I need to get in there. Snookums might not even have food." I followed her into her apartment. The promotional materials were right; one wall was totally glass and offered a sweeping view of the Capitol building, with the UT Tower in the background. The solid walls were festooned with what looked like African masks, and zebra skins were flung across the sleek hardwood floors. Unusual décor for a woman in her seventies. Not a tea cozy in sight.

"Why don't you have a seat," she said, "and I'll track down Evan's key. He gave it to me a few months ago, for emergencies, but I don't remember what I did with it."

"Thank you," I said, perching on an armchair strewn with some kind of woven tribal fabric. "Your decorating sense is incredible. What wonderful things you have here."

"You think so? Henry and I spent years and years in Africa. They're just a few things I picked up along the way." I eyed a mask that looked something like a cross between a saber-toothed tiger and a rabbit.

"I'm worried," I said. "Are you sure the police didn't say what had happened to Evan?"

"Not a word, I'm afraid. They were quite close about it all. Now, where did you say you went to school with Evan?"

I swallowed. "Oh, just a small college up north."

"Really? I thought he was a big UT fan."

"Oh, of course," I stammered. "We used to tease him, call him Tex." I laughed lightly. "It was such a long time ago. Seems like another lifetime. I always thought he was cute, though. Tell me, is he dating anyone?"

"Oh, so you're single?"

"Yes."

"Then why are you wearing that wedding ring?"

The ring again. I sucked in a deep breath while I fumbled for an explanation. "The wedding ring?" I tried to laugh lightly, but it came out sounding like a sheep being strangled. "Oh, yes. I keep forgetting about that." Willie's sharp eyes examined my face. "Well, you see, the thing is, my husband and I are . . . are . . ."

She gave me a knowing look. "Separated?"

The air whooshed out of my lungs. "Exactly. That's it. We're separated."

"Oh, I'm sorry, dear. Really, though, in this day and age, you shouldn't be ashamed of it." She'd misinterpreted my panicked bleat as shame. "What with all of these loose morals, it's happening more and more. But shouldn't you wait a bit before you start dating around? I mean, don't you want to see if things will work out?"

I blinked.

"When we were in Africa," she continued, "my Henry fell for a chief's daughter. They met at the Chibuku Neshamwari festival. Suddenly, he was coming home smelling like an incense pot every night. For a month or two there, I thought he'd abandon us and take up the native life, but he eventually came to his senses. They almost always do, you know. Once the wild sex wears off, they start to miss the domestic comforts, the familiarity."

I was speechless, but it didn't matter. Willie wasn't done yet.

"Did you give him plenty of back rubs? I've found it always helps to have a nice cocktail waiting for them when they get home, and a hot dinner on the table. Henry once told me that the chief's daughter made a mean groundnut stew, but she didn't know the first thing about pot roast. Turns out it was my pot roast that brought him around in the end. I'll give you the recipe if you'd like." She shook her head. "Men may wander, but if you keep a nice hot meal on the table and their slippers waiting for them, they'll almost always come back."

I managed not to choke. Here was this prim-looking lady, talking about her husband's sexual escapades with some kind of Zambian princess, and recommending I save my marriage by learning to make a good pot roast. Maybe she had a point, though. Our life in the bedroom had never been earthshaking, but it had tapered off lately. I'd attributed it to having two kids under the age of six, but maybe there was more to it. Was I being a good wife to Blake? I'd stopped making his favorite dishes lately because most of them were heavy on cheese and beef. Had I gone too far in the other direction? What if I started cooking steaks again? Or met him at the door with slippers and a glass of wine?

I was on the verge of confiding my worries to this kind woman in a turban when I remembered that the marriage I had told her about was fictitious. I was here to find out about Evan Maxted, not look for marital advice. I sighed mournfully. "I'm afraid my marriage is beyond saving. He's filing for divorce. I guess I just wear the ring because I'm not ready to let go yet."

"Poor dear. Well, then, I suppose it is time to start looking for greener pastures. And Evan is a nice-looking young man, with a good job, too. You may be a bit older, but if you're a good cook, that can make up for it. I don't know if he's dating anyone. He has a lot of men friends, like all young men do . . . I imagine they go out carousing together, and I've seen a lovely woman coming and going from time to time."

"A woman?"

"Oh, yes. A beautiful blonde. She comes by some evenings, usually in a ball gown. Dressed to kill, you know. Funny, though, I never see them going out together. I saw her just last night, in fact."

"Has anyone else been by recently?"

"Why?"

"Oh, I just thought maybe they'd know why the cops were there this morning. Maybe it would be someone I know."

"Let me think. I'm here most of the time, and since my door is at the end of the hall, I can peek out the peephole and see what's happening." She blushed slightly. "Not that I'm nosy. I just worry about security. They promised us a doorman when we bought the place, but they keep giving notice. So I keep an eye on things, just in case."

"I understand," I said. "You can never take enough precautions."

"Exactly." She nodded, seeming relieved that I had bought her explanation. "Anyway, the police have been in and out all morning. I can't think why. But other than that, Evan had two visitors recently. One was an attractive older woman. At least I think she was attractive. It was hard to tell with the hat and sunglasses. Very nice figure, though, and the cutest little skirt and jacket—all mauve, done up with embroidery on the lapels. She stopped by Monday night, around seven, and stayed for a half hour. She didn't look happy when she left, though. She jabbed at that elevator button as if she wanted to poke it right out of the wall."

"And who was the other visitor?"

"A gentleman, in his fifties, I'd say. Quite good-looking, even though his hairline has receded. I hadn't seen him before. He was here Sunday. We met in the hall when my Henry was taking me out to dinner."

"Huh. Doesn't ring a bell. What did he look like?"

"Oh, he was quite debonair." She tilted her head to one side coquettishly. "Reminded me of Sinatra, in a way. A voice like melted butter." She sighed. "Anyway, you didn't come here to pass the time of day with me. Let me get that key."

As she bustled away, I sat and stared at the masks on the wall. As she disappeared into the other end of the apartment, unsettling thoughts began passing through my mind. I hadn't heard anyone when I first checked on Maxted's door, but that didn't mean there wasn't someone there. What if we burst into the room and Bunsen was there?

By the time Willie returned, brandishing a silver key, my hands were clammy with sweat. "Ready?" she asked.

I gulped. "Sure."

As I padded down the hallway in the older woman's wake, I fought the urge to disappear into the elevator. I'd gotten this far, hadn't I? And if someone was in the apartment, I would have heard it, wouldn't I?

She was about to fit the key into the lock when Evan Maxted's door swung open.

CHAPTER NINE

It wasn't Bunsen.

It wasn't a whole lot better, either.

The woman who opened the door was dressed in blue polyester, with a nice shiny gold badge to match. "Can I help you?" she asked in a clipped voice.

I opened and closed my mouth a few times. Fortunately, Willie jumped into the gap. "Yes. This is a friend of Evan's. Prudence Schultz. He was keeping her cat, but she can't seem to get in touch with him." Her delicate face squinched into a worried look under her turban. "We saw the crime scene tape, and now you're here . . . Is he all right?"

"I'm afraid Mr. Maxted passed away last night. This is a crime scene, ma'am."

Although it wasn't news to me, I widened my eyes and raised a hand to my mouth. "Oh no!" I said. "How did it happen? He was so young . . ."

"Oh my goodness," Willie said, drawing in her breath. "How awful!"

I blinked at the cop. "But if you're here, does that mean . . . Does that mean somebody killed him?"

The policewoman nodded curtly.

"Oh dear. Such a tragedy. Such a young man . . ." Willie shook her head and adjusted her turban. "But what shall we do about Prudence's cat?"

"She can get her cat." The officer, whose name was Carmes according to her name tag, turned her slate-hard eyes to me. "You say you're a friend of Mr. Maxted's?"

I nodded.

"When was the last time you saw Mr. Maxted?"

"I don't know. This is all just such a shock, I can't even think . . . When I dropped off my cat, I guess."

"And when was that?"

How the hell was I supposed to know? So far, the cat-sitting plan wasn't working out too well. "Um, two weeks ago, I guess." I sniffled. "Poor Evan!"

"And were you out of town?"

"Yes. That's right. Of course, if I had known *this* would happen, I never would have left."

"Where were you?"

"Pardon me?"

"I asked where you went on your trip."

I blinked. I'd heard her the first time. I just couldn't think of an answer. "Paris," I blurted.

Paris? What was I thinking?

Fortunately, this seemed exotic enough to satisfy her. "Your cat's in there," she said. "I'd go get it myself, but it almost bit me when I tried to contain it earlier. Besides, forensics has already been all over this place, so I guess it's okay. Good thing you showed up, though. Animal Control is due here in a half hour."

"Thanks," I said with a twinge of misgiving. I hadn't expected there to be an actual cat. Now that there was one, and one that wasn't afraid to use its teeth, I was worried. What was I going to do when my supposed cat attacked me?

"Follow me, ladies," the cop said. Willie fell in behind her, and I brought up the rear.

We marched through Evan Maxted's tastefully decorated Art Deco living room, with an expensive entertainment center and vintage posters of old movies, into his master bedroom, which was dominated by a round bed with a red satin comforter. Officer Carmes flipped up the shiny spread and pointed under the bed. "It's under there."

I approached gingerly and lowered myself to peer under the bed. "Here, Snookums," I crooned.

A paw flashed out and raked across my face. I dropped the coverlet and leaped back, pressing my hand to my bleeding cheek.

The cop eyed me suspiciously. "I thought it was your cat."

"He is, he is. He's just . . . temperamental. I guess all the activity has thrown him off kilter."

I knelt down again and peered in. Huddling under the bed, about a foot out of arm's reach, lurked an enormous orange cat with eyes that glowed like green fire. I swallowed hard and dropped the coverlet.

"Anyone have a broom?" I asked.

"A broom?"

"I can't reach him, and he won't come out."

"He won't come to you?" Officer Carmes piped up. "Isn't it your cat?"

"Of course he's my cat. It's just been a rough day for him." And me.

"It doesn't look like you brought your carrier. Shall I get a box for you to put him in for the ride home?" Willie asked sweetly.

I looked at her gratefully. "That would be a good idea. An old towel might not be a bad idea, either. I'll wrap him up in that so he won't scratch anyone." I'd learned that trick taking Rufus, my Siamese, to the vet. "He seems a little upset."

As Willie returned to her apartment, Carmes's radio burbled to life. She stepped into the hall to respond, leaving me alone in Maxted's bedroom with Snookums and the big red bed.

I wasn't thrilled with the idea of snooping around with a cop right outside the door, but this could be my only opportunity to find out more about Maxted.

I crept over to the closet. Inside was what looked like the wardrobe of a businessman married to a Hollywood starlet: gray and blue suits marched soberly up one side, ending with a rack of red and blue ties, while the other side was ablaze in sequins and lamé in a rainbow of flaming colors. A row of wigs sat on a shelf above the dresses—auburn, blond, and one that was shiny and black as a raven's wing. One of the wig stands was empty, and I shivered. I had seen the wig at the Rainbow Room, ripped away from Evan Maxted's head. I tore my eyes away from the wigs and examined the rest of the closet. On the top shelf were a few intriguing cardboard boxes, but with a policewoman standing ten feet away, I didn't feel it was the right moment to pull one down and start sorting through the contents.

I backed out of the closet and listened. Carmes was still occupied in the hall, so I tiptoed over to Maxted's dresser and picked up the one photo: a framed shot of Maxted in a mortarboard, beaming and standing next to a middle-aged blond woman. His mother, probably. She looked faded, but happy, in a baggy print dress. I imagined the bottles she must have fed her son, the soccer practices she'd driven him to, the pride she must have felt at his graduation. Had she known about his double life? If not, what a terrible way to find out. Tears welled in my eyes again. I thrust the photo back onto the dresser and wiped my eyes.

Next to the photo lay a thick ivory envelope. Whoever was on the radio with Carmes was still going, so I slid it open. It was a wedding invitation. The bride was Anna Maxted. Evan's sister? The wedding, to be held in Sausalito, was slated for late October. The reply card was missing.

I had just slid the invitation back into the envelope when Carmes stepped back into the room.

"What are you doing?" she asked.

"Oh, just looking at this photo. It's so sad, don't you think?"

"The photo?"

"No. I was thinking of Evan's poor mother. Has she been notified yet?"

"I don't know. I assume so. I'm just here to close the place up."

At that moment, Willie swept through the door, carrying a large cardboard box, a towel, and a broom. "Will this do?"

I eyed the box. The lid consisted of four flimsy flaps. "Do you have any duct tape or string?"

"I brought a roll of packing tape."

"That'll work." *I hope.*

As Willie and Officer Carmes watched, I grabbed the broom and knelt beside the bed again.

Willie said, "I'll close the door, dear, so he doesn't escape."

"Can you throw the towel over him when he comes out?"

"I'll try."

I lifted the comforter and peered under. "Here, Snookums," I crooned. Once again, a paw shot out at me. On the plus side, this time he was too far away to make contact. He had relocated himself to right under the middle of the bed.

I poked the broom under. He hissed at it and raked his claws through the straw. I tried to shove him to one side, but he sank his claws into the carpet and refused to budge. After several attempts to dislodge him gently, I gave him a good hard thwack.

He yowled and streaked toward me, sinking his claws into my thigh before using it as a springboard to rocket toward the door. Willie threw the towel over him, and I hurled myself at the yowling ball, hugging him to my chest and dumping him into the box.

"Where's the tape?" I yelled, pushing down the flaps. An orange paw thrust through the crack in the middle.

"Oh, I'm sorry, dear. It's still in the box."

I sucked in my breath and shoved my arm under the flap. Snookums's claws fastened onto it immediately, and as my fingers made contact with the roll of tape, he sank his teeth into my thumb.

I jerked my arm out and howled. Snookums exploded out of the box and shot toward the door. A loud thump sounded as his head made contact with the solid oak. He dropped to the floor like a downed duck.

"Well," I said, nursing my thumb and eyeing the unconscious tabby. "That went okay."

Willie bent down and peered at the massive feline. "That's Snookums? I thought that was Evan's cat."

Suspicion flared in Carmes's eyes. "That's not your cat?"

How was I supposed to know that Evan had a cat? Or that Willie would be acquainted with him? My throat closed with panic. *Think, Margie, think.* "Well," I said, "we kind of have a joint custody thing going. Had, I mean."

Willie looked confused. "You keep calling him Snookums. I thought Evan called him Lothario."

"Yes, well, we never could agree on a name," I stammered, "so we each did our own thing. At Evan's, he was Lothario, but when he's with me, his name is Snookums." I gave the cop a toothy smile. "It works out for both of us that way. See?" She didn't look like she was buying it. I couldn't blame her.

Fortunately, at that moment, her cell phone piped up with the theme song to *Law & Order*. Carmes glanced at the phone. "I need to take this call. But before you leave, I'll need to see some kind of identification."

Identification? Despite a strong breeze from the air-conditioning, the areas of my body most frequently mentioned in antiperspirant ads were drenched. As Carmes walked into the next room and delivered rapid-fire responses into the phone, I stuffed the unconscious cat into the box and pulled Willie aside.

"I really have to run before this cat—I mean Snookums—wakes up and gets through the cardboard. Could you tell her I'll call down to the station as soon as I get home?"

"Sure, honey. I'll tell her. And if things change with your marriage, swing by for my pot roast recipe. I'll write it out for you."

"Thanks," I said. "I may do that." As I was about to dash through the door, I hung back for a moment to ask the question that had been plaguing me since I'd met Willie. "By the way," I said, "where did you get the idea for the turban? Is it an African thing?"

She shook her head. "No, dear. I'm undergoing treatment for ovarian cancer. The chemotherapy made my hair fall out."

I swallowed. "Well, I think it looks great," I said. "Thanks for all your help."

I hadn't just lied. I'd lied to a seventy-five-year-old cancer patient and a cop. I scurried out of the apartment toward the stairs and leaped down them two at a time.

• • •

I kept glancing over my shoulder on the way home, looking for a police car or signs of an orange projectile emerging from the flimsy box in the backseat of the minivan. Fortunately, nobody followed me, and Snookums didn't wake up. This was a good thing, because I didn't relish the thought of driving home with a ball of fur and teeth ricocheting around under my legs. I deposited the box in the laundry room, which was already crowded due to the week's worth of unwashed laundry spilling from a stack of baskets, and filled two bowls, one with water and the other with cat food. Then I opened the flaps and backed away quickly, closing the door tight behind me.

Rufus had already stalked over to the laundry room door, the fur on his back bristling, when I ran upstairs to get some first-aid cream and a couple of Band-Aids. I examined my wounds in the mirror; thanks to Snookums, it now looked like I had racing stripes on my left cheek. At least the bleeding had stopped. I slathered cream on my face, bandaged my swollen thumb, and headed out the front door to pick up my kids.

Nick was feeling much perkier by the time I got to Becky's house. As I buckled him into his car seat, Becky hovered beside me.

"Thanks for watching him for me," I said. "Did he throw up any more?"

"No, he didn't. And the fever's completely gone." She eyed my cheek and my bandaged thumb. "But what happened to you? I didn't realize car repair shops could be such dangerous places."

"Oh, I had a run-in with a cat. It's a long story."

"Any word on the minivan?"

I glanced at the mangled back end. "I called around, but I don't have a quote yet."

"Did you find out anything about the transvestite?"

What was this, Twenty Questions? I shook my head. "No, but Peaches is looking into it for me." Becky was my best friend, but I wasn't ready to tell her what I had found on the Christmas party list at Blake's office.

"Peaches?"

"The woman who runs the agency."

"Oh. That's nice of her."

I changed the subject. "Do you want me to pick up Zoe and Josh this afternoon?"

"No, that's okay. I promised to take them to Zilker Park anyway. Want to join us?"

Part of me wanted to, but another part of me wasn't ready to talk yet. And it would be impossible to spend two hours with Becky without spilling everything. "I'd love to," I said, "but I've got to swing by Randall's and pick up a cake for Prue's birthday."

Becky stood at the end of the driveway and waved as I drove away. As I waved back, part of me wished I'd told her everything.

The dull ache in my heart might be relieved by talking it over with someone who cared about me.

But part of me wasn't ready to admit what I had discovered to myself, much less to anyone else.

● ● ●

Ten minutes later, I pulled into the drive-through pickup lane at Green Meadows. As Elsie hurled herself into the car, I accosted the perky twenty-year-old teaching assistant whose job it was to make sure the kids were buckled in. "How did it go today?" I asked. "Any problems?"

"None at all," she said.

None at all? Mrs. Bunn had told me Elsie was acting like a wolf-hound in the late stages of rabies. I'd expected to see her foaming at the mouth, a fragment of another child's shirt hanging from her clenched teeth.

I smiled, relieved. "Well, that's good to hear."

The teaching assistant's smooth forehead wrinkled. "But Mrs. Bunn wanted to talk to you . . . Did she get in touch with you?"

"I met with her this morning," I said.

She tightened Elsie's buckles. "Well, then, I guess you're good to go!"

Despite Attila's grave admonitions, Elsie was chipper, cheerful, and anything but doglike. Relieved, I put on a June Cleaver smile as we pulled onto the freeway.

"How was your day, sweetheart?"

"Great. Mommy, what happened to your face?"

"A cat scratched me," I said.

"Rufus?"

"No, a different cat. I'm fine, though." I glanced back at her. "So, did everything go okay today?"

"It was Madeline's birthday today, so we got cupcakes for a snack." Her chubby face darkened. "Miss Lawson took mine away, though."

"I thought Miss Grayson said everything went fine."

"Oh, she wasn't in my classroom today."

Well, that explained the glowing review. The pit in my stomach started to deepen again. "Why did Miss Lawson take your cupcake away?" I asked.

Elsie shrugged. Had she been eating off the floor again? I inspected her in the rearview mirror for telltale frosting smudges, but both her dress and face were clean.

"Mrs. Bunn tells me you've been pretending you're a dog," I said. "Is that true?"

"Mom. It's just a game." She sounded exactly like a sullen thirteen-year-old. I shivered.

"That may be," I said calmly, "but you need to do that at home, not at school."

She was silent for a moment. Good, I thought. She was thinking about it. Then her voice reverted to a five-year-old's again. "Mommy, did you find my fry phone?"

I stifled a groan. "Not yet, honey. But I'm still looking."

● ● ●

We swung by Randall's to pick up the cake, a card, and a bouquet of electric-blue carnations Elsie insisted we buy for Grandma. I'd voted for a tasteful blend of purple irises and yellow roses, but Elsie had stood firm. "But blue's her favorite color, Mom," she whined. Normally I wouldn't have given in, but after everything that had happened that day, I was in no mood to argue.

We made it the entire way home without any evidence of doglike behavior from Elsie. She even helped me carry the groceries into the house, one roll of paper towels at a time. Was this something she saved just for Attila? I wondered.

I slid the cake box onto the counter and filled a vase of water for the carnations. Then I emptied a package of graham crackers and some grapes onto a plate for the kids' afternoon snack. As I returned the bag of grapes to the fridge, I was confronted by a photo of the four of us smiling in Zilker Park. Nick was clinging to his daddy's leg; Elsie had her arms around my waist. I touched my husband's face in the picture. There he had been grinning, carefree. Things had changed lately. Why?

As I closed the fridge, my thoughts turned to our most recent squabble. When I'd suggested getting a part-time job, Blake's reaction had surprised me.

"What about the kids?"

"Blake," I had said, "we're not living in the 1950s anymore. Most women work full-time. It'll only be fifteen or twenty hours a week. I'll still have plenty of time for Elsie and Nick."

"I guess it's okay, at least until my promotion comes through," he said. But when I came home and announced I was working for a private investigator, he looked at me as if I'd announced I was taking up nude hang gliding. And now he was trying to get me to join the Junior League.

I knew that his suggestion that I get involved with the organization Herb McEwan's wife chaired was another way of ingratiating himself with his boss and moving up the ladder.

My thoughts turned to the promotion Blake kept striving for—the one that never came. I had always wondered how a person could work so hard and never reap the benefits. Now, the unpleasant thought occurred to me that maybe the reason he never got promoted was that those night hours weren't spent at the office. I had always trusted him implicitly. Now, I wasn't sure about anything. My stomach churned. If he wasn't spending those hours at the office, where was he spending them?

As I filled two sippy cups with apple juice, I thought with a pang of our early years together. When I met Blake my senior year in college, I was bowled over by his self-assurance. Our first date had been at Paggi House, a romantic Italian restaurant twinkling with candles and out-of-season Christmas lights.

Unlike most of my previous boyfriends, who considered going Dutch to be chivalrous, Blake was a gentleman. He opened my door for me, pulled my chair out for me, stood when I stood. Over the lobster ravioli, Blake talked about his passion for his future career. He had wanted to be a lawyer since sixth grade and had pursued it ever since. He was so serious, so sincere. I had fallen for him by the time the waiter delivered a plate of cannoli with two forks.

Although his passion for me never seemed to equal his passion for schoolwork and his future career, I told myself that once he had made it through law school and had established himself with a firm, he would have more energy for me and for the children I already imagined us having. He was never particularly romantic, with the exception of that first Italian dinner, but he was solid, a man of integrity, and exactly what I was looking for in a future husband. After my years shuttling from apartment to apartment with my single mother, security was important to me. And with Blake, I would always feel safe.

Which was why the lie he had told me this morning was so shattering.

I paused at the sink, blinking back tears. Where had things gone wrong?

I squared my shoulders and wiped my eyes on the back of my arm. Even though my life was in an uproar, it was important to keep things steady for Elsie and Nick. As I turned to carry the snack plate to the kitchen table, I glanced at the phone. I had three voice mails. Had Peaches found something out already? I slid the plate onto the table and picked up the phone.

The first was a call from my mother, asking about tea again. Then Mrs. Bunn's voice burbled into my ear. "Mrs. Peterson, I need you to call me as soon as possible regarding the photographs from the school festival." I sighed and jotted down the number. Probably not enough of them featured Attila herself.

Detective Bunsen's drawl was next. "Mrs. Peterson, this is Detective Bunsen. A few things have come up during the investigation of the Maxted homicide. We need to talk. Call me."

I copied his number down below Attila's.

Had they already figured out I had visited Maxted's building? For the first time, I felt a prickle of fear.

CHAPTER TEN

We arrived at Sullivan's only ten minutes late. Elsie carried the blue carnations, which I had removed from the vase and wrapped in wet newspaper and a Target bag. Not the classiest presentation, but it was better than tipping over a vase and swamping the minivan—or my mother-in-law—with a half gallon of smelly water.

Blake strode ahead of us and held the door open as we straggled through. We had been in such a rush to get out of the house that we hadn't had much of an opportunity to talk. This was good, because I wasn't sure I'd be able to hold it together if we did. Besides, I wasn't ready to spring the news about the rabid cat in the laundry room just yet.

Prudence and Phil were already seated at a round table by the window. When we made our entrance, Prudence stood up and rushed over, looking natty as always in a royal blue Chanel suit that matched her eyes. "Darlings, where were you? We were worried something had happened!" Her eyes alighted on my striped face. "Margie, what happened to your face?"

"Just an accident," I said.

"A cat scratched her," Nick said.

"Oh, that Rufus. He's been trouble from the beginning, hasn't he? What you need is a nice terrier, or a poodle." She kissed Blake on either cheek, a habit she had picked up during the seven days she had spent in Paris the previous year. Then she turned to the children. "How are my sweet grandchildren? Elsie, come here, darling. Your face is smudged. And let me tuck that shirt in for you."

"Happy birthday, Gramma." Elsie proffered the bouquet.

"She picked them out herself," I said hurriedly.

Prudence formed her mauve-lined lips into a faint moue of distaste. "Did she? Well. They certainly are interesting." She laid them on the table and hugged her granddaughter. "Thank you, sweetheart. That was very thoughtful of you." Elsie beamed.

Then my mother-in-law turned and pinched Nick's cheek. Her powdered brow furrowed as she looked up at me. "He's looking kind of skinny, Margie. Are you sure you're feeding him enough?"

I pasted on a smile. "He must have inherited your great metabolism, Prue. I just took him for his annual checkup. He's doing fine."

She eyed him critically. "It's not all metabolism, my dear. It's willpower." She sighed. "Well, we'll get him a big, fat steak tonight, anyway."

I bit my tongue and turned to my father-in-law. He was a quiet, benevolent presence in my in-laws' household, and I'd grown quite fond of him over the last eight years. As I watched, he squatted down and enfolded Elsie into a big hug. "How's my favorite girl?" he asked.

"Good, Grandpa. Do they have spaghetti here? Because Lady likes spaghetti."

Uh-oh.

But Grandpa took it in stride. "Oh, so you're Lady today?" He chuckled. "Well, Lady, we can order whatever you like."

Phil stood up and pulled me into a brief hug. "You're looking lovely tonight, Margie. Thank you for coming to meet us."

I flushed. My black pants were still wrinkled. Someone had yanked them off their hanger, and I had found them crammed into the corner of my closet. The blouse was one I had bought in better, slimmer times, and I was just praying the buttons would hold.

"Thanks," I said. "I wouldn't have missed it." We all took our places at the table, and after I had distributed crayons and coloring books to Elsie and Nick, I turned to Phil, who was sitting to my right. "How's work?"

"Oh, same-old same-old," he said. Although retirement age had come and gone for Phil, he continued to put in fifty-plus hours a week at 3M. He said it was so he could keep up with his wife's spending habits, but I harbored the private suspicion that he just couldn't face twenty-four hours a day at home with her. "How about you?" he said. "I heard you got a part-time job."

Before I had a chance to answer, Prudence leaned toward me. "Margie, darling, I was wondering if you wanted to help me organize the Junior League fashion show. I know decorating's not your thing, but we could really use help addressing and stamping the invitations, and arranging for rentals."

The Junior League again? I shot Blake a look, but he was focusing on arranging his napkin in his lap. "Actually," I said, "I'm really pretty busy right now." I had nothing against the Junior League fashion show. After all, it consumed my mother-in-law's attention for fully half of each year, for which I was grateful. But I just wasn't very interested in clothes or fancy events. Or in the Junior League itself.

"It'll be so much fun," she said. "Bitsy McEwan's debuting her new line," she said. "All the profits go to charity, of course."

"How nice," I said.

Blake perked up. "She is?" He turned to me. "You should think about it, Margie. It's a good networking opportunity. It could really help with my career."

I gave him a tight smile. "I'll think about it."

At the mention of career, Prudence's blue eyes brightened. "Any word on that partnership yet, sweetheart?"

Blake flushed. "The vote isn't until February, Mother."

Despite my anger over his lie, my heart twinged for him. Part of the reason he worked so hard was because his mother had spent her married life castigating her husband for his failure to elevate the family to country-club status. Although Phil had moved up the ranks at 3M, where he was a senior manager, he'd never made VP, and Prudence's dreams of living in a mansion by Lake Austin had never come to fruition. Although they lived in a very nice house next to a golf course, it still wasn't enough for Prudence. So she'd set her sights on her son.

"Well, let us know when it happens," my mother-in-law said. "We'll have a celebration!"

"How's the redecorating going?" I asked Prudence as a distraction. Last year the style had been Tuscan. This year she was changing everything in her 1950s ranch to resemble a French chateau. No wonder Phil still had to work.

"Oh, the redo is fine, but Graciela's work has fallen off terribly," she said.

"Is she okay?" Graciela had been Prudence's housekeeper for fifteen years. She was a hard worker, and always reliable.

"Well, her husband went to Mexico to see his dying mother or something, a few months ago, and he hasn't come back yet. Bitsy tells me she's been slacking off at her house, too." She leaned over the table and whispered hoarsely, "He's illegal, you know. He uses those wolf people to get across the border."

"You mean coyotes?" I said.

"Yes, that's it. Anyway, he was supposed to be back a few weeks ago, but she hasn't heard from him. Probably fell for some senorita back in the old country."

I felt a flicker of worry. That didn't sound like Eduardo to me. I thought of Graciela's teenaged daughters, now in high school. Without their father around, how was Graciela making ends meet? "Is there anyone she can talk to, to find out?"

Prudence shrugged a Chanel-clad shoulder. "I don't know. I just hope she gets this straightened out soon. Her work has really fallen off . . . It's been a month since she's done the windows."

"I have to go potty," Elsie announced.

"Excuse me," I said, and got up from the table.

Prudence stood up and shouldered her massive Coach purse. "I'll join you."

As Elsie closed the stall door behind her, Prudence pulled me aside. Her breath, as always, smelled like mint. I raised my hand to my mouth. Had I had onions with lunch?

Prudence spoke in a low voice. "I've noticed things seem a little tense between you and Blake lately, so I brought you a few things to help out."

"Oh no, we're fine," I protested.

She opened her purse and pulled out two books. "Here. These are for you." I stared at the paperbacks she shoved into my hands. The one on top was *How to Be a Domestic Goddess*.

"Prudence, no, really," I said. "Blake has just been under a lot of stress at work . . ."

"It's the other one that really made the difference in our marriage," she said. I slid the top book aside and almost gagged. The one underneath was titled *Sex Secrets of Happy Wives*.

I could feel my face turning beet red. My mother-in-law had just handed me a sex manual. "Prudence . . ."

"Just read it. Between that book and a nice diet and exercise regimen—I'll give you the number of my personal trainer if you want—you'll have Blake eating out of your hand in no time." At that moment, Elsie's thin voice piped up from behind the stall door. "Mommy, can you wipe me?"

"Sure, honey!" I shoved the books into my purse and escaped into Elsie's stall. I'd never been so eager to wipe a bottom in my life.

"If you have any questions, give me a call. And I'll set you up with Rocco whenever you're ready. He's really the best."

"Uh, thanks."

"I'll see you back at the table, dear," she called over the stall door.

As I pulled Elsie's skirt down and flushed the toilet, I reflected that this was the second time today I'd gotten unsolicited marital advice. I thought about the Domestic Goddess book in my bag. Was it that obvious that my marriage was in trouble? And could pot roast and a working knowledge of the Kama Sutra really make a difference?

By the time we got back to the table, the salad had appeared, and we made it through the appetizer phase and into the main course without any barking or biting from my daughter, or my mother-in-law. Although Elsie ate her spaghetti by sucking it from the plate strand by strand like Lady—I'd insisted she leave the bowl on the table, rather than moving to the floor—I kept Prudence on the safe topics of redecoration and the upcoming fashion show. The evening went smoothly, right up to the moment when I lifted the lid to the birthday cake box.

The waitresses and waiters who had gathered around to wish my mother-in-law a happy birthday fell silent. I flushed and jammed a few candles in. As we began to sing, a smothered titter sounded from the back of the crowd of black-and-white-clad waitstaff.

Across the top of the cake, in bright blue letters, the woman at the bakery had scrawled *Happy Birthday, Grandma Prude.*

• • •

"How could you have missed that?" Blake threw the minivan into reverse, and we jerked backward out of our parking place.

"What do you mean? I ordered the cake. I picked it up. How was I supposed to know they'd screw it up?"

"You didn't check?"

The anger I had suppressed all day flared up. "No," I hissed. "I didn't check. I was too busy trying to find something presentable to wear for Sullivan's."

"This wouldn't have happened if you'd ordered it from Lucy's."

"Yeah, but we would have been out an extra thirty bucks." I glanced over my shoulder. Nick's eyes were saucer-size. I lowered my voice. "Look . . . Can't we talk about this later, when the kids are in bed?"

"Not tonight. I have to go back to the office."

"What?"

"I have a deposition tomorrow. I told you about it last week."

My stomach churned again. Another late night at the office . . . or was it something else? I sighed. "I guess it's up to me to get the kids to bed, then."

"I did it last night, didn't I?"

We rode home the rest of the way in silence.

• • •

Blake was already gone by the time my alarm clock rang the next morning, and I wondered if he'd even come home. His sink bore a film of whiskers and shaving cream. He had been back at least long enough to shave.

I threw on a pair of shorts and a T-shirt, gave the kids a wake-up call, and headed downstairs to down a cup of coffee and a bagel. As the caffeine percolated through my sluggish body, I assembled peanut butter and jelly sandwiches, dressed, shod, and finger-combed my children. Then I grabbed my tennis shoes, distributed cups of dry Cheerios, and herded everyone to the car. For the first time that week, we were going to be on time.

It was only when I pulled into the parking lot of Green Meadows that I realized I'd left my shoes on the driveway beside the minivan.

As I padded past the office in white athletic socks, Mrs. Bunn waved furiously through the window. At first I thought she was applauding my punctuality; then I remembered she had wanted to talk about the school picnic photos. I delivered my children to their classrooms and crept back to the office, hoping she wouldn't notice the absence of shoes.

"Mrs. Peterson," she trumpeted as I closed the door behind me. "We need to talk. In my office, please." She paused for a moment. "And what is wrong with your face?"

"Cat injury," I said. I followed her into the antiseptic room she called an office. My eyes roamed the crowded room. Not a speck of dust sat on any object, and the walls were festooned with photos of previous students. Judging by the hair in the photos, she'd been at Green Meadows at least since the seventies. I sat gingerly on a diminutive wooden chair. Attila closed the door with a thud and waddled across the small room, wedging her bulk behind her desk with some difficulty. Her little eyes focused on me as she sank into her leather chair with a huff.

"Mrs. Peterson," she wheezed, "something has come to my attention that simply *must* be discussed. I knew things at your household were a bit . . . a bit *unorthodox*, but until now I didn't realize the level of depravity we were dealing with."

I blinked. "Depravity?"

"Depravity," she repeated, enunciating each syllable.

As I tucked my sock-clad feet under the chair, Attila opened her desk drawer and extracted a photo. "Mrs. Belmont discovered this when she was selecting photos for the school newsletter." As she slapped the four-by-six rectangle down on the desk, I shriveled in my tiny chair.

It was the photo of Pence.

I snatched it off the desk. "I'm so sorry. I've taken a new job . . . I'm a private investigator . . . and I guess I printed them all. I can't believe I didn't take it out."

Attila narrowed her green eyes at me, sniffing as if trying to scent a lie. I suppressed a groan. Why had it been Lydia Belmont who had found it? I could imagine the look on her laser-treated face when she found the photo. I would have bet my last nickel it wasn't shock. A gleeful smile was more likely. By lunchtime, every parent in the school, including several of my husband's coworkers, would know I had submitted a picture of an obese man clad in Saran Wrap to the school newsletter.

I slouched in my chair, trying not to think about Blake's reaction when he found out.

"You're a private investigator?"

My focus snapped back to Attila. She was chewing her lip and eyeing me as if I were a chicken she was considering turning into potpie. She was probably deciding whether to call Child Protective Services. "Yes," I said. "I mean, well, not officially . . ."

Her bushy black eyebrows shot up. "Not officially?"

"I mean, I don't have a license . . . but I'm working as an investigator for a local firm. Chasing down adultery cases, mainly."

Attila licked her bottom lip. Potpie, indeed. "What firm do you work for?"

"It's called Peachtree Investigations."

"And are the children aware of your new . . . occupation?"

"They know I work, but they're a little hazy on the details."

"Good, good," she said.

Good? What had happened to depravity?

"Any progress on the psychologist yet?"

I blinked. No castigation? No accusations? Either Attila had begun attending anger management classes, or something was up.

When I confessed that I hadn't gotten around to it yet, she gave me an understanding nod. "I can't recommend Dr. Lemmon enough. I think you'll be pleased with the results."

"I'll call today," I said. Attila continued to study me. I cleared my throat. "Is there something else you wanted to talk to me about?"

She leaned back in her chair, adding a fourth chin to the collection that nestled above the collar of her dress. "When you work," she said slowly, "I presume you do so with the utmost confidentiality."

I nodded.

"Good." She leaned toward me and lowered her voice. "I need your assistance with something."

What had been a twinge of misgiving escalated to major foreboding. What was it she wanted me to do? Trail her husband? Track down a love child? I shifted in the tiny chair and tried to maintain a pleasant facial expression.

"What I am about to tell you," she continued, "must not leave this office." Her jowly face hardened. "Do you understand?"

I nodded again.

Attila pried herself from the chair and waddled over to the window. Her rippled back jiggled slightly as she spoke. "We have an unfortunate . . . situation at Green Meadows Day School that has developed since the school year began."

"Oh? What's going on?"

Attila turned to face me. Her fleshy lips were a thin line. "I will be blunt with you, Mrs. Peterson. Significant amounts of money have been disappearing, and I have been unable to trace the source of the problem." She sighed. "It appears, I'm afraid, that someone at the school is a thief."

"A thief?"

"Yes. Someone has been embezzling funds."

I glanced at the filing cabinets that lined the office. Did she expect me to go through all of the school's financial records? I suppressed a groan. "And you want me to . . ."

"I want you to find out who is responsible."

I slumped in my chair. I'd read somewhere that companies often hired forensic accountants or something to track down missing money. Trained accountants. Accountants who were good at math. I hadn't balanced my own checkbook since sometime in the midnineties, and I could barely remember how to do long division.

"Why do you need a private investigator? Wouldn't an accountant be the right person for the job? I mean, someone to do an audit?"

Attila shook her head sharply. "This must not be made public. I want no taint of scandal associated with the school. I started this institution forty years ago, and since then we have been a paragon of virtue and honesty. I will not have the good name of Green Meadows Day School tarnished by a common thief."

"But it's not the school's fault. How were you to know that someone was going to embezzle money from you? I'm sure people would understand . . ."

Attila drew herself up as only a three-hundred-pound woman can. "Mrs. Peterson, I do all the hiring, and the parents who entrust me with their children trust my judgment. If it came to light that a dishonest person was employed here . . ."

I grimaced. My experience as a private investigator was virtually nonexistent. I knew zip about embezzlement. The thought of spending hours going through the school's books and making sure pages full of numbers added up was about as appealing as cleaning bedpans. Besides, most of my free time was dedicated to investigating my husband and avoiding Detective Bunsen. On the list of priorities, finding out who was funding his or her Starbucks habit from Green Meadows Day School's petty cash drawer was right up there with cleaning the fan blades in the living room.

On the other hand, helping Attila the Bunn might keep Elsie from getting expelled. Heck, she might even give me a discount on tuition if I played my cards right. I gritted my teeth. "I'll give it a shot."

Her body relaxed, and her doughy face split into a smile of satisfaction. "Good. You can start this Saturday."

"Saturday?"

"Why, you can't do your work with people in the office, can you? Not if we're going to keep things quiet."

She wobbled toward the door. "I'll provide you with a key to the office tomorrow."

I followed her, wondering who was going to watch the kids while I rifled through the school's office.

As we exited her office and walked to the front door, she said, "One more question, Mrs. Peterson."

"What?"

"Is there any particular reason you're not wearing shoes?"

I muttered something about dogs stealing them and padded out the door.

As I trudged back to the minivan, I thought about the case Attila had plopped into my lap. Even if it was possible for me to figure out how much was missing, and from where, I had no idea how to find out who was responsible. I thought of Peaches. Had she had experience with embezzlement? Maybe she could tell me what to look for.

As I crossed the grassy lawn to the parking lot, something squelched under my sock. As I looked down, a familiar odor wafted up from my feet.

I had just stepped in a giant pile of dog doo-doo.

CHAPTER ELEVEN

I hopped into the house a half hour later, barefoot. After rinsing my foot and tossing my socks onto the growing pile of dirty clothes outside the laundry room door, I poured myself another cup of coffee and sat down at the kitchen table to think.

A low rumble sounded from the laundry room. Snookums was evidently up and around. In response, Rufus, who had stationed himself right outside the door, arched his back and hissed. He had already left a deposit in front of the door that morning that I'd cleaned up before my first cup of coffee.

My thumb throbbed as I lifted the cup to my lips. Blake had enough trouble with Nick's toilet-training lapses: I doubted he'd be delighted by the addition of Snookums to the household menagerie. I peeked under the Band-Aid. The area around the bite was pink and puffy. I added "call the doctor" to my mental list of things to do.

I had just set down my coffee cup when the phone rang.

"Marigold!"

I suppressed a groan. "Hi, Mom. What's up?"

"Did you get that tea I sent you?"

"It came yesterday."

"I can tell you haven't used it yet, though. There's a lot of gray in your phone aura."

"My phone aura?"

"Oh yes, darling. Usually yours is more yellow."

Who knew? "How's Karma?" I asked, anxious to change the subject. Karma was her latest boyfriend, an herbalist from San Diego.

"Oh, he's wonderful. We went to the most fabulous retreat last weekend at an ashram up in Massachusetts . . . but anyway, I didn't call to talk about me. How are you? And how are my two darlings? When can I come to visit them?"

I stifled a sigh. "Everyone's fine, Mom. Aren't you coming down for Thanksgiving?"

"Oh, but that's such a long time! And I picked up a few new crystals the other day that I want to give the kids—"

"Mom, I hate to run, but I need to call a psychologist this afternoon—"

"A psychologist?"

Damn. I hadn't meant to let that slip. "It's for Elsie, just a little thing with school—"

My mother tsked. "Things aren't going well with Blake, are they? It turns up in the kids every time. I knew he was the wrong aura for you. Too clouded, too blocked—"

"Mom." Sometimes I wondered if my mother really was psychic. "Everything's fine with Blake and me," I lied. "It's just a little developmental hiccup, that's all."

"Do you need me to come down and help you with the kids?"

"Mom, I appreciate the offer, but things are a bit hectic right now. Can I call you back later?"

"Honey, you know you can always talk to me. In the meantime, make sure you use that tea! And I'll ask Karma what will work for Elsie."

"I love you, Mom. Got to go."

"Love you, too, sweetheart. Bye! And don't forget the tea!"

I hung up the phone and took another swig of coffee. How had I let that little tidbit slip? Now I was in for daily phone calls until I managed to reassure my mom that our auras were all okay.

I forced my mind to focus on the problem at hand. If I solved my issues with Blake, maybe my phone aura would turn yellow again, and my mother would leave me alone. I wasn't ready to confront Blake until I had some information to go on, so that meant finding out more about Evan Maxted. I'd gone to his apartment building, but what should I do next? After my experience at Maxted's apartment, I wasn't ready to take on a visit to International Shipping Company yet. My thoughts turned to Cassandra Starr. She had known Evan. But it was nine in the morning, and I doubted the Rainbow Room was open for breakfast.

I was about to dial Peaches when the phone rang again. I picked it up on the second ring.

"Hello, Margie? This is Bitsy McEwan."

"Oh. Hi." I gripped the phone. Great. My husband's boss's wife. Had Lydia already told her about the Pence photo?

"I was just talking to your mother-in-law this morning, and she mentioned that you were interested in volunteering for the Junior League fashion show."

"She did?"

"Yes, and I'm so delighted you'll help us. The proceeds go to the Children's Fund, you know. Such a wonderful cause, don't you think? Helping the little children?"

"She did say something about addressing invitations."

"Yes, well, the invitations are already in the mail—you should be receiving yours any day now—but we do have an opportunity available to help out during the event."

"Oh?"

"Yes. It'll be a wonderful chance to meet some of the other ladies. Prue said you were thinking of joining the League."

"She did?"

"Yes, and I think it's a wonderful idea. We have so many opportunities to do good things in the community, and it's important to take advantage of them. Anyway, I'll just put you down, then."

I bit my lip. I had enough on my plate without volunteering to help out at the Junior League fashion show. But if it would help defray some of the damage Lydia's discovery of the Pence photo was sure to do, how could I say no?

"Okay. What will I be doing?"

"I've got you down as a volunteer, darling. Now, will you also be attending the event?"

If I was volunteering for it, I might as well attend it. "Sure."

"Wonderful, wonderful. I'll just put you down next to Prue." I stifled a groan as she continued. Attending a Junior League fashion show with my mother-in-law was up there with having a root canal done. "Tickets are two hundred dollars each, you know. You can buy them on the League website."

I gulped. "Two hundred dollars?"

"Yes, but I assure you, it will be worth every penny. Wait till you see the new collection . . ."

"And what is it I'll be doing?" I asked.

"Oh, I put you down for cleanup, dear. After the event. You know, washing dishes, sweeping up . . . Just girl stuff, though. We've got some of the men to move the tables."

I was paying two hundred dollars to sit next to my mother-in-law and then wash dishes?

Bitsy continued undaunted. "Well, anyway, I'd love to chat, but I've got to run. You know how it is, busy, busy! I look forward to seeing you at the show, and if you have any questions, just call me at home. I'm sure we can figure out a way to sponsor you."

Sponsor me? "Um . . ."

"We'll talk at the show. Toodle-oo!"

The phone clicked, then went dead. Bitsy McEwan was something. I almost felt sorry for her husband.

I sighed and dialed Peachtree Investigations. Once again, the line was busy, which worried me.

I put down the phone and grabbed my coffee cup. Evan Maxted was a dead end this morning. *Blake is at work*, my mind whispered. *His desk is right here, in the next room.* I pushed the thought from my head and topped off my coffee cup.

Two cardinals flitted around the bird feeder outside the kitchen window as I considered my next step. Peaches was right about expanding my investigation. In order to figure out Blake's connection to the dead transvestite, I needed to find out more about my husband. And as much as I hated the idea of prying into my husband's things, it might be the only way to find out how he was connected to Maxted.

But wasn't that dishonest? I had never held anything back from my husband. Then again, that was when I thought he never held anything back from me. Which apparently wasn't the case.

I had asked him point-blank about Evan Maxted, and he had denied knowing him. Obviously the straightforward approach wasn't working, which meant if I had any hope of finding out about Blake's connection to the dead transvestite, I had to be sneaky.

I finished my coffee and walked to our bedroom, feeling like every step was a chink in the mortar of our marriage. Here I was, preparing to go through my husband's drawers, looking for incriminating evidence. The coffee soured in my stomach. What had our marriage come to?

I started with his dresser. I didn't know what I expected to find. Part of me was dreading the discovery of a hidden cache of lace thongs and garters. But the drawers yielded nothing but socks, boxer shorts, and semifolded T-shirts. This wasn't surprising, since I was the one who put away the laundry. His closet was equally boring— the only thing out of place was a sock that had missed the laundry hamper. I allowed myself a sigh of relief. At least Blake wasn't a closet cross-dresser. Or if he was, he didn't use this closet.

I headed back to the kitchen with increased optimism. Maybe Blake had denied knowing Maxted because of a confidentiality agreement. Then again, I had no idea what a confidentiality agreement covered. Did it extend to denying knowledge of your client?

I climbed the steps to the little room above the garage that Blake used as an office. The desk was a squat mahogany thing we had picked up at an antique fair and that had barely made it up the stairs. Once there, it took up at least half of the seven-by-ten room. A green banker's lamp sat atop the scarred surface, which in contrast to the rest of the house was uncluttered by anything but two fountain pens in a wooden case.

Squeezed in next to the desk was the glass-fronted barrister cabinet. It looked impressive, but I always had to smother a grin when I dusted it. Except for one shelf dedicated to the *Law Review*, the dark wood shelves were filled not with legal tomes, but with paperback thrillers.

I eased myself into his leather chair and pulled open the top drawer. Paper clips, staples, and a package of rollerball pens. The fountain pens were just for show.

The top drawer on the right was locked, but that wasn't a big surprise. Blake had a phobia about burglars getting our credit card information. I poked around in the office, and within five minutes, had located the key. He had tucked it into the corner of one of the barrister cases.

The drawer was dedicated to bills, and I flipped through it quickly: electric, gas, phone, cell phone.

Cell phone.

I pulled the file out and spread it across the desk.

A quick scan of the most recent bills yielded a list of familiar numbers: Blake's office, Becky, our home phone number. A few other numbers popped up from time to time, none of them regularly. I grabbed a rollerball and a Post-it note and jotted them down anyway.

Then, in April, one number started showing up regularly. I didn't recognize it, but Blake had called it at least three times a week; while some of the calls were only for a few minutes, one was for as long as forty. I leafed through the March and February bills. Same number, same pattern. Then, in mid-January, they stopped abruptly.

I scanned the bills again. Except for a few one-minute calls, all of the calls had occurred during business hours. Had he been calling a client?

I restacked the bills and slid them back into the folder. As I pulled out the file marked *Visa*, a thump sounded from somewhere in the house.

I froze. Was Blake home? I slammed the drawer shut and pocketed the key, then crept down the stairs. "Hello?" I called.

Nothing.

When I got to the kitchen, Rufus thumped the laundry room door with his tail. I sagged against the wall as Snookums growled on the other side. That was the thump I had heard. Just to be sure, I checked the driveway. Blake's parking spot was empty.

As I hurried back upstairs, I chided myself for spooking so easily. After all, I was just going through the family files. What was wrong with that? If Blake did come home, I could tell him I was just making sure I hadn't been overcharged on the credit card.

I opened the drawer and pulled out the *Visa* file again, laying it open on the desk. No unusual charges. A few local restaurants, Target, Randall's, Macy's. I went all the way back to January, and the only thing I discovered was that I was spending way too much money at Dr. Chocolate.

I was about to close the drawer when I spotted a slim file labeled *Jones McEwan*. As I opened it, a stack of pay stubs slid out, fanning across the desk. I shoveled them back into the folder, disappointed. As I replaced the last slip of paper, my breath caught in my throat.

According to Blake, he hadn't gotten a raise in a year and a half. But the amount recorded on the pay stubs was a thousand dollars higher than it had been last year. I flipped through the stack; the amount had shot up in January. The same time the calls started happening. But while the calls had stopped, the extra money hadn't.

I grabbed the file marked *Bank Statements*, wondering if he'd just forgotten to tell me about it.

I scanned the August statement and blinked in disbelief. My husband had lied about knowing Evan Maxted, but that wasn't the only thing he had been keeping from me.

Despite the increase on the paychecks, the deposits were exactly the same as they had been for the last eighteen months.

Where was the extra money going?

And what was my husband involved in?

My mind ricocheted through a series of terrible scenarios as I returned the file to the drawer. Drugs? A mistress? My thoughts flashed on Evan Maxted's body, askew on the toilet. Could it be something even worse?

I closed my eyes. *This can't be happening.* Not my husband.

But it was.

I pushed myself away from the desk and stared out the window. A woman with a baby carriage strolled down the sidewalk outside, looking tired, but happy. A stab of envy shot through me. Her little world was intact: playgroups, late nights with the baby, a kiss from her husband when he got home from work. That used to be my world, too. Not anymore.

Why was Blake hiding money from me?

And what else was he hiding?

I watched until the woman disappeared around the corner. Then I returned the files to the drawer, locked it, and tore through the rest of the desk. The question burned like fire. Where was the extra money going? Finally, I sat back, drained and disappointed. The money was missing, but nothing in Blake's desk told me where it was going. The only other surprise had been an illicit bag of Snickers bars tucked in with the reams of extra paper. I had just closed the last drawer and returned the key to its place in the barrister cabinet when the phone rang.

My eyes scanned the little room to make sure everything was in place. Then I scurried down the stairs and picked up the phone just before it went to voice mail. "Hello?"

"Margie? It's Peaches. Did I interrupt something? You sound like you've been running."

My whole body felt as if I had just spent a few hours on a rack—when in fact, my whole life was ripping apart at the seams—but I focused on making my voice sound normal. "Just doing some housework."

"I was calling to let you know I did the background check on Maxted."

I swallowed hard. "And?"

"He's pretty clean. Graduated with honors from UCLA, got an MBA from Texas. Worked for a couple of Internet companies, then started at International Shipping two years ago. Never married, no kids."

"That's not surprising. Anything else?"

"His dad's a big preacher type out in California. Plus he's got a sister in San Diego. His folks live in LA. No police record."

I slumped into a kitchen chair. "Another dead end."

"Just because nothing shows up in the background check doesn't mean it's a dead end. Did you talk to the neighbors?"

My husband is lying to me! I wanted to scream. *My marriage is a sham!* Instead, I said, "Yeah. A nice old lady down the hall." The coolness of my voice startled me. "Apparently two people visited him," I said, "but I have no idea who they are."

"What you need is to get into that apartment."

My eyes shot to the laundry room door. Rufus still hovered outside, but the rumbling had stopped. "I already did."

"You got in? How?"

"I told the neighbor he was watching my cat for me."

She snorted. "And that worked?"

"Yeah. The only problem is, there was a cop there."

"I should have told you to wait a few days for them to clear out," she said. "What did you do when there wasn't a cat in the apartment?"

"There was one. It's now in my laundry room."

She wheezed with laughter, which turned into a hacking cough. "You're shitting me. What are you going to do with it?"

"I don't know," I said. The cat was the least of my problems. First I had to figure out what to do about my husband. "By the way," I said, straining to keep my voice casual, "I did a little research on my friend."

"Yeah?"

I swallowed hard. *Steady, Margie. Steady.* "One number kept popping up on the cell phone records. Any idea how to track it down?"

"Have you tried calling it?"

"Um, no. I hadn't thought of that."

"Give that a try first. Say you're a pizza delivery service, and you're calling to tell them they won a free pizza, so you need their address."

"Really? People fall for that?"

"Sometimes. If they hang up on you, it's no big deal. If you call from home, make sure you block the number. Everybody's got Caller ID these days."

"What if no one answers?"

"If nobody answers, I have a friend who can track it down, but that costs money. Find anything else?"

If I said it, somehow, it would make it more real. I squeezed my eyes shut, feeling the prickle of hot tears. "Missing money," I croaked.

"Missing money? What do you mean?"

My voice wobbled slightly. "There should be more money in a bank account than there is."

"How did you find that out?" There was something in Peaches's tone that made me wonder if she'd figured out exactly how close my "friend" was.

Shame burned through me as I tried to think of what to tell her. My husband had stolen money from our family, and I'd had to go through the family files to find out. No, no. I couldn't tell Peaches that. I couldn't even admit it to my best friend.

"Okay, okay," Peaches said finally. "You don't have to tell me. How much is missing?"

I gripped the phone. "About two thousand a month," I whispered.

She let out a long, low whistle. "You can do a lot with two thousand a month. Drugs, a second apartment for a mistress . . . Can you get the credit card records?"

Nightmare scenarios reeled through my head. "I already did," I said. "Everything's in cash."

"Well, unless you know where he stashes his receipts, you're out of luck. We could always put a tail on him."

"No," I said hurriedly. Putting a tail on him would mean I would have to admit to Peaches that I was checking out my husband. "Let me see what else I can find out first."

My eyes fell on the latest newsletter from Green Meadows, and I remembered my conversation with Attila that morning. "By the way, do you know anything about tracking down an embezzler?"

"Your friend's embezzling, too?"

"No, this is for someone else. Another friend."

"Christ. And here I thought you were a meek little housewife. What kind of people are you hanging out with? You gonna call to ask about busting up a drug deal next?"

I blinked back tears. "I hope not."

CHAPTER TWELVE

The Rainbow Room wasn't quite as busy at noon as it was for the Tuesday Night Showdowns, but it did a pretty brisk lunch trade. After Bitsy had hung up, I'd called and found out it opened at eleven thirty. I drove downtown and arrived just after twelve. If Cassandra was there, I'd have plenty of time to ask her a few questions about Evan Maxted before picking up my kids at two.

The cold air raised goose bumps on my arms and legs as I walked past clusters of men in business suits and a few women—or were they men?—in low-cut tops and abbreviated skirts. Fortunately, this time I'd remembered to bring a sweatshirt with me, and I pulled it over my head as I settled myself at a bar stool. Adonis wasn't on duty, but a short Hispanic guy named Domingo was.

"What can I get you?" he asked. The diamond stud in his nose sparkled pink under the neon lights.

"Just a Diet Coke," I said. "And could I have a lunch menu?"

He slid a sticky laminated menu across the bar toward me and turned to fill a glass with ice. When he plunked my Diet Coke on the counter, I asked if Cassandra was around.

"Cassandra?" He eyed my sweatshirt. "Why do you want to talk to Cassandra?"

"We have a mutual friend," I said.

"She'll be here at one," he said. "Let me know when you've decided."

I nodded, and deliberated for ten minutes between the Bunlovers' Burger and the Fetish-ini Alfredo. I decided on the Alfredo and was pleasantly surprised by the plate Domingo brought out fifteen minutes later. I was just scraping up the last bits of sauce when Cassandra swept into the bar. She no longer looked like an orange Popsicle. Today, she was dressed like Dale Evans in a short denim skirt, red cowboy boots, and a straw hat. Only the heavy makeup and furry eyelashes were the same.

"Cassandra!" Domingo called.

She turned and fluttered those eyelashes at him, which was quite a feat, given their tonnage. "Domingo! Did you miss me?"

"Sure, Cassandra."

She pouted at him as he pointed at me. "Lady here wants to talk to you."

Cassandra's fringed eyes sought me out, but instead of sparking with recognition, they clouded with confusion. "Do I know you?"

"We met the other night. The night Evan—Selena—died."

"Did we?"

"I was a little more dressed up." She still looked confused. "Remember Emerald?" I said. "Emerald Divine?"

She blinked. "*You're* Emerald?"

I nodded. "Margie, actually."

She sat back, exposing an awful lot of thigh. "Well. It's amazing what a little makeup and hair spray will do. Miracles, really. I mean, you took third place the other night, and now, who would guess?"

"Gee, thanks." I resisted the urge to reach up and fluff my hair. Did the makeup really make that much of a difference? "I wanted to ask you a few questions about Selena, if that's okay with you."

"Oh yes. Poor dear." Her chandelier earrings—miniature silver horses and spurs—jingled as she shook her head. "I can't imagine who would do a thing like that to a beautiful girl like Selena."

"That's what I want to ask you. Do you know who would have wanted to . . . to hurt her like that?"

"Why are you interested?"

I shrugged. "It turns out she's a friend of a friend of mine. Besides, I found her . . ."

"So? The police will handle it. And that gorgeous detective seems able to handle just about everything." She sighed. "Too bad he's straight. But why should I talk to you?"

"Because I'm a private investigator," I said. The title sounded awkward to me.

It must have sounded awkward to Cassandra, too, because she eyed me skeptically. "You? A private investigator?"

"Actually, I was on a job the night I came here."

She blinked. "No kidding."

I forged ahead before she could ask for details. "Do you know if Selena was seeing anyone?"

"That's just what that handsome Detective Bunsen asked me. I told him, a girl like Selena always has suitors. She's been in here with a lot of men."

"Anyone in particular?"

Cassandra pursed her purple lips. "Well, the last couple of months, she's been hanging around with one guy more than the others. Good-looking guy, wears a lot of black leather, and his *muscles* . . ." She moaned. "He must live at the gym. I tell you, you've never *seen* such a tight bottom. And in those leather pants . . ."

"Did he have a name?"

"I think Selena called him Marcus. I told Detective Bunsen about him, too."

"Any idea where he lives?"

"I don't know, but Veronica might."

"Veronica?"

"She runs the only tranny school in town." I must have had a blank look on my face. "You know what a tranny school is, don't you?"

"Kind of . . ."

Cassandra fumbled in her purse for a cigarette, which she jammed into a silver holder and perched on a purple lip. After fluttering her eyes at Domingo for a moment, she gave up and lit it herself. "Miss Veronica's Boudoir," she said finally. "It's a place that helps men get in touch with their feminine side, if you know what I mean." She winked at me, but I still wasn't getting it.

Finally, she rolled her eyes. "For transvestites. You know, to teach them girl stuff. Picking out bras, stockings, how to apply makeup." She tittered. "Of course, I never needed the help. Fashion sense came naturally to me. But a lot of these men, well, they couldn't tell you the difference between a mule and a slide for a million dollars."

I didn't know the difference, either, but I didn't tell Cassandra. "Do you know where I can find her?"

"Sure. She's down on South Congress. Even though I don't need the instruction, I like to order a few things from time to time." She leaned forward, lowering her voice to a whisper. "Her thongs are to die for. You should check them out while you're down there. She's got lace, rubber . . . even some with plastic fruit, would you believe?" Cassandra pulled a pen from her leather-fringed purse, jotted the address on a cocktail napkin, and pushed it toward me. "There you go. Can't miss it. It's right behind the Hot Chicken."

"The Hot Chicken? What's that, a gay bar?"

She blinked her eyelashes at me. "No, dear, it's a take-out chicken place."

• • •

It was only one thirty when I stepped out of the Rainbow Room and slid into the oven that was the minivan. I had a few minutes before it was time to pick up the kids, so I decided to cruise by Miss Veronica's Boudoir. Cassandra was right; it was tucked into the trees directly behind the Hot Chicken. I don't know what I was expecting, maybe a strip mall, or something concrete and grungy like Peachtree Investigations, but Miss Veronica's was a little gingerbread Victorian, complete with lace curtains at the window and a porch swing. It looked like a knitting store, not a training facility for wannabe transvestites.

I pulled into the driveway and peered at the hours sign posted next to the front door. "Monday through Friday, ten to six. Walk-ins welcome, appointments preferred." Appointments? What kind of appointments? As I stared at the building, a curvaceous woman in a chiffon miniskirt opened the front door, accompanied by a conservative-looking young man in slacks and a dress shirt. Was the woman really a woman? The young man smiled at her, and I was reminded with a pang of Evan Maxted's driver's license picture. I wondered if he was a transvestite in training.

As I peered at the couple, the woman in chiffon turned to look at me. Even from a distance, I could see that her eyes were a startling violet. She reminded me a little of Elizabeth Taylor. I turned my head away and blushed, embarrassed to have been caught staring. Then I threw the minivan into reverse and pulled back onto South Congress, resolving to come back tomorrow after dropping the kids off at school. Hopefully, the woman in the chiffon skirt wouldn't remember me gawking at her.

I rolled into the Green Meadows parking lot five minutes early—on time twice in one day!—and spent two of them practicing facial expressions in the rearview mirror. What I was going for was the "Everything is just fine, and your daddy didn't lie about knowing a murdered transvestite and isn't hiding money from your mommy" look. I settled on a smile that I hoped wasn't too strained and stepped out of the car, right into Lydia Belmont.

"Oh. Hello." Every inch of her professionally tanned, expensively manicured, and stylishly slender figure tensed. The nostrils of her aquiline nose flared slightly, as if she'd gotten a whiff of something, or someone, nasty.

"Hi," I said. My carefully rehearsed facial expression melted. "I heard you found one of my work photos in the school pictures. Did Mrs. Bunn get a chance to explain it to you?"

"Explain why you're walking around with disgusting photographs? Need I remind you that this is a school?"

"I know it's a school, and I'm mortified that that photo got in there." I swallowed. "But it's not what you think. I'm a private investigator, Lydia. It was proof for an infidelity case."

Her penciled eyebrows rose. "Oh?"

"Yes."

"Well," she huffed. "You can call your . . . your *perversion* whatever you want to, but I will not have my daughter exposed to such influences!"

"It was an accident. I promise it won't happen again."

"No, I should think not. In fact, I'm determined to see that it doesn't." She took a breath, and her nostrils quivered. "That's why I've started a petition."

I stepped backward. "A petition?"

"Yes. A petition. This is a private school, and the parental body should be able to choose whom we allow to attend."

"Whom we allow . . ."

"And that is why I have started a petition that would allow the removal of influences we deem unsafe for our children."

I clenched my fists. "You mean you've started a petition to have my children expelled?"

"That is correct, Mrs. Peterson. Now, if you will excuse me, I need to retrieve my daughter."

Heat rose to my cheeks as she strode toward the school gate, her Dooney & Bourke handbag bouncing against her bony hip.

Lydia Belmont was trying to have my children expelled from Green Meadows Day School. And her husband was one of Blake's colleagues.

On the plus side, I thought as I trailed her to the gate, at least Attila was on my side.

For now.

Elsie and Nick raced toward me as I entered the playground area. "Mommy!" Nick hollered, his Stride Rites churning up the pea gravel, Elsie tripping along behind him in pink strappy sandals. For a moment, as my kids wrapped themselves around my legs and hugged me as if I were the only thing that mattered, everything that was going wrong in my life—Lydia, Evan Maxted, Green Meadows Day School, even my troubles with Blake—faded away.

Then Elsie burst into tears.

"What's wrong, sweetheart?"

Her little face was mottled from crying. "Cherie . . . Cherie says our family is a bunch of perbers!"

"Perbers?" I looked up and focused on Cherie. Her mother, Lydia, glared at me and threw a protective arm around her before hustling her away. Perbers. *Perverts.*

My eyes scanned the playground, searching for one of the kids' teachers, focusing finally on Elsie's teacher, who was stationed by the porch steps. "Miss Lawson? Could you keep an eye on Nick and Elsie for a moment? There's something I need to discuss with Mrs. Bunn."

Miss Lawson, a kindly looking woman in flowing, gauzy fabrics, smiled at me. "Sure." I bent down and kissed Elsie's wet cheek. "I'll be back in a moment, sweetheart." Then I gave Nick's arm a quick squeeze. "Mommy has to go into the office for a few minutes. Will you stay with Miss Lawson?" He nodded, his blue eyes wide.

I shepherded them over to the porch steps and marched to the office. Mrs. Bunn was alone behind the front desk. I slammed the door behind me.

"I've got a big problem, Mrs. Bunn."

Attila's bushy black eyebrows rose in surprise. "Oh? What is it?"

"My daughter is in tears because Cherie Belmont is calling our family a bunch of perverts. And Cherie's mother just informed me in the parking lot that she's putting together a petition to have Elsie and Nick expelled."

Attila shifted uncomfortably in her chair. "Yes, well, she was quite upset over the photograph."

"Upset? So what? I explained the photograph to you. It was a mistake. Are you going to let them tar and feather my children because of a small error?"

Mrs. Bunn shrugged. "Unfortunately, I have no control over Mrs. Belmont's actions."

"Okay. Maybe not. But you can sure as heck make sure her daughter isn't spreading nasty rumors about my family on the playground."

She sighed. "I'll talk to the teachers this afternoon."

"What about the petition?"

"I'm afraid the petition is out of my hands. While you're here, though, I wanted to give you a copy of the key to the office."

"What?"

"So you can commence your investigation."

"Oh yes. The investigation." I crossed my arms. "I'd be happy to look into things for you—and to keep it quiet—but I need something in return."

Mrs. Bunn's jowly face stiffened. "What do you mean?"

"I need you to talk to Mrs. Belmont and put a stop to this."

"To the petition?"

I nodded.

The whiskers on her chin bristled as she shook her head. "I don't know if I can do that."

"That's too bad." I turned and put my hand on the doorknob. "With everything that's been going on in my life, I'm afraid I may not be able to start the investigation for another couple of weeks. Maybe even a few months."

"A few months?"

My hand turned the knob. Mrs. Bunn let out an exasperated sigh. "All right. I'll talk to her. But I can't make any promises."

"What about the teasing?"

"As I mentioned earlier, I'll be discussing the matter with the children's teachers this afternoon."

"Good." I walked back to the desk, and she handed me a set of keys. I couldn't believe it. Mrs. Bunn had just agreed to run interference for Elsie and Nick.

"All the financial files are in here." She gestured toward an imposing file cabinet that could easily have worked as an anchor for the *Titanic*. I gritted my teeth. Victory didn't come without a price.

"I'll get started this weekend, then."

"Marvelous. But there's one more thing, Mrs. Peterson."

"What?"

"I spoke with my friend Dr. Lemmon yesterday. Apparently you haven't called to schedule an appointment for your daughter yet."

I bit my lip. "I'll call this afternoon," I said, and then strode out of the office, stuffing the keys into my pocket.

A few minutes later, I retrieved Elsie and Nick from beneath Miss Lawson's wing, holding their hands tightly as we trotted to the parking lot. "I'm sorry that happened to you today, Elsie. I've just spoken with Mrs. Bunn, and your teachers are going to make sure nobody calls you any more names."

She sniffled. "What's a perber, Mommy?"

Christ. "Whatever it is, it's not very nice. The important thing is that you know that it doesn't matter what other people say. You're a wonderful, kind, smart little girl." I gave her small hand a squeeze. "And when people say mean things to you, all it does is tell you something about them."

"What do you mean, Mommy?"

"It tells you that they're not good people to have as friends."

"Oh."

I buckled Elsie and Nick into their car seats and exited the driveway right behind Lydia Belmont's silver Mercedes SUV. It was all I could do not to slam the gas pedal and smash into her sparkling bumper. I limited myself to sticking my tongue out at her as she turned right.

As I maneuvered the minivan out of the parking lot, Elsie piped up from the backseat. "Why did you stick your tongue out at that lady's car, Mommy?"

"Did I? Oh, I must have been thinking about something else."

CHAPTER THIRTEEN

The phone started ringing the moment the front door closed behind me. I raced into the kitchen and picked it up halfway through the fourth ring.

"Hello?"

"Margie?"

"Becky. What's up?"

"Lydia Belmont just called me and asked me to sign a petition to have Elsie and Nick expelled from Green Meadows. What's going on?"

I sank into one of the kitchen chairs, thinking of the discovery I'd made in Blake's office. *Oh, not much. Just my marriage is falling apart, that's all.* Instead, I said, "Remember that photo of Pence I told you about?"

"You mean Mr. Saran Wrap?"

"Yeah. I accidentally left a copy in with the pictures from the school picnic."

"You didn't."

"I did. And guess who found it."

Becky groaned. "I can't believe it."

"On the plus side, Attila promised she'd try to talk her out of it."

"Attila? As in Attila the Bunn?"

"The very same."

"How did you manage that?"

"Don't ask." *And don't ask about Blake, either.* I forced a light tone to my voice. "By the way, are you going to the Junior League fashion show?"

"What does that have to do with Lydia Belmont?"

"Nothing. I got roped into going, and I was hoping you'd be there, too. They put me next to Prue."

"Did you tell her about your new job yet?"

"What do you think?"

"I didn't think you had." She sighed. "I guess I have to go, then. Otherwise you might end up in jail for matricide. Or do they call it something different when it's your mother-in-law?"

"Self-defense?" Becky laughed. "You wouldn't believe what she gave me the other night," I said.

"What? A lecture on the importance of Kegels?"

"It's much worse. When we were in the bathroom, she handed me two books. One's a cookbook—that Nigella Lawson one, *How to be a Domestic Goddess*."

"So?"

"The other's a sex manual."

A snort sounded from the other end of the phone line. "Oh my God. She didn't."

"She did." My voice wobbled through the forced gaiety. "And if things don't work out for Blake and me, I'll donate them to you." Tears gathered in the corners of my eyes.

Becky was silent for a moment. "What do you mean, 'if things don't work out'?"

A wave of anger and despair swelled up in me. I was aching to talk to someone, to have someone tell me everything was going to be okay, even though I knew it wasn't. I checked to make sure the kids were out of earshot. "I think Blake is hiding something from me," I whispered into the phone.

"Hiding something? You mean he's having an affair?"

"I don't know." A lump expanded in my throat, squeezing my words. "He said he didn't know Evan Maxted, but he was one of his clients. And now there's missing money."

"Oh my God. You poor thing. How much? How did you find out?"

"I snuck into his office and went through the files. He got a raise in January, but he never told me about it. When he deposits the checks, he takes a thousand dollars off the top."

Becky sucked in her breath.

"I can't believe this is happening," I said, my voice thick. "Blake always seemed so solid, so dependable. And now this . . ."

"Have you said anything to him?"

"How could I? I've hardly seen him. He's at work all the time. At least that's what he says."

"Well," she said slowly, "on the plus side, you're now a private investigator."

"I know." I took a shuddery breath. I couldn't control my husband's actions. But what I could do was find out everything I could about what was going on. Then I'd confront him with everything I'd discovered, and if he couldn't come up with a good answer . . . "I've already been to Maxted's apartment," I said. My voice was surprisingly firm.

"*You what?*"

"And I was thinking about going into Blake's office at Jones McEwan one night, to see what I can find out."

"Isn't that illegal?"

"I also want to go to Maxted's office."

"That's *definitely* illegal."

"Not if I go asking them to handle a shipment for me." The pain receded a bit as I tackled the problem, allowing my mind to sift through the possibilities. It was still there, still waiting, but no longer engulfing me. "Isn't your brother in the shipping industry?"

"Michael?"

"Yeah. Think he could give me a few tips, so that I can sound convincing?"

"You know, maybe you're taking this private investigator stuff too seriously."

"Becky, my husband lied about knowing a murder victim and is hiding money from me," I hissed. "Unless I tell the police about everything—and I don't want to do that when I don't know what's going on myself—it's up to me to figure out what's going on." I gripped the phone so hard it hurt. "And I *need* to know."

She sighed. "I guess you're right. I'll call Michael this afternoon."

"Thanks." A growl sounded from behind the laundry room door. "By the way, do you want a cat?"

"A cat?"

I eyed Rufus, who hadn't left his post by the door. "Never mind."

Becky promised to call me back as soon as she'd talked to her brother and told me to call her if I needed anything. "I'm sure it will all work out," she said.

I wasn't, but I thanked her anyway. Then I hung up the phone and pulled out the yellow pages to look up Dr. Lemmon's number. I needed to stay busy to keep my mind from diving back into the nightmare that was my marriage. Besides, I might as well get it over with.

I was about to pick up the phone and dial when it rang again.

"Hello?"

"Mrs. Peterson?"

"Speaking."

"This is Detective Bunsen. I left a message for you yesterday."

My body went cold. "Oh yes. Sorry. I haven't had a chance to call you back yet. How's the investigation going?"

"We need to schedule a time to talk, Mrs. Peterson."

I swallowed. "You mentioned that in your message. I'm afraid things are really busy right now." What with my husband being a lying snake and all. "Can we try for sometime next week?"

"Mrs. Peterson, this is a homicide case. I understand you have a busy schedule, what with all of the *investigations* I'm sure you're handling, but this isn't fun and games we're talking."

I switched hands, wiping my sweaty palm on my shorts. "Okay. Fine. I just need to set up child care for my kids. I don't want them around when we're talking about . . . you know."

"Murder?"

"Exactly. Can I call you back later this afternoon? After I've set up a babysitter?"

"You have my number?"

"It's on your card, right?"

"Uh-huh. And I'd better hear from you by five."

"Got it. Thanks."

"Talk to you later this afternoon, Mrs. Peterson."

"Yes. Great. Bye."

I hung up the phone and glanced at the clock. It was two forty-five. I had two hours and fifteen minutes before I had to call Detective Bunsen and set up a time. My hands felt icy at the thought of being stuck in an interrogation room with Detective Bunsen. Had I left any fingerprints on Maxted's wallet? Did they know about his connection with my husband? And what if Officer Carmes was there?

Maybe I should call an attorney. Unfortunately, the only ones I knew worked with my husband.

I closed my eyes. *Calm down, Margie.* Worrying about the police was only going to stress me out more. I hadn't done anything wrong—well, I hadn't murdered anyone, anyway—so what did I have to worry about? I took a few deep, cleansing breaths and opened my eyes. The open phone book lay on the counter in front of me. What had I been doing when Bunsen called? Oh, yes. Calling the psychologist so I could have my daughter's doglike tendencies examined. As my finger moved down the line of numbers, the doorbell rang.

The cops?

It couldn't be. I had just spoken with Bunsen two seconds ago. It was probably another solicitor. I jogged to the front door, ready to tell whoever was selling miracle cleaning products or overpriced magazine subscriptions that they'd picked the wrong housewife.

But when I opened the door, my mother-in-law's housekeeper stood on the doorstep.

"Graciela?"

"Miss Margie," she said. "I am so sorry to disturb you, but . . ."

"Come in, come in," I said, overly aware of the mélange of shoes, dirty socks, and Matchbox cars decorating my front hallway, not to mention two overflowing laundry baskets on the couch in the living room. Usually my house was pretty presentable, but with everything that had been going on the last couple of days, it was looking a little like the inside of a Dumpster. I pushed my hair out of my eyes and forced a smile. Other than my husband, and possibly my husband's mother, the last person I wanted to talk to right now was my mother-in-law's housekeeper.

"Are you sure?" she asked tentatively as she stepped through the front door.

"I'm sure," I said. "As long as you don't mind a bit of a mess. With two kids . . ." I laughed hollowly, resisting the urge to scoop up the cars and shove them into my pockets. "You know how it is."

She followed me into the kitchen and perched gingerly on one of the chairs, which was wise, as they still bore a patina of Elmer's glue from a recent art project. "Can I get you a drink?" I asked. "Water? Iced tea?"

"No, thank you. I'm fine."

I filled a glass with water and sat down across from her, my thighs adhering instantly to the wood chair. My eyes fell on the picture on the fridge—the picture of Blake, smiling—and my stomach clenched.

"If you want," Graciela said, "I can come help you."

"What?" My head whipped around to Graciela, who was inspecting the sticky floor. I rubbed my eyes and forced myself to focus on what she was saying.

"I said I can come help you."

"Oh, thanks," I said. "I know you're great. Prue's house always looks fabulous. But with both kids in private school, we just can't afford to have you come." Of course, if the money from Blake's raise actually made it into our bank account, that might be a different story.

She eyed a sippy cup, which lay sideways in a puddle of congealed strawberry milk. At least I'm pretty sure it was strawberry milk. "With the kids, you need help. I could make a special offer."

"No, really. Thank you, but we're doing okay." I took a sip of my water and forced a smile. "How are things with the girls? Is everything okay?"

Her brown eyes looked desperate. "I talk with Miss Becky, and she tell me you work as an investigator."

Uh-oh. "I just started a week ago," I said. I remembered my conversation with Prudence about Graciela's missing husband, and a warning bell went off in my head. I wasn't the only one with problems. "Does this have something to do with Eduardo?"

Her eyes filled as she nodded. "My Eduardo, his mother was sick, very sick, so he went back to Guadalajara last month. We set every thing up with the coyote. Eduardo was supposed to come back three weeks ago. The coyote said he would call when they got to Austin. I wait by the phone, check for messages. Nothing." She wrung the straps of her black vinyl purse. "I don't know what to do. Can you help me?"

I closed my eyes and leaned back in my chair. Less than fourteen days after starting a job as an investigator, I had taken on two adultery cases, an embezzlement case, and was investigating my own husband's lies. Now Graciela wanted me to track down *her* husband.

"Graciela," I said, "I wish I could help you. But the truth is, I just started. I know squat about looking for a missing person, much less one that's been smuggled over the border."

Her shoulders slumped in her Mickey Mouse T-shirt. "I don't know where to go," she whispered. "Without Eduardo, I can't pay for the apartment. My kids and me, we have nowhere to go. My whole family is in Mexico, and they have nothing. I have nowhere to turn."

"But Graciela . . ."

"I do anything. I clean your house, I do your laundry . . . just please, please, help me." The rawness in her voice pierced my heart.

I stared at her pinched face, her eyes swollen from crying. "Graciela," I said, "I don't know what I can do for you. I've got a lot going on right now, and I'm just figuring things out on my own. But I'll see what I can do."

Her brown eyes opened wide, which made me feel even worse. She thought she was hiring a real private investigator. She probably thought I would actually be able to locate Eduardo. The problem was, not only did I not have an "in" with any local smuggling rings, but I didn't even speak Spanish.

"Really?" she said, eyes bright.

I sighed. "Really."

She stood up and trotted to the sink, turning on the faucet and grabbing a sponge. "I clean house, I cook for you . . ."

"No, no," I said, hurrying to turn the water off. "That won't be necessary."

"But how do I pay you?"

"Consider it pro bono."

"Pro bono?"

"Free," I said.

"Thank you so much, Miss Margie. I don't know how to thank you." As I sipped my water, she opened her handbag and pulled out a sheaf of papers. "Here is all of Eduardo's information. And this is the number they gave me to call. The name of the coyote was La Serpiente."

"La Serpiente? What's that?"

"It means snake."

I winced.

"How long do you think it will take?" she asked.

I shook my head. "I'll do my best, but I have no idea. Like I said, I have a lot going on right now." Like a dead transvestite, an embezzler, and a lying husband. "And I can't guarantee I'll find him."

"Oh, thank you, Miss Margie, thank you." She trotted out the front door fifteen minutes later, a new spring in her step.

With a sick feeling in my stomach, I watched her Ford Pinto recede down Laurel Lane. Whatever I found out, chances were it wouldn't be good. For either of us.

CHAPTER FOURTEEN

I've got good news," Becky said when she called a half hour later. After Graciela had gone, I'd left a message with Dr. Lemmon's answering service, arbitrated a squabble over a fire truck, cleaned up Rufus's most recent offering outside the laundry room door, and plowed through half a bag of Dove chocolates. I still hadn't gotten around to setting an appointment with Bunsen.

"I'm glad someone does," I said. "My mother-in-law's house-keeper just swung by."

"Why?"

"Oh, it was just a casual call. All she wants is for me to find her missing husband."

"When are you going to find the time to do that?"

"It gets worse. He disappeared while being smuggled over the border."

Becky sucked in her breath. "Gosh. I hope he's okay. Doesn't she have two kids?"

"Yeah. Don't remind me. Hey, you don't speak Spanish, do you?"

"Sorry."

"Me neither. Apparently the coyote's name is the Snake."

"Oof."

"Exactly." I sighed. "Anyway, what's your news?"

"I just got off the phone with Michael. He knows the guy who runs International Shipping, and he's agreed to set up an appointment with him."

"And?"

"Duh. For a private investigator, sometimes you're not very smart. You and I are going to go along, of course."

"Whoa. I don't want to get your brother involved in this. Or you. Besides, I don't know anything about shipping."

"So what? It'll be fun. Even if we don't find anything out, it's good for you to stay busy. I told Michael you're working on a case, and he's all excited about it—he loves all those spy novels. And we won't have to know a thing about the shipping industry. He'll say we're employees in training, and that he wants us to meet some of his contacts."

"How are we going to get into Maxted's office if we're all in a meeting together?"

"Well," Becky said, "I figure we'll ask for a tour. Then, later, when we're all sitting back in some conference room, you can excuse yourself to go to the ladies' room and hightail it back to Maxted's office."

"You've got this all worked out," I said. "What if someone sees me?"

"Just tell them you're lost," she said. "Or you needed a pen, and ducked into the nearest office."

"And who's going to watch the kids?"

"Do you *not* want this to happen, or what? I'm trying to help you here."

"Sorry. I know."

"It'll be a morning meeting, doofus. When the kids are in school. You think I'm going to leave them out in the car or something?"

I smiled into the phone. "You know, you're a pretty cool Mary Kay salesperson, Becky."

"I'm dropping the order form in your mailbox this afternoon. I'm hoping for a pink Cadillac by Christmas."

"But I don't wear makeup."

"After this, I'm counting on you to start."

I glanced at the clock as I hung up the phone. It was three forty-five; I still had plenty of time to call Bunsen back. Instead, I took care of vital tasks like emptying the dishwasher and clearing my water glass from the table. I was about to scrub the glue off the chairs when Elsie trailed into the kitchen with Nick in her wake.

"Mommy, did you find my fry phone?"

I paused with the sponge in my hand. "No, sweetie, not yet. But I've been meaning to call someone about it. Let me just finish getting the glue off this chair and I'll see what I can do."

As Elsie watched, I picked up the phone and dialed Peachtree Investigations, hoping that Peaches had had a chance to talk with Mrs. Pence. The line was busy. "They're not answering, sweetie," I told Elsie. "I'll try again in a little bit."

Her eyes filled with tears. "Did someone steal it?"

"Steal it?" I knelt down and cradled her face in my hands, hoping a missing fry phone was the worst catastrophe my daughter would have to face. "No, sweetheart. Of course not. I'm sure it will turn up."

I gave her a big hug and steered her in toward Nick, who discarded the two babies Elsie had been walking around the house and filled the baby stroller with Matchbox cars and a toy fire truck instead. Fortunately, her outrage over Nick's impropriety eclipsed her concern over the fry phone. I lured them into the kitchen with the promise of drinkable yogurts and escaped to the computer, where I pulled up eBay.

Fry phone, McDonald's phone, Happy Meal toy, toy phone. Nothing. And the line at Peachtree Investigations was still busy.

I punched the "Off" button and leaned back in my chair, feeling like I was up against a brick wall. The investigation of Maxted would have to wait until tomorrow, when I could visit Miss Veronica, and I couldn't get in touch with Peaches. I should probably see what I could find out about Eduardo, but I wasn't ready to tackle a whole new problem yet.

Then I remembered the cell phone numbers from the file in Blake's office. I fumbled in the back pocket of my shorts. The list was still there. Should I call them now? I listened for sounds of discord from the kitchen. Nothing.

The first thing was to figure out how to block my phone number. That turned out to be easy; to my relief, the phone book devoted an entire section to it. All you had to do was dial *67 before the phone number.

I closed the bedroom door and took a deep breath, steeling myself for whatever it was I was about to find out. I dialed the first number and prepared to deliver my free-pizza speech.

"Thank you for calling Jiffy Lube. May I help you?"

I hung up.

Blake might be up to something, but I doubted getting the address of Jiffy Lube was going to get me any closer to finding out what.

I didn't need my pizza speech for the next four numbers, either. I inadvertently contacted a barbershop, the Dodge dealership, and two longstanding clients, who conveniently identified themselves when they picked up the phone. I hung up on all of them, feeling only a twinge of guilt when I put the phone down on Dwight Merkum. He was a nice guy I'd met at the last Christmas party. Then I dialed the fifth number.

It rang four times before a woman picked up. "Hello?"

For a moment, I couldn't think of a thing to say.

"Hello? Hello?"

I recovered my voice. "Hi. My name is Mandy, and I'm calling from Widgit's Pizza. We're doing a promotion, and you won a free pizza. I just need to know where to have it delivered."

"A free pizza? I don't eat pizza. Too many carbs."

"If you'd like," I stammered, "maybe we can substitute a salad."

"Look, Amanda. Or Amelia, I don't remember what you said your name was, but I am a *very* busy woman, and you are contacting me on my *cell phone*."

"Um . . . sorry about that. So, do you want a salad?"

"No. I most definitely do not want a salad. And please remove me from your phone list, or I will be in touch with your CEO. Good day." She hung up.

I hadn't gotten the address, but it didn't matter.

I recognized her voice.

I put down the phone, puzzled. Why had Blake called his boss's wife on her cell phone?

Then I dialed the sixth number, the one Blake had called several times between January and March. "Hi, this is Evan Maxted with International Shipping Company. Please leave a message and I'll get back to you as soon as possible." I sat motionless, listening to a long beep, before clicking "Off." His voice was so young, so vibrant. And he wouldn't be making it to the phone ever again.

My stomach twisted. My husband, who had denied even knowing Evan Maxted, had called him at least a dozen times.

I took a deep breath and closed my eyes. At least it was Evan's office phone; he could have been calling him at home. Since Evan was a client, it would be reasonable to call his office.

But then why had my husband said he didn't know him?

As I tucked the list of phone numbers into my back pocket, an unearthly sound came from the direction of the kitchen, and Elsie screamed.

I burst through the bedroom door and pounded toward the kitchen. Elsie and Nick stood frozen, watching a furry ball of beige and orange writhing around in front of the open laundry room door.

"Out!" I yelled. They didn't move. *"Out!"* I scooped the kids up and pushed them toward the hallway. "Go to your rooms and close the doors. *Now!"*

As they stumbled down the hall, I turned to face the cats, who by now had disengaged from each other and were streaking toward the living room. I grabbed a broom from the laundry room and raced after them.

"Snookums!" I yelled. "Rufus! Scat! Go away!"

Yeah, right.

I advanced slowly, holding the broom out like a sword.

I scooted them around the room for a bit, but they didn't loosen their death grips. Then I tried thrusting it between them. It worked for a moment, but then they just shifted position and re-embedded their teeth and claws. On the third thrust, Rufus disengaged for a moment and leaped to the top of the pile of laundry. Snookums followed, and the two started writhing through the clean laundry and yowling again.

Water. A good shot of water would get them apart long enough for me to separate them.

I ran to the kitchen and grabbed a pot from the drawer. As it filled in the sink, the sound of the cats' moaning and growling in the living room intensified.

"Mommy?" It was Nick.

"Go back to your room!" I barked. The last thing I needed was to have my son mauled by a renegade cat. Then Attila really would call Child Protective Services.

I yanked the pot out of the sink half-full and ran to the living room. The room looked like it had been hit by a laundry bomb. Socks, towels, and underwear were strewn around the room like shrapnel. And Rufus and Snookums were locked in a death embrace on my six-month-old Broyhill couch.

I sucked in my breath and emptied the pot over the cats.

It worked.

Rufus and Snookums streaked out of the room, each in a different direction. I chased down Rufus first, tossing him into my bedroom and locking the door. Then I grabbed a towel from the laundry explosion and began tracking down Snookums. I found him crouched in the corner of the kitchen, fur standing up on his back and teeth bared. I lunged for him, towel extended.

He flashed past me—and right into the laundry room. I slammed the door behind him and sagged against the wall.

The living room had looked better. Soggy laundry and tufts of cat fur were everywhere, and in addition to a huge wet spot and a few artful spatters of blood on the new couch cushions, yellow foam stuffing protruded where one of the cats had slashed through the upholstery fabric. The laundry could be rewashed, but I wasn't sure the couch cushions could be repaired. I released the children from their rooms and checked on Rufus. His ear was slightly tattered, but he was otherwise okay. I had just started loading a laundry basket with wet socks when the front door opened, and my husband walked in.

"Blake!" I dropped the socks. All of the emotions I had pushed down bubbled right back up. I glanced at the children and struggled to keep my voice calm. "What are you doing home?"

He blinked. "What happened to the couch?"

Before I could come up with a response, Nick supplied the answer. "The cats were fighting."

"Cats?"

"I'm watching a cat for a friend," I said, flustered. "I was keeping him in the laundry room, but the kids accidentally let him out."

"You're keeping another cat in the laundry room? For how long?"

"Oh, I don't know."

"Jesus, Margie. That's the new couch. We spent fifteen hundred dollars for it, and now look at it. First the minivan, now the couch. What are you going to do next? Burn the house down?"

I gritted my teeth, suppressing the rage that boiled up in my throat. Since at least sixteen thousand dollars was unaccounted for, I felt that complaining about a fifteen-hundred-dollar couch was a bit unreasonable.

"I'm sure it can be fixed," I said through clenched teeth. "What are you doing home? It's not even five o'clock."

"I had a client meeting right nearby. It ended early, so I figured I'd work from home tonight." He stared at the mess in the living room and shifted his briefcase to his other hand. "I'll be in my office. Let me know when dinner's ready." He bent down to give each of the kids a perfunctory kiss, then headed upstairs to his office.

I jammed the wet, fur-covered clothes into laundry baskets, hardly seeing what I was doing. Every cell in my body was aware of my husband's presence, and each one was yammering at me to lay it out on the table now.

But first I had to find out more.

I tossed the chicken onto a baking pan and put a pot of water on the stove to boil while I scrubbed at the stains on the couch, taking out some of my anger on the mutilated upholstery. The couch didn't look a whole lot better when I was done. I didn't feel any better, either. A half hour later, I sent Elsie to retrieve her daddy for dinner.

Blake stalked into the kitchen, glaring at the laundry room door before taking his seat at the table. Rufus was stationed outside, flanked by the piles of wet laundry I had rescued from the living room. I hadn't been brave enough to actually open the laundry room door and shove them in. When I offered Blake the salad bowl, he tore his eyes from the door and spooned a bit of lettuce onto his plate.

"Ick, spicy chicken," Elsie said. "Do I have to eat it?"

"Yes," I said. I deposited a chicken breast on her plate. She wrinkled her nose as if I had just served her a dead rat. I glanced at Nick, who fortunately had not picked up his sister's eating habits; he was already halfway through his dinner.

I spooned some noodles onto my plate and addressed my husband in a tone that I hoped came off as light. "How was work?"

"Fine." He popped a piece of chicken into his mouth, and his eyebrows rose. "Not bad."

What I wanted to say was, "I was rifling through your desk today, and there seems to be an accounting error . . . to the tune of two thousand dollars a month." Instead, I said, "Glad you like it. Oh, by the way, I've decided to volunteer at the Junior League fashion show."

Blake looked up from his plate. "Really? What made you change your mind?"

"Bitsy called me today and talked me into it. I suppose it's for a good cause."

His face lightened, thoughts of minivans and couches temporarily dismissed. "Absolutely. And good for my career, too."

I glanced at Elsie's plate. It was empty, as was the place mat in front of it. "Elsie!" I barked. "Your plate needs to be on the table, not the floor. You are a girl, not a dog."

"But Mommy . . ."

"On the table. *Now!*" Blake raised his eyebrows. Elsie's head jerked up from under the table. She hastily slid her plate back onto the place mat, staring at me wide-eyed. I ate a few bites of salad and turned back to Blake. "Have you talked much with Bitsy McEwan?" I asked, as if I hadn't just bitten my daughter's head off. "She seems like quite a woman."

"Not much," he said. "Only at company events, really."

The children ate in uncharacteristic silence, their eyes trained on my face. A growl sounded from the laundry room. Blake grimaced.

I swallowed a mouthful of chicken and stared at my plate. "Anyway, she's got the most terrific phone voice, don't you think?"

Blake's eyes were on the laundry room door. "Who?"

"Bitsy McEwan."

He poked at his salad and shrugged. "I don't know."

A loud slurping sound came from Elsie's end of the table. "Use your fork, Elsie."

"But Lady doesn't."

I spoke through clenched teeth. "Lady is a cartoon dog. You are a child. And you will use your fork or you will leave the table." Elsie retrieved her fork and poked at her chicken. I turned back to Blake. "You mean you've never called Bitsy?"

His head jerked up. "What? Of course not. Why would I?"

"Oh, I don't know. Maybe if you had a message for her husband, and he couldn't be reached . . ." I took a sip of water.

"Nope," he said. "But we really need to get my car cleaned. I've been driving with the windows open all week. And I want to find out how much it's going to cost to get the minivan fixed. I don't want you driving around in that thing. It looks bad. Why don't I take the minivan tomorrow, and you can take the Audi to the Finish Line?"

Normally I'd be happy to, but I wasn't feeling particularly cooperative tonight. "I don't know. I kind of have a busy schedule tomorrow."

"Busy? How so?"

"Junior League stuff." I wasn't about to tell him I was headed to Miss Veronica's Boudoir. "Plus, Attila"—I glanced at the kids—"I mean, Mrs. Bunn has some work she wants me to do for her."

"Volunteering for the school? Great. I'm glad to hear it." He took a last bite of chicken and pushed back from the table. "I'm bushed. Would you mind getting the kids down tonight? I've got to get up early again."

I pulled my lips into a thin smile and grabbed his plate from in front of him. "No problem."

He rumpled the kids' hair and headed upstairs. As I washed the baking pan, it occurred to me that he hadn't mentioned Lydia or the petition. Maybe Attila had shut her down before she spread the word about the Pence photo too far. On the other hand, he hadn't said a word about his phone call to Bitsy McEwan, either.

I took my time putting the dishes away and getting the kids down, stretching it out as long as possible to avoid having to go up to the master bedroom. I briefly considered sleeping on the couch, but I decided against it. I didn't want Blake to know that there was a problem until I had as many facts as I could find.

When I got to our bedroom an hour and a half later, Blake was already in bed, eyes closed, lights off. I brushed my teeth and changed in the bathroom, then slipped into my side of the bed, listening to the slow rhythm of his breathing. Although only three feet lay between us, it felt like we were on opposite ends of the world. I picked up a paperback thriller, but my mind kept churning up all kinds of terrible scenarios. Drugs, mistresses, gambling . . . Finally, three hours later, I gave up and turned off the light.

I was about to drift off to sleep when an explosion shook the house.

CHAPTER FIFTEEN

The kids screamed as I hurled myself out of bed and thundered down the hall. Elsie and Nick stood at their doorways, eyes wild.

"It's okay, it's okay, it's okay," I murmured, clutching their trembling bodies to my chest. "Everything's all right."

"What the hell was that?" Blake rushed up behind me.

"I don't know. I think it came from outside."

"Stay here. I'll go see."

I sat and held the kids for a few minutes until their breathing slowed to normal. "What was that noise?" Nick asked.

"I don't know, sweetie. Your daddy's going to check."

My daughter said, "Was that a gun? Because it sounded like a gun."

"How do you know what a gun sounds like?"

"Bethany's mommy watches a lot of shows with guns in them."

"I didn't know that," I said, making a mental note to scratch Bethany off the playdate list. "Can you two stay together while I go and find Daddy? Everything's okay. I just need to find out what happened."

Elsie nodded and grabbed for Nick's hand. "Stay here," I said. "I'll be right back."

"I love you, Mommy."

"I love you too, sweetie pie."

A whiff of acrid smoke wafted toward me as I crept down the hall. The front door was ajar. When I stepped through to the front porch, the front yard was bathed in orange light.

Blake's car was on fire.

As I stared at the black skeleton of his Audi, orange flames leaping from the broken windshield toward the star-flecked sky, my husband staggered up the walk. "Someone blew up my car." My eyes jerked from the burning car to my husband, his pale face illuminated by the inferno in the driveway. His normally robust trial-attorney voice was thin and strained. "Why would someone do that?"

I eyed him coolly. "I don't know," I said. "Do you?"

His eyes darted to mine. Then he shook his head and turned away.

"I'll call 911," I said. One of the neighbors was already approaching the house. I glanced at Blake's boxer shorts and T-shirt, and realized I was wearing nothing but a short nightshirt decorated with lobsters. "I'm going in to get changed. You'd better get a bathrobe."

He nodded dumbly and followed me into the house.

• • •

"It's too early to tell, but it looks like a Molotov cocktail."

The firefighters had drenched the inferno and finally put out the flames. Now Blake's car was a smoking, black skeletal thing in the driveway. Fortunately, although it had blackened the left side of the minivan, the explosion hadn't destroyed both cars.

"What's a Molotov cocktail?" I asked the young police officer. Laurel Lane was lined with emergency vehicles, and Blake, who had positioned himself at the curb, was back in attorney mode, explaining to curious neighbors that the reason his car had exploded in the middle of the night was probably "a short in the engine."

The officer glanced back at the smoking wreck in the driveway. "It's pretty primitive. They fill a bottle with gasoline, stuff a rag in it, then light it and toss it. But it can still do a lot of damage. Do you have any idea who might have done this?"

I shook my head. "None."

He hitched up his belt. "We'll be out of here in a little while, but the investigators will be back to examine things more thoroughly in the morning. But in the meantime . . ." He pulled a card out of his pocket and handed it to me. "If you think of anything, or have any questions, call me."

"Thank you," I said. "Can I go in to check on my kids now?"

"Your husband seems to have things under control, ma'am." He gestured toward Blake, who held a gaggle of bathrobe-clad neighbors in thrall at the curb. "If we need any more information, we'll ask him."

"Thanks."

As I turned toward the house, he called after me. "And ma'am?"

"Yes?"

"If I were you, I'd watch my step until we find out who did this to you."

"Thanks," I said. "I will."

My stomach clenched as I closed the front door behind me and climbed the stairs to the kids' bedrooms. The smell of burning plastic permeated the air, even inside the house.

Someone had blown up my husband's car.

Would they attack the house next?

I shivered and tried to think positive thoughts. On the plus side, at least I wouldn't have to worry about getting vomit stains out of the backseat.

• • •

The investigators hadn't arrived yet when I pulled the minivan out of the driveway the next morning, my eyes glued to the blackened hulk that used to be an Audi coupe. Blake sat beside me, staring at his car with mournful eyes. I was driving him to the car rental agency, then taking the kids to school.

"I hope that insurance money comes through soon. I don't want to be stuck driving a Chevy Cavalier for the next month." He shook his head. "So, which one of your clients' friends did this?"

"It wasn't *my* car that got blown up."

"Yeah, but nothing like this ever happened until you started working for Plum."

"Peaches."

"Peaches. Right. I still can't believe someone blew up the car. Jesus. What's next? Carpet-bombing the neighborhood?"

The thought chilled me, too. But something told me the explosion had more to do with Blake's activities than mine. I glanced at my husband. "The police said they thought it was a Molotov cocktail. Did they come up with any new theories after I went up to bed?"

He shook his head. "Nope. No idea. They'll know more today. I just hope it doesn't make the papers. I told all the neighbors it was just a fluke."

"Well, when the investigators come out today, the neighbors may start to wonder."

"I told everyone they were sending an investigator out as a routine precaution." He glanced at me. "Why are you all dressed up?"

"Oh, just trying to take better care of myself," I said, smoothing down the skirt I had salvaged from the depths of my closet. Actually, I was planning a visit to Miss Veronica's Boudoir later in the day, and after Cassandra's comment about my appearance at the Rainbow Room yesterday, there was no way I was going into a drag queen school without at least a little feminine armor. So while the kids were waking up, I had dug through the closet until I found a blouse and a skirt that weren't too tight and put on a bit of mascara and lipstick.

"Why?" Blake asked. "Are you meeting with Bitsy McEwan today?"

"No," I answered. Why was he suddenly so curious? "Just felt like dressing up. Polishing my image a bit."

"Good." He nodded approvingly.

I gritted my teeth as I turned into the Hertz parking lot.

A half hour later I cruised through the drop-off lane of Green Meadows Day School. As we waited in line behind a dozen Lexus and Mercedes SUVs, I turned around to address Elsie. "I talked with Mrs. Bunn yesterday, and you shouldn't have any more trouble with Cherie. But if you do, tell me about it."

She sucked on her lower lip. "Okay." Then she asked, "Mommy, what happened to Daddy's car?"

We'd been over this last night, but I smiled at her reassuringly. "There was a fire. It was an accident. But you don't need to worry about it. The car is replaceable, and the most important thing is that everyone's okay."

"Is your car going to catch on fire and go boom?"

"No, sweetheart." I patted her chubby leg. At least I hoped not. "But don't worry about the cars. Mommy and Daddy will take care of that."

"Okay."

"And today? If someone does say something mean? Just tell them they're not being a very good friend and find someone else to play with. Got it?"

She nodded solemnly. A few minutes later, the kids disappeared behind the wood picket fence enclosing Green Meadows Day School, and I was on my way to Miss Veronica's Boudoir.

• • •

Since Miss Veronica's didn't open until ten, I grabbed my knitting bag and headed to Starbucks for one of my guilty indulgences—a tall nonfat vanilla latte. With everything that had happened since Tuesday, I felt I deserved it. Images of Blake's blackened car and the bank statements I had found in his office kept popping into my mind, so knitting didn't create the relaxed feeling it usually did; but it still felt good to do something constructive, even if I kept adding extra stitches. I ran my hand over the rows I had finished and told myself the lumps gave it extra character.

At five minutes past ten, I parked behind the Hot Chicken, fully caffeinated and with another fifteen rows of my niece's rainbow scarf complete. I refreshed my lipstick in the rearview mirror and practiced a smile. Then I marched across the parking lot and walked into Miss Veronica's Boudoir.

The inside was much like the outside, with an ancient pine floor, lace curtains, and hundred-year-old furniture. The room looked like an antique store, except for the merchandise displayed in the glass-fronted hutches. Wigs, thongs, bras, and false eyelashes were featured prominently, and when I peered through the warped glass of a huge breakfront, I was confronted by a line of dildos in an astonishing variety of shapes and colors. As I bent forward for a closer look at one called the Venus Vibrato, a throat cleared behind me.

I whirled around to face a young man in black slacks and a thin cashmere V-neck sweater. It was the one I'd seen yesterday. "May I help you?" he asked.

Heat crept up my neck to my cheeks as I sidled away from the dildo display. "Yes, actually. I mean, I hope so."

"Do you need help with one of those?" He gestured toward the case.

I jumped away from it. "Oh no."

"If you're here for the wives' group, it's moved to Tuesdays at noon."

"Wives' group?"

He blinked at me from behind wire-rimmed frames. "Yes. The support group for spouses."

"What spouses?"

"Spouses who are letting their husbands explore their feminine side."

And I'd always thought transvestites were gay. "Um, no. No, I'm not here for the group. Is Miss Veronica here?"

"She's in her office. Do you have an appointment?"

"No."

"May I tell her your name?"

"Margie. Margie Peterson."

He backed into a cabinet, knocking over a display of breast forms.

"Are you okay?"

"Oh, I'm fine," he said, fumbling to fit the artificial breasts back onto their stands. He replaced the last one, turning it so that the nipple faced straight ahead, like a soldier at attention, and closed the cabinet. "I'm just clumsy this morning. Not enough coffee. I'll tell Miss Veronica you're here."

"Thank you."

I settled myself on a pink velvet divan while he disappeared down a hallway. "Miss Veronica's Boudoir and Finishing School . . . For the Fabulous Woman Inside!" read the hand-painted wooden sign above the front desk. I was pondering the breast forms, which looked like oversized truffles, when voices approached from down the hall.

"Can you do Brandy on Friday afternoon? It's her first night out, and she's really nervous about it. You might want to do her wife, too. Give her a little boost."

"Sure thing, Miss V."

"Trevor, why don't you call her and set it up?"

"Of course, Miss Veronica." The young man who had greeted me emerged from the doorway and slipped behind the desk.

Then the Elizabeth Taylor look-alike I had seen from the parking lot appeared in the doorway. Yesterday's chiffon dress had been replaced by tight white pants and a silky blue blouse that set off her vivid eyes and plunged down to reveal a sizable amount of cleavage. Above the cleavage, her full lips were painted into a sultry pout. My eyes drifted back down to what her clingy blouse barely concealed. Her clients must be rabid with jealousy.

Then her companion stepped through the doorway, and I forgot all about Elizabeth Taylor.

It was the transvestite from the Como Motel.

Mr. Legs was still looking good. He had replaced the raspberry miniskirt with a clingy vinyl dress, but his legs were still a mile long, stockinged, and hairless. His blue-gray eyes widened with recognition when he spotted me.

"Aren't you the lady from the Como?" He turned to the woman in blue. "This lady's old man got a thing for cling wrap. And he needs a *lot* of it, if you know what I mean." Mr. Legs turned to me. "How'd that go, anyway? He into thongs now, too?"

The woman placed a manicured hand on Mr. Legs's arm. "Please, Topaz, let's not embarrass the poor thing." She walked over to me, extending a slender hand with pearl-painted nails. "I'm Miss Veronica." She nodded at the sign above Trevor's desk. "The proprietor of this establishment, as you may have guessed. And this is Miss Topaz, our dean of cosmetology. I see you've met before."

"Well, we haven't been formally introduced, but yes." I turned to face Miss Topaz. "What were *you* doing at the Como?"

"Oh, I used to hang down there all the time. You know, before I came here? Now I just go visit sometimes."

"Yes," said Miss Veronica, "before she became a dean here, Miss Topaz used to live a very different life. But then we discovered her talents, and she's been a fixture here ever since. She's a wonder with a mascara wand, don't you think?"

I ran my eyes over Miss Topaz's long lashes and satin skin, and I had to agree.

"If you'd like a makeover," said Miss Veronica, "I'd be happy to arrange it."

"Actually, no. That's not what I'm here for."

Miss Veronica settled herself on the divan next to me. "Then what can I help you with?" She took my hands in hers and gazed into my eyes. I found myself mesmerized. "Is your husband interested in exploring his feminine side?" she said gently.

I jerked my hands back. "No, no. This isn't about my husband."

Miss Topaz hmmphed from the doorway. "If I saw my husband doing that . . ."

"You're married?" I asked.

"Oh yes," she said. "Been married to the man of my dreams for almost ten years now, and he still brings me flowers on our anniversary. Have a nice place off South Congress. Picket fence and everything." Miss Topaz grinned. "We're thinkin' of adopting in the next year or two."

"That's terrific," I said, feeling a twinge of jealousy at her obvious happiness. Roses and picket fences? That was how it was supposed to be for me, too. Where had I gone wrong?

Maybe I needed to get lessons on more than cosmetics from Miss Topaz, I reflected.

"Well then, what can I do for you?" Miss Veronica asked, bringing me back to the issue at hand. Which did involve my husband, but not in a roses-and-picket-fences kind of way.

I swallowed hard. "I came by because Cassandra Starr told me you knew Evan Maxted."

"Oh. You mean Selena," said Miss Topaz from the doorway. Trevor continued to shuffle papers.

Miss Veronica's violet eyes clouded. "I heard about what happened to her at the Rainbow Room. Just terrible."

"I was wondering if you had any idea who might have killed her."

"Maybe that nasty ol' Marcus," said Miss Topaz.

My head swiveled toward the doorway. "Cassandra mentioned Marcus. Did they have a falling-out?"

"She broke up with him a month or so ago," said Miss Topaz, picking a piece of lint off her vinyl dress. "The man's got the nicest ass you ever seen, but he's mean as a snake. Marcus was always smackin' her around."

"How did you know Selena?" asked Miss Veronica.

"I was the one who found her," I said.

Miss Veronica raised a hand to her glossy red lips. "Oh, how awful for you. But aren't the police handling it?"

"Do you know someone named Blake Peterson?" I blurted.

Trevor dropped something behind the desk and reached for it with a curse. A furrow appeared in Miss Veronica's ivory brow as she considered the question. "Peterson? Isn't that your name?"

I blushed. "Just a coincidence."

Miss Veronica nodded in a way that made me think she wasn't buying it. Then she turned to her employees. "Ring any bells for you, Trevor? Miss Topaz?"

"No, ma'am," said Trevor, who had recovered the wayward file.

"Never heard of the guy," said Miss Topaz.

Miss Veronica turned back to me. "What does Blake Peterson have to do with Selena?"

"I don't know," I said. "Maybe nothing. At any rate, the reason I'm involved with the case is that I'm a private investigator."

"Private investigator?" Miss Topaz pushed herself away from the doorway. "So Mr. Cling Wrap *wasn't* your husband . . ."

I blushed again. "No, he wasn't."

"Well, that's a relief. For you, anyway. Who you workin' for?"

"I can't tell you that." No need to share the fact that I was the client. "Client confidentiality . . . I'm sure you understand." Particularly since Miss Veronica worked for a company that specialized in helping men realize their cross-dressing fantasies. "Anyway, other than Marcus, is there anyone else who might have wanted to hurt Ev . . . I mean, Selena?"

"Wasn't Selena the one havin' trouble tellin' her family?" said Miss Topaz. "Did she ever get around to it?"

"I don't know," said Miss Veronica. "But that's a problem for several of our clients. Wives, in particular, seem to have difficulty with the idea that their men like to be ladies from time to time."

Gee, I couldn't think why. "Trevor said something about a wives' group," I said. "Is it common for . . . er . . . transvestites . . . to be married?"

There was pity in her eyes. "Honey, sixty percent of the men who come visit us have families. The spousal support group is one of our more popular programs. That and the transformation class."

"Transformation class?"

"Oh yes. It's a weekend workshop. That's when our deans turn the ugly ducklings into swans. We've got a dean of cosmetology, whom you've met . . . a dean of seduction, a dean of high heels, a ballet mistress . . . even a dean of femmenergy."

I blinked. How come I didn't have these resources available when I was an adolescent girl? Miss Veronica continued. "The new ladies join the sorority. Most of the ladies who have come through here stick together, and the community in Austin's a pretty close-knit group. And the deans get to play fairy godmother and wave their magic wands." I glanced around at the array of feminine accoutrements and wondered what the final products looked like.

"Yeah, I been tryin' to get Cassandra in my chair, but she won't budge. That girl got an eyelash problem. Looks like she's growin' mustaches on her eyelids."

I shifted the conversation from the topic of Cassandra's eyelashes. "So, Selena was having trouble with her family?"

"She was thinkin' of talkin' to 'em, but I don't think she had a chance."

Since she died in a ball gown, I was guessing the cat was out of the bag now. "So other than Marcus, you can't think of anyone who might have wanted to hurt Selena."

"Nope," said Miss Topaz. Miss Veronica shook her head sadly.

"Do you know where I can find Marcus?"

"He lives down off South Congress. Trevor, can you get the lady Marcus's address?"

Miss Topaz narrowed her blue-gray eyes at me. "You got a gun?"

I shook my head.

"Well, if you're goin' to see Marcus, it might be a good idea to get one."

CHAPTER SIXTEEN

A s I climbed into the minivan, my cell phone bleeped.
"Hello?"

"Margie?" It was Becky. "I'm sorry for the short notice . . . Can you be at International Shipping in thirty minutes? Michael's contact is going out of town for a month tomorrow, so he moved up the meeting."

"But I haven't had a chance to find anything out about the shipping industry!"

"You don't need to. You're a new employee, remember?"

"Yeah, brand-new. Okay. Where is it again?"

"On Sixth Street. That big silver building. What's it called?"

"The Frost Tower?"

"That's the one. By the way, your name is Priscilla Anderson."

"Priscilla?"

"I had to come up with something fast. Anyway, I've got to run and get dressed. See you at eleven."

Becky hung up the phone before I had a chance to tell her about Blake's car or my trip to Miss Veronica's Boudoir. I put the Caravan in gear and headed toward downtown. Thank goodness I had spiffed myself up this morning.

I arrived at the Frost Tower with fifteen minutes to spare. It was a glass monolith not far from Maxted's apartment, and as the parking garage attendant handed me a ticket, I wondered if Maxted had walked to work. It would certainly be more cost-efficient than paying the three-hundred-dollar monthly rate advertised at the entrance.

I took the elevator to the lobby and parked myself on a leather couch while I waited for Becky and Michael to show up. A stream of men and women in tailored suits flowed by. Although Austin was known for "business casual," evidently the workers in this building didn't subscribe to the city's laid-back approach to life, or at least not to the slacker wardrobe.

"Margie!" Becky and Michael appeared near the giant glass front door. Becky looked like anything but a mother of two small children in a perfectly cut blue suit that curved in and out in all the right places. Her brother, Michael, looked as good as she did in a double-breasted charcoal Brooks Brothers suit. Although I had felt nattily dressed an hour ago, as Becky approached with her brother, I found myself wishing I had thrown a jacket on over my blouse.

"I thought you said my name was Priscilla," I said.

"Sorry, sorry."

"Hi, *Priscilla*." Michael thrust out a hand and engulfed my own. "You look great."

I felt myself blush. "Thanks. So do you. And thanks for doing this."

"No problem." He squeezed my hand before releasing it, and a little tingle traveled up my arm. Michael had always been tall and stocky, and although he was a little thicker around the middle than he had been, he was as appealing as he had been twenty years ago when Becky and I were in high school. I'd had a terrible crush on him. Evidently I still wasn't completely over it.

For God's sake, Margie, you're a married woman, I reminded myself. *Think of Blake.* Then I remembered the missing money and the dead transvestite and decided to focus on my kids instead.

Michael directed another high-wattage smile toward me. "Ready?"

I swallowed hard. "Anything I need to know?"

"Nope. I've told them you're training to be a client contact, and that you're new to the industry. I'll do all the talking. If they ask you any questions, just tell them you started last week."

"Okay. I can do that."

As the elevator door closed behind us, I studied my distorted reflection in the shiny brass doors and whispered to Becky, "Do I look okay?"

She squeezed my arm. "You look great. At least my brother thinks so."

I was about to poke her, when the elevator doors opened, and we were there.

Becky and I hung back while Michael talked with the receptionist. The lobby of International Shipping was heavy on the mahogany and granite. The company's name was emblazoned in silver on the wall above the front desk.

"Somebody blew up Blake's car last night."

Becky's face paled. "Oh my God. You're kidding me. Is everyone okay?"

"Yeah. The investigators should be out at the house right now. It was a Molotov cocktail, they think."

"Do you think it has something to do with the missing money?" she whispered.

Now that the kids were at risk, I kept thinking I should tell everything to the police. But something held me back. I still didn't know how Blake was involved with Maxted—and I was afraid that my husband might be wrongly tied to the transvestite's death. A wave of anger and pain threatened to engulf me. I pushed it back. "Right now, I don't know what to think."

"God. I can't believe it. Blake's car." Her mouth twitched up into a sly smile. "I bet he was pissed. He was mad enough about Nick throwing up in it."

Despite the knot of despair in my stomach, I giggled. Then I told her about my trip to visit Miss Veronica.

"So he's got a violent ex-boyfriend?" she said. "Maybe that's what happened. Evan broke up with Marcus, and he snapped."

"Could be," I said. "I'm planning to swing by and talk with him later."

She fished through her purse and pulled out a small blue canister. "If you do, take this."

I picked it up and gave the trigger an experimental push. "What is it? Hair spray?"

Becky's hands flew out. "No! Don't spray it! It's pepper spray!"

I hastily released the trigger. "Oops. Sorry."

"Just keep it handy, okay? And don't let the kids get their hands on it."

"Got it. Thanks."

As I tucked the pepper spray into my purse, I remembered that there was something else I wanted to ask. "By the way, can you help me with some accounting stuff?" I murmured.

"Accounting stuff? Does this have something to do with Blake?"

"No, not this. But if I tell you, you have to promise me you won't say a word to anyone."

"Cross my heart and hope to die."

"Okay. Attila wants me to find out if someone's embezzling money from Green Meadows."

"Embezzling?" Becky's voice rang out clear as a bell. The receptionist looked up from the phone. Michael's eyebrows rose as he turned to look at his sister.

"Shhh! No need to announce it to the world!" When Michael had engaged the receptionist in a conversation, I continued. "I'm supposed to go in and look through the files this weekend, but I have no idea what I'm looking for. I need someone who knows something about accounting, so I thought of you."

Becky hesitated. "I've done accounting, but never auditing."

"Well, you're ten steps ahead of me, then."

"I don't know . . ."

"Becky, please help me. Just tell me what to look for. Attila's promised to call Lydia off my daughter if I help her. And maybe I won't have to go see that stupid child psychologist."

"I can't believe someone's embezzling from the school. It's no wonder the tuition is so outrageous!"

"Will you help me?"

Becky smiled. "I can't promise you I'll track it down, but yes, I'll help you."

"I'll hire a babysitter, then."

"No need. Rick is already planning on keeping the kids while we go to the Junior League thing. He'll just have them longer."

"The Junior League fashion show? That's *this* Saturday? I thought it was next week! I don't have anything to wear!" My voice rose as I spoke, and the receptionist glared at us.

Becky patted my arm and shot a reassuring smile to the receptionist. "We'll find something."

"And then I've got a memorial service to attend on Sunday . . ."

"Who died?"

"Maxted," I whispered. "I saw the notice in the paper this morning. Figured I'd go and see who turns up."

"After the meeting today, won't his coworkers recognize you?"

I hadn't thought of that. "Crap. You're right."

"Don't worry. We'll think of something."

"Ready, ladies?" We looked up. A large bald man in a too-tight suit stood beside Becky's brother. We stood up and joined them at the reception desk.

"This is Calvin Pitts, the CEO of International Shipping," Michael said as I held my hand out. Calvin's palm was sweaty, and he smelled strongly of Brut cologne. "Calvin, this is Priscilla Anderson and Becky Hale."

"Nice to meet you," I murmured, withdrawing my hand and pressing it against my skirt to surreptitiously wipe off the sweat.

"Mike here says you're two bright girls." His small eyes roamed up and down Becky's curvy figure, and I resisted the urge to knee him in the balls.

"Shall we give them a tour?" Michael said brightly.

"Well, there's not that much to see—these are just the corporate offices—but it can't hurt to get to know a few of the people you'll be working with, can it?"

We followed Calvin down a thickly carpeted hall, meeting and greeting the corporate cream of ISC. Calvin walked behind Becky, ogling her derriere, and placed his hand on her lower back every time he introduced her to someone new.

I paused at an empty corner office. Although the nameplate on the door was blank, files lay strewn across the desk inside. "Whose office is this?" I asked, interrupting a monologue about the risks of dealing with Brazilian trucking companies.

Calvin tore his eyes from Becky. "Oh, that office belonged to our former CFO." His face sagged slightly. "He passed away this week, I'm afraid. We haven't found a replacement yet."

"I'm so sorry."

Calvin shrugged, and a shadow crossed his features. Then his eyes found Becky, and he perked up again. Soon we were back on Brazilian companies and following him into a small conference room, where we sat in front of burnt coffee in tiny Styrofoam cups.

He had just launched into a description of freight containers when I decided to make my move.

"Would you please excuse me for a few minutes?"

Calvin nodded at me and turned back to Becky, who appeared to be hanging on his every word. Her eyes flashed to me. Then Michael asked something about Pacific transport, and I was out the door.

I shouldered my purse and hurried down the hallway, resisting the urge to break into a sprint. I was three doors from Maxted's office when a woman in a plum-colored suit appeared from one of the offices. I remembered meeting her. She was one of the few women who worked at ISC, and she had an arched nose that reminded me of some kind of predatory bird. But I couldn't remember her name.

"Can I help you?" she asked.

"Oh. I was just looking for the ladies' room."

"Then you're going the wrong way." She pointed her beak toward the conference room. "It's down there."

"Thanks," I said. She watched as I backtracked almost the whole way to the conference room. I turned to smile at her and stepped into the ladies' room.

After thirty seconds, I poked my head out again. The plum-colored suit was gone. I eased the door shut behind me and trotted down the hall, staying close to the far side of the hall and picking up speed as I passed the door she had emerged from a minute earlier.

I finally got to Maxted's office. As my hand reached for the door-knob, voices sounded from the woman's office. I slid into the corner office and closed the door with a soft click behind me.

My stomach tightened as I surveyed the files strewn across every surface of the large office. I only had a few minutes. What was I supposed to be looking for?

I slid behind the desk and flipped through the nearest stack of files. Invoices from E. M. Hernandez Trucking Company. Each file was stuffed with papers marked *Bill of Lading*. A couple had red stars on the top-right corner, but I had no idea why.

I tried a few more stacks, but they contained equally incomprehensible financial records. Incomprehensible to me, anyway. I should have sent Becky instead.

I gave up on the files and swiveled around to the computer, shivering as I touched a key. Had Evan Maxted's been the last fingers on this keyboard?

To my surprise, the computer hummed and came to life. A thrill of excitement rippled through me.

Then it died.

The screen that appeared required a password.

I pushed away from the desk in frustration. I had already used up at least half of my time, and I still had no idea what I was looking for.

I scanned the room, looking for something—anything—that would help me. The police had probably been all over the room; I was just hoping they had left something for me to find. I swung around to try the computer again, when my shoe caught on something that had fallen between the desk and the filing cabinet. I reached down and pulled out a small black leather book. As I flipped it open, the door opened.

I whirled around and dropped the book into my purse.

It was the woman in the plum-colored suit.

"What are you doing in here?" Her eyes hardened as my brain fumbled to come up with a response.

"Checking my e-mail!" I spouted. "I noticed this office was empty, so I figured I'd just slip in and see if I could get into my account."

"I thought you had to go to the restroom."

"I did. Just checked my lipstick. Then I decided to check my e-mail."

Her eyes narrowed. "On someone else's computer?"

"Oh, I have one of those things where I can pick it up anywhere. You know. I think it's Yahoo, or something." Brilliant, Margie. "Anyway, I didn't realize the computers had passwords." I grabbed my purse and stood up. "Sorry about that. I'll just get it back at the office."

The woman's eyes were hot on my back as I hurried down the hall and slipped into the conference room.

Calvin looked up from Becky's cleavage. "What happened to you? We were about to send out a search party!"

"Oh, I just got turned around," I said. "Did I miss anything?"

"I'll fill you in later," Michael said. "We were just about to wrap up, anyway." He turned to Calvin. "Thank you for your time, Calvin."

"My pleasure," he said, watching Becky as she got up from her chair. "Any time you want to stop by, just let me know. Maybe we could meet for lunch, and I could fill you in on the business."

Becky smiled. "Thank you, Mr. Pitts. That's so kind of you to offer."

I huddled behind Becky and Michael as we walked back to the lobby, scanning the hallway for the beaky woman in the plum-colored suit. Fortunately, she was occupied elsewhere.

"What happened to you?" Becky asked when the elevator door slid shut behind us. "I thought I was going to have to do a striptease to keep Pitts distracted."

"And I was afraid I was going to have to destroy a good client relationship to defend my sister's honor," Michael said.

"And he's married," Becky said. "He's even wearing the ring. Can you believe it? If my husband did that . . ." She looked at me and colored.

I flushed in response and muttered, "Thanks for covering me. Sorry it took so long."

Becky recovered. "So? What did you find out?"

"Not much, I'm afraid. There were tons of files, but I just glanced through them, and I couldn't make heads or tails of them. And his computer needed a password."

Becky's face dimmed. "Did you get anything?"

"I did get his appointment book. At least I think I did."

She perked up again. "Well, that's good. What's in it?"

"I haven't looked yet. I don't even know if that's what it is. Someone walked in on me, so I shoved it in my purse."

"Oh my God. How did you get out of that one?"

"I said I was checking my e-mail."

"And she believed you?"

Michael laughed. "Quick thinking."

"Thank you so much for doing this, both of you," I said. "I just hope it was worth all the trouble."

"Trouble? I had a great time," Michael said. "Calvin Pitts is such a sleazeball, I have no qualms about taking up his time. Besides, it was fun feeling like a special operative. Kind of like James Bond." He struck a pose as the elevator door opened. "Do I look the part?"

Becky rolled her eyes. "See what I had to put up with growing up?"

I laughed. "It could be worse. Anyway, thanks, guys." We walked into the lobby together. "Becky, call me when you're ready to go tomorrow, okay?"

"Will do." She gave me a hug, and Michael clasped my hand again. More tingles. I headed toward the parking garage, trying to slow my heart rate, as Michael and his sister crossed the lobby to the front door.

Once I was safely in the minivan, I pulled the little black book out of my purse and opened it. I was right; it was his appointment calendar. I leafed through the last month of Maxted's life. The days were riddled with notations and names, and my heart plummeted. How would I track all of these people down?

I decided to focus on the last week of his life. The day after he died, he had an appointment at the offices of the *Austin American-Statesman*. It was an appointment he had never shown up for, I thought with a sick feeling. The rest of the meetings were all associated with companies; there was only one address. At the bottom of Tuesday, September 15, an address was scrawled across the blocks for seven o'clock to eight thirty: 1516 East Seventh Street.

Still, it didn't say whom he was meeting, or even the company name. In fact, I wasn't even sure it was an appointment. Unlike the other entries, which were carefully hand printed, this one was a quick slanted scrawl. Was he meeting someone there? And if so, who was it?

As I flipped back a few pages, I noticed a tab marked *Addresses*. A lump formed in my throat as I turned until I found the page labeled *P*.

The first entry was my husband's name.

I closed my eyes, feeling sick, and forced myself to look again. No address was listed, but there was a phone number. His office phone number. Which would be normal, I reasoned, if Maxted had been a client. I checked the other side of the page for entries—cell phone, home phone. Nothing.

Then how had Maxted known our home phone number?

I remembered my conversation with Miss Topaz earlier in the day and flipped through to the section labeled *L*. Marcus Lassiter. There were three phone numbers and an address.

I glanced at my watch. I still had an hour and a half before it was time to pick up the kids.

Just enough time to pay Maxted's ex-boyfriend a visit.

CHAPTER SEVENTEEN

Marcus Lassiter lived only a few miles south of downtown. As I pointed the minivan south, my thoughts turned to Blake, and the missing money. Sixteen thousand dollars. Where had it gone?

As the minivan passed the Bartleby Bank building, my eyes counted up the glass windows to my husband's office. The building was open twenty-four hours a day. I was sure it was in an attempt to wring as many billable hours as possible from the overworked attorneys of Jones McEwan.

I remembered Peaches's question: *How much access do you have?* Well, I had access to Blake's keys, which also meant I had access to his office. I was wondering whether to plan a nighttime foray into Jones McEwan, when my cell phone burbled again. I glanced at the display but didn't recognize the number. I hit "Talk."

"Hello?"

"Mrs. Peterson?"

Adrenaline shot through me. It was Bunsen.

"Hello?" I said, louder.

"This is Mrs. Peterson? You never did return that phone call yesterday."

"Hello?" I yelled. "Is someone there?" I whacked the phone against the steering wheel a couple of times and put it to my ear again. "I'm sorry. You're breaking up." I hit "End" and tossed the phone onto the car's front seat.

A moment later, it rang again.

I ignored it and focused on the road, wondering what the penalty was for avoiding a police interview. A slap on the wrist? A few days in a holding cell? Or serious jail time?

After what felt like ten minutes, the phone finally stopped ringing, and I pushed thoughts of Bunsen and state penitentiaries from my mind. I was deep in SoCo, a hip part of town that specialized in lava lamps, saggy couches on peeling front porches, a few "new vintage" homes, and a growing number of ultramodern concrete monstrosities that the Style page of the *Austin American-Statesman* loved to feature.

I turned my eyes from a new block of upscale apartments that was under construction and peered at street signs, concentrating on finding Annie Street among the gaggle of streets that 1920s developers had named after their daughters.

The green rectangular sign was buried in an ancient magnolia tree. I was halfway past it when I spotted it, and the station wagon behind me almost plowed into my back bumper as I slammed on the brakes and veered right. Once on Annie, I consulted the address on the scrap of paper Trevor had handed me. I drove a few blocks, scanning the mix of decrepit and recently expanded wooden houses for numbers, but it turned out the house wasn't too hard to spot. Three police cruisers were parked in front of it.

As the minivan crept by, two women in blue stepped out from the yellow front door, flanking a tall, muscular man. Marcus Lassiter, I guessed. Despite his violent reputation, I could see why Maxted found him appealing; he looked like something out of a Calvin Klein underwear ad. As the trio approached the street, I hunched down in the driver's seat; I didn't think either of the cops was Carmes, but I wasn't sure. Just before they got to the mailbox, the man turned back toward the house for a second, and something metallic flashed in the sun.

Handcuffs.

As I stared at Lassiter, my foot left the gas pedal and the minivan slowed to a crawl. The cop on the right fixed me with a hard stare. I hunched down farther and accelerated, hoping that the cop hadn't seen enough of me to pick me out in a lineup. On the plus side, now that they'd arrested Marcus Lassiter, my odds of ever being in a lineup had just dropped dramatically.

I turned at the end of the street and steered the minivan back to South Congress. Despite the relief of not having to ask a violent man whether he was involved in his ex-lover's death—and, by the way, did he know my husband?—something akin to disappointment washed through me. The cops had figured things out before I had. In fact, that was probably why Bunsen had called—to tell me they'd arrested someone. I should be happy, right? I was no longer a suspect.

But Lassiter's arrest didn't mean all of my problems were solved.

Someone had blown up my husband's car last night. My husband had lied about knowing a murdered transvestite. And sixteen thousand dollars was still missing from our joint bank account.

I glanced at my watch. I still had forty-five minutes before it was time to pick up the kids. Enough time to swing by Peachtree Investigations and see if Peaches had any advice on tracking down car bombers. I should probably also call Bunsen back; since the cops had already arrested someone, it would be a good time to get in touch.

I scrolled through to "Missed Calls" and hit "Talk."

"Detective Bunsen here."

"Hi. This is Margie Peterson. Did you try to call me a few minutes ago?"

"When we had the 'bad connection'?"

"Um, yeah. I need a new phone; it does that all the time, lately. Anyway, sorry I didn't get a chance to call you back last night."

"We need to schedule a time for you to come in and talk, Mrs. Peterson."

I blinked. "But I thought you arrested someone!"

"Excuse me?"

"I just drove by Marc . . ." I trailed off.

"You just drove by what?"

"McDonald's," I stammered. "And I heard on the radio that someone had been arrested. For a homicide."

"Well, I don't know what station you listen to, but we've made no homicide arrests today."

I swallowed.

"But if you're talking about Marcus Lassiter, yes, he was arrested just a few minutes ago on drug charges."

"Who?" I croaked.

"Mrs. Peterson, for someone who never met Evan Maxted before, you seem to know an awful lot about him. And he seemed to know you, too. Unless he accidentally dialed the wrong number the night he died."

My throat closed up. I had erased my number from his phone! Then it hit me. *Cell phone records.* Duh. The same way I had tracked Blake's calls. I forced myself to focus. Bunsen was still talking.

"Mrs. Peterson, I expect you in my office at eight o'clock Monday morning. If you don't show up, I will issue a warrant for your arrest."

"A warrant?" *Oh God.* My palms went slick. He thought I had murdered Evan Maxted. "A warrant for what?" I finally managed to croak.

"Obstructing justice." My body went limp. *Still safe.* For now, anyway. "Now," Bunsen continued, "can I count on you showing up?"

"Yes. I mean, of course." I reviewed my schedule mentally. Eight was too early. I'd have to ask Blake to take the kids into school for me. But what would I tell him I was doing? Going to talk to the cops about the dead transvestite he had denied knowing? "Actually," I said, "could we make it eight forty-five? I have to drop my kids off first . . ."

He sighed. "Fine. But if your ass is not in my office by eight forty-six, I'm sending someone to get you."

"Got it," I said. He hadn't mentioned the explosion in my driveway the night before. How seriously were the police taking it? I wondered. "By the way," I said, "someone blew up my husband's car last night."

He was silent for a moment. "Blew it up?"

"Yeah. They think it was a Molotov cocktail."

"Well, thank goodness there was a private investigator in the house. Got the case solved yet?"

"No. I was hoping you guys could do that."

He sighed. "What's your husband's name?"

I paused for a moment, considering telling him about the money, about my worries about my husband . . . everything. But loyalty held me back. "Peterson. Blake Peterson."

"I'll look into it."

"Thanks. See you Monday."

"Remember. Eight forty-five or else."

"Got it."

He hung up.

I hit "End" and turned onto South First, my hands trembling on the steering wheel. Why had I opened my big mouth about Marcus Lassiter? Maybe Peaches could help me figure out a way to talk myself out of it. It might be time to come clean with her about my husband, anyway.

Five minutes later, I pulled into the parking lot of Peachtree Investigations.

All that was left of the building was a smoking pile of cinder blocks.

My body turned cold. *Another bomb?*

First, my husband's car had been blown up. Now my office. I had thought Blake was the reason for the Molotov cocktail. Now, I wasn't so sure.

I swung open the minivan's door and stared at the scorched remains of the building, cordoned off by flapping yellow police tape. With those stacks of files, it must have gone up like a torch. Then an awful thought occurred to me. Had Peaches been there?

A cold knot formed in my stomach. If she had, had she gotten out? I started to search the parking lot for her car. Then I realized I didn't know what she drove. *Oh God.* Why would someone burn down Peachtree Investigations? Was it a coincidence?

It was always possible that the fire started on its own. Maybe one of the ashes from Peaches's Ultra Slims had landed on a file folder or a pile of dried-up doodlebugs. But the police tape made me think otherwise. Peaches's desk—1950s army issue, solid metal—was the only thing still intact. What was left of her chair lay on its side in the middle of the rubble like a dead three-legged spider.

A prickle of fear crept up my back. Had someone done this to warn me away?

I thought about my actions for the last few days. I'd gone down to the Rainbow Room to talk with Cassandra about Maxted. Had that been what motivated this? Was someone telling me to stop asking questions about Evan Maxted? Personally, I would have preferred a nice handwritten note.

On the plus side, if it was Marcus Lassiter who was unhappy about my asking questions, he wouldn't be able to commit any more acts of arson from jail. Looking at the remains of Peachtree Investigations, I was thankful that whoever had thrown that Molotov cocktail last night had aimed at my car and not at my house. Still, if bad things happened in threes, I didn't even want to think about what might be next.

As I stared at the blackened rubble, a chilling thought crept into my head.

What about Elsie and Nick?

I fumbled for my phone and picked out the number for Green Meadows. The line was busy.

Just like the line at Peachtree Investigations had been all day yesterday.

I dashed back to the minivan and gunned the engine, punching the redial button as the minivan screeched out of the parking lot.

Still busy.

I raced up South First, running two red lights and scanning the northwest horizon for signs of smoke. Surely they wouldn't go after my children.

Would they?

Horrible thoughts passed through my mind as I dodged slow-moving SUVs and almost took the front bumper off a Mini, cursing the traffic lights. The ten minutes it took me to get to my children's school felt like an hour. I roared off at the Enfield exit and then gunned the engine and ran the last red light, breathing a sigh of relief as Green Meadows Day School came into view. No smoke, no flames. It looked just like it had when I dropped the kids off. At least something was going right today.

And then I saw the ambulance.

I hurled myself out of the minivan and across the parking lot to where a group of mothers huddled, looking white-faced and somber.

"What happened?" I gasped. "Why is the ambulance here?"

Nina Jeffreys looked at me with big, soulful eyes. "Didn't you hear?"

"No!" I yelled. I resisted the urge to grab her by her scrawny throat. "That's why I'm asking you!"

Marina Helden said, "Relax, Margie."

"How can I relax when there's an ambulance in the parking lot? Will someone tell me what the hell is going on? Are my kids okay?"

Betty Flanagan patted my arm. "They're fine, Margie."

Relief gushed through me. "Oh God. Thank God." I sagged against somebody's SUV. "But why is the ambulance here?"

"Mrs. Bunn collapsed in the office." As Marina spoke, a gaggle of paramedics and firemen staggered through the school's front door, struggling to maneuver a stretcher over the rough stone pathway. From a distance, Mrs. Bunn looked like an immense loaf of half-risen dough covered with a massive floral dish towel. I caught a glimpse of her face when one of the men carrying her stumbled on a rock. Under the oxygen mask strapped over her face, her skin looked like pork roast that's been in the fridge a few days too long.

"Is she going to be okay?" Marina asked as they approached the ambulance.

One of the paramedics grimaced and shrugged. As they heaved the stretcher into the back of the ambulance, I asked him, "Do you have any idea what's wrong?"

"Can't say," he huffed. "We won't know until we get her to the emergency room."

Then they slammed the back door shut and hustled to the front of the ambulance. A moment later, the siren started, and the ambulance pulled out of the parking lot, flashing its lights as it sped down Enfield Road.

I turned back to Nina, who I knew volunteered in the office on Fridays. "How did it happen?"

Tears welled in her brown eyes. "She had just come back from circle time and fixed herself a cup of tea. I walked into her office to ask her whether she wanted to order *I Love Fire Trucks* or *Bluebonnet Bunny* for one of the birthday books, and she was sitting there in her chair, all purple, looking like she was choking or something. I tried to help her, but then she fell out of her chair." She blushed slightly. "I . . . I tried to help her up, but I couldn't move her, so I called 911, and . . ." I put my arm around her as she started to sob.

"Could it have been a heart attack?" Marina asked.

I shrugged. "I don't know. I've never seen one."

"Well, I have," piped up Melissa Steck. "And that doesn't sound like a heart attack. Maybe someone finally got tired of the old witch and poisoned her."

A stunned silence fell over the little group. Nina's shoulders shuddered as she sobbed quietly.

"We've all had issues with Mrs. Bunn from time to time," Marina said finally, "but I just can't imagine anyone would want to poison her."

I could think of a lot of people, but all I said was, "I guess we'll just have to wait and see."

CHAPTER EIGHTEEN

I had just gotten the kids a snack and settled them in with *Lady and the Tramp* when the phone rang.

"Hello?"

"It's Peaches."

"Peaches!" I gripped the phone. "Are you okay?"

"I'm fine," she said. "But the office isn't." Her gravelly voice wobbled a bit, and I could hear her sucking in smoke.

"Thank God you're all right. I saw it this morning, but I didn't know how to get in touch with you. What happened?"

"Arson."

I sank into a chair. "I was afraid of that. How did they do it?"

"They think someone got in and soaked the place with gasoline. Went up like a torch."

"Any idea who?"

"Not a clue. Thank God for insurance, though. I've been meaning to get a new place for years, actually, but I was hoping to take my files with me."

"Gosh. I hadn't thought about that. What does that do for some of your cases?" My mind touched on Pence. Would I have to follow him to the Como Motel again?

"Fortunately, all of my clients have copies of their reports and photos. And I'd just done the billing on Wednesday." She sighed. "I still lost a lot of important stuff, though."

"Your office wasn't the only place that went up in smoke. Someone bombed my husband's car last night."

"What?"

"Yeah. They said it looked like a Molotov cocktail."

"Looks like you're getting into some heavy shit. Maybe you need to back off. You got kids, don't you?"

I swallowed hard. "Yeah."

"People like this, who knows what they'll do? If I were you, I would just cool it with your 'friend.'"

I bit my lip. Since my friend slept in the same bed with me and was the father of my children, that was going to be tough to do. "Wouldn't it be better to find out what's going on?"

"Honey, you've done a great job. Better than I thought you would. But this stuff is getting serious. I've got a bad feeling about this. I think you need to let things die down a bit."

I gritted my teeth. Italian music swelled in the living room. It must have been the big spaghetti scene. "I can't."

"Why not?"

"Because the 'friend' I've been telling you about is my husband."

"Shit." She sucked on her cigarette again. "I was afraid of that."

I told her everything I'd found out. "What do I do next?" I asked.

"So, you've looked through his home office, but you haven't gone to his work office yet."

"No. Not yet. I've been thinking about it, though."

"Do they have a security person?"

"I think so. But I don't think they make you sign in or anything. Blake just uses one of those security cards to get in and out."

"Is the building open twenty-four hours a day?"

"Uh-huh."

"That would be my next move, then. Wait till he's sound asleep. Then grab his keys and go. I'd tell you to search his car, too, but I guess that ain't gonna happen now."

"What do I do if the security guy asks me what I'm doing?"

"You got into a dead person's apartment while the police were there and then snooped through his office and stole his appointment book, and you're asking me how to deal with a security guard?"

"Good point. I'll think of something."

"And make sure you get into his computer, too. People hide lots of stuff on computers. I'd go with you, but it might look a little weird, the two of us going up to McWatson and Kinks at three in the morning."

"Jones McEwan," I said.

"Whatever. Anyway, let me know what happens. Then we'll figure out what to do next. Want me to run a background check on him?"

"On my husband?"

"Can't hurt. You never know."

I sighed. "I suppose you're right. It can't hurt, can it?"

"I'll see what I can do. And let me know what you find out tonight." Her voice was suddenly serious. "Be careful."

"Thanks. I will. Are you going to be okay?"

"Once that insurance check comes through, I'll be right as rain. What do you think . . . Should we move downtown? Or maybe one of those redone bungalows, over where all the lawyers are?"

"How much was the place insured for?"

"Let's just say it's a good thing I called my ex last night."

"Why?"

"'Cause the insurance company is going to do everything it can to wriggle out of paying up. But Buck and I were dancing at the Broken Spoke till they closed it down, so I've got a solid alibi. We were probably doing the schottische while some asshole was torching the place."

I grinned. "Normally I'd say going out with exes is a bad idea, but in this case . . ."

"Yeah. Now go find out about your hubby and call me in the morning. Okay?"

"I don't have your home number."

"Oh. I guess you're right."

She reeled it off to me, and I jotted it down. "And Peaches?" I said.

"Yeah?"

"I'm glad you're all right."

She took another drag off her cigarette. "Thanks, honey. Me, too."

• • •

I couldn't wait for Blake to go to bed. I briefly considered adding the contents of a few antihistamine capsules to his Friday night Amstel Light. Then I remembered Marina's poison theory from this afternoon and changed my mind.

After the kids went down, Blake parked himself in the living room and stuck *Gladiator* into the DVD player. I picked up the case: one hundred forty minutes. Why were movies so much longer these days? I poured myself a glass of leftover Chardonnay and sat down at the kitchen table, listening to the tinkle of the wind chimes on the back porch and the sound of swords clanging in the living room. Everything looked just like it had last week—the lace curtains over the kitchen window, the kids' rock collection decorating the sill, the front of the fridge thick with family photos, finger paintings, and school reminders.

But nothing was the same. In just a few short days, everything I had spent the last eight years building—my marriage to Blake, the little house that was the center of my family's life—had been thrown into jeopardy. Rufus growled at the laundry room door, and

Snookums snarled back. I had just poured myself another glass of Chardonnay when my mother called.

"How are things with you and Blake, darling?"

I gritted my teeth. "Fine," I lied. "Just fine."

"I can tell you haven't started taking that tea yet."

"Mom . . ."

"I think maybe you'd better go see someone. Let me talk to Karma. I'm sure he knows a good herbalist in the area. Have you thought about Rolfing?"

I sighed. I knew she meant well, but this was one of those marital situations where eating weird plants or having my spine readjusted wasn't going to make much of a difference. "Mom, thanks for thinking of me, but everything's okay."

"I still hear gray in your aura."

I took a swig of my wine. "Why don't you have Karma look up a few names, and I'll think about it. And I promise I'll drink that tea. Can we talk about this in a day or two?"

"Oooh, Blake must be there. Well, I understand. Let me know when I can come down to see my sweethearts! And maybe you and Blake can take a weekend and go to the ashram."

I almost snorted wine through my nose at the image of Blake at an ashram. "Thanks, Mom. I'll talk to you soon."

"I love you, sweetheart."

"Love you, too."

A few minutes later, Becky called.

"You doing okay?"

"My mother-in-law is giving me sex manuals, and my mother thinks my phone aura is too gray, but other than that, as well as can be expected." I glanced toward the darkened living room and took a slug of wine. "Any word on Attila?"

"She's still in the ICU, but no word on what happened."

"I hope she's okay. Are you still up for a trip to the school office tomorrow?"

"Yeah. Is ten o'clock okay?"

"Perfect."

"And when we're done there, I'm taking you clothes shopping. You need a pick-me-up. And then we'll do a makeover, and you can put in your order."

"That's right," I said. "You're going for the pink Cadillac."

"After going through Attila's files, I might just put you down for one of everything."

I groaned and tossed back the rest of the Chardonnay.

By the time Blake was snoring, I had drunk two Diet Cokes and eaten half a Cadbury Dairy Milk bar. The combo would never get written up in *Food & Wine*, but it was fine for medicinal purposes.

I prodded my husband a few times. Nothing. Then I slid out of bed and pulled on a pair of khakis and a polo shirt. I took one last look at Blake, sprawled under the covers. *Who are you really?* I asked him silently.

Then I slid the keys from the top of his dresser and tiptoed out to the minivan.

· · ·

Sixth Street is a different place by night than it is by day. The business suits and khakis of daylight had morphed into painfully tight jeans and dresses that looked more like fabric swatches than clothing. The shiny SUVs and luxury sedans had been replaced by sleek sports cars and low-riding coupes. Under the bright lights of the bar marquees, my crumpled minivan felt like the automotive equivalent of a maiden aunt.

I was almost relieved when I pulled into the garage beneath Blake's building, flashing his blue parking card at the attendant and pulling into a corner spot. I grabbed Blake's keys from the ignition and caught the elevator to the lobby. As the doors slid open to reveal the lobby, I thought, *So far, so good.*

That came to a screeching halt a moment later.

I don't know what I expected to find. Maybe a slot to stick Blake's card into that would allow me to whisk up the fourteen floors to his office unchallenged? What I got was a beetle-browed security guard who looked like she'd just found her husband cheating on her with a two-hundred-pound baboon.

She glared at me as I tripped across the cool terrazzo floor. "Can I help you?" Her voice made it clear that helping me wasn't high on her list of things to do.

"Yes. I'm headed up to Jones McEwan."

She squeezed her eyebrows even tighter together. "Then you'll have to sign in." She pushed a clipboard toward me. "Name?"

"Um, Priscilla Anderson."

She opened a binder and ran her fingers down a list of names. Then she looked up at me, suspicion in her close-set black eyes. "You're not in here."

I panicked. Her black eyes bored into me, suspicion growing with each moment I failed to supply an answer. Finally, I let out an exasperated sigh. "You're kidding me! They told me last week that everything would be taken care of." I thrust Blake's security card at her. "Here. Maybe this will help."

She peered at the number on the card and ran her finger down the list of names in her binder again. "Says here the card's registered to a guy named Blake Peterson."

I rolled my eyes. "Oh, for God's sake. They let him go last month. I'm his replacement."

The hard certainty in her eyes wavered.

"Look," I said. "Why don't you take my name down and check it out with Herb McEwan tomorrow? I've got a big case going to trial on Monday, and if I don't get everything together, heads are going to roll." I gave her a pointed look, hoping that she would take it to mean that hers might be among them.

"Well, it's not standard procedure . . ." Her resistance was faltering.

"If anyone gives you a hard time over this, I promise I'll go to bat for you."

She chewed on her lip. Just when I thought *Victory!*, she shook her head. "I'm sorry, ma'am, but I can't bend the security procedures."

Crap. I gazed at the elevator with longing. So near, yet so far . . . "Would it help if I called Annette Morton?" She glanced at her list. "She's a senior partner of Jones McEwan," I supplied helpfully.

"Well, with her permission, I suppose . . ."

"Great." I whipped out my cell phone and dialed.

"Hello, Annette? Sorry to bother you. This is Priscilla Anderson."

A sleepy voice came through the phone. "Margie? Is that you?"

"Sorry to disturb you, but I'm standing at the front desk of Jones McEwan, and I need you to tell"—I glanced at the guard's badge—"Melissa here that it's okay to let me into my office."

Becky's voice was confused. "What?"

"Can you just do that for me?"

"Where are you again?"

"Like I said, I'm in the lobby. Here's Melissa. She's running security tonight." Then I handed the phone over the desk and prayed that Becky would figure it out.

"Ms. Morton?" Melissa was silent for a moment, and I crossed my fingers tight behind my back. Finally, her eyebrows relaxed. "Okay. Will do." She handed the phone back to me. "She says it's okay."

Thank you, Becky. "Great," I said, trying not to sound too relieved. Melissa got up, lumbered over to the elevator, and punched the "Up" button for me before returning to her desk.

That the security guard didn't find it odd for me to call one of the two senior partners of Jones McEwan after midnight made me wonder about the quality of security these days. On the other hand, she had given me a really hard time. But it didn't matter.

I was in.

Blake's security card slid into the key slot of Jones McEwan as if it were greased. The door opened with a click.

I turned on the lights to the lobby and the hall and trotted to Blake's office, my hands damp with sweat. I needed to get in and out before Melissa thought too hard about my midnight phone call.

Blake's office door was unlocked. I flicked on the light and made for the desk. Like the desk in his home office, the slab of dark-stained walnut was clear of anything but a pair of Blake's beloved Montblanc pens.

I slid into his leather chair and did a quick survey of his desk drawers, not knowing what I was hoping—or dreading—to find. Motel receipts? Crack cocaine? Thong underwear with plastic fruit? But the contents were uninspiring: nothing but paper clips, plastic rollerball pens, and rubber bands.

I flipped the switch on the computer. While it booted up, I swiveled around and opened the top drawer of the credenza. Client files. Nothing that would indicate where two thousand dollars a month was going. I was about to close the drawer when three fat green files labeled *International Shipping Company* caught my eye. I pulled them out and laid them on top of the credenza. They were stuffed with half a dozen manila files.

The first few folders were for cases connected with what looked like unhappy clients. I raised my eyebrows. Apparently International Shipping Company wasn't as rigorous as it could be in recording and shipping the correct amount of stuff. My thoughts turned to Calvin Pitts, the lascivious CEO we had met that morning. He was so sleazy, I couldn't say I was surprised. I opened the fourth file. Apparently the company wasn't too good at recording profits, either. The corporate offices might look luxurious, but unless their coffers were well lined, the company might have to downgrade its office space soon. The IRS was suing for back taxes to the tune of a couple million dollars.

The computer bleeped, and I turned to look at the screen. Another password request. I typed in a few likely candidates: social security numbers, children's names, mother's maiden name. Nothing. My name didn't work, either. I sighed and turned to the next manila folder, which was labeled *E. M. Hernandez*—the same name I had seen on the files in Maxted's office that morning.

I flipped through the file. Once again, bills of lading. Apparently Hernandez had shipped several loads of piñatas from Guadalajara to a company called Innovative Imports. I looked at the address and blinked. It was the same as the one scrawled at the bottom of the page on Maxted's appointment book.

I flipped past the bills and was about to read Blake's notes on the case when a squeak sounded from the hall.

I jammed the files back into the folder and shoved them into the credenza, pushing the drawer closed with my foot. Then I dashed around the desk to switch off the lights. *Damn!* I had left the hall lights on, but there was nothing I could do about it now. I pushed the "Off" button on Blake's computer and scurried under the desk.

My breathing was so loud I was convinced whoever was approaching would hear me from the hall. Was it the security guard? Had she called someone and found out I was a fraud? I concentrated on regulating my breathing and making myself as small as possible.

The footsteps paused outside the door to Blake's office. I pressed myself deeper into the dark well under the desk.

Then the lights went on.

I glanced up at the credenza to make sure the drawer was closed and cursed silently. The drawer was closed, but Blake's keys gleamed on the edge of the credenza.

The footsteps approached the desk. I fought to still my breathing and pressed my back into the hard walnut desk.

A pair of gray slacks came into view, ending in polished black wing tips. Whoever it was, it wasn't the security guard. She'd been wearing blue polyester. I squeezed my eyes shut, praying that whoever was prowling around my husband's office wouldn't look under the desk. Then I opened them again. Who the heck *was* prowling around my husband's office? And why?

As I watched, the top drawer of the credenza slid open. After a moment, it slid shut again. And then I heard the sound I had been dreading.

The jingle of keys.

Fortunately, they were in fact my husband's keys, and therefore it was reasonable for them to be in his office. The problem was, if whoever it was walked off with them, I had no way to get the minivan home. And it would be darned hard to explain to my husband why the minivan was in the parking garage of his office.

Please, please, please put them back. A split second later, I added, *And please don't look under the desk, either.*

After a moment that felt like an eternity, the keys thunked down on the credenza. The pants disappeared, the lights went off, and the footsteps receded down the hall.

I waited a few minutes, then clambered out from under the desk and slid the credenza drawer open.

Even in the faint reflected light of downtown, it was obvious what was missing. The files on International Shipping Company were gone.

I slid my keys off the credenza and stuffed them into my pocket. Then I crept to the door. The hall was empty. I dashed to the end of it and peered around the corner into the lobby.

Nobody.

I crossed the room and slipped through the front door, jabbing at the elevator button and trying to disappear behind a potted ficus tree. I'd made it out of the office okay. With my luck, I'd be caught waiting for the elevator. When the door finally opened, I ducked inside and punched the "Door Close" button. I sagged against the mirrored wall and prepared myself for the lobby, where Melissa, the security guard, was waiting for me. Maybe if I moved fast, I could get out before she had a chance to stop me.

When the door opened, I broke into a trot, but the efficient guard called out before I had taken three steps. "That was quick." Her voice was icy. "I thought you had a mountain of work to do."

I plastered a smile onto my face. "Oh, the computers were down, so I figured I'd get a good night's sleep and try again tomorrow."

Her brows beetled with suspicion again. "You need to sign out."

"Oh. Sure." I hurried over to the register and jotted *12:45 a.m.* next to my name, glancing at the lone entry under mine.

Herb McEwan.

"By the way, I talked with Herb McEwan a moment ago," Melissa said, "and he said he never heard of a Priscilla Anderson."

I forced a tinkly laugh. "Men never know what's going on, do they? Oh, well. I'm sure Annette will fill him in at the next partners meeting." I tapped my forehead. "It's always us women who keep things running, isn't it?"

Before she had a chance to answer, I turned and hustled toward the garage elevator. As I crossed the lobby, a whirring sound came from one of the lobby elevators. Someone—probably Herb McEwan—was on his way down.

I picked up the pace, skipping the elevator and ducking through the door marked "Stairs." Melissa took a step toward me, calling, "Wait! Wait a moment!"

I pretended not to hear, instead turning to give her a brief wave. "See you later!" I called, and disappeared through the door.

Just before the door to the stairwell snicked shut, the lobby elevator dinged.

I pelted down two flights of stairs and burst through the door, sprinting for the minivan. I needed to get out before Melissa had a chance to alert the parking attendant.

A moment later, I roared past McEwan's black Mercedes and held up my blue pass for the parking attendant, who waved me by. I smiled at him and sailed past the parking booth. His radio crackled to life behind me as I pulled out of the garage and disappeared into the neon-lit traffic on Sixth Street.

CHAPTER NINETEEN

B ecky's taking you shopping for clothes?" Blake slurped his coffee
and smiled. "That's a great idea! She always looks so put together.
I'm sure she can find something that will look nice on you."

I scowled and poured myself a second cup of coffee, reflecting
that it was becoming increasingly difficult to remember why I had
married this man in the first place.

I had made it home without incident last night, exhausted, but
also revved up. Blake was still in the same sprawled position when I
slid under the covers. As I lay in the darkness, trying to calm myself
down enough to sleep, it occurred to me that Peaches was right: I
hadn't needed any help getting into Blake's office. My marriage might
be headed down the toilet, but at least I was turning out to be a pretty
decent private investigator. Frankly, it wasn't much consolation.

This morning, when I floated my idea about doing a little "volunteer" work at the school office and then shopping for an outfit to
wear to the Junior League fashion show, he'd been thrilled. "Great!
I'm so glad you're taking better care of yourself. Image is *so* important." But when I told him I needed to go back into the office the next
day (that was my cover for Maxted's memorial service), he shook his
head. "I've got a client meeting. You'll have to get a babysitter or do
it another time."

I was dying to ask him why Herb McEwan would take the ISC files from his office in the middle of the night. Instead, I kissed the kids, poured a third cup of coffee into a travel mug, and announced that I was on my way out. "Take your time!" he called as I headed for the front door, feeling churlish. If I'd known he'd be so delighted to watch the kids while I went clothes shopping, I would have started faking mall expeditions years ago.

Becky was waiting in the parking lot when I pulled into Green Meadows. "What was *that* all about last night?"

"Thanks for covering for me."

"No problem. I still can't believe you broke into Blake's office. Did you find out anything?"

I recounted what I'd found in Blake's credenza—and what McEwan had done while I was hiding under the desk. When I got to the part about my escape from the lobby, she shook her head.

"So you ran away from the security guard?"

"Sort of. Not exactly."

"I don't know how you do it."

My voice was sharper than I meant it to be. "Hopefully, your husband will never start skimming money from the family bank account, and you'll never have to find out."

"Sorry, Margie. I didn't mean . . ."

"No, no. It's okay. I shouldn't have lashed out at you like that . . . I guess I'm not dealing with this very well."

We walked toward the office together in silence. As I unlocked the door, Becky said, "Why do you think McEwan took the file? Do you think he was just borrowing it?"

"Wouldn't he do that during office hours? I can't see making a trip to the office at midnight on a Friday just to borrow a file."

"Good point. By the way, any word yet on the car?"

I shook my head. Then I opened the door and flipped on the light. "Well," I said, waving a hand at the enormous metal file cabinet with a flourish, "there it is."

Becky walked over and pulled open a drawer. "Let's get started. The sooner we're done here, the sooner we can start on your new look."

"Oh joy."

"Did she give you any idea of what we're looking for?" I shook my head. She sighed. "Well, at least things are filed. I worked at an office once where they just threw everything into boxes and shoved them in a storage room."

"Where do we start?" I asked.

"Since she didn't tell you how she figured out the money was missing, I'd say we start with the bank statements."

"I wish I'd thought to ask."

"Well, maybe when she gets better, we'll go visit her." She tossed me a bulging file. "You get started on last year's stack, and I'll take a look at the most recent statements."

"What am I looking for?"

She brushed a strand of hair from her cheek. "Anything that doesn't look like a school expense. Or just anything weird."

"Gosh, that narrows it down." I opened the file with a sigh. "Sure you don't want me to make a coffee run?"

"Stop talking and get working."

I was halfway through the first pile of statements and starting to get a tension headache from the long rows of numbers when my cell phone rang. Normally I wouldn't be that excited to talk to my mother, but right now, I was looking for an escape.

"Hi, Mom."

"Hi, Marigold. I just decided to call and check up on you . . . Your aura's better today! Are things looking up?"

I made a mental note that embezzling investigations were aura-enhancing and proceeded to dodge her question. "How are things with you?"

"Fine, fine . . . I just called to tell you I popped another little package into the mail . . . Some crystals you can put around the house, to help the chi. Also, I found the most wonderful CD. It's got Tibetan monks on it. We heard it at the ashram."

"Thanks." I smiled, thinking of my childhood room, where my mother hung crystals alongside the Holly Hobbie pictures "to soothe my spirit." Even now, the smell of incense, which for most people evoked their teenaged years, sent me zinging back to childhood. It was ironic. For most kids, tie-dyed clothes and weird music alienated and appalled their parents. For me, the best way to irk my mother had been to wear polo shirts and khakis.

"Anyway, Karma and I are planning to drive down next weekend, to help out with the kids."

"Mom—"

"No, no, dear. I can tell you need the help."

"No, really—"

"I have to run, darling, but I'll call you in a few days. Toodle-oo!"

She hung up, and I hit "End." Great. As if things weren't bad enough, I was going to have my mother and my husband in the same house for a weekend. And Karma, the herbalist boyfriend from California. Maybe I should start drinking now.

Becky eyed me over a stack of statements. "What was that all about?"

My smile was strained. "My mother just announced that she and Karma are coming to visit next weekend."

"Karma? What, or who, is that?"

"Her new herbalist boyfriend."

Becky cringed. "Oof. Train wreck." Then she brightened. "Maybe you can move in with me."

"I may take you up on it," I said, returning to the lines of numbers in front of me with what I was sure was an extremely gray aura. "For now, let's just get this over with."

Becky shook her head and went back to poring over the papers. A moment later, she squealed. "I think I've got something!"

I dropped the statement I had been staring at for the last ten minutes and hurried over to her. "What is it?"

"Starting last July, one or two checks a month aren't showing up in the monthly statements."

"And Attila didn't notice that?"

"Not until now, anyway. I guess there's so much money coming and going, whoever did it figured a couple checks a month would be easy to miss."

"How much?"

"Just a little at a time. Fifty here, a hundred there. Always even numbers, though." She sifted through the stack of statements, put her finger on an entry, and riffled through a stack of canceled checks. "But the amounts start creeping up. Look—here, in November, there's one for two hundred fifty dollars." She looked up at me. "Who handles the accounting for the office?"

"I'm guessing it's Alicia," I said, "but we'll have to ask Mrs. Bunn."

Becky flipped through a few more statements, comparing entries with the stack of checks. "I'll bet they have copies of these at the bank. At least they'll know who the checks are going to."

"But it's Saturday."

"We'll check on Monday. By then, maybe Attila will be doing better, and she can tell us how the accounting is handled."

I flipped my file closed. "So we're done, then."

"Nope. We have to go through and find all of the missing checks. And it wouldn't hurt to go through the accounting books, either."

"The accounting books?"

"It could turn out that the checks are legit. We've got to cover all our bases." She pursed her lips. "Too bad they don't use Quicken. It would make things a lot easier."

I groaned and resumed studying the stack of statements, resolving to turn down any future embezzling cases.

By the time Becky closed up the accounting book, it was after one. "Done?" I asked.

"Yup. The checks are the only thing out of place, and just like I thought, they aren't recorded in the books." She stood and shoved the big book back onto its shelf. "Let me do one more thing, and then we're out of here!"

I replaced the files I had been looking through while she did some figuring on a calculator. "Wow," she said. "Almost ten thousand dollars is missing."

"It thought it was only disappearing in small increments."

"That was at first. Whoever it was got brave. Or else something happened that made him—or her—need more."

"I guess we'll find out Monday." I slammed the drawer shut. "Now let's get some lunch."

"And then," Becky said triumphantly, "the mall!"

• • •

It was almost five o'clock when we emerged from Barton Creek Mall, burdened with a flotilla of plastic bags containing three dresses, a couple of pants suits, four pairs of shoes, and a bottle of temporary hair color.

"But I like my hair color," I had complained when Becky plucked a bottle of "Darkest Ebony" off the shelf of the beauty shop.

"It's for the memorial service, dummy. So that jerk from ISC doesn't recognize you. You're still planning on going, aren't you?"

I was torn, actually. "Do you think it's worth it?"

"Don't murderers usually show up at memorial services?"

"They do in the Agatha Christies I read, but I don't know how that transfers to real life. And I'm not so sure that identifying Maxted's killer is going to shed any light on what's going on with my husband. Besides, Blake can't watch the kids."

"Margie, your husband was one of the last people Maxted called before he died. Don't you think there's a teensy chance that might be relevant?" She pursed her lips. "And it sounds like that Bunsen guy hasn't crossed you off his list of suspects yet."

"What if Bunsen shows up? Won't that just make him suspect me more?"

"You've got a reason to be there. You found the guy dead. Besides, you're going as a brunette, remember? And why can't Blake watch the kids?"

"He's got a client meeting."

She rolled her eyes. "On *Sunday*?"

"I know. Ridiculous, isn't it? Maybe I'll ask Prue if she can babysit."

Becky smiled a wicked smile. "Oh, that's right. You get to sit next to her at the fashion show. I wonder if this time she'll give you a vibrator."

"The way things are going in my marriage, that might be my only option soon."

"Well, at least she won't be able to complain about your wardrobe." She handed me her cell phone. "Call your husband and tell him you're coming straight to my house. I'll do your hair and makeup."

I remembered what she'd done to me before my first trip to the Rainbow Room and hesitated. "Nothing too major, okay?"

She laughed. "No, I'm not going to do you up like a femme fatale this time. I only did that because you were *supposed* to look easy." Well, that was a relief. "This time, think Laura Bush."

"Couldn't we go for Hillary, instead?"

"Trust me," she said. "When I'm done with you, you'll look great. Besides, you owe me a Mary Kay order."

• • •

Once again, I didn't recognize the reflection in the mirror when Becky finished poking and prodding me. Instead of a slightly chunky, shorts-clad mom with lank hair, a svelte woman in a tan pants suit and a shiny French twist stared back at me. It wasn't quite Hillary Clinton, but I'd take it.

I struck a pose in the mirror, then glanced back at Becky. "How did you do it? I *never* look like this."

"It was all there," she said. "You just need to bring it out."

"I would love to look like this every day. I just don't want to have to get up at five to make it happen."

"It's not that bad. Getting a good haircut will help; it won't take as long to fix up. I'll teach you how to do the rest of it."

I turned and glanced at the unfamiliar woman in the mirror again. "You're a miracle worker."

"Nonsense," she said, putting the finishing touches on her own makeup. "Now, let's get going. It starts in a half hour."

• • •

Twenty minutes later, I took a last glance at myself in the flip-down mirror of Becky's Suburban before facing Austin's female upper crust.

"Stop worrying," Becky said. "You look great." She looked pretty good, too, in a pale blue dress that plunged a little in the front, but not too much, and ended just above her shapely knees. Her hair and makeup, as always, were impeccable, as, for a change, were mine. Before we left Becky's, I'd placed a huge Mary Kay order with enthusiasm. I might have to put the kids' next tuition payments on my Visa, but it would be worth it.

As we rode up in the elevator, I leaned over to Becky. "You know, if Miss Topaz ever quits Miss Veronica's, you should apply for the job."

She laughed. "Thanks, I think. On the other hand, I guess catering to transvestites would expand my potential clientele."

"And then there are the metrosexuals . . ."

Before she could respond, the elevator door opened, and we plunged into the thickly carpeted front lobby of the Metropolitan

Club. Although I had felt impeccably dressed as we rode the elevator up, my suit felt almost casual among the throng of peacock-colored dresses. A startling amount of bony décolletage was visible as we wove through the crowd toward the registration table. We passed the sign advertising the show—*Couture with a Conscience*—and I murmured to Becky, "Bitsy's going to need to sell a lot of clothes to cover the tab for this place."

"Not really," she whispered back. "Have you seen the price tags on the dresses?"

"How much are we talking?"

"I was in her shop a month ago. She's asking up to two K for a cocktail dress."

"Christ. People pay that much?"

"For a Bitsy McEwan creation, they do."

"Are the designs that good?"

Becky shrugged. "I didn't buy anything. But in Austin right now, she's very hot. The whole Couture with a Conscience thing is going over big."

"If you ask me," I hissed as we approached the registration table, "two hundred smacks a ticket is unconscionable."

"Not if it all goes to help the starving children."

We registered, hung laminated name tags around our necks, and merged with the heavily perfumed crowd. The main room was paneled in dark wood, and the emerald carpet was so plush that my heels sank into it as Becky and I entered. A runway dominated the space, and the perimeter was lined with candlelit tables. In the center of each table was a ring of candles and an extravagant floral centerpiece that probably cost as much as my weekly groceries. Next to the glittering dresses dotted around the room, the suit that had seemed so classy a few minutes ago felt more like a burlap sack.

I made a beeline for the nearest waiter and reached for a champagne glass, hoping a glass or two would help me feel less like a goose at a convention of swans. "I can't believe I'm doing this," I murmured to Becky. "My life's a total wreck, and here I am shelling out two hundred bucks to go to a Junior League fashion show."

"But Bitsy McEwan's here," Becky said, nodding toward a tall blond woman in the center of the room.

"So?"

"So, it was her husband who was sneaking into Blake's office. Maybe she knows something about ISC."

I studied Bitsy, who was holding a glass of champagne in her slender hand and gesturing to one of the waitstaff. "Somehow I don't see that coming up in casual conversation."

"You never know," said Becky, draining her champagne and scanning the room. "Oh, look. There's your mother-in-law." I followed her gaze to Prue, who was holding court with a gaggle of satin-clad women a few tables over. "Oooh. Are those shrimp toasts over there? I'm getting one. Do you think they'll have crab cakes?"

"How do you stay so skinny?" I asked.

"Good genes," she said, grabbing my arm and looking completely at home. I envied her. "Let's go forage for hors d'oeuvres. And where's that guy with the champagne?"

We stationed ourselves near the kitchen, where we could snag things off the trays as they came through. Although Becky looked right at home, selecting tidbits off the trays that whisked by and washing them down with generous sips of champagne, I felt like an alien in the fashionable crowd that ebbed and flowed around us. I had always wondered who bought the tiny, sparkly dresses displayed in the front windows of the Arboretum stores. Likewise the gigantic diamonds, some of which looked to be in the five-to-ten-pound range. Now I knew. "I bet they take their engagement rings off before they get on the scales," I said to Becky through a mouthful of shrimp.

"Can you imagine wearing a rock like that?" she asked, nodding toward a particularly massive specimen perched on the scrawny, taloned hand of a redhead.

"I bet it comes in handy as a weapon."

"Yeah. You could knock a guy out with that."

I reached for another glass of champagne with a conspicuously unmanicured hand and was onto the third flute of bubbly and my fourth shrimp toast when Becky and I drifted into Bitsy McEwan's orbit. "Now's your chance," Becky whispered, and nudged me toward her.

"What do I say?"

"You'll think of something."

I gulped down the rest of my champagne.

Bitsy McEwan was perfectly dressed in a silver and lavender cocktail gown that made her china-white skin glow. Her pale blue eyes settled on me as I approached, Becky a couple of steps behind me.

"Margie! How lovely that you could come." Her eyes registered Becky. "And who is this?"

"Bitsy, this is Becky. She's a good friend of mine. Becky, this is Bitsy McEwan."

She extended a pale hand. "Becky! So pleased to meet you." She narrowed her eyes. "I believe I've seen you in the shop before, haven't I?"

Becky smiled. "I've been in from time to time."

"Well, lovely to see you. And is that Vera Wang you're wearing? Stunning, simply stunning on you. If you're interested, I'm always looking for models. Not for this year, of course, but maybe next." Bitsy turned to the woman next to her. "This is Maria, my store manager. Much more than that, really. She handles all the operations for me."

Maria held out a slender hand. "Nice to meet you." Her skin was cool and dry to the touch, and she didn't look a day over twenty-five. Her ruby-red dress clung to her curves, and I felt a twinge of envy at her shiny black hair and smooth, dusky skin. If one of Bitsy's gowns could make me look half as good as Maria, I'd buy it in a second.

"We're really looking forward to seeing this year's collection," Becky said.

Bitsy glanced at me. "I'm surprised, actually. I never thought Margie cared much for clothes." I felt a flush suffuse my neck, moving up toward my cheeks. She smiled. "But you look stunning tonight, dear. I'm surprised you could make it, with Blake working so many hours. Did you get a babysitter?"

"No, he took a few hours off." Becky nudged me with a sharp elbow. I plowed ahead. "He tells me Herb has been helping out with one of his clients—International Shipping Company?"

Maria took a step toward her employer, whose blue eyes shifted from my face to scan the room behind me. "Yes, yes," Bitsy said. "Of course, Herb and I never talk business. Now, I hate to run, but will you excuse me? I have a couple of things to take care of before the show begins . . ."

She slipped past us gracefully, Maria in her wake, and glided toward the stage.

Becky eyed me critically. "Smooth."

"Well, what was I supposed to do?"

Becky stared at Bitsy's receding back. "She disappeared in a hurry, didn't she? Well, I'm sure you'll get another chance. In the meantime, I'm going to go and see if I can find another one of those shrimp toasts."

I was considering a fourth glass of champagne—after all, I wasn't driving—when Bitsy took the podium and invited everyone to sit down to dinner. I parted ways reluctantly with Becky—"If she gives you a dildo, I want to see it"—and headed toward my mother-in-law's table.

Prudence's eyes widened as I sat down. "Darling, you look marvelous. What did you do to yourself?"

"Becky and I went shopping," I said, wishing I had gone for the fourth glass.

"She's a miracle worker," Prudence breathed. Mercifully, Prudence's best friend, Miriam, took her seat at that moment and related a juicy tidbit of gossip, and soon the table was oohing and aahing over somebody's poor choice of shoes and digging into Caesar salads adorned with little shrimps. No crab cakes, unfortunately.

The conversation ranged from personal hygiene to personal trainers as we plodded through the menu. Some kind of greenish sorbet followed the salad, and after a hiatus of about twenty minutes, during which I considered cutting my wrists with a butter knife, we moved on to overcooked lemon sole and wilted broccoli. The meal culminated in a discussion of mildly revolting pedicure stories and a slice of my least favorite dessert, Italian cream cake.

Finally, the lights dimmed, and for the first time in my life, I found myself looking forward to seeing what next year's fashion forecast would hold.

CHAPTER TWENTY

Couture with a Conscience is the only fashion show I've ever attended, so I wouldn't know what to compare it to, but the concoctions that paraded down the stage during the next several minutes were unlike anything I'd ever seen a grown woman wear. I stared open-mouthed at the ragged bits of fabric that clung to the young models' bony bodies, trying to figure out how the outfits on the stage had evolved from the country-club style of their creator. Some of the dresses were so small and so sheer, you had to squint to see them, and the overall effect was something like Oliver Twist meets Gypsy Rose Lee.

From the lackluster applause that followed the scrawny women back up the catwalk, it occurred to me that I wasn't the only one struggling to make the connection. I leaned over to my mother-in-law as a skeletal model in a scrap of distressed fabric sashayed onto the stage. "Is this what all of her dresses look like?"

"No," she whispered back. "She's doing a few avant-garde things to break into the New York market. I think Maria helped her with the new line. We'll see some traditional things in a minute, I'm guessing."

She was right. A few minutes later, I found myself wondering if Bitsy McEwan was suffering from a split personality. The next "collection" featured a lineup of dresses that Scarlett O'Hara—and

Cassandra Starr—would have died for. Sequins, glittery beads, feathers, and lots of plunging necklines were the order of the day for the Tara collection. The applause picked up measurably, and murmurs of approval echoed from the silk-clad walls. My eyes had begun to glaze over, when a particularly sparkly creation hit the runway—"the Ariel," purred the announcer. I could see why: the glittery blue-green dress looked just like a mermaid's tail. By the time we got to business wear, I was about to slump into my Italian cream cake.

Finally, the last model exited the runway, and Bitsy McEwan herself took the stage to a roar of applause. The ladies might not have been crazy about the New Horizons collection, but the Tara line had won them over.

"Thank you, ladies, all of you, for attending this year's *Couture with a Conscience* show. We raised over half a million dollars for the Children's Fund last year, and it's all thanks to your support." She smiled broadly as the ladies gave her a big round of applause.

"And of course," she continued, "a big thank-you to everyone who made *Couture with a Conscience* possible, particularly Maria Espinosa." She gestured toward the lovely raven-haired woman who had accompanied her earlier. She sat at a front-row table. A spotlight lit up her red dress, and she dipped her head in acknowledgment as Bitsy continued. "Not only does she keep the day-to-day operations going, but her cutting-edge style helped me create the New Horizons line, which will debut in New York this fall." Feeble applause followed this declaration, but both Bitsy and Maria kept smiling. "I hope you enjoyed yourselves," Bitsy continued. "Feel free to mingle for as long as you like, and I look forward to seeing everyone at the shop."

I glanced at my watch as everyone rose from their tables and stretched. I wasn't too interested in mingling. What I really wanted to do was go home and sleep. But I still had to help with the cleanup.

"No dildos?" Becky asked when we reconvened.

"No, but she did offer to take the kids tomorrow."

"What time?"

"Ten."

"What time's the memorial service?"

"Noon."

"Then come over as soon as she gets there. We don't have a lot of time to get you ready."

"Thanks," I said as we walked toward the kitchen. "Want to help me wash dishes?"

She made a sour face and gestured at her dress. "In Vera Wang?"

"Don't worry." I laughed. "Why don't you hang out or go to the bar? I'll catch up with you later."

"Thanks," she said. "See if you can find out anything else."

"I will," I promised, and followed the white-jacketed serving staff into the kitchen.

Fortunately, the hotel staff was taking care of the dishwashing. An efficient-looking brunette set me to work returning the stacks of plates and glasses to their carrying cases.

"I haven't seen you around before," said Doris, the short fiftyish woman who was partnered with me. "Are you new?"

"Oh, my mother-in-law is a member, and Bitsy asked me the other day if I could help out."

Doris sighed. "She's such a noble woman. She puts all of her time and effort into the design studio, and it's all for the children . . ." She closed up a box and opened a new one. "I thought tonight's designs were wonderful. Didn't you just *love* that blue tulle? And the one with all the sequins, that looked like a mermaid—*fabulous.*" Doris was wearing a green satin gown she proudly told me was from the previous year's McEwan collection. Either she had bought it a size too small or she had grown in the past year, because pink flesh oozed over the low-cut bodice, and the seams were stretched to capacity.

I loaded another stack of Junior League–monogrammed plates into a box. "I've never bought a McEwan design before," I said, "although I did like a few of the ones I saw this evening."

Doris squinted at me. "I think that blue tulle would look marvelous on you. You should go try it on! Used to be you had to have them ordered specially, but now she's got all the sizes in the shop."

I closed up another box. "How long has Bitsy been designing clothes?"

"I think she's been doing it for forever, really, but the shop just opened up two or three years ago. It didn't work too well at first—like I said, they didn't ever have much in stock—but about a year or so ago, she really got it going." Doris bent to retrieve another box, and I winced, expecting a seam to pop. Regardless of how you felt about the design, the McEwan dress sure took top marks for endurance. Doris stood up and huffed a couple of times before she continued. "Now she's got loads of clothes, and she's even taking some of the collection to New York. I heard she's even thinking of doing a *Couture with a Conscience* show in Paris next year. Paris. Can you imagine?"

I closed up another box, but the stack of clean dishes seemed to be growing faster than our ability to box them up. "Why didn't they just use the hotel dishes?" I asked.

"Oh, Bitsy's *such* a perfectionist. She ordered these for all functions just a few years ago. I love the little crest, don't you? Makes it *so* special."

"Still," I said, "if all the profits are going to charity, wouldn't it be cheaper just to use standard-issue dishes?"

Doris blinked at me. "The shop raised more than half a million dollars for charity last year. Mrs. McEwan knows *exactly* what she's doing."

I shook my head in wonder. With dresses going for two thousand dollars a pop, I guess it made sense.

"And she could be making that kind of money for *herself*," Doris continued, her pink-painted lips a tight line. "But instead, it's all going to charity. She's a great lady."

We closed up another box and lapsed into silence for the next few minutes. The slingbacks Becky had picked out for me were digging into my heels, and my bladder was sending up distress signals. "I'll be back in a minute, Doris."

I stepped out of the noisy, steamy kitchen into the ballroom. The staff was pushing the tables to the edges of the room, and Prudence was directing a few women who were loading the tablecloths into plastic bags. "Light starch," she said, "and make sure you fold them immediately so they don't get wrinkled." Thank God I hadn't gotten laundry duty. With Snookums hanging out next to the washer and dryer, chances were the tablecloths would come back looking like lace designed by a pack of angry squirrels.

As I headed for the restroom, I noticed Bitsy and Maria Espinosa. They were walking, deep in conversation. I hustled across the room as they disappeared into a corridor. As I sidled up to the hallway, Bitsy said, "Let's go in here." I glanced around the corner just in time to see a door on the right-hand side swing shut.

I padded down the hallway and put my ear to the door, but I couldn't hear anything. *Damn.* I stared at the plate over the door. "Magnolia Ballroom: Room E." I took a few steps down the hall; the next door down was labeled "D." It was one of those big ballrooms hotels partition off to make smaller spaces.

I crossed my fingers and slipped through the doorway to room D. I was in luck. On one side of the room was stacked a huge pile of metal chairs. On the other was a sliding room divider with a two-foot gap.

I hurried across the room to the gap.

"Why has production been off?" It was Bitsy McEwan. Her normally chipper voice was low and urgent.

"Morale's been down," Maria answered. "Also, the demand is increasing. We've got twice as many orders as we did last year."

"Well, start turning it around."

"I'll talk with them tonight. There are two deliveries scheduled for tomorrow. One's a brand-new batch. Hopefully that will help."

"Maybe we need to expand operations."

"I've thought about that. I'll get in touch with Xenia, see what she can find. We've got the capital now. Maybe it *is* time to expand."

"We need to be careful, though. Remember what happened with Ernesto . . ."

"I know, I know. But that's taken care of now, and I think the new procedures will ensure that won't happen again."

Maria's voice sounded closer. I took a step back and banged into a table.

"What was that?"

"Is someone in here?" Bitsy asked. I scrambled across the room and dived behind a stack of chairs. "Is anyone in there?" I held my breath and peered through the metal chair legs, thankful I was wearing carpet-matching beige instead of something sparkly and bright pink. I ducked my head and shrank as low as I could as Bitsy approached my hiding spot. Just when I was sure she would see me, she said, "I think we're okay." My body went limp as they retreated into the next room. "Anyway, Maria, see what you can do. I want a better report by the end of next week."

A moment later, a door clicked. I waited a few minutes and crept to the door, peering out carefully. The hallway was empty. I smoothed a few dust bunnies from my jacket and closed the door to room D behind me.

Bitsy and Maria were nowhere to be seen when I reentered the main ballroom. Before returning to the kitchen, I slipped into the restroom and made a quick examination of my fading makeup. Becky knew what she was doing; although the lipstick had worn off, everything else was pretty much intact. I refreshed the lipstick, took advantage of the facilities, and headed back to plate stacking.

"What took you so long?" asked Doris when I returned to my station in the kitchen.

"Oh, I ran into an old friend."

Forty-five minutes later, we loaded the last box, and I went up to the bar in search of Becky.

She had tucked herself into a big leather chair, and sucked down the rest of a gin and tonic when I approached. "Finally done?"

I sank into the chair opposite her. "No thanks to you."

"Hey. Who got you into International Shipping? And who gave you this glamorous makeover?"

"I know, I know," I said, waving away the waitress. I leaned forward. "Guess what I overheard?"

Becky's eyes widened as I related the conversation between Bitsy McEwan and her assistant. "Have you ever heard of someone named Xenia?" I asked.

"I think she's one of Bitsy's cronies," Becky said. "A real estate agent. Works for Callum and Higgins."

"They said something about expanding operations. Do you think maybe they're looking to open a new store?"

Becky wrinkled her nose. "Maybe," she mused, "but I don't see how that's going to help with their production problems."

I sighed and closed my eyes. "It doesn't make sense, but I'm too tired to think."

"Then let's get you home. You've got another big day tomorrow." She paid her tab, and I followed her down to her Suburban.

As I fumbled in my purse to pay the parking attendant, Evan Maxted's appointment book caught my eye. I pulled it out and flipped to the page with the scrawled address. "Do you have a few minutes?"

"Sure," Becky said as we pulled out of the garage. "Why?"

"I want to swing by this place on East Seventh Street."

"Why?"

"Because we're kid-free and we're only a few blocks away."

"Okay. That still doesn't tell me what's so interesting about East Seventh."

"Because this address showed up in Maxted's appointment book a few days before he died, and it was also in those ISC files that McEwan took."

"Don't you think the police are going to check it out?"

"They don't have his address book. And McEwan has the ISC files."

She sighed. "It's worth a shot. Now, where am I going again?"

Ten minutes later we were coasting down East Seventh Street. The skyscrapers and fancy restaurants of downtown had given way to taquerias whose bright pink paint glowed in the streetlamps, and billboards blaring "*Envios dinero a Mexico!*" The Suburban passed a brightly lit bakery named La Victoriana. "I wonder if they have good churros?" Becky murmured. She had an avowed weakness for the doughy, cinnamon-sugar dusted pastries.

"Turn here!" I barked.

She wheeled the car around. "They're open twenty-four hours," she said.

"We can get it on the way back. Didn't you get enough Italian cream cake?"

"That was two hours ago." She peered through the windshield at the dimly lit street. "What are we looking for?"

"Number fifteen-sixteen." I pointed to a dilapidated warehouse hunkering next to the railroad tracks. Ancient washers and refrigerators dotted the weedy strip of ground between the building and the street, like debris washed up on a beach. The windows were covered with sheets of plywood, and even by the dim light of the streetlamp it was obvious that the building suffered from years of neglect. "That's it."

Becky looked at me. "Great. An old warehouse. Now let's get churros."

The headlights flashed across the front of the building as we turned a corner. "Not yet. It hasn't been boarded up that long. Look, the plywood is new."

"So?"

"There's a light on inside."

She squinted. "How can you tell?"

"That door." I pointed to a metal door in the corner. "There's a slit of light at the bottom. See?"

"So it's not abandoned. Great. Now can we go to the bakery? Do you think they have those little chicken things Josh likes?"

"I'm going to get a closer look."

She sighed. "Whatever. I'll park over there."

My feet complained as I crossed the street and navigated through the appliance graveyard to the rusted door. Although the door itself looked as old as the concrete surrounding it, both the knob and the dead-bolt lock gleamed like new. As I reached out to try the knob, headlights came around the corner. On instinct, I sprinted toward the nearest dead washing machine and squatted down behind it.

The car crunched to a stop in front of the building, and a moment later I heard the clip-clop of high heels on pavement. Then came the jangle of keys. I peeked around the washer just in time to see a flash of shiny satin disappear into the building.

It was Maria Espinosa.

A moment later I scurried back to Becky's Suburban. "Did you see that?"

Becky nodded. "What is Bitsy's assistant doing here?"

"I don't know," I said, "but I intend to find out. Let's see how long she's in there."

We didn't have to wait long. Ten minutes later she slid out the door and hurried back to her car. We huddled in our seats as her car, a silver Mercedes, zipped by us and turned onto Chicon Street.

"Nice car for an assistant," Becky said. "How did you find out about this building again?"

"The address was in Maxted's appointment book. And in the ISC files in Blake's office."

"What does Maria Espinosa have to do with ISC?"

"I don't know," I said, "but the address shows up in Maxted's book on September fifteen. Five days later, he was dead."

Becky's mouth was a thin line. "You don't think the McEwans had something to do with it, do you?" She was quiet for a moment. "Or Blake?"

"That's what I've been asking myself. The only thing is, if Blake is involved, then why did McEwan sneak into his office to take the ISC files? Why not just ask him for them?"

"Good point. But he signed in downstairs, didn't he? So Blake could figure out who was in the office."

"Yeah, but lots of people come in on weekends. They're attorneys, remember? Besides, who would suspect the principal partner of stealing?"

"I see what you mean. What do you think is going on?"

I gazed at the dark building. "Something tells me the answer is in there. The problem is, I don't know how to get in."

CHAPTER TWENTY-ONE

Blake hadn't woken up yet when Prue stopped by to pick up the kids the next morning. She waltzed through the door, resplendent in a peach twin set that I was betting would be covered in peanut butter before noon.

"What happened to Blake's car?" she asked.

"It blew up," Elsie answered helpfully.

"Blew up?"

"Oh, a short in the wiring." I reminded myself to ask Blake later if there was any more information on the Molotov cocktail. "The insurance will take care of it. Blake is renting a car in the meantime."

She glanced out the window at the blackened metal, which sat next to my still-crunched minivan. "Not having much luck with cars lately, are you?"

"My mommy is a vestigator now," Elsie said proudly.

Prue's tweezed eyebrows shot up. "A what?"

"A vestigator. She follows people around."

"Follows people . . . Margie, what on earth is she talking about?"

My face turned scarlet. "It's a little part-time thing," I mumbled.

Comprehension dawned on my mother-in-law's powdered face. "You're a private investigator?"

I nodded.

She raised a manicured hand to her forehead. "Dear God." For a moment, I thought she was going to pass out in my front hall. You'd think I'd admitted to selling children on the black market, or performing human sacrifices and baying at the full moon. Then she opened her eyes. "What does Blake think?"

"Well, I don't think he's crazy about it . . ."

"I can see why." Her voice was waspish. "No wonder you're having problems."

I blinked at her. "Problems?"

"Margie, I know that staying home can be . . . challenging sometimes. But a private investigating job . . . well, it's dangerous, and just . . . just *inappropriate*." She sighed and put a hand on my arm. "I'll tell you what. Why don't I call Bitsy. I'll sponsor you, she'll sponsor you, and we'll get you involved in the League. It'll keep you busy, although Lord knows there's enough that needs doing here. . ." She eyed the messy living room meaningfully.

"I'll think about it."

"A private investigator," she murmured, shaking her coiffed head.

"Thanks so much for taking the kids." I said, trying to change the subject. "What do you have planned for the day?"

"We're going to go shopping," she said, still looking pale. She leaned down to smooth Elsie's wayward hair. "Won't that be fun, sweetie?"

"Can I get a new dress?" Elsie asked eagerly.

"We'll get a couple of new dresses. And maybe some new shoes."

"Oh, Prue, you don't have to do that . . ."

"I'll have them back by five," she said briskly. "We'll talk more about this then."

I kissed the kids and watched them trail their grandma to her shiny new Camry, sure that Prudence would spend the rest of the day quizzing my children, looking for evidence of maternal neglect. When the Camry disappeared around the corner, I jotted a quick note to my husband, grabbed the Nordstrom bag, and headed to Becky's.

. . .

"I thought this was supposed to come out black." Becky and I stood at her mirror, staring at my formerly reddish-brown hair.

"Well, it said *Darkest Ebony* on the label." Becky picked up a lock of my wet hair and squinted at it. The she picked up a hair dryer and a brush. "Maybe it'll look different when it dries."

Twenty minutes later, we stared into the mirror again.

"The hair dryer just made it brighter."

"Hmmm. Well, I think it looks kind of stylish. I was reading the other day that aubergine is all the rage in Paris."

"Aubergine?"

"It's French for eggplant."

"Eggplant! Becky," I said, turning to face her, "my hair is purple. Purple! I have a memorial service to attend in"—I glanced at my watch—"forty minutes, and my head looks like it just came back from a bad acid trip. I was going for incognito, remember? This is *not* going to help!"

"Let me try one more rinse of color."

"There's no time!"

"I could always try shoe polish."

"No!" I stared at my bright purple hair.

She pursed her lips. "I might have a hat you could borrow. Big, black, floppy—if we put it up in a bun and stick the hat on, it'll cover it."

We gazed at my hair in the mirror, fascinated by its brilliance. "How long does it take this to wash out?"

Becky squinted at the bottle. "About ten shampoos, it says."

I sighed. "Damn. I hope there's enough time to get it out before Prue comes back with the kids."

"Oh, that's right. How did it go this morning?"

"Elsie spilled the beans about my new job."

Becky winced. "Oh no."

"Oh yes. I thought Prue was going to have a stroke in my living room."

"Your life just keeps getting better and better, doesn't it?"

I sighed. "Honestly? I don't see how it could get any worse."

• • •

I walked into Lakeside Baptist Church two minutes before the service was scheduled to start, clutching my floppy hat and ducking my head. The orange and green stained glass obviously dated from the seventies, and thirty years' accumulation of must and lilies assaulted my nostrils as I snatched a program and hurried to one of the dark wooden pews.

I scanned the backs of the heads in front of me. A woman in a black turban was three rows from the front, accompanied by a stooped, bald man. It was Willie and her husband. I stared hard at the backs of the rest of the heads, hoping I wouldn't see Bunsen, but men are hard to recognize by the backs of their heads. A few women were smattered among the crowd, including a blonde in the front row. I found myself wondering if she or the handful of other women were transvestites. Then again, this was a Baptist church, so maybe not.

As the elderly organist began cranking out a wheezy dirge, I examined the program in my hands. My heart twinged at the photo of Evan Maxted on the front—smiling, young, full of life and hope.

Nothing like the dead body in the ladies' room at the Rainbow Room.

I opened the program and blinked. The officiant was Rev. Ronald Maxted. Peaches had said Evan's father was a preacher out west, and now I recognized the name.

Ronald Maxted was a fundamentalist televangelist.

For a moment I wondered why the memorial service was being held in a small church in Austin, instead of in Maxted's sprawling church compound in California. Then I remembered the circumstances of Evan Maxted's death. Rev. Maxted probably wanted to avoid the publicity. After all, his son had been wearing a ball gown when he died, and he'd been found in the ladies' room of a gay bar. That probably wouldn't go over too well with his national audience.

The dirge died away, and the Reverend Ronald Maxted walked down the aisle, a woman I recognized as Evan's mother clutching his arm in a tragic parody of a wedding procession. She wore an ill-cut black dress, and the bleakness in her tear-streaked face hit me like a blow. Tears sprang to my eyes as she stumbled to the front pew, helped to her seat by the blonde I had noticed earlier. As the younger woman put her arms around the grieving woman, it occurred to me she must be Evan's sister, the woman who was to be married in October.

While Mrs. Maxted was obviously falling to pieces, Rev. Maxted's lips were set in a grim line. As he mounted the steps to the altar and turned to address the small congregation, I could understand why he had such a following. His high cheekbones and shock of dark hair gave him a boyish look, and I could see millions of lonely housewives swooning over this handsome man and his promises of salvation. Beside her husband's good looks and charisma, Violet Maxted seemed small and washed out. It was an odd match.

"Thank you all for coming to honor the life of my son, Evan Maxted." A keening noise came from the front of the church, where Violet Maxted doubled over in her pew. "God giveth," he said, his voice like warm chocolate despite the circumstances, "and God taketh away."

As he moved through the service, I found myself hypnotized by his voice, which was low, soothing, and bore an undercurrent of authority that was somehow comforting. Were it not for their shared last name and the blown-up photo of Evan that stood in a place of honor by the altar, the young man's cheekbones and dark eyes an eerie mirror image of the man speaking, I wouldn't have known Rev. Maxted was officiating his own son's memorial service.

It wasn't until he began the eulogy that a current of raw emotion pulsed through his voice. "Evan was a kind, good boy. His mother and I always taught him to walk in the light, in the way of the Lord." He paused and looked down for a moment. "We are all sinners," he said slowly, "each in our own way. Let us hope that our misdeeds, and those of my son"—his voice cracked—"will be washed clean in the next lifetime, and that we will all be spared the fires of hell."

The church was silent for a long moment, except for a choking sob from Evan's mother. My heart tore for both of them, and I thought of my own precious babies, safe at home. How could the Maxteds bear to go on living when their child was dead? Life was so unfair.

There was a long, painful moment. Then Rev. Maxted jerked his head toward the organist, and she cranked out another dirge. He stood at the front of the church, eyes closed, until the last strains died away. He looked up slowly. "Thank you all for coming to honor my son. May the Lord be with all of us, and lead us all in the paths of righteousness. Amen."

He stepped down to join his wife, and the service was over.

As the people in the pews rose and moved toward the aisle, I pretended to search for something in my purse. Calvin Pitts, the lecherous man from ISC walked by my pew, followed by the woman who had caught me in Evan's office. I ducked my head and peeked out again just in time to see Willie hobble down the aisle on the arm of a stooped, liver-spotted man. I tried not to imagine his exploits with a Zambian princess and glanced instead at the rest of the group coming down the aisle. I was surprised to see Trevor among them, wearing a black turtleneck and black horn-rimmed glasses. His eyes slid to me, and I lowered my head again, focusing on the contents of my purse. When I looked up again a moment later, my heart stopped.

A few steps behind Trevor was my husband.

I buried my hands in my purse, hands shaking, trying to control my body. My husband had lied about his client meeting so that he could attend Evan Maxted's memorial service. Bile welled up in my throat. Did I know my husband at all?

When the murmur of voices dissipated, I staggered to my feet and stumbled into the nave. I opened the heavy double doors to the outside just in time to see my husband's rented Subaru pull onto Loop 360.

Somehow I made it across the parking lot to the minivan. My fingers trembled as I slammed the door behind me and dialed Becky.

"How'd it go?" she asked.

"Blake was there," I croaked.

Becky sucked in her breath. "Oh, Margie . . ."

All of the pain and anger—the betrayal—swamped me. I clutched the phone to my ear as a deep, heaving sob racked my body. The steering wheel was hot against my forehead, and tears coursed down my cheeks.

"Margie . . . Where are you?"

"I'm at the church," I whispered, my mind reeling through all the lies: Maxted, the pay raise I never found out about, my husband's face at the memorial service. "I don't know what Blake is mixed up in. I thought it might be me they were going after when they blew up the car. Now I just don't know . . . I don't know anything anymore."

"Ask him about it."

"No," I said. "Not yet." I took a shuddery breath and straightened in my seat. "There's one more thing I need to do."

"Margie . . ."

"I'll call you later," I said, and hung up.

I gripped the steering wheel for a few minutes, ignoring the frantic ring of the phone. Then I wiped my tears away, reversed out of the parking spot with a jerk, and headed toward town.

• • •

The warehouse on Seventh Street looked even more dilapidated in the blazing afternoon sun than it had the night before. I circled the building and discovered a loading dock I had missed the night before. Then I drove a short way up a neighboring street and turned around, parking in front of a sagging bungalow, its yard littered with dead cars. I put the minivan in park and stared at the building.

Graffiti covered the peeling brown paint in places, and the rusted-out appliances adrift among the weeds gave the building a forlorn and dangerous air. The loading dock door was probably locked, but it wouldn't hurt to check.

I got out of the minivan and scuttled across the pitted street, my high-heeled shoe slipping on a slick of old oil. Then I trotted up to the loading dock door and yanked at the handle. It didn't budge. I snuck around the corner of the building to the door Maria Espinosa had used last night. It, too, was locked.

As I returned to the minivan in defeat, I remembered what Maria Espinosa had said last night. Two more deliveries were due. Was this their destination? A freight train rumbled by just ten feet from the building as I closed the van door behind me, the events of the past week a jumble in my head. Maxted, International Shipping Company, the McEwans, Maria Espinosa—everything intersected here. My eyes bored into weather-stained concrete. I was more convinced than ever that the answer to the puzzle of Maxted's murder, and my husband's lies, lay behind that rusty metal door.

An hour passed, then two, and nothing happened. The air-conditioning was on, and the gas gauge was dropping perilously low. I probably had another twenty minutes left. Maybe the delivery Maria was talking about was destined for the store, not this abandoned warehouse. I had just decided to wait another ten minutes and leave to confront my husband when a dirty white truck rolled down the street and backed up to the loading dock.

I shrank down in my seat, peering out the window as the driver got out and rapped at the loading dock door. A moment later, it rolled open. I craned my neck to see inside but glimpsed only a concrete wall.

The driver fumbled with the back of the truck, and a moment later the white doors swung open. A few Hispanic-looking men in threadbare jeans emerged from the warehouse's open door and helped pull out the loading ramp. Then they began unloading something that resembled long rolls of paper from the back of the truck.

Paper? Why paper?

I watched as they hauled dozens of rolls into the building, wishing I could figure out a way to slip inside while the door was open. When they finished, the older of the warehouse men pointed back toward the building. His two helpers disappeared inside, and he pulled the door down behind them before walking around to the front of the truck. A moment later, he and the driver each lit a cigarette and leaned against the driver's door.

My eyes darted to the loading dock door. When he rolled it down, it hadn't gone all the way. A foot-high gap remained at the bottom.

I shoved my keys into my skirt's tiny pocket and shoved the cell phone and the pepper spray Becky had given me into the waistband of my skirt. Then I slid out the door, closing it softly behind me, slipped off my shoes, and sprinted across the road toward the warehouse.

As I darted past the appliances, a stab of pain lanced through my foot. I ignored it and hobbled around the truck. The sound of Spanish floated to me from the driver's side, along with the smell of smoke. I crept to the open door and crouched down, peering under it. I could see the rolls of paper, but the men had gone. I dropped to my belly and scooted inside, losing a button from my new suit to the rough concrete lip.

I scrambled to my feet and scanned the dim room, which was lit by a single bulb dangling from the ceiling. The paper rolls had been deposited in a corner next to a pair of big double doors. A whirring sound came from the other side of the doors, and something told me it wouldn't be a good idea to go in that way. My eyes focused on a dark doorway near the other corner. I tiptoed over to it. As I peered around the corner into a darkened hallway, a volley of Spanish sounded just outside. I whirled around to see two pairs of feet in the gap of the bottom of the loading dock door.

I dashed through the door and ducked through the first doorway on the left just as the loading dock door rumbled open behind me.

CHAPTER TWENTY-TWO

The room around me was pitch-black and oppressively hot. The air smelled like mildew, automotive oil, and something else—something rotten. I pressed myself against the wall and inched to the side as the door outside screeched shut again. A clicking noise that sounded ominously like a lock followed, and I held my breath, half expecting the voices to round the corner and flick on a light. Instead, the whirring sound grew louder; then it faded along with the voices, and I thought I heard the snick of a door shutting. The big double doors, probably.

I waited a few minutes, listening for any further sound, but I heard nothing but the faint whirring in the background. I cursed myself for not thinking to bring my flashlight. It was safely tucked away in the glove compartment of the minivan, not fifty yards from where I stood.

I inched back toward the doorway, fumbling for a light switch. It was risky, but it was the only way I could figure out what was going on in this building. Besides, I was pretty sure I'd hear someone coming. My fingers found the switch, and I let a couple of long minutes pass, during which no sound but the whirring and the faint drip-drip of water somewhere nearby reached my ears. Then I took a deep breath and flicked it up.

Bluish fluorescent light flooded the room, and I cringed, half expecting one of the men to burst through the door and grab me. But nobody did. My eyes roamed the cramped room. Plywood covered windows along the back wall, and the concrete floor was crowded with several mismatched tables, most of them brown or gray laminate, the chipped tops exposing stained particleboard underneath. They were ringed by metal chairs. Here and there, a few stray kernels of corn were strewn across the dirty concrete floor. I took a step forward, and a movement caught my eye. It was a massive brown roach. I wrinkled my nose. What was this place? Some kind of lunchroom?

I flipped the light off again and was plunged into inky darkness. Cautiously I maneuvered back toward the hall, working on what I remembered seeing of the dim hall before the lights from the loading dock went out.

A few feet down the hallway was another door, and the single bare bulb that flared when I hit the light switch revealed a small, somewhat dirty kitchen. The rotten smell was stronger in here. Giant cans of vegetables and beans stood in the corner, and a heap of empties poked out of a plastic bag beside them. As in the first room, plywood covered the only window. Two massive, dented pots stood on a decrepit-looking stove. The sink was stained orange with rust.

The smell of urine from the last door on the left side of the hallway told me what kind of room it was before I switched on the lights. I took a brief glimpse, seeing a single, lidless toilet and a sink with a leaking faucet, the source of the maddening drips. Backing out quickly, I extinguished the light and promised myself that I'd never complain about the state of our bathroom again. Then I crossed the corridor and felt my way down to the only door I remembered seeing on that side.

The stench of unwashed bodies hit me as the door opened, and I staggered back, pulling my shirt up to my nose and swallowing back bile. Although the smell was strong, I sensed the room was empty; no one spoke, and there was no rustle of movement. I stepped forward again, clutching my shirt to my face, and felt the wall for a light switch. The whirring was louder in here. The room must adjoin what I assumed was the main part of the warehouse, the one on the other side of those double doors.

Another bank of fluorescent lights, greenish this time, illuminated a floor littered with scraps of foam and old mattresses so stained and mottled with mildew that the original fabric pattern was indecipherable. A few old blankets were scattered around. The concrete walls were bare, and a roach scuttled under one of the blankets. I shuddered and doused the lights, backing out of the room quickly and trying not to vomit.

I stood in the dark hall for a moment, debating my next move. I was dying to see what was making all the whirring noise behind the double doors but was pretty sure that opening one up to peek through would be tantamount to blowing a whistle and announcing my arrival.

My other option was the stairs I had glimpsed at the end of the darkened hallway. Maybe they would lead to offices, or something that would tell me what the building's purpose was. My main concern with that option was whether or not I'd find anyone up there. Since it was a sure bet that the area behind the double doors was occupied, though, I figured my odds would be better on the stairs.

I felt my way to the end of the hallway, discovering the stairs when my shin banged into the bottom step. I climbed slowly, wincing when something crunched beneath my stockinged foot. At the first landing, I felt around for a door, but my fingers found only concrete. I climbed the second flight and discovered the end when my nose bumped into a door.

I put my ear to it, listening for voices or footsteps. Silence. After several long minutes, I risked easing the door open a crack.

Light flooded the staircase. I closed it and backed away, waiting for the thundering of feet. As my heart hammered against my rib cage, I realized that it hadn't been the sickly green light I had seen downstairs, but softer, like filtered sunlight. I cracked the door open again and peered into the room. An old wooden table sat in the center of the room, papers stacked neatly on the scarred surface, with a row of filing cabinets on the wall behind it. Apparently I'd located command central. Fortunately for me, no one seemed to be at the helm today.

I swung the door open a little wider and slipped inside. The whiff of pine deodorizer was a welcome improvement on the aroma downstairs. The light came from clouded skylights dotting the metal ceiling, and from the huge plate glass windows that stretched across the inside wall. Excitement coursed through me. The office looked down on the area hidden by those big double doors. I crouched down immediately, not wanting to be spotted from below, and crab walked over to the huge window, squatting beneath it, and peered over the sill. Now I understood the whirring sound—and the purpose of the giant rolls.

They weren't paper.

They were fabric.

Huge sewing machines and tables heaped with bolts of brightly colored cloth crowded the warehouse's concrete floor. As I watched, a hundred pairs of brown hands measured, stitched, or hauled new bolts of fabric over to one of the huge cutting tables.

The watery sunlight from the skylights glinted off a bolt of fabric being carted to a table. It was the same fabric in the mermaid gown I had seen at the *Couture with a Conscience* show.

So Bitsy wasn't having the dresses delivered from factories in Mexico after all. They were being made right here.

All the secrecy must be because the workers were illegal aliens, doing their jobs for less than minimum wage. The Junior League wouldn't be pleased to find that out, but the truth was, most of them employed illegal aliens to clean their houses and mow their lawns. It wasn't quite on the scale of running a factory, but it was the same basic concept. If Bitsy were discovered, what would the punishment be? Back taxes plus a penalty? I couldn't imagine that would be enough to murder Maxted. Not in such a savage fashion. And how was ISC involved? Or my husband?

As I watched the workers below, mesmerized by their quiet efficiency, something caught my eye. One of the men carting fabric looked familiar under his red ball cap. My eyes followed him around the huge room, willing him to move closer, or at least take off his cap so I could get a better look at his face. Finally, he stopped at one of the big tables and heaved the bolt onto the table. Then he mopped his brow, pushing his cap up and giving me a full view of the puckered skin on the left side of his face.

It was Graciela's husband, Eduardo.

Heart thundering against my ribs, I ducked down, putting it all together. Eduardo had disappeared a month or two ago, using a coyote to transport him back and forth over the border. Graciela knew he'd made it to Mexico, but he had never come back.

Only he had.

I sat back against the hard wall, stunned as the truth hit me. Bitsy McEwan wasn't just employing illegal aliens.

She was using them for slave labor.

I'd read stories in the paper about enterprising business owners who promised aliens safe transport, only to hold them hostage and force them to work for free. Many of them eventually let the immigrants go. After all, what were the poor people going to do, turn them in? If they approached the authorities, they'd risk being deported.

Now the small kitchen, the decrepit toilet, the horrible mattresses downstairs, made sense. The workers below were being held prisoner. And the "new batch" Bitsy had been talking about yesterday wasn't fabric. It was people.

I fumbled in my waistband for my cell phone. I needed to call the police. I had dialed 9-1-1 and was about to press "Talk" when it occurred to me what would happen to Eduardo.

He'd be deported, and Graciela would be alone with her kids again.

I cleared the display and shoved the phone back into my waistband. I had to get him out of here. But how?

I peered over the windowsill again. Two men loitered by the double doors below me, but the smaller door—the one Maria had gone through last night—was unguarded. I squinted harder at the lock, and my hopes faded. It required a key from the inside, too.

I hunkered down again, trying to think. I probably couldn't do it on my own. Whom could I call for help?

Peaches. I pulled the phone out and dialed, then hit "Talk." As I raised the phone to my ear, I heard voices. My eyes darted to the stairway door. I had left it ajar. I hit "End" just as the first footstep hit the stairs.

I scanned the room, looking for a place to hide. My eyes flew to a small doorway at the far end. I scooted over to it as the footsteps approached the first landing.

The doorknob turned, but the door wouldn't budge. The footsteps grew closer. I hurled my shoulder against it, and it opened with a crack.

"What was that?" a woman said. The door to the stairwell began to open wider.

I scrambled through the doorway and pulled it shut. It wouldn't wedge back into the doorframe, so I left it slightly ajar and hoped no one would notice, and took a few small steps backward, my hands out cautiously behind me. I had glimpsed several stacks of paper and a few old chairs in the cramped closet. The last thing I needed to do was knock one of them over.

"Probably a rat," a man's voice answered.

"A rat? You don't think they'll chew on the fabric, do you?" I recognized the voice as Maria Espinosa's.

"I set some traps," the man said in heavily accented English. I edged forward and peered through the slit in the door. It was Maria Espinosa, talking to a tall, dark-haired man.

"Do you have those production numbers?" Maria asked. "She's been asking for them." I heard a door slide open and then thunk shut a moment later.

"*Sí.* It is not so good this time. The *patrona*, she want to give less food, so they work harder."

"I think it's a mistake to cut the food back. They need the energy to work . . ."

He shrugged. "That's what she tell me. She the boss."

Maria sighed. "Whatever she says, I suppose we have to do it. I'll let Sergio know."

A cell phone rang. "It's her," Maria said, then, "Hello?" A moment later, she said, "Xenia told me she's got a few new prospects, but the property values have gone up lately, and it's not going to be cheap. There are some inexpensive factories down by Mexico City, though. We could hire one of the . . ."

Silence again.

"I suppose you're probably right," Maria said after a long pause. "Still, we might want to work on the conditions. I think cutting rations is a mistake."

She was quiet for a moment. Whoever she was talking to evidently disagreed and had changed the subject, because the next time Maria spoke, she sounded excited. "It just came this afternoon. I think it's going to be great. I so appreciate you letting me help you design it . . ."

Bitsy. Of course. I shook my head in disbelief. If what I was hearing was correct, the president of the Junior League was using slave labor to create her Couture with a Conscience.

Maria continued, her voice still excited. "Once we get the new factory online, we'll be fine. If I place the order for the machines now, I should have them by next month. I've got a new group ready to come up at any time, and we'll get things going as soon as you close on a property."

She was quiet again, and then said, "That will increase our production by seventy percent. More than we need right now, but it's good to plan for the future. I was down at the shop earlier, and the orders are starting to pour in. The show was a big hit." After a moment, she said, "Don't think twice about it. I'll talk to Sergio immediately. Call me if you need anything else."

She evidently hung up then, because she let out a big sigh and said, "Well, I tried."

"It is all you can do," he said. Their footsteps receded as they headed toward the stairway, and I let the air out of my lungs. I had escaped undetected.

Then a loud ring sounded right behind me.

It was my cell phone.

CHAPTER TWENTY-THREE

I fumbled in my waistband and jabbed at buttons until it stopped. But it was too late.

"That wasn't a rat." Maria sounded scared.

The man spoke, his voice menacing. "Who's there?"

I froze, waiting for the door to open and expose me. Why hadn't I turned off the ringer? I crouched down, ready to explode out of the room.

Then the door swung open, and I found myself staring down the barrel of a gun.

"What are you doing here?" Maria gasped from where she stood, a few paces behind the man with the gun. Her dark eyes were fixed on my face; the whites showed around them. "Nobody's supposed to be here!"

"Oh, I was just in the neighborhood."

"How did you find this place?" Maria's voice was panicky.

I said nothing.

The man with the gun ignored her and looked at me. "Out."

Maria stepped aside, her hands at her mouth, as I emerged from the closet.

Maria's voice wobbled. "How did you get in?"

"When the delivery came . . . I slipped in through the bottom of the door."

The man narrowed his eyes at me. "Call the *patrona*."

Maria pulled the cell phone from her purse and hit a button; she still looked like a spooked deer.

"I am so sorry to bother you," she said when the caller picked up, "but one of the ladies from the fashion show is here." She was quiet for a moment, but I could hear an angry voice coming through the phone. "I don't know." She looked at me. "What's your name?"

"Margie," I said, without thinking to lie. "Margie Peterson."

She told Bitsy—I was assuming it was Bitsy, anyway—and from what I could make out, she did not sound pleased. "How did you know to come here?"

"I saw the address in one of the International Shipping Company files."

She relayed the message, and then said, "Which files?"

"The ones in my husband's office," I said.

I didn't hear Bitsy's response to that, but I was guessing I wouldn't have liked what she said, because when she hung up a moment later, Maria was looking very grim.

"So," I said, my stomach flip-flopping as I smiled my brightest smile, "what do we do now? If I promise not to mention any of this to the authorities, can I go home?"

She looked at the man. "She said you'd know what to do, Carlos." Her words sent a chill down my spine.

"Get Jorge," he said.

"Fine."

As she turned and hurried down the hallway, he looked at me. "Give me the cell phone." I pulled it out of my waistband and handed it over to him. "And your car keys." I fished them out, too. We stood there for a moment, evidently waiting until Jorge showed up, which he did—all too soon.

"Put your arms out," Carlos ordered. I extended both arms, and Jorge, who had a scary set of tattooed tears on his right cheek, patted me down roughly. Normally I had an assortment of wadded-up tissues and broken toys in my pockets, but the suit was new and contained only my keys. Fortunately, he missed the pepper spray, which was tucked into the back of my skirt.

"Now what?" I asked.

"Turn around," Carlos said in a flat voice. Fear coursing through me, I reached under my jacket for the pepper spray as I shifted around to face the closet. But before I could grab it, something heavy crashed down on my head, and I crumpled to the floor.

• • •

It was the smell that woke me. My face was pressed into a filthy blanket, and my stomach heaved in protest as I opened my eyes to darkness. When I tried to shift my head around, I discovered that my hands and feet were bound.

Although it was black, I recognized the whirring of the sewing machines, and the slow drip-drip of the bathroom's leaky faucet. I was in the sleeping room on the first floor.

As I rolled away from the reeking blanket, my head throbbed. Vomit rose in my throat, partly from the smell, partly from the panic that had begun pressing on my chest. I wasn't dead. But I didn't imagine they were planning to let me go with a wink and a handshake, either. I strained to move myself to an upright position, pain stabbing through the base of my skull from where Carlos had brained me. My mind was skittering in a number of unpleasant directions, including death and dismemberment by a variety of methods, and the disturbing possibility that I might never see Elsie and Nick again. I struggled to corral my racing thoughts and focus on what to do now.

I raised my bound hands, feeling for the pepper spray canister. It was still there. I wasn't sure it was going to be any help—after all, if I couldn't get my hands free, it was useless—but it was a comfort to know I wasn't completely unarmed.

Then I tested the bonds on my hands. They didn't feel rough, like rope, and from the way they pulled at my skin, I was guessing Carlos had used tape. Whoever had bound me hadn't taken any chances. The tape dug into my wrists and ankles, and my hands and feet were tingling from lack of blood. The first thing to do was get my hands free. Had I seen any sharp objects in the room from before? I tried to heave myself to my feet. My head throbbed as I lurched to a half-sitting, half-kneeling position, trying to contain the panic that rose in my throat like a scream.

I paused to rest for a moment, waiting for the pain in my head to subside. Then I shifted to a kneeling position and rocked back onto my toes, only to fall over into a mound of stinking blankets.

Ugh.

I tried again, only to go lurching into another pile of blankets, thinking of Elsie and Nick. On the third try, I made it up.

The whirring was strongest behind me, which meant the door was in the other direction. I hopped across the room, tripping once on a rolled-up blanket and coming down hard, on my shoulder. I forced myself to my feet again, making it on the first try this time, and managed to hobble to the wall. Shuffle-hopping along it with my back to the concrete, I groped for the light switch. After about ten feet, I found it. I listened for footsteps, or voices, but the only sound was the steady thrum of the machines in the next room. Then I flipped it on with my shoulder, squinting at the bright bluish light that flooded the space.

As I scanned the room, the sound of voices echoed in the hall. I ground my shoulder against the switch. Had they seen the light? I was preparing to throw myself to the floor again and feign unconsciousness when the voices faded, and a door slammed shut in the distance.

I didn't bother turning the light back on. In the brief moment it was on, I had confirmed that the only thing in the room was a pile of unwashed blankets. Instead, I hopped through the doorway into the hall and turned right.

Both the base of my skull and the foot I had hurt in the grass outside throbbed as a breeze of stale urine wafted over me from the bathroom. Almost there. At the next doorway, I hopped inside and felt for the light switch with my shoulder, illuminating the tiny room with sickly yellow light.

The pots stood on the stove, just like I remembered, and although a couple of ladles and spatulas hung from hooks beside the stove, I didn't see what I was looking for. My eyes swept the peeling paint of the small cabinets, stopping at the room's two drawers. I hopped over and turned around, grabbing the handle of the top drawer and leaning forward. Something metal rattled as the drawer slid open.

The good news was it was filled with silverware.

The bad news was, the sharpest thing available was an ancient butter knife. I squatted as best I could and opened the drawer beneath it. Can openers, ladles, and spatulas. *Damn.*

As I shoved the second drawer closed, a clanging sound came from the end of the hallway. My eyes leaped to the light switch; there was no way to make it there in time. I squeezed my eyes closed and waited.

Nothing.

The breath shuddered out of my chest as I slid the first drawer open again, fumbling through its contents until my fingers closed on a knife handle. After one last survey of the dingy room, I returned to the doorway, pushed the light off with a shoulder, and began the long hop back to the smelly room I had started in. I'd work on freeing myself once I was back where I started. That way, if anyone came in suddenly, I could pretend to still be unconscious.

I moved back to what I hoped was my original position and dropped down to the floor. Despite the smell, it was a relief to be off my feet again. As things skittered around me in the darkness, I clutched the knife and clumsily shoved the dull blade into the tight gap between my wrists. Then, as the water dripped and little feet pattered around me, I pulled the blade back and forth, back and forth, praying that it would make some impression on the taut tape.

As I sawed away at the tape, my wrists aching from the repetitive motions, I considered my situation. I'd discovered that the president of the Junior League was using slave labor to produce her Couture with a Conscience clothing line, and that International Shipping Company was likely providing the immigrants' transportation. I guessed that Jones McEwan was working with ISC to cover it all up.

Now I was trussed up like a turkey in a disgusting warehouse, and I still didn't know who had killed Evan Maxted. The missing sixteen thousand dollars and the bomb that had destroyed my husband's car were still mysteries. And I hadn't bothered to tell anyone where I was going, so my chances of an outside rescue were pretty much nonexistent.

Still, Carlos hadn't killed me yet. That was a good sign. On the other hand, I knew enough about their operation that they probably weren't going to just let me go.

I thought of Elsie's laugh and trusting blue eyes. I thought of the softness of Nick's chubby face when he slept, and the heaviness of his downy limbs. Tears rose to my eyes. Elsie hadn't even started first grade yet! That I would be robbed of sharing their childhoods with them, helping them with homework, struggling through the middle school and high school years, picking a college, getting married. It was unbearable.

I attacked the tape binding my hands with new vigor, the blunt end of the knife digging into the soft flesh of my wrists. A few minutes later, I was rewarded with a soft ripping sound.

Just then, footsteps sounded in the hall. I froze. A light flipped on in the hall, and I jammed the knife up in between my wrists and closed my eyes, struggling to slow my breathing. Somebody turned on the light, and I heard Maria's voice. She said something in Spanish, and a low voice responded. They seemed to be debating something. I heard the word *Mexico*, and also *camion*—truck? Then someone nudged me with a foot. A moment later, the footsteps receded, and I worked furiously on the tape between my wrists.

I had sawed through maybe a quarter of an inch of tape, and was attempting to tear it further, when the footsteps returned. Then two pairs of rough hands grabbed me. I squeezed my eyes shut and concentrated on staying limp—and not dropping the knife—as they carted me out of the room. The smell receded, and I caught the drone of a lone cicada in the distance, and the smell of hot asphalt, before they dumped me onto a hard, rough surface.

Then a door slammed, an engine rumbled, and the floor lurched beneath me.

CHAPTER TWENTY-FOUR

I'd been right when I thought they'd been talking about a truck. Evidently the discussion had centered on tossing me into one. Except for a few bright pinpoints where the late-afternoon sun leaked through the loading door, everything was dark, and suffocating heat bore down on me. My new suit clung to my body like a wet towel as I eased the knife out of the tape and continued sawing away at it. Where were they taking me? A shiver passed through me despite the heat. I hoped their destination wasn't an abandoned field on the outskirts of town.

As I dragged the knife blade back and forth across the tape, blood trickled down my hands, mixing with sweat to loosen my grip on the blade. Then the truck suddenly swerved to the right. As my body slammed into one of the walls, the knife slipped from my grasp, skittering across the floor.

Panic rose to my throat as I writhed on the floor of the truck, listening for the slide of metal as the truck turned again. When my ears picked up a scraping sound over by the door, I inched toward the back of the truck like a caterpillar, trying to detect the flat piece of metal through the sweat-soaked rayon of my suit. Finally, I found it. But every time I got my hands into position to pick it up, the truck surged forward with a jerk, sending it skittering out of reach.

Just as the knife had escaped my grasp for the fifth time, the truck made a sudden swing to the right, sending it right up against my hand. I grabbed the handle just before the truck veered in the other direction, smacking me into a metal wall.

Ten minutes later, I ripped my wrists apart, gasping at the pain as the tape tore my skin. The truck lurched again, but this time I was ready. I steadied myself with a numb hand, and then set to work freeing my feet. Now that I could grab the edge of the tape and pull, it only took a few minutes. I flexed my hands and feet, encouraging the blood to flow through them, wincing at the prickly feeling that comes with restored circulation. Then I fumbled with the latch on the back of the truck. If I could open it, I could signal to the cars behind me, or even jump out when the truck came to a stop.

It was locked. After testing the walls for weaknesses and finding none, I had no choice but to sit and wait. The truck floor jounced beneath me as I leaned against the side, watching as the sunlight in the cracks faded, replaced by darkness and the white flicker of head-lights.

I don't know much time passed before the truck lurched to a stop, but afternoon had long ago faded into night. The engine sput-tered and died, and I crouched by the back door, pepper spray in hand. My heart pounded in my throat as the front door opened and closed. The whir of automobiles was distant, replaced by the chirr of crickets and the crunch of footsteps, and two men talking in Spanish.

A moment later, the latch jiggled. Then the doors swung open. I pressed the button on the pepper spray, swinging my arm in an arc before me. I had a brief glimpse of two men staggering, clutching their faces, before the wind swept a cloud of the chemical back at me.

I leaped out of the truck, eyes burning like fire, and stumbled across a few feet of pavement into something that felt like grass. A burst of Spanish sounded behind me, and a hand grabbed my shoul-der, spinning me around. I thrust the canister out and sprayed again. A curse sounded as I struggled to regain my balance, but no one grabbed me. I stumbled ahead blindly, tears streaming down my face. I had been hit by the spray, but not as badly as the men behind me. The moon was full, and I could make out what I thought was a clump of trees ahead of me. When I glanced back, the two figures were falling behind.

The sharp grass tore at my legs as I ran, and stickers and nettles dug themselves into the soft skin of my feet. When I got to the trees, I paused for a second. I could hear the sharp retort of Spanish behind me. I blundered forward again, clambering through a wire fence and pushing through to the other side of the trees before taking off across another field. I finally stopped in a stand of sycamore trees, their silvery bark ghostly in the moonlight, and listened for sounds of pursuit. The crickets chirred as a breeze stirred the leaves, and somewhere far above me an owl hooted, but the sound of the men had faded into the night.

I leaned against a tree, the air like fire in my lungs, my eyes still stinging from the pepper spray. A shallow pool of stagnant water gleamed in the moonlight, and thirst gripped me. I had been sweating for hours, with no food or water. I was thirsty, hungry, and tired, and although I couldn't hear the men, I was sure they were still searching for me. I surveyed the land around me, looking for a farmhouse. Nothing. Then the distant rumble of an automobile floated to my ears, and a pair of headlights pierced the darkness in the distance. Fear coursed through me. Was it the truck?

As the rumble faded into the distance, I limped out of the grove of sycamores and hobbled toward the road. Roads led to towns, and towns had phones. And what I needed right now, more than anything, was a phone.

The cracked strip of pavement was farther than it looked. Although it felt like an hour, it must have been no more than twenty minutes before I stumbled out of the field onto the gravel shoulder. I winced as the pebbles ground into my wounded feet, feeling exposed. What if the truck came back? Fields stretched out on either side of the road. Would I have a chance to hide in time? And how far was the next town? In rural Texas, the distances between towns could be twenty miles or more. I set off in the direction of the moon, hoping I was picking the right way—and hoping I would get to a phone before my captors got to me.

I had walked for about fifteen minutes, alert for the sound of the truck, when the low thrum of an engine sounded ahead of me.

There was nothing higher than a short clump of grass along the side of the road. Where could I hide? I couldn't even move off the road; barbed wire gleamed in the moonlight. I scooted down into the furrow beside the road and lay down behind a tussock of grass. A few minutes later, a pickup truck rattled by, and I realized I had just hidden from a potential ride to town.

I climbed out of the shallow ditch and hobbled down the road again, my feet stinging with every step, ears pricked for the sound of pursuit. Tears still leaked out of the corners of my eyes from the pepper spray, and I was beginning to despair of ever reaching a phone, when a yellow light twinkled on the horizon. I ignored my feet and quickened my pace.

Almost a half hour later I teetered across a cattle guard onto a dirt driveway. Old cars, their dulled metal gleaming in the moonlight, lined the rough track. The farmhouse sat about a quarter mile back from the road, its sagging front porch lit by a single bulb. As I passed the remains of a fifty-year-old Chevy, a low growl froze my blood.

Fifteen feet in front of me, a dog the size and shape of a large wolf rose to its feet, yellow teeth bared. I tore my eyes from it and looked away—I'd read somewhere that looking away shows submission—and hunched down in an attempt to look small and nonthreatening. But the dog advanced, snarling. Although I was focusing on a rusted bumper, I could see the dog in my peripheral vision—ten feet away, now five—and was about to squeeze the trigger on the pepper spray when the screen door slammed open. My head jerked up as a man with a shotgun appeared on the front porch.

"Lucy! Heel!"

The dog didn't exactly dash to its master's side, but at least it hesitated. The man on the porch squinted into the night and leveled the shotgun at me. "What are you doin' on my property?" His rough voice was anything but friendly.

I stared at the gun in his hand, then at the dog. "I'm sorry. Sorry for trespassing." I swallowed, and the dog growled, exposing another half inch of teeth. "I know it sounds crazy, but somebody kidnapped me in a truck. I managed to escape a few miles from here . . ." As I recounted my story, it sounded ridiculous even to me.

"Kidnapped?"

I nodded.

"Step a little closer, where I can see you."

I glanced at the dog, which didn't seem to think this was a good idea.

"Lucy!" the man yelled. "I said heel! Now!" She reluctantly retreated toward the porch, her yellow eyes still trained on me. When she had settled back onto her haunches, I shuffled forward a few steps. The man's eyes widened, and his voice lost its menacing edge. "You look like hell!"

Glancing down at what was left of my brand-new suit and the shreds of my taupe panty hose, I realized he was right. With the dog semi-safely at her master's heel, I relaxed a little bit. "Could I have a glass of water?" I asked. "And maybe use your phone?"

"Sure thing, honey. Those fellas still out there?" The harshness in his voice was gone, replaced by warmth and compassion.

As the tension seeped from my body, I swayed on my feet. "I think so," I rasped.

He scanned the horizon. "Well, Lucy here'll let us know if they decide to drop by. Won't you, girl?" He patted her bristling fur. "In the meantime, let's get you inside."

I edged toward the front porch, and he reached out a rough hand to help me climb the two steps. My eyes flitted from his friendly brown eyes to Lucy's cold yellow ones, and I was relieved when the door slammed shut behind us, leaving the wolf-dog on the porch.

"Sit down," he said. "Take a load off."

"Thanks." I sank into the nearest chair and surveyed the kitchen. Tacked up next to the ancient fridge was a farming-supply company calendar featuring a tractor. Behind it, faded floral wallpaper peeled from the walls, and the linoleum on the floor had worn away in several places, but no dirty dishes littered the chipped Formica counter. A woman had lived here in the past, but not now, I was guessing.

"I'm Jess Howard," he said, rummaging through a drawer and pulling out a couple of safety pins, which he tossed onto the table.

"I'm Margie," I said. "Margie Peterson." I picked up a safety pin. "What are these for?"

He nodded toward my shirt. I looked down. Two of the buttons had torn free, exposing a few inches of rippled flesh and the clasp of my bra. I grabbed the edges of fabric and pulled them together, blushing, as he turned and pulled a glass from a cabinet.

By the time he had filled it with water and ice and slid it across the table to me, I was decent again. "Thanks," I muttered.

"No problem," he said, pulling up a chair across from me. "So, you were kidnapped?"

I nodded and gulped down the water.

He rose to refill the glass. "I heard kidnapping was big business in Mexico, but I didn't know it was going on here, too. Where did they pick you up?"

"Austin," I said. "It wasn't a ransom kidnapping, though. I found out something I wasn't supposed to know."

His thick eyebrows rose. "Drugs?"

"Nope. I found a factory that someone's staffing with slave labor—illegal immigrants. They caught me before I could get out and call the police."

"No wonder they wanted you out of the way. Where were they headed when you got away?"

"I don't know." I shivered as I considered the possibilities.

He glanced at my tattered suit. "Well, whatever it was, I'm bettin' it wasn't good. How did you escape?"

As I recounted my story, his brown eyes widened. At first, all I had noticed was the shotgun, but now I realized he was a good-looking man. He was going to seed a little around the middle, maybe, and his brown hair was receding a little from his weathered face, but he was still attractive in a rugged way. In his fifties, probably. When I finished, he said, "You want to call the cops? I'll bet those fellas are still in the area."

"No, not yet. There's one more thing I have to do." I gulped down another swig of water. "Can I use your phone? It may be long distance, I'm afraid . . ." I looked at him. "Where are we, by the way?"

"Utopia."

Suddenly, Lucy began to growl. Headlights flashed against the fading wallpaper as the sound of crunching gravel eclipsed the crickets. A shiver ran down my back. "Are you expecting anyone?"

"Nope." Jess grabbed his shotgun. "Stay in here. In fact, why don't you head back down the hall?"

I nodded and ducked down the narrow hall as the screen door squeaked open. I slipped through the first doorway on the right, into a tiny bathroom, it turned out, and pressed myself against the wall, listening. Sweat broke out on my brow as Jess's taut, rough voice filtered down the hall toward me. I couldn't make out his words, or hear whomever he was talking to. Then the gravel crunched again, and when the sound had receded into the distance, the screen door banged shut.

"You okay back there, ma'am?"

I ventured out of the bathroom. "Fine. Who was it?"

He grimaced. "The fellas you got away from, I reckon."

My heart thumped against my ribs. "What did you tell them?"

"They said they was lookin' for a woman. Said she got lost. Said there was a big cash reward out for her." He shrugged. "I told 'em I ain't seen no one. They said they'd come back later, maybe. I told 'em not to bother."

I slumped against a wall. "Thanks for covering for me. I can't believe they had the balls to come up the driveway and ask you."

"Well," he said, "this house is the only one for miles 'round here, so I guess they figgered this is where to find you." His lips twitched into a mischievous smile. "I got somethin' from 'em, though."

"What?"

He held up a scrap of paper. "Plate numbers."

"You're kidding me!" I resisted the urge to run up and hug him. "You know, if I weren't already married, I think I might propose."

He laughed. "It ain't worth *that* much."

"I don't know about that," I said. "Now, before they come back, can I borrow your phone?"

He smiled. "It's all yours. And when you're done, can I interest you in a bite to eat?" My stomach gurgled, and he chuckled. "I'll take that as a yes."

• • •

An hour and a half later, not long after I finished a third bowl of chili, the driveway crunched again. I slunk back down the hall while Jess picked up his gun.

A minute later, I heard a familiar husky voice and burst into the kitchen. "Peaches!" My boss stood in the kitchen, one hand on her hip, her generous curves clad in a lime-green spandex minidress.

She ran an eye over me. "You look like hell."

"Thanks." I grinned. "Jess, this is my boss, Peaches."

Jess smiled big and swept an imaginary hat off his balding head. "Pleased to meet you, miss."

Peaches's eyes swept up and down Jess's tall frame, lingering at his dark brown eyes. "Likewise," she purred.

"I hate to run," I said, "but we've got somebody else to rescue. Jess, I can't thank you enough for everything you've done . . ."

"Don't forget this," he said, handing me the scrap of paper with the plate numbers. "I put my number down there, too," he said, glancing at Peaches. "Margie here tells me you've got a little rescue operation going on. Anything I can help with?"

"Jess," I protested, "you've done so much already. I can't ask you . . ."

Peaches put her hand on my arm. "Hold on there, sugar." Then she turned to Jess. "That shotgun there might come in mighty handy."

"Peaches!"

Jess smiled at Peaches. "Why don't I just follow you all into Austin? I could be there as backup . . . just in case . . ."

"But . . . ," I stammered.

Peaches just looked at me. "Honey, we need all the help we can get."

CHAPTER TWENTY-FIVE

He's cute," Peaches said as we bumped over the cattle guard in her Buick Regal.

"I thought you were already seeing someone," I said.

"Yeah, well, that ended last night."

"What happened?"

"I ran into him down at the Broken Spoke with a twenty-year-old."

I winced. "What a jerk. Are you okay?"

She glanced at the rearview mirror, and the reflected glare of Jess's headlights lit up her carefully rouged cheeks. "It's just like my mama said. Men are like buses. They come around every twenty minutes, but you have to get off one before you can get on another."

I eyed her dress. "I guess that means you weren't sitting home moping tonight."

"Nope. Good thing, too. You don't want to meet a man like Jess when you're wearing a T-shirt and a ratty pair of shorts."

"Thanks for coming to pick me up," I said.

"No problem. You did a good job getting out of that truck. I'm just hoping we can get to the warehouse before they clear everything out of there."

"I didn't think about that. You think they'll do that tonight?"

She glanced at me and shook her head. "Of course. They figure the first thing you're gonna do when you get to a phone is call the cops. As soon as those goons call in and say you got away, they'll empty the place. I'm just hoping they're afraid to call and tell their boss they lost you."

"They stopped by Jess's place."

"I know. And it's a good thing you hid. If they knew you were there, they probably would have killed him and taken off with you." She grinned. "They must be scared shitless to tell their boss they lost a little *gringa* like you. I'm guessing they won't be getting their Christmas bonuses this year."

"So what are we going to do about getting Eduardo out?"

"See that bag there?" She nodded toward a canvas bag on the floor between us. "Take a look inside."

I opened it and peered inside, but it was too dark to see. I slid my hand inside and felt something cold, hard, and slick. "A gun?" I whispered.

"Yup."

"What do I do with it?"

Peaches rolled her eyes. "Jesus. What do you think you do with it? You shoot people with it. If you look underneath, you'll find a couple of stun guns, too."

"Can't I just take a stun gun?"

She shook her head. "Not with these people."

"So what's the plan?"

"Don't worry, sweetheart. I've got it all worked out. Now why don't you get a few minutes of shut-eye? I'll wake you up when we get to Austin."

I sank back into the bench seat and relaxed, watching the fence posts flash by in the headlights and drowsing while a singer on the radio crooned about a woman in Tennessee.

• • •

"Margie! Margie!" Somebody was shaking me. "Wake up!"

I swam up through a dream about snakes wrapping themselves around my wrists, their forked tongues darting out to caress my skin. "What?"

"Where exactly is this place?"

I looked around, disoriented. The fence posts were gone, replaced by darkened storefronts and a few people in baseball caps slouching on street corners. "Where are we?"

"East Austin. Where did you think we were, New York?"

I rubbed my eyes and sat up straight, suddenly remembering why we were here. "The warehouse. It's on Seventh Street. Over by Chicon. But what are we going to do when we get there?"

"You said you only saw a few heavies, right?"

I thought back to the guards I had seen in the main room of the warehouse. "Yeah. Three or four of them."

"Well, I'm guessing at least one of them is out looking for you now, so that puts us at two or three. Maybe even just one."

"Okay. So?"

"So. We knock on the door . . ."

"We knock on the door? You're kidding me, right?"

"How else are we going to get in? You said the windows were boarded up, right?" I nodded. "Okay," she continued. "So, we knock on the door and yell 'Immigration!' When someone answers, we take him out with the stun gun, and then go in and secure the place."

"That's it? We 'take him out' and then 'secure the place'?"

She beamed at me. "Yup. Piece of cake."

"Forgive me for sounding dense, but how exactly are we supposed to secure the place?"

"Take out the other guys."

"What do you mean, 'take out the other guys'?"

"Remember the guns?"

"Yeah. But I thought we were going to use the stun guns."

"Yeah, well, they only work at short distances. You gotta have the guns for longer-range stuff."

"So I'm supposed to use a gun—which I've never even *held* before, much less used—to take out a few, possibly several, members of the Mexican Mafia." My stomach turned over at the thought of holding a gun, much less pulling the trigger. I hated what they'd done to Eduardo, but I wasn't sure I could shoot someone over it—or should.

Peaches's eyebrows rose. "They're involved with the Mexican Mafia?"

I threw up my hands. "I don't know! I just don't think this is a good idea."

"You want to call the cops instead? Because if you do that, Eduardo is going straight back to Mexico on a one-way ticket."

I sighed. "There's no other way to do this?"

She shook her head. "Not unless you can come up with something better. Besides, we've got that hunk Jess looking out for us. I'll bet he's real good with a shotgun."

"Let's just get it over with," I groaned.

"You worry too much," Peaches said, patting my leg. "You'll be fine."

• • •

Five minutes later, we pulled up across the street from the warehouse. Peaches parked the car and as Jess pulled up behind us, she dug through the bag and tossed me a gun and a stun gun. "How does it work?" I said.

"See that? That's the safety. You flip that back, and then all you gotta do is pull the trigger."

I flipped it back experimentally and held it out in front of me. "Like this?"

She grabbed my hand. "Careful with that thing! I just got the windshield replaced last week."

I replaced the safety. "Sorry. And what about the stun gun?"

"You just press this end—the one with the metal pointy things—up against the guy and hit the button, and they go down like a sack of potatoes." She checked her makeup in the rearview mirror. "Do I look okay?"

"We're about to go raid a warehouse filled with armed men, and you're worried about your lipstick?"

"Hey. Once this thing is over, I'm planning on taking that handsome man out to the Spoke. Show Buck a thing or two. I'll bet he's a great dancer."

"Let's just hope we get a chance to find out."

We climbed out of the car and met up with Jess, who was leaning against the front of his truck and eyeing Peaches's legs appreciatively. "What's the plan, ladies?"

When Peaches told him, he nodded.

"You think it's okay?" I said, relieved that he wasn't rolling around in the grass and laughing.

"It's all you got, so it'll have to be. I'm coming with you."

"Oh no," I said. "We couldn't ask you to do that."

"If there are three of them and two of you ladies, you're going to need help."

"What a man," Peaches purred. Even in the dim light of the streetlamp I could see Jess blush.

Peaches turned to me. "There are two entrances, right?"

"That's all I know of. There's the main door on the corner, there, and then there's the loading dock in the back."

"Why don't I take one of the doors?" Jess said. "That way, if they try to sneak out the back, it's covered."

Peaches nodded. "Good idea. If you'll cover the loading dock, we'll take the main door."

"Sounds like a plan," Jess said, and trotted around the building. When he'd disappeared, Peaches adjusted her cleavage. "Are you sure this dress doesn't make me look fat?"

"You look fine. Now, can we get this over with?"

She tightened her grip on the gun and the stun gun. "Ready?"

"I guess it's now or never." We set off across the street, my still-bare, torn-up feet howling with every step.

A chill swept through me as we crossed the appliance graveyard. What was I doing? Last time I went in there, they had taped me up and stuck me in a delivery truck destined for God knows where. This time I had a gun, and Peaches, but I wasn't sure how much good it would do me. I remembered seeing only a couple of guards, but I wasn't really sure. Maybe the rest of them were on their lunch break.

As we approached the door on the corner of the building—the small one, not the big one on the loading dock—Peaches pointed to a spot a few feet to the left of the door. "Stand there," she hissed. "Right next to me."

I moved toward the peeling concrete wall and squeezed the stun gun hard.

"Ready?" Peaches whispered.

I nodded.

She hauled off and whacked the door with the butt of her gun, yelling, "Immigration! Open up!"

Silence.

She banged again. "Immigration! We have the building surrounded! Open up *now*!"

A moment later, a shuffling sound came from behind the door. Peaches flattened herself against the wall beside me as the dead bolt clicked back. When the door opened, Peaches thrust her gun through the opening and yelled, "Come out with your hands up!"

When a short dark man in a grubby T-shirt and jeans inched through the doorway, looking surprised to find himself face-to-face with a buxom woman in lime-green spandex instead of a guy in blue polyester, Peaches gave me a quick nod. I stepped forward and hit the button on the stun gun. Instantly, the man crumpled to the ground.

Peaches peered through the open door. "That was easy." Then she waved to me. "It's clear. Come on."

We slid into the darkened warehouse, the massive machines lit only by the pale light of the moon seeping through the skylights. "Where is everyone?" I whispered.

"I don't know. But I bet we'll find out soon. Try to stay covered." We darted from the doorway to crouch behind one of the cutting tables. "Where are the workers?"

I pointed to the doorway to the loading dock. "Through there," I whispered. "But there's a big glass wall up there," I said, nodding toward the black glass on the second floor. "Anyone who's up there can see what we're doing."

"We'll just have to be careful, then."

We had made it halfway across the floor when the glass shattered above our heads, and a piece of the sewing machine next to us flew into the air. A split second later, the hard ping of metal on metal ricocheted around the room.

"Stay down!" Peaches hissed. I was already flat on my belly under a table, but I appreciated the tip. She ducked behind a machine and let off a few rounds in the direction of the window. The glass exploded. Then it was silent, except for the occasional tinkle of a piece of falling glass. "Come on!" Peaches darted forward. I scrabbled out from under the table and tried to keep up with her. We were just ten yards from the door when three more bullets whizzed past us. I ducked again, smelling burnt hair.

"Peaches! Are you okay?"

"Took a chunk out of my hair, the bastards."

"At least that's all they hit," I hissed back.

She peered over the edge of a machine and popped off a few rounds in the direction of the gunshots. Then she grabbed my arm. "Let's go!"

Another bullet zinged by as we dashed toward the door and flattened ourselves against the wall. Peaches listened for a moment. Then she crept over, pulled the door open, and retreated to the wall. When nothing happened, she edged over to it and peered in. Then she slipped through it, waving to me to follow.

Except for a pale sliver of moonlight through the open door, the room was pitch-black. "At least there's no welcoming party in here. They must be short-staffed. Where are they keeping everyone?" Peaches asked.

"Over there," I said, pointing toward where I remembered seeing the hallway. "Should we let Jess in?"

"Maybe," she said. "If we can do it without getting shot. Where's the loading dock door?"

I stepped forward, hands in front of me, until my fingers touched metal. "It's here." A second later, she bumped into me. "What do we do now?" I asked.

"I wish we had radios, or something. I guess we just knock and hope he can hear us."

"What about the other guys?"

"Can you cover the hallway?"

"I guess so." As I walked over in the general direction of the hall-way door, the silence was broken by a gunshot. "Don't count on it, though."

I felt for the wall in the darkness and fumbled along it until I got to the opening that led to the hall. Then I planted myself next to it and gripped the stun gun in my hand. There was no way I was going to go down that hallway alone, but at least I could surprise anyone coming through it. As I guarded the doorway to the hall, Peaches knocked on the loading dock door.

"I don't know if he can hear me," she said.

"I'm not sure you can open it even if he could," I said. "I bet it's locked."

A moment later, she said, "You're right. But I have the key."

"You found the key?"

A crack sounded, followed by the ping of a bullet ricocheting around the small room. "Yup," she said.

"Peaches! You could have killed me!"

"In case you forgot, there're a couple of guys at the end of that hallway who have just that in mind. And unless you want to head back across the floor out there, we were gonna need another exit, anyway. Now, let's just hope Jess recognizes me before he takes my legs out. I just bought these shoes, and it would be a shame to have to give them away." Something rumbled from the direction of her voice—the door opening, I realized—and the faint light of sodium streetlamps filtered into the room, silhouetting Peaches's curvy form.

"So far, so good," she said.

A moment later, Jess trotted through the open loading dock door. "Are you two okay? I heard gunshots."

"We're fine for now," said Peaches. "But we've got a problem at the end of that hallway."

He squinted into the darkness. "Is that where we're going?"

"Of course," Peaches said.

Jess turned to me. "You know where they're keeping them?"

I nodded. "First door on the right."

"Tell you what. Why don't I fire a few shots down there, clear out whoever's down there." He glanced at the loading dock door. "We should probably close that, though. The light behind us will make us sitting ducks."

I walked over and tugged at the door. Although the room was darker, the double doors were still open. "Is that going to be okay?" I asked, pointing to the moonlight leaking in from the factory floor. Unfortunately, the only way to get to the double doors was to cross in front of the hallway door, providing an easy target to the gunmen who were doubtless lurking at the other end of the hall.

"It would be better to close it," he said. "How about I take a couple of shots, and then one of you gals run over and close it up?"

"I'm on it," Peaches said. A moment later, a shotgun blast exploded from the door to the hallway. Peaches scuttled across the room and swung the double doors closed, plunging the room into darkness. Jess emptied two more rounds down the hallway and then called to me, "Ready, Margie?"

I swallowed hard. What was I doing here? Saving Eduardo, I told myself. And potentially making my children motherless, I realized, thinking of Elsie and Nick. Would I ever see them again?

I forced down the lump that was growing in my throat. Graciela's children deserved both parents, too—as did the children of all the other workers. I would just have to be careful. Wishing for a helmet and a bulletproof vest, I said, "I guess so."

"I'll go first. Stay behind me."

I stumbled over and grabbed a handful of Jess's soft shirt. He smelled of tobacco and soap.

"I'm going to stay on the right side of the hall," he said. As we pressed ourselves against the wall and sidled down the hallway, a gunshot cracked in front of us. "How far?" he whispered.

"Just a few more feet, I think." A moment later, a doorknob rattled, another gunshot sounded, and something whizzed by my head. It was followed by two reports I recognized as Jess's shotgun.

"It's locked," he said.

"Let me do it," I hissed. "There's a dead bolt above the knob."

I fumbled past him and snicked the dead bolt back. Then the door swung open, releasing the fetid smell of unwashed bodies and fear, and we tumbled into the room.

The room was dark, but we were surrounded by whimpers and urgent whispers. "What do we do now?" I asked Jess.

"Wait for them to come to us."

"What do you mean?"

"There's only one shooter."

"How do you know?"

"Because of how far apart the shots are. This door locks from the outside. If we bide our time, I'm betting our friend will try to lock us in."

"Then what?"

"We shoot him."

"Kill him?" The thought turned my stomach. Hadn't I spent the last five years telling my children that guns are bad? What was I doing here?

"You got a better idea?" Jess asked.

"Can't we just use the stun gun?"

"Too risky."

"Jess, I don't want to murder someone."

"They've been keeping these folks here prisoner, and God knows what they were gonna do to you."

"We'll know it when he goes to close the door, won't we?"

"Yup."

"Well, when that happens, why don't you give it a hard kick? When he goes down, I'll get him with the stun gun."

"It's too risky."

As he spoke, a squeak came from the direction of the door.

There was no time to think. I tightened my grip on the stun gun and hurled myself toward the noise. With a crack, my shoulder connected with the door. The door swung open sharply, then stopped with a thud. At the same moment, a gunshot sounded. I thrust the stun gun out and down, making contact with something soft. Then I punched the button, and something thumped to the floor.

"Shit!" It was Jess's voice from behind me. "Margie? Margie? Are you okay?"

"I'm fine," I croaked, my legs wobbling as I stepped back. "The guy's down."

"He could have killed you!"

"Yes, but he didn't."

Jess had reached over to steady me when another gunshot rang out, and he groaned in pain.

CHAPTER TWENTY-SIX

Jess!" I yelled, reaching for him in the darkness. As I crawled back
into the room, pulling him behind me, another shot rang out.

I fumbled with the safety on my gun. It was bad enough having
to use the thing at all, much less in a pitch-dark building with inno-
cent lives depending on my accuracy.

I aimed at what I hoped was the hall, said a small prayer asking
for forgiveness, and was about to squeeze the trigger when a volley
of shots rang out from the direction of the loading dock.

I'd forgotten about Peaches.

"Hang in there, guys! I'm comin'!" she called.

The shooter returned a few rounds. Then Peaches let off another
volley of shots, and somebody cried out in pain.

"Put down the gun!" Peaches hollered. *Now!*

A moment later, harsh light flooded the hallway. I flinched, then
edged toward the hallway and squinted. One man lay next to the
door. A few steps farther on, another man slumped against the wall,
holding his side. Blood oozed from between his fingers.

Peaches strode down the hall, her gun trained on the wounded
man. "Is there anyone else here?" she asked.

The man responded in Spanish. She rattled something back to him, then turned to me. "He says only three of them were here. All the other guys are out looking for you."

"Thank God you know how to use that gun."

Peaches walked up to the bleeding man. His gun lay beside him, and she kicked it out of reach. "Margie, can you cover him for me? I'll make sure Jess is okay."

"I'll be fine," said Jess in a weak voice as I stepped forward and held my gun up with a shaking arm. I glanced back at him. Blood leaked from his left arm.

"You will be once we get you to a hospital," Peaches said. "First, though, we got to get these guys out of here." She motioned to the men and women huddled behind us in the dim room.

"But they're going to need to get in touch with their relatives. How are we going to manage that?"

A tall, thin man stepped forward into the light from the hallway. I recognized him from the puckered skin on the side of his face: Eduardo. For a moment, I forgot about the two thugs lying in the hallway. "Eduardo! Thank God you're all right! Graciela and the girls will be so happy to see you!"

"Thank you so much for coming to help us, Miss Margie."

I surveyed the crowd behind him. Their faces were scared and tired, but there was hope in their eyes. I wanted to send them to their families . . . but how were we going to be able to prove what Bitsy was doing?

I turned to Eduardo. "Now what do we do?" I asked. "I don't want to turn them over to Immigration. They'll just try again with another coyote, and who knows what will happen the next time."

"I will take them to my house," he said. "I know where this building is. I recognized it when they brought us here. It is near La Victoriana. Graciela and I live on Eleventh Street, not far from here. They can telephone their families from our house."

Bitsy would likely escape prosecution if that happened, but at least these people would earn their freedom. I didn't like it but didn't see any other options. And after all, that was why we'd come here in the first place, rather than calling the cops an hour ago and avoiding the whole gun-battle thing. "Are you sure that's okay?"

"It will be fine. Everyone has a contact here, waiting to hear from them."

"I hate for you to have to walk. I don't even have my car keys, though, and there are so many . . ."

"It is no problem. My house is only ten or fifteen blocks from here. A short walk. I will lead them, and you can call the *policía*."

Peaches nodded. "Good idea, Eduardo. Then, when they get here, they've got witnesses, but we can just say everyone escaped in the commotion."

I hugged Eduardo. "Tell Graciela I said hi."

"I will. And thank you for helping us." He turned to Peaches and Jess. "All of you."

"Our pleasure," Jess said softly. Peaches nodded. Eduardo turned and said something in Spanish, and everyone hurried past us out of the squalid room, touching us lightly in gestures of thanks and murmuring in Spanish as they jostled one another down the hallway. The loading dock door squeaked open, and in less than two minutes, the men and women who had been enslaved for months—years, maybe—disappeared into the night.

"We'll give them ten minutes," Peaches said. "Anyone got a cell phone?"

I grimaced. "Maria took it from me when she caught me."

Peaches sighed. "I left mine out in the car."

"I've got one," Jess said. "The holster's on my belt, if you can find it."

After a bit of fumbling that I suspected neither of them minded, she held up the phone. "Ready?"

"Give it five more minutes," I said, "and we'll call."

"I'm worried about that fella over there," said Jess.

I glanced over at the man in the hallway. His brown face had an undertone of gray, and the pool of blood beneath him had grown alarmingly.

Peaches said, "Forget him. What about you?"

"I think Jess is right," I said. "We need to call for help."

"I hate to put those poor people at risk on his account." Peaches jabbed a finger toward the guy in the hall.

"Better to call now," Jess said. "I don't know how long that stun gun works."

She sighed. "I guess you're right. Let's just hope Eduardo gets a move on." She dialed, and a few minutes later, sirens wailed in the distance.

"I don't think you need to worry about Eduardo and the others," Jess said. "Those sirens will put a spring in their step. Besides, we'll just put off telling the cops the details for as long as possible. Give 'em a chance to get away."

"I hope you're right," I said. "Peaches, why don't you stay here, and I'll go out and meet the police."

"Don't forget your stun gun," she said. "Just in case that guy by the door wakes up."

• • •

When the firefighters and paramedics arrived, the man by the front door was still passed out. The police rolled up as the paramedics wheeled stretchers into the ambulances, and we spent the next hour repeating the story about everyone scattering into the night when the doors opened. The fifth time Peaches and I went through it, they finally gave up and let us go home.

"So they're going to question the president of the Junior League about using slave labor," Peaches said as we pulled away from the warehouse in the Buick. The keys to my minivan hadn't materialized, so she was taking me home. "I'll bet that'll raise some eyebrows when the next society page comes out."

"And her assistant. I hope Maria doesn't take the fall for her, but I'm betting that's what's going to happen." I glanced back at the warehouse, which was still swarming with police. Jess's gunshot wound was minor, but the paramedics had insisted on taking him to the hospital anyway, along with the guy Peaches shot. "It's a shame, really," I said. "The organization could have done a lot of good." I shivered. "She ordered Carlos to 'take care of me.'" I didn't want to think of what that would entail. Mexico? Or something more final? "I think she's got a few screws loose."

Peaches rolled her eyes. "You can say that again. Charity is one thing. Keeping people locked up in a disgusting warehouse so you can look good in the papers is nuts. Besides, I'd be willing to bet a good portion of the cash went right into her little Donna Karan purse."

"I hope the police figure it out when they finish the investigation." I'd told them I thought Bitsy was involved, but I was betting she'd claim ignorance and say it was all Maria's doing. I leaned back into the Buick's seat. "I'm glad that guy you shot is going to be okay."

"Yeah, it's too bad, isn't it?"

"Peaches!"

She reached over and patted my knee. "You know, I was right about hiring you. You've been working what—two weeks?—and you've broken up a high-society slave ring that's been going on for years. Pretty damned impressive, if you ask me."

I slumped into my seat. "Thanks. Too bad I can't figure out what's going on with my husband. Or who killed Maxted, for that matter." I sighed. "Maybe I should have stuck with gardening."

Peaches pursed her lips. "There may be a few rocks you haven't turned over yet."

"What do you mean? I've been to Maxted's apartment, Maxted's office, the Rainbow Room, Miss Veronica's Boudoir . . ." I ticked them off on my fingers. "I tried to talk with Maxted's boyfriend, but they locked him up on drug charges before I got to him."

"Well, you've *been* to Maxted's apartment, but the way I hear it, you didn't get much of a chance to look around."

"Yeah, but how am I going to get back in? Even if Willie believed the story about the cat, why would she let me in a second time?"

Peaches shrugged. "I don't know. Make something up."

"I did that last time. Now I'm stuck with a homicidal cat, my new couch is destroyed, and I've got a week's worth of dirty clothes stacked up in my kitchen because I can't get into my laundry room." I sighed. "Still, I guess it couldn't hurt."

"We'll go tomorrow." Peaches turned left onto Laurel Lane. "What number?"

"It's two down from the corner, on the left." A moment later, the Buick rolled to a stop in front of my house. "You want me to pick you up at ten? I'll swing by the hospital and check on Jess. Then I'll come here."

"Oh, that's right. I still don't have a car." I bit my lip. "I know you're busy . . . Are you sure?"

She rolled her eyes. "Honey, I just helped you storm a warehouse full of armed men hiding illegal aliens, and you want to know if I'll give you a ride to an apartment building?"

I hugged her impulsively, breathing in her musky perfume. "Thanks, Peaches. You're the best."

As I hobbled up the front steps past the lavender, she rolled down the window. "Nothing dangerous, though, you hear? I've got a date at the Spoke this Friday night."

I laughed. "Good thing Jess didn't get shot in the leg. I'll do the best I can."

• • •

My husband leaped up from the couch, his white face drawn with worry, as I closed the front door behind me. "Margie! Where have you been? What the hell happened to you?" His eyes lifted to my hair. "And why is your hair purple?"

I sighed. "I found out Bitsy McEwan was running a factory on the east side of town."

Blake's brow wrinkled. "What are you talking about?"

"She was using slave labor—illegal aliens held against their will—to do it. I found out about it, but her assistant caught me before I could go to the authorities."

He blinked. "Bitsy McEwan? The president of the Junior League?" He narrowed his blue eyes at me. "You've been drinking your mother's weird concoctions, haven't you?"

My temper flared. "Do you really think I'd be making this up? She decided it was cheaper to use slaves than to pay workers in Mexico ten cents an hour for labor. She's a criminal."

Blake paled. "You're kidding me, right?"

"No, I am not."

My husband took a step back. "But she's in the Junior League . . . and Herb is a partner at Jones McEwan . . ."

"Look. I don't care what she is. She had me tied up and stuck in a truck headed for Mexico, or God knows where. I managed to escape before they killed me, or whatever they were planning to do. Then Peaches and I headed back to the warehouse to get Eduardo and the other people out—she was keeping Graciela's husband hostage, you know—before we called the cops."

"I don't believe it." He stood looking disoriented for a few seconds. Then with a hurt-sounding voice, he said, "You called Peaches instead of me?"

"I called Peaches because I knew she'd believe me," I said, suddenly feeling very tired. "Anyway, the authorities will hopefully be arresting Bitsy shortly. Maybe Herb, too."

"I just can't believe it. Bitsy McEwan." He shook his head. Then he suddenly pulled me into a fierce hug that stirred an ache in my heart. "I don't know what to think of all this, but I'm glad you're okay," he whispered.

"Me, too," I murmured, tears pricking at the backs of my eyes. I didn't know what to think of my husband right now, either, but I still loved him. After a long moment, he stepped back and studied me. "That still doesn't explain why your hair is purple."

I smiled weakly. "I needed a change." This wasn't the time to discuss my incognito visit to Evan Maxted's memorial service. Or why my husband's "client meeting" was being held at such an event. The clock in the front hall chimed four. "Look, I'm beat. Can we talk about this tomorrow?"

He was surprisingly solicitous. "You go take a bath. I'll just call my parents and let them know you're okay. By the way, your mom called. Wanted to know if you'd tried some tea she sent you, and said something about our auras and karma, and coming to town next weekend . . ." He rolled his eyes. "Lord only knows what she was going on about. I'm not sure *she* knew. Anyway, I didn't tell her anything, because I didn't want her to worry."

"Thanks," I said, and trundled down the hall to the bathroom, where I stripped off my clothes and threw them into the trash. Then I filled the claw-footed tub with hot water, poured in a capful of lavender bubble bath, and sank into a mound of fragrant bubbles. A half hour later, my feet bandaged and my hair still dripping, I slipped into bed beside Blake and fell asleep.

• • •

I woke up at nine fifteen the next morning and hurried downstairs, cursing under my breath. Although the police officers had agreed to postpone my appointment with Detective Bunsen, I'd still overslept, and the kids would be late to school. I was tossing Pop-Tarts into the toaster when I noticed a note on the kitchen table; Blake had taken the kids to school, and Prue would pick them up for me. My eyebrows shot up in surprise. Had my husband been replaced by an alien during the night? If he had, I was thinking I might be able to get used to it.

After putting on a fresh pot of coffee, I headed upstairs to throw on jeans and a T-shirt. My hair was still the color of an eggplant, but today, that was the least of my worries. Peaches honked her horn at ten minutes after ten. I took a last swig of coffee and headed out the door.

"Your hair's still purple," Peaches said when she saw me. She had traded in her green dress for a short black skirt and a close-fitting white top.

"Thanks for noticing," I said. "According to the bottle, I've got about nine more washes to go. Then again, the bottle said my hair was supposed to turn black, not purple, so who knows? Maybe I'll start a new trend." As I closed the Buick door behind me, Peaches pointed to the Mexican sage, its cascade of velvety purple blooms a perfect foil to the jewel-like orange flowers of a butterfly weed. "Nice place you got here. You're quite a gardener."

"Thanks," I said, looking back at the stone cottage nestled among leafy ferns and pale impatiens, with honeysuckle clinging to the chimney. Despite the overgrown lawn, it looked idyllic, like a fairy-tale house. It was amazing how much had changed. Two weeks ago, I was happy, secure, relatively content, and the queen of my little domain. Now, everything had been turned upside down. I watched the house until it slid out of sight. Then, I turned to Peaches. "God, what a week. Do you think they arrested Bitsy?"

She nodded grimly. "I sure hope so. I just hope they put her away for a long time."

"Me, too," I said, wondering how well Bitsy had managed to cover her tracks—and how expensive her legal bills would be. It was not worth worrying about now, though. There were other things to deal with. "How's Jess?"

"He's heading home this morning. He's going to call me later."

"Looks like you caught yourself another bus," I said as we turned onto Congress Avenue.

"Any idea how you're going to get into Maxted's apartment today?"

"I figured I'd wing it."

Peaches grinned. "Well, if what you did yesterday was 'winging it,' I'd recommend you take a parachute."

"I'm hoping a seventy-five-year-old woman will be a bit less hostile than a group of heavily armed thugs."

"You thought that about the Junior League lady, too."

"Good point. But I doubt Willie is running a slave-labor factory in her bedroom closet."

"You want me to come with you?"

"The more the merrier," I said as we pulled into a parking spot across the street from Evan Maxted's apartment building.

"Pretty swanky place," Peaches said as we tip-tapped across the marble floor toward the elevator. The doorman's mahogany desk was still vacant.

"Maxted was doing pretty well for himself, I guess."

"So, what are you going to do when we get up there? Tell this Willie woman you forgot to pick up the cat food?"

I sighed and stabbed the button for the ninth floor. "To be honest, I'm considering telling her the truth."

"The truth? Are you nuts?"

I shrugged. "You haven't met Willie. Somehow I think she'd be okay with it."

Peaches groaned. "I was wrong. You need more than a parachute, honey. This is a frickin' suicide mission. Why don't you say your cat was on some kind of medication, and you have to go through the apartment and look for it?"

"I don't know. I'm not sure she bought the cat story last time." The elevator dinged, the door slid open, and we stepped out onto the plush carpet of the hallway. As we walked past Maxted's door on the way to Willie's apartment, I noticed that the crime scene tape was gone.

"Why don't you just try the cat thing first? Then if it doesn't work, you can spill the beans."

"This is it," I said as we stopped outside Willie's door.

"Couldn't you just tell her you forgot the litter box?"

I knocked three times, and the door swung open.

CHAPTER TWENTY-SEVEN

P rudence! How are you?" Willie was wearing a purple and orange turban today, above a silky lilac housedress that hung loosely on her thin frame.

"I'm fine," I said. "How are you?"

"Oh, I just had another round of chemo, but I'm not in the hospital yet!" Her eyes twinkled as she smiled at me. "Who's your friend?"

"Willie, I'd like to introduce you to Peaches Barlowe."

Peaches stuck out a hand. "Hi, Willie. I've heard wonderful things about you."

"Oh, thanks. Lovely to meet you, my dear. And what a beautiful skirt that is! You have such nice legs. Oh, but here you are standing in the hallway . . . Do come in. I love a bit of company." As we followed her in, she said, "How's Lothario?"

"He's just fine," I said.

"Good, good. Sit down, sit down," she said, waving us toward the animal-print couches. "Now, can I get you a cup of tea?"

"No, thanks," I said. "I just had coffee."

"And I'm a Dr. Pepper woman, myself," Peaches said.

"Well, then," she said as we settled ourselves into the massive sofas, "what can I do for you girls?"

I took a deep breath. "I'm sorry to bother you, Willie, but I came to ask you a favor."

"Is it about Evan? You know, that policewoman was awfully miffed when she found out you'd gone. I would have told her your last name, only I didn't remember it."

I sighed. "Willie, I have something to tell you."

Peaches kicked me.

"What is it, dear?"

"I feel awful about this . . . but my name isn't Prudence. It's Margie. Margie Peterson." It was like telling my grandmother that I had broken her favorite cookie jar. Only worse. I looked up to gauge Willie's reaction.

"Margie." She nodded. "That's a much nicer name." She squinted at me. "Wasn't your hair auburn last time?"

"Yes, it was." I bit my lip. "And I have to admit that the reason I came here last time was not because Evan was watching my cat."

She smiled. "I figured that was the case. Although I didn't worry about it when you took him, because you seemed like a good person."

"You knew Snookums—I mean Lothario—wasn't my cat?"

Her eyes sparkled. "I may be old, but I'm not stupid. A cat with two names?" She rolled her eyes. "But I figured you had a good reason to be there. I can usually tell with people, you know." She pursed her lips. "So why did you come?"

I took a deep breath. "I was the one who found Evan. He was dressed as a drag queen when he died, and my home phone number was on his cell phone." I closed my eyes and leaned back into the overstuffed sofa. "I'm not divorced. I'm happily married—or at least I was until a week or two ago." Tears bit at the back of my eyes. "I'm afraid my husband was mixed up with Evan somehow. That's what I was trying to find out."

When I opened my eyes, Willie was holding a tissue out to me. "I'm so sorry, dear. Thank you for being honest with me. Marriage can be a difficult thing, and if you think your husband is involved with someone else . . ." She trailed off. "I can understand your wanting to know. Particularly if there are children involved?"

I nodded.

She sighed. "I was afraid of that."

"I hate to ask," I said, swiping at my nose with a tissue, "but is there any way you could let me into Evan's apartment? I just need to know."

Willie pursed her lips, considering my request for a moment, then spoke. "Normally I would have to say no, but under the circumstances, I think I can make an exception. Wait right here, and I'll get the key."

As she disappeared down the hallway, Peaches turned to me, bug-eyed. "I can't believe it worked!"

I reached for another tissue and blew my nose. "I told you she'd understand. Now let's just hope we find something."

"I'll bet he's got some good wigs."

"That's not exactly what I had in mind."

Willie returned to the room a moment later, a key dangling from her knotted fingers. "Ready, girls?"

Peaches and I stood up. "Thanks, Willie," I said.

"Don't mention it," she said. "All I ask is that you come back and visit me from time to time. Let me know how things are going."

"I would love to."

We followed her down the hall, and a moment later we were standing in Evan Maxted's apartment.

Peaches eyed the Art Deco entertainment center, the sleek black leather couches, the 1920s prints, and the panoramic view of downtown Austin. She let out a low whistle. "Heck of a pad."

"It's a shame he's not alive to enjoy it," I said, remembering the youthful face in his driver's license picture and the horrible way he'd died.

Willie shook her head. "I still can't believe he's gone. He was such a nice young man."

"I know. Or at least I've heard. I never got a chance to meet him." I sighed. "Well, let's get this over with. Where do we start?"

"How about you take the bedroom, and I'll start with the living room?" Peaches said.

"I'd be happy to go through the kitchen," Willie volunteered. "But what am I looking for?"

The kitchen probably wasn't going to produce much useful evidence, but I said, "Letters, photos . . . anything that looks like it might be useful."

"I'll see what I can find."

As Peaches opened the entertainment center and Willie started rattling through the utensil drawer, I stepped back into Evan Maxted's bedroom.

The red satin coverlet lay neatly on the round bed, just as it had when I lured Snookums out from beneath it. Evan's business clothes and dresses still lined the closet, looking just as incongruous, and the wigs were still on their stands. All but one—the one he'd been wearing the night he was killed, I thought with a shudder.

I walked farther into the bedroom and opened the drawers of Evan's black lacquer dresser. One side of the dresser contained boxer shorts, dark socks, white T-shirts, and a stack of polo shirts. The other side was filled with lacy things that looked like they'd belong to a Playboy Playmate.

I shivered and returned to the closet, averting my eyes from the empty wig stand, and noticed that the top shelf was still lined with shoe boxes. I stood on tiptoe, pulled down the nearest box, and peeked under the lid, hoping the box wouldn't contain stiletto heels. It was filled with letters and photos. *Bingo*. Heart thumping, I carried the box to the bed and sat down.

The first box was filled with notes and snapshots from high school and college, all jumbled together as if someone—the police, probably—had rifled through them.

Although Veronica had told me that a lot of transvestites were heterosexual, evidently Evan wasn't among them. If his collection of high school notes was any indication, he hadn't gone through the awkward stage many gay men do of trying to date girls. Based on the scrawled missives from people named Toby and Jacob, he'd known pretty early. The photos showed a younger version of Evan—fit, smiling, a sparkle in his dark eyes, always with other boys.

Once he hit college, his mother started writing him letters in which she implored him to "keep an open mind," and "not discuss it with the family yet." College appeared to have brought another succession of boyfriends. I leafed through the photos of handsome young men interspersed with what appeared to be family shots, including one of Evan with an arm around the blonde I had seen at the memorial service.

The contents of the second box were of a more recent vintage. There were several photos of Evan with men I didn't recognize, Valentine's Day cards, and a few candid shots of handsome Marcus with his arm locked around Evan, who looked like a tall Hollywood starlet in a blond wig and a sequined red ball gown. There were more letters from his mother, increasingly desperate as she realized her son wasn't going to change his ways, including a fervent plea that he enroll in a Christian program in Florida designed to "rehabilitate" gay men.

I was almost through with the box when I spotted a small photo tucked into the corner. I picked it up with a shock of recognition, and after a long moment, set it on the dresser. Then I forced myself to go through the rest of the box and return it to the shelf.

I had just sorted through the third and final box when Peaches arrived at the doorway.

"Well, he had a thing for Audrey Hepburn, but other than that, I came up empty."

Willie was stooped over in the kitchen, rifling through Evan's pot drawer. When she saw me, she straightened up slowly, holding her turban with her left hand. "Nothing here, I'm afraid."

I wished I could say the same.

• • •

As we pulled away from Evan's building, Peaches said, "I gotta hand it to you. You got us in."

"Yeah, but I'm still no closer to figuring out who killed him." Despite my success getting into Maxted's apartment, I still felt morose. And not just because of the photo I'd slipped into my purse. "I still feel bad about lying to Willie the first time."

"You do what you gotta do," Peaches said. "By the way, what's with the turban?"

"She's got ovarian cancer," I said.

Peaches winced. "Ouch."

I sank back into the vinyl seat, thinking I still didn't know who had killed Evan Maxted, or what had happened to the money my lying, embezzling husband had been spiriting out of our account. How had everything turned into such a mess?

"I'm sure Maxted's death had something to do with that warehouse," I said, watching the runners on the Lady Bird Lake trail as the Buick motored down First Street, "but I still don't know what the connection is. And what's worse is that Bitsy will probably claim Maria was handling everything at the warehouse and get away scot-free."

"Let's think about it," Peaches said. "We know Maxted knew about the warehouse. We don't know if he knew what was going on in there, but we can guess he might have. So there's some motive."

"He did have an appointment to go and talk to a reporter at the *Statesman* the day after he died," I said. "Do you think he was going to do an exposé?"

"It's a thought," she said.

"It still doesn't explain what was going on with the International Shipping Company files," I said. "Why would Herb McEwan take them?"

"Could be unrelated," Peaches said. "Or could be that he was just being cautious. Maybe whoever was working on the account did some funny accounting, and he wanted to get rid of the paper trail."

My stomach lurched. Could Blake be involved in that?

"But why would Maxted talk to a reporter about the warehouse if there were problems with his own company? Wouldn't that be risky?"

"It would," she said, "but maybe he wasn't in on whatever was happening. Or maybe he figured McEwan had cleaned up the paper trail and would keep his mouth shut."

"If Bitsy knew Maxted was going to blab to a reporter, she would certainly have a motive," I said. "The problem is, there's no link to the crime. Bitsy's very good at insulating herself. If she did get Maxted, I'll bet she had someone else do her dirty work."

"From what you've told me, she doesn't seem the Rainbow Room type," Peaches said, echoing my thoughts. "Her assistant, Maria, maybe?"

"Or Carlos," I suggested.

I thought again of the body on the toilet in the Princesses' room, running the entire evening over in my mind and trying to remember if I'd seen anyone who resembled Carlos or Maria. My mind re-created the scene, and I suddenly remembered the earring on the floor nearby. The earring. I had seen it before, but where? As I stared out the window at the light glittering on the lake, a memory that had been floating just out of reach finally rose to the surface. "Holy shit," I said, sitting up straight.

"What?"

"I can't believe I forgot about that."

"Are you gonna tell me, or are we going to play Twenty Questions?"

"Sorry. I found an earring near the body," I said. "I know where it came from."

"Can you prove it?"

"Maybe." I thought about it for a moment; then I pulled out my phone and typed in a name.

Could it be? I wondered as I scanned through the images the search had brought up. I cast my mind back to that awful night—and to the person who had looked strangely familiar. Out of context, yes, but familiar.

I found the photo I was looking for on the third page and let out a whoop. "I think I've got what we need," I told Peaches, feeling adrenaline surge through me. "But I need to double-check. We need to go to the Rainbow Room," I told Peaches. "I need to talk to Cassandra."

"I knew I'd hired the right woman," Peaches said, grinning at me. "Let's just hope you're right."

• • •

We pulled into a parking space on Fourth Street, and Peaches squinted at the old brick building with the neon rainbow over the doorway. "Are you sure this place is going to be open?"

"It opens at noon. It's eleven forty-five now."

Peaches opened the car door. "Let's just knock and ask. It's not like we want to buy a drink or anything."

"Are you sure?"

"Come on," she said, and slammed the door behind her. I scurried out of the Buick and followed her to the front door of the Rainbow Room. She had already started hammering at the plate glass.

When Domingo appeared at the doorway, sunlight glinting off his diamond studs, Peaches said, "We need to ask Cassandra Starr a couple of questions."

Domingo raised his eyebrows. "Is she in trouble?"

"No," I said. "It's about the man who was murdered in your bathroom a week ago."

He shrugged and opened the door.

"See?" Peaches hissed as we stepped into the air-conditioned darkness, which smelled like stale cigarette smoke and sautéing garlic. Lunch preparations must be under way in the kitchen. "It just takes a little authority."

I turned to Domingo. "Where's Cassandra?"

"Up at the bar."

"Thanks."

The only woman at the bar was dressed in a white clingy dress, and her hair was a platinum pouf. Dale Evans had been replaced by Marilyn Monroe.

"Cassandra?" I said as I pulled a stool up next to her.

"Margie, right?" She took a drag from her e-cigarette, leaving a ring of her trademark purple lipstick on the white cylinder.

"Nice outfit," Peaches said.

"Who's this?" Cassandra narrowed her furry eyes at Peaches's short black skirt and clingy top.

"This is Peaches," I said. "A friend of mine. I'm sorry to bother you, but I want to ask one more question."

Cassandra rolled her eyes. "What?"

I showed her the image on my phone. "Was this person here the night Evan—I mean Selena—died?"

I held my breath as she glanced at the image. "That was the night of the Showdown, right?"

"It was."

She picked up my phone and peered at it. "Nice dress."

"You don't know her?"

She sucked on her e-cigarette and blew out a plume of vapor. "Don't get too many of the society ladies in here. That blue's a good color on her, though. Goes with her eyes."

My heart sank as she peered down at the image again. Then, suddenly, she straightened a little bit. "Wait a moment."

I leaned forward, holding my breath. "You've seen her before?"

"There's something about the eyes . . ." She pondered the phone. "She's not wearing quite as much makeup, and the hair is different, but yes, I think she was here."

"Bingo," Peaches murmured.

"What do you remember?" I asked.

Cassandra took another drag before answering. "I'd never seen her in here before, and I'm always interested in new men, so I went over and tried to start up a little conversation. He was older, but very convincing . . . cleavage, even!" She narrowed her eyes at me. "The cleavage is real, isn't it?"

"He's a she," I confirmed. "When did you approach her?"

"Before the Showdown started, of course; once the girls are lining up, I'm too busy to even *think*! And then, afterward, with Selena . . . "

"Did she talk to you at all?"

She shook her blond pouf and sighed. "She just looked at me with those ice-blue eyes and got up and walked away. Can you believe how *rude* she was? That's why I remember her—those cold eyes. And I was wearing my best Chanel and everything." She pouted, and I noticed the beauty mark she had penciled in above her lip had smudged. "Some people have no taste. No taste at all."

I took my phone back and tucked it into my bag. "Thanks, Cassandra. You've been a big help."

"Sure," she said, sucking on her cigarette and fluttering her eyelashes at Domingo, who was now polishing glasses behind the bar.

• • •

"So I guess we call the cops now," I said as we pulled away from the Rainbow Room.

"What?"

"We call the cops," I repeated.

"No way. We're professionals, remember? We call the cops when we have all the evidence. I think a taped confession would do nicely, don't you?"

I turned to face Peaches. "We're about to confront a murderer. Personally, I'd be more comfortable accompanied by a bunch of people in polyester carrying guns."

Peaches pulled a pack of Ultra Slims out of her purse. "Look. This is going to be a piece of cake. I'll keep my gun in my purse, and you can carry your stun gun. We go in, get the confession on tape, and call the police."

"It's that easy, right? Just like the warehouse was supposed to be a snap."

She tapped out a cigarette, lit it, and took a deep drag. "We did what we meant to do, didn't we? And Eduardo is free."

"Yeah, and we almost got killed. Look. There's no reason *not* to call the cops this time. Besides, I don't even know where we're going. She could be anywhere."

"When's the next League meeting?" Peaches asked.

I Googled it on my phone. "This afternoon," I said. "Two o'clock. At the Austin Country Club."

"Well, that's convenient," she said. "Now we know where to go."

CHAPTER TWENTY-EIGHT

We arrived at the Austin Country Club at a quarter to two, parking the Buick between a Lexus SUV and a BMW coupe. Peaches was resplendent in fuchsia spandex, with boots and a rhinestone belt, and her stiletto heels clicked on the limestone flagstone as we climbed the steps to the front door.

"Nice place," she said.

"Far cry from the warehouse," I said, looking around to take in the stately oaks and the expanse of Lake Austin, glittering in the sunshine. "Got the recorder ready?" I asked.

"Of course," she said.

Together we walked into the building. I found myself smiling at the raised-eyebrow looks in the lobby and was not surprised when one of the ladies behind the reception desk intercepted us.

"Can I help you?" she asked in a nervous, chirpy voice, eyeing first Peaches's fuchsia-encased décolletage, and then my eggplant-colored hair.

"We're looking for the Junior League meeting," I said.

She blinked. "Really?"

"No, actually, we're looking for the morgue," Peaches drawled.

"The Junior League meeting," I reiterated, elbowing Peaches.

"Um, it should be down the hall in the Magnolia Room. Are you a guest?"

"Yes," I said, smiling. "Of Prudence Peterson. I'm her daughter-in-law."

"Ah. And this is . . . ," the young woman said, her eyes sliding to Peaches.

"A friend," I said. "Now, if you'll excuse us, we don't want to be late."

I didn't wait for a response but breezed down the carpeted hall in the direction the woman had indicated. The door was open; inside were ten tables, all with white tablecloths and plated spinach salads on them. "We need to bring up the salads at our next board meeting," I heard a woman say. "No one eats the onions, and they just make the room stinky." The look on her companion's face must have alerted her to something; a moment later she turned, eyes wide, to look at Peaches and me.

"Hi," I said.

"Can I help you?" the woman asked, archly, looking at Peaches's prominently displayed décolletage, and then at my purple hair.

"Margie!" Prudence hurried over to me, looking absolutely mortified. "What have you done to your hair? And who is . . . this?" She stabbed a manicured finger at my boss. "Let's talk about this out in the hall," she said, trying to shepherd me toward the door.

"Not yet," I said. "Have you seen Bitsy?"

"Bitsy McEwan? Of course. She's at the head table."

"Wonderful," I said, smiling and walking past my mother-in-law to where Bitsy stood, looking at us with narrowed eyes.

"But . . ."

Peaches and I left Prudence behind us and focused on Bitsy, who looked no worse for wear after her conversation with the police. I wondered if they'd even contacted her.

"So glad you decided to attend more League functions," she said as if she hadn't ordered her henchmen to get rid of me just last night.

"If you don't mind, though, the meeting is about to begin, and I'm afraid we didn't know you were coming. Perhaps the next meeting?"

"I have a few things I need to talk to you about," I said.

"Perhaps after the meeting."

"Perhaps now," I said. She opened her mouth as if to protest, then gave a sharp nod. She turned to the woman next to her, a petite woman wearing a lavender suit and a somewhat shocked look. "Janice, will you excuse me for a moment?"

"Of course, Bitsy. But we're about to begin . . ."

"The ladies can get started on their salads if they get restless," she said to Janice, then turned to us with a polite smile. "This way, please, ladies."

"You have it running?" I murmured to Peaches as we followed Bitsy out to the carpeted hallway.

"Just started it," she whispered back.

"Let's go in here," Bitsy said, stepping into the next room down. It had been divided from the League's luncheon room by one of those movable accordion-style walls, but in here, the tables were pushed to the walls, alongside stacks of chairs. Peaches and I followed her in, and she shut the door behind us. When she turned, all trace of the genteel Junior League president's smile was gone.

"Why are you here?" she barked.

"Like I said, I have a few questions." I crossed my arms. "For starters, Bitsy, what are you doing with all the money you made off the slave labor in the warehouse on Seventh Street?" I asked. "It wasn't really all going to charity, was it? Some of it was lining your pockets. A lot of it, in fact."

"You came all the way here to ask me that?" she said. "I have no connection to that warehouse. Maria handles production. Now, if that's all . . ."

"What about your earring?" I asked.

Bitsy blanched, but her face didn't even twitch.

"You know . . . the prototype pair you wore to the gala last fall. Remember? Your photo was in the society pages."

"I don't know what you're talking about," she said.

"I didn't notice the earrings when I saw you—the wig must have covered them—but I knew the one on the restroom floor at the Rainbow Room looked familiar. You know. The one near Evan Maxted's body." I took a deep breath and realized she was wearing Anaïs Anaïs, the same perfume I'd smelled outside the restroom at the Rainbow Room.

She stared at me.

"The police have it," I said. "All I have to do is show them the picture. They were one-of-a-kind, weren't they?" I smiled. "And Cassandra remembers you, too. The one with the furry eyelashes? She told me you weren't too chatty, but that you had very realistic cleavage."

"You can't prove anything," she hissed.

"How did you know Evan was going to be there?" I asked. "That's the thing I can't figure out. He'd found out about your trafficking operation, hadn't he? I'm betting you figured if you murdered him in a gay bar, no one would connect his death with you."

"Do you need a phone so you can call the police?" Bitsy asked, opening her clutch. Before I knew it, she had a pearl-handled gun in her hand.

"Shit," Peaches said.

"You're smarter than Prue gives you credit for," she said. She sighed, exasperated. "All right. I knew he'd be there. I'd had him followed. He went every week."

"Why didn't you have one of your people do it?" I asked.

"No time. He had a meeting with a reporter the next morning."

I was right. "He'd figured out what was going on in the warehouse, hadn't he?"

"He knew there were some accounting issues we were working on, but I don't know how much he was aware of. Still, it was best not to take chances. And speaking of husbands," she said, raising a plucked, penciled eyebrow, "yours isn't lily-white, either."

My stomach dropped. "What do you mean?"

"Who do you think helped us fix the books?" she asked. "He was a company man."

I felt sick as I thought of Blake helping Bitsy launder money and cover her slave operation. "Did he know about the warehouse?"

"No, but he didn't ask a lot of questions," she said. "He knew we were shipping something illegally. It didn't seem to bother him."

I thought of the files I'd seen at Jones McEwan—the ones Herb had taken. "Who's E. M. Hernandez?"

"He transported the workers, and made up fake bills of lading to cover his tracks. The only problem was, the IRS was onto him. Plus, he got searched at the border a month or two ago, and had to bluff his way through."

"The IRS? Don't you mean ICE—Immigration and Customs Enforcement?"

"No, it was the IRS. His accounting wasn't in order. That's where your husband came in." Bitsy chuckled. "Why do you think he got that nice raise?"

The raise I hadn't seen, I thought, my stomach churning. Well, that explained why Blake had called Bitsy a while back. But it didn't explain the money Blake had spirited from our joint account. "There's still one thing I don't understand," I said. "Where did the money go?"

"What money?"

"The money Blake was taking off the top of his paychecks."

Bitsy shook her head. "I don't know about that. Looks like you've got some trouble on the home front, my dear. Prue was right. She thought your marriage had hit a rough patch."

For a moment, I was relieved Blake wasn't directly involved in Bitsy's slave-run factory, but the feeling was short-lived. My husband had evidently helped launder money; he had denied knowing Maxted; and he was still skimming money from the family bank account. If the money wasn't connected with the factory, where was it going?

But I didn't have time to worry about my husband right now. Bitsy was pointing a gun at me—and evidently didn't have qualms about violence.

I shivered involuntarily, thinking of Evan's bloodied body. "You were pretty ruthless at the Rainbow Room. What did you use?"

"A pistol with a silencer," she said, waving the pearl-handled gun as if to remind us it was there.

I knew I should shut up and try to figure out what to do, but adrenaline was pulsing through me, and I couldn't seem to stop talking. "When did this trafficking start, Bitsy? And has it ever occurred to you that it's a bit hypocritical? You know, hiring slave labor and sending the profits to charity?"

Bitsy pursed her pink-frosted lips. "It's business. They don't stay here forever—just long enough to pay off the debt from the trip. And conditions are better than they have at home. So everything works out for everyone, really."

"You're wrong about things being worse where they came from," I said. "I know one of your workers. Eduardo. His wife is named Graciela, and she and her two teenaged daughters are sick with worry. He was supposed to be home weeks ago, and she thinks he's dead. Hernandez was La Serpiente, wasn't he? Or is that what they call *you*?"

"Start moving," she said, pointing to a door in the back of the room.

"That's not a revolver. That's a .22," Peaches said, pointing to the gun.

"The revolver wouldn't fit in the clutch," she said. "Now move."

"Okay," Peaches said, putting her hands up. "But I don't think you're going to do much damage with a .22." She glanced at me and flicked her eyes to the accordion wall. "Hang on a second," she said. "I think there's something in my shoe."

"Just move!" Bitsy barked.

Peaches bent down, then hurled herself at Bitsy's shins. I froze for a moment.

"Go, Margie!" Peaches bellowed.

I stumbled to the accordion wall and yanked at the handle. The wall reeled back, bringing a waft of onion with it. I caught a glimpse of several shocked ladies, most with their forks in midair, before there was a popping sound, and one of the lights exploded behind me.

I whirled around, terrified that Bitsy had killed Peaches. I needn't have worried. Peaches sat straddling the Junior League president, her tight skirt hiked up to her lime-green underwear, the .22 in her hand. Bitsy's patrician face was purple, and her blue eyes bulged as she squirmed on the carpet.

"Are you okay?" I asked Peaches.

"She missed," Peaches said, grinning, and held up the recorder. "But the tape's still running."

"Bitsy!"

I turned around to see Prudence, one bony arm extended, staring in horror at the Junior League president. She turned her eyes to me and made a whimpering sound.

"So embarrassing," she murmured. And then she fainted.

CHAPTER TWENTY-NINE

Peaches had finished her first cigarette and started on a second by the time we pulled into the parking lot of the Green Meadows Day School. Prudence hadn't offered to take me—and frankly, after the fainting fit, I wasn't sure I wanted her to, anyway. Fortunately, Peaches had stepped into the breach.

"By the way," I said as we crossed the parking lot, "did you ever find out who burned down your office?"

Peaches paused to light a cigarette. "Oh, didn't I tell you? It was Irwin Pence. His wife accidentally left my card by the phone. After Mrs. Pence broke the news about the photo you took, he got pissed one night, came and drenched the office with gasoline, and lit a match."

"How did they catch him?"

"He left the gasoline can fifteen feet away. His prints were all over it."

"Huh. I wonder if he's the one who blew up Blake's car."

Peaches shrugged. "Maybe. Oh, and I almost forgot." She dug through her purse and pulled out a red plastic object. "I think this is yours."

"Elsie's fry phone!"

"Mrs. Pence dropped it off at my house yesterday. Said she figured it was the least she could do." Peaches took a drag from her cigarette. "Now that that's taken care of, why don't you go get your kids."

. . .

A few minutes later, over the protestations of the teaching assistants, we loaded the kids into the back of the Buick without car seats. "Cool," said Elsie, and turned to Nick. "You know what this means, don't you?"

"What?"

"We're adults now."

I tossed my daughter her fry phone as Peaches pulled away from the pickup zone. Elsie was still squealing with delight when Peaches dropped us off at my house a few minutes later.

"Got a big date tonight," she said. "Gonna see if I can fit in a few hours of beauty sleep."

I gave her a big hug. "Thanks, Peaches. Thanks for everything."

She gave me a long, hard look. "I'm forwarding my home phone to my cell. If you need anything tonight, you give me a call, okay?"

I swallowed hard and nodded.

"Any time of night. Understand?"

I nodded again. "Got it."

Peaches gave me another big, musky hug. Then she clicked down the stone walk to the Buick.

As Peaches revved the engine, Elsie sidled up behind me and wrapped her arms around my waist. "Why did that lady say for you to call her, Mommy?"

"Because she's a friend, Elsie. A good, good friend."

I waved until the Buick disappeared down the street. Then, my children at my side, I walked back into the house to wait.

• • •

The phone rang almost as soon as the door closed behind me. It was Becky.

"Margie! Where have you been? I've been calling you all day . . ."

"It's a long story," I said.

"I've been dying to talk to you. I checked with the bank first thing this morning, and you're not going to *believe* who's been stealing money from Green Meadows."

"Who?"

"Lydia Belmont."

"No. It can't be. Sign-the-petition-Lydia? With the silver Mercedes?"

"Yup. I called Attila about it—she's home, by the way; they thought it was a heart attack but it turned out to be just a scare—and she called Lydia right off. She confessed to everything. Apparently she used some of the money on laser treatments and plastic surgery, and the rest she invested with Bitsy McEwan."

"Lovely," I said.

"She didn't want her husband to know about it, so she embezzled the cash she needed from the school. That's why she took so many 'vacations' last year—she was having surgery done in Costa Rica, then staying there for the recovery."

"Why didn't she want him to know about it?"

"She didn't want him to think she was getting old. She was afraid he was going to divorce her for a younger model."

"You're joking."

"Nope. And there's more. Apparently Bitsy promised her big gains on whatever she invested into the fashion line, and Lydia fell for it. For all the fancy cars, her hubby put her on a tight budget. The profits were going into a rainy-day divorce-attorney fund."

"You're kidding me." How many other Junior Leaguers had helped fund the slave-run factory? I wondered. Probably my mother-in-law, although I doubted she'd admit it. I was guessing it would all come out as the police investigation got under way.

"On the plus side, I'm guessing that petition won't be going anywhere soon."

"I hope you're right."

"Also, there's this rumor going around that Bitsy McEwan was arrested for running some kind of immigrant ring. Does this have something to do with the fashion line?"

"She was," I said. "Remember that warehouse we visited the other night?"

"The one where we saw Maria?"

"That's where all the clothing for Couture with a Conscience was made. Bitsy was transporting illegal immigrants over the border and holding them hostage there, making them sew clothes."

"You're kidding me. How do you know all that?"

"She was also arrested for murder," I said.

"What?"

"She was the one who killed Evan Maxted."

"Oh my God. Bitsy McEwan?"

"It's a long story," I said. And one I wasn't ready to tell right now. I had other things I wanted to get off my plate, first. "I'll tell you all about it soon . . . but for now, can you do me a favor?"

"Sure, Margie. Wow." She paused for a moment, still digesting what I'd told her. "Sorry. What do you need?"

"Can you watch the kids for a while this afternoon?"

"Of course! Why? What's going on?"

When I told her, she breathed, "Oh God. I'll be over in ten minutes."

"Thanks," I said. Then I hung up the phone and dialed another number.

• • •

I was sitting on my Broyhill couch when the front door opened.

"Hi," I said.

Blake closed the door behind him. "What's going on? Where are the kids?"

I pointed to the armchair across from me. "Please sit down."

He put down his briefcase and approached the chair warily. "What's the emergency?"

"How long have you been seeing Evan Maxted?" My voice was ragged.

"What?" He paled. "Evan's a client. I don't know what you're talking about."

I slapped the photo I'd found in Evan's apartment on the table between us.

He reached out and snatched the picture. "Oh God. I didn't want you to find out."

A wave of dizziness washed over me. "How long have you been hiding this from me?"

He leaned forward with his head in his hands, rocking back and forth on the chair, staring at the floor between his feet. "I've always been this way," he whispered.

Although I already knew it, his admission hit me like a shock wave. A sob escaped my chest. Even with my eyes closed, the image in the photograph was burned into my retinas. Blake, reclining on a leather couch with a blue-sequined Selena Sass in his lap.

Tears squeezed out of the corners of my eyes. "Even when we got married?"

"Since high school," he said. "I tried so hard to be normal, to be the pride of the family . . . I hated that part of myself, tried to destroy it . . ."

"Did you ever love me?" I whispered.

He crossed the gap between us and put his arm around me. I flinched, and he backed away. "Of course I loved you. I still do."

"I saw you at the memorial service the other day."

"How do you know about the memorial service?"

"I was there. The woman in the black hat."

Blake blinked.

"How could you do this to me?" I raged. "And you were stealing money, too!"

"Stealing money?"

"Two thousand dollars a month," I hissed. "You never told me about your raise. Or that you cooked the books to get it."

"I had to," he said. "To protect you."

"Where's it all going? To Evan?"

"No, no," he said. "Evan and I broke up months ago."

"Oh really? Then how come he called you on her cell phone the night she died?"

He closed his eyes and leaned back against the couch. "Selena—Evan—thought there was something going on with International Shipping that wasn't quite right, and he thought it had something to do with Bitsy McEwan. He was calling me for help. Not that I could do anything about it." He gave a bitter laugh. "The thing is, I couldn't say anything; I was the one who covered it up."

"You knew they were transporting illegal immigrants?" I asked.

"No," he said, his eyes widening in horror. "I would never do that. I knew they were shipping something, but I didn't know it was . . . people. Herb and Bitsy told me it was fabric for her clothing line. To cut costs."

That explained the calls to Bitsy, but not the missing money. "That still doesn't explain where the money went."

He sighed. "I was being blackmailed."

"Blackmailed? By whom?"

"By a man named Trevor."

An image of Trevor backing into a display at Miss Veronica's Boudoir flashed into my mind. It must have been because he recognized my name, I realized now. "The one who works at Miss Veronica's Boudoir?"

"How did you find that out?"

"I went there the other day to ask about Evan Maxted. So you were paying Trevor money that should have come to the family just to keep your affair quiet."

"I felt awful about it. I even threatened to stop making the payments. That's why he blew up my car."

"He blew up your car?"

"To scare me. Yes."

I cradled my head in my hands. "Jesus Christ. I don't believe this."

"Selena . . . I mean, Evan and I met two years ago, when ISC first became a client. There was a mutual . . . attraction there, and things just kind of happened." He held my gaze with his blue eyes. "It was my first time," he said.

I looked away.

Blake's voice was thick. "About a year ago, we went to a party together. Somebody snapped a few photos, and somehow Trevor got hold of one. He contacted me about it six or eight months ago." He sighed. "I didn't want to destroy our family. So I paid."

We sat in silence for a moment. A breeze ruffled the roses outside the front window and made the wind chimes hanging from the eaves tinkle. I fingered the tear in the couch. How could everything around me seem so normal when my life was falling apart?

I looked at my husband, with his patrician nose and remorseful eyes. "Is that why you've been such a jerk lately? Because of the blackmailing?"

"I'm so sorry, Margie. Yes, it was that. I was worried it was all going to blow up in my face."

"It did blow up. In the driveway, actually," I said acidly. "You blamed me for that, too, if I remember correctly."

"I know, and I'm sorry. I was also worried about the ISC thing. Everything just went wrong, and I didn't handle it well."

"You made me feel like it was my fault," I said. "And all the time, you were lying to me."

We sat together for several minutes, the air thick with anger and unspoken words.

When Blake spoke, his voice was soft. "Where do we go from here, Margie?"

I buried my head in my hands. "I don't know. I don't know anything anymore."

"I love you. And I love the kids."

I raised my head and looked at him. "How can we stay married if you only want to sleep with men?"

"Maybe I could change . . ."

"No. No, I don't think so. I need some time, time to think."

"Maybe I should leave for a while."

"I think that would be a good idea," I said, crossing my arms.

He sighed. "I didn't want it to happen this way."

"Me neither," I whispered. "Me neither."

He sat beside me on the couch for a moment. "I guess I'll go pack my bags, then." I wiped my eyes and nodded. He sat beside me for another minute. Then he got up and climbed the stairs to our bedroom, the wooden steps creaking under his heavy tread.

Twenty minutes later, he was gone.

• • •

Becky arrived first, holding a bag of chocolate chip cookies and a bottle of Chardonnay.

"Where are the kids?" I asked.

"Rick came home early. They're with him." She set the food down on the table and put her arms around me. "Oh, Margie. I'm so sorry."

My body heaved with sobs, and tears poured down my cheeks. Becky held me for a few minutes; then she guided me to the couch and went searching for a tissue box.

"They're in the laundry room," I snuffled.

"Hang in there," she said. "I'll be right back."

A moment later, a yowl sounded from the direction of the laundry room, and an orange streak whizzed across the living room. It was Snookums. Only instead of turning to face down Rufus, he jumped onto the couch and cowered beside me. Becky appeared at the doorway a moment later, Rufus bristling at her feet.

"I'm so sorry. I forgot about the cat."

I stroked Snookums, who had burrowed in beside me. "It's okay," I said. The orange tabby trembled under my touch.

"Isn't that the lunatic cat? The one that bit you the other day?"

"I think he's just had a rough time of it lately," I said.

Becky went to the kitchen for a corkscrew and glasses while Snookums pressed his warm body against me.

"You may just need a little TLC," I crooned to Snookums, fondling the orange cat's ears. Rufus hissed from the doorway. "Cut it out, Rufus. Becky, could you let him out?"

Becky returned with two full glasses of wine. She handed one to me and opened the front door, and Rufus stalked out of it, giving me a baleful look.

"There's a weird-looking woman with red hair and a miniskirt coming up the walk," Becky hissed.

"That must be Peaches," I said. A moment later, her stiletto heels clicked on the hardwood floors, and she set a fifth of tequila down on the front-hall table with a clunk. Then she walked over to the couch and gave my shoulder a squeeze.

"How are you doin', sweetheart?"

I smiled feebly and raised my glass. "I'm still upright, aren't I?"

"Then you're not drinking enough," Peaches said. She turned to Becky. "I'm Peaches," she said, thrusting a hand out. "You must be Becky."

As my friends introduced themselves, I looked around at my living room, the soft, squishy couches, the petit-point rug on the hardwood floor. The family and the life I had so carefully designed—the house we were going to redo together, the plans we made for the future—were falling apart around me. As I stroked Snookums, Peaches plopped down beside me and threw an arm across my shoulders.

"Remember what my momma said."

"Men are like buses?"

"Bingo. It's gonna suck for a while, but you'll make out all right. I raised two kids on my own."

"You went through this, too?" I wasn't sure I was ready to get off my bus just yet, but it was comforting to know that other women had—and had survived.

She nodded. My husband wasn't hitting for the other team, like yours is, but he had himself a whole harem goin'. One of them was just sixteen. Man, was he an asshole."

I sniffled. "Did the kids . . . Were they okay?"

"Both of 'em happily married, got kids of their own."

I leaned back into the couch and closed my eyes. It was going to be tough; there was no way around it. If Blake and I split up, who would get the house? Who would have primary custody of the kids? I didn't want to think about either of those questions, but they would have to be dealt with. And if we didn't split up, how could we manage to live in the same house together? I knew being gay wasn't a lifestyle choice. Could I spend decades with a man who was my friend, but who I knew wasn't attracted to me? Should I, if it was what was best for Elsie and Nick?

Peaches squeezed my shoulder. "It's gonna be hard either way. You're gonna want to crawl into a hole and die for a while. But it won't last. And after what you've been through? You're gonna come out of this smellin' like a rose."

"My mother and father split up, too," Becky said. "And I turned out okay."

I thought about my mother, and the effort she'd put into raising us after my father left. She was a little loopier than most moms, but the truth was, I'd turned out okay, too. I hated to think of my kids growing up in a split household, though. I'd always wanted them to experience the intact family I'd never had.

But sometimes, I knew, you didn't get your wish.

"And who knows?" Becky continued. "Maybe you and Blake will patch things up."

"Maybe so. Of course, I might have to have an operation first," I said, smiling despite the ache in my heart. "Even so, I don't look that good in a cocktail dress."

Peaches snickered first. Then Becky snorted. A moment later, the room exploded with laughter.

As she wiped a tear from her eye, Peaches said, "By the way, did I tell you I got another call this morning? Another infidelity case." She winked. "After the last few days, you should be a pro."

"Another one?" At least I wouldn't have to worry about finding a job, I realized. It wasn't much, but it was something. "Please tell me he's not gay this time."

Peaches shrugged. "At least this time, if he heads for the Rainbow Room, you'll know."

As Peaches poured everyone a round of tequila and Becky tore open the bag of cookies, I took a sip of Chardonnay. I didn't know what the next chapter of my life held for me. The jury was out on my marriage. I might have to sell the house and move to an apartment, just like my mother had.

But Peaches was right. It was going to be hard for a while. But one way or another, it was going to be okay.

ACKNOWLEDGMENTS

Thanks as always go first to my sweet husband, Eric, who supports me in all my ventures, and to my terrific kids, Abby and Ian, neither of whom has anything at all in common with Elsie and Nick, incidentally. Except perhaps for the skort incident.

Thanks also to Jessica Faust, who encouraged me to write this book in the first place, to Jessica Park, who encouraged me to resurrect it, and to Barbara Burnett Smith, my late mentor, who was a terrific encouragement during the initial writing of the book. Jim Thomsen helped me figure out the (originally flawed) ending, and my wonderful parents, Dave and Carol Swartz, and friends Bethann and Beau Eccles all gave thoughtful reads to early drafts. (Beau also saved a McDonald's fry phone for me. For seven years. That's friendship!) Love always to my fabulous in-laws, Dorothy and Ed MacInerney, without whom so many things, including this book, would not be possible. And thanks to Austin Mystery Writers for thoughtful comments: Mary Jo Powell, Sylvia Dickey Smith, Dave Ciambrone, Kimberly Sandman, Rie Sheridan, and Laney Hennelly all made their marks, usually in No. 2 pencil. Thanks to Anh Schluep for giving Margie an opportunity to reach a wider audience, and to Charlotte Herscher, who once again helped me polish my work.

And last but not least, thanks to my wonderful readers and Facebook friends, who named approximately 50 percent of the characters in this book for me. You make days at the desk go by so much faster, even if you do lure me away from the word processor!

ABOUT THE AUTHOR

 Karen MacInerney is the author of numerous popular mystery novels, including the Agatha Award–nominated series The Gray Whale Inn Mysteries and the trilogy Tales of an Urban Werewolf, which was nominated for a P.E.A.R.L. award by her readers. When she's not working on her novels, she teaches writing workshops in Austin, Texas, where she lives with her husband and two children.